Belinda Alexandra is the author of eight bestselling novels and has been published around the world, including in the United States, Spain, France, Germany, the United Kingdom, Turkey, Hungary and Poland. She is the daughter of a Russian mother and an Australian father and has been an intrepid traveller since her youth. Belinda is the patron of the World League for the Protection of Animals (Australia) and lives in Sydney with her three rescue cats, Valentino, Versace and Gucci, and a garden full of interesting wildlife.

f BelindaAlexandraAuthor
𝕐 belinda_alexandra_author
⧠ belinda_alexandra_author
www.belinda-alexandra.com

Also by Belinda Alexandra

The
MYSTERY
WOMAN

BELINDA ALEXANDRA

HarperCollins*Publishers*

HarperCollins*Publishers*

Australia • Brazil • Canada • France • Germany • Holland • Hungary
India • Italy • Japan • Mexico • New Zealand • Poland • Spain • Sweden
Switzerland • United Kingdom • United States of America

First published in Australia in 2020
This edition published in 2021
by HarperCollins*Publishers* Australia Pty Limited
Level 13, 201 Elizabeth Street, Sydney NSW 2000
ABN 36 009 913 517
harpercollins.com.au

A catalogue record for this book is available from
the National Library of Australia.

ISBN 978 1 4607 5850 2 (paperback)
ISBN 978 1 4607 1230 6 (ebook)
ISBN 978 1 4607 8467 9 (audio book)

Cover design by Lisa White
Cover image: Woman © Lee Avison/Arcangel; landscape by Robert Lang/
stocksy.com/1490750
Author photograph by Elizabeth Allnutt
Typeset in Bembo Std by Kelli Lonergan
Printed and bound in Australia by McPherson's Printing Group
The papers used by HarperCollins in the manufacture of this book are a
natural, recyclable product made from wood grown in sustainable plantation
forests. The fibre source and manufacturing processes meet recognised
international environmental standards, and carry certification.

For Dali

CHAPTER ONE

The train burst from the tunnel and the bay came into view. Rebecca squeezed her eyes shut before opening them again, and twisted the gloves in her lap. She had not expected the scenery to be so magnificent. Mountains, verdant with lilli pilli, wild cherry and cabbage tree palms, shadowed the town, which was tucked into the elbow of the bay like a babe in the crook of a mother's arm. On the other side of it, flat rock platforms jutted out into the ocean. The sea beyond the bay was vast. It spread to the horizon and shimmered with a spectacular shade of sapphire blue. The surface was calm but Rebecca knew there was nothing more treacherous than the sea. A fluttery feeling disturbed her stomach and she looked away. It was ironic that she should have been assigned to this coastal town when there were dozens of inland centres equally in need of her services. Perhaps it was fate. Perhaps a divine reminder of mistakes made that could never be forgiven.

The train slowed and came to a stop in front of a station with a weatherboard office and waiting room. The 'Welcome to Shipwreck Bay' sign was sun-bleached and in need of paint, but below it somebody had planted a bed of purple pigface, which was vibrant with blooms. Rebecca tugged down her suitcase from the rack and pulled on her gloves. She stepped onto the platform at the same time as the stationmaster appeared from his office, rubbing his bald head before he replaced his cap and hitched his trousers over his substantial belly. He stopped in his tracks and his eyes widened when he saw her. 'Are you on your way to Melbourne, Miss?'

His gaze slowly ran over Rebecca from her pump shoes to her calot hat. She was used to that look. Even girdled and clothed for business in a nipped-waist tweed jacket and pencil skirt she couldn't hide her curvaceous figure. Men – young, middle-aged, old, ugly or handsome – always regarded her like a delicious cake they wanted to devour. It bemused her now that she was no longer young. At thirty-two years of age she was as good as a spinster. And with her round face and hooded grey eyes, she did not consider herself especially beautiful. Yet men always stared, even when there were far more attractive women in the room. 'You've got something magnetic about you, Becky,' her friend, Marion, always told her. 'Men just can't look away.'

The train guard blew his whistle and the train chugged out of the station to continue its journey south. Rebecca's eyes followed it.

'Are you visiting someone then?' the stationmaster asked her, as if he still refused to believe that she had got off the train intentionally.

She turned to him. 'No. I am the new postmistress. The Postmaster-General's Department sent me.'

★

Rebecca hadn't wanted a lift and asked about a taxi, but the stationmaster had told her that in a town as small as Shipwreck Bay there was no such thing.

'The house Doris is renting you is up that hill,' he said, taking his eyes from Rebecca's legs for a moment and indicating a street that ran straight from the town and disappeared somewhere among the trees on the mountainside. 'It's too far to walk, Miss ...'

'Wood.'

He nodded. 'I'm Ernest Mullens. But everyone calls me Ernie.'

He swung her suitcase into the boot of his black Holden and Rebecca flinched. 'You travel light,' he remarked. 'Are you sure you remembered to pack? Doesn't feel like there is anything in there.'

'The rest of my things are coming later.'

Ernie opened the car door for her and watched her slide in before waddling around to the driver's side. The car dipped when he got in and sat down. Rebecca wound down the window, trying to create more space between them. The breeze blew in a sudden stench of fish oil and rotting seafood. The smell was so pungent it left a foul taste in her mouth and she gagged. She reached into her purse for a handkerchief and brought it to her face.

Ernie looked puzzled then realised what the problem was. 'Oh that? You'll get used to that soon enough. The whalers caught a big blue earlier today. They're processing it down at the station.'

'I thought this was a mining town,' Rebecca said, winding the window up again. Ernie turned the ignition. 'It is now but it was built on whale oil. The road into town is made from crushed whale bone.'

The town centre could have been missed in the blink of an eye. The sun was setting and the shops' shutters were closed. There was the ubiquitous memorial hall, as well as a pub, greengrocer, butcher and general store. The post office, where Rebecca was due to start work the following day, was on the corner of the main street. It was a single-storey dwelling of rendered cream brick with chimneys and a filigreed porch. A large fig tree stood in front of it. The foundation stone read 1887.

'The town will be glad to have you,' Ernie told her. 'It's been chaos for the past few months without an official postmaster. The delivery boy, Johnny, is a good soul but a bit of a dope. People have been travelling to Twin Falls to post their mail just to make sure it arrives at its destination.'

The road to the top of the hill was bordered by cottages with corrugated iron roofs. Some of them had neat gardens of geraniums and daisies while others were unkempt and chickens picked their way through the overgrown lawns. About halfway up the hill Ernie came to a stop outside a freshly painted cottage with a gabled roof. An elderly woman in a belted striped dress and blue cardigan was waiting on the veranda. She seemed to be deep in thought but as the car engine cut out she moved like a statue coming to life. Rebecca got out of the car before Ernie could open the door for her. She looked back towards the town and realised from this point she had a view of the ocean beyond it to the horizon, as well as the train station. The woman must have seen her arrive. She shivered, not liking the idea of having been watched.

'I'm Doris Campbell,' said the woman, stepping through the gate and reaching her age-spotted hand out to Rebecca. 'Welcome to Shipwreck Bay, Miss Wood.'

Doris was about sixty years of age, with a ramrod straight spine. As tall as a man, she towered over Rebecca. But the masculine effect was softened by her large protruding eyes and the floral scent of Lux soap that wafted from her each time she moved.

Ernie carried Rebecca's suitcase to the front veranda. Then he returned to the car and straightened his cap. 'I'll be off, then,' he said.

'Thank you, Ernie,' Doris told him. 'Tell Marge I'll drop in and see her tomorrow about the flowers for Sunday's service.'

Doris turned back to Rebecca. 'Well, you are a pretty thing,' she said, admiring Rebecca's clothes and figure. 'My granddaughter has hair the same red copper tone but with your pale complexion I would say yours is natural.' She took Rebecca's arm and led her up the path to the house with an ease that made it seem as if they had known each other for ages. 'I hope you will find the house comfortable,' she said. 'You're from Sydney, aren't you?'

Doris opened the front door and led Rebecca straight into the living area of the cottage. A wood stove stood in one corner and the walls were pine, painted cream. The entire house took less than a minute to inspect. Its two small bedrooms each contained a single bed covered in a rose quilted spread, and white frilly curtains. Between the two bedrooms was a grey and pink tiled bathroom. The house was half the size of Rebecca's old apartment in Potts Point which had looked out over Elizabeth Bay and been decorated in silver velvet furnishings and a teak cocktail cabinet. The walls had been papered in teal blue damask. She wondered what her Sydney friends would make of this tiny doll's house with its hanging cord light switches and laminated plywood furniture. For a moment she was sure she heard Ned laughing. 'Come on, Becky! Has it really come to this?' But she knew it was her imagination because she doubted Ned was giving her a moment's thought. She hid her grimace from Doris but then lifted her head and regarded the house with greater courage. Wasn't this exactly what she had wanted? A sanctuary? A hideaway? It was not the kind of place people would come looking for her.

'It's lovely,' she said, pressing her hands together. Doris led her into the eat-in kitchen.

'I've put milk in the fridge and there is bread and jam in the cupboard,' the older woman told her. She pointed to some plastic canisters on a shelf. 'You'll find tea and sugar in those.'

Rebecca nodded, glad her landlady had provided some basic supplies. She hadn't given any thought to what she might eat that evening, or the following morning. Doris eyed her with sympathy. 'I'm sure you must be tired after your journey so we'll have a chat tomorrow. I'll come by the post office at nine o'clock.'

A pair of sulphur-crested cockatoos landed on the lawn at the back of the house and began eating the grass seed. Rebecca forgot where she was for a moment and stared at them foraging together. Hadn't she heard somewhere that the birds mated for life? And that if one of the pair died the other often stayed alone for the rest of its life? How come animals managed monogamy better than humans? Then, screeching, the rest of the flock flew overhead and the pair took flight to join them. Rebecca's eyes followed the birds' ascent until they disappeared into the distance. She turned to Doris. 'When I was given the assignment I was told that the last postmistress only stayed two weeks.'

Doris's face clouded. 'Yes, she was a nervous, jittery thing. Too young for the responsibility.' A slight frown wrinkled her forehead. 'I shouldn't have told her about Mabel, I suppose.'

'Mabel?'

Doris picked up her handbag from the table. 'Mabel was the town's postmistress for over twenty years. She spoiled us with her efficiency which we didn't fully appreciate until she suddenly passed away earlier this year.'

Rebecca followed Doris to the front door. The landlady reached into her handbag and slipped Rebecca the house key and another key with a tag that labelled it as belonging to the post office. 'I do hope you are not foolish enough to believe in ghosts, Miss Wood. People imagine such silly things. That last young girl was convinced the post office was haunted.'

Rebecca noticed the subtle change in Doris's posture, the shifting of her feet. Country people could be so superstitious. 'The foundation stone for the post office says 1887,' she replied lightly. 'I'm sure there are plenty of ghosts haunting the place and I should be very glad of the company.'

Doris's face pinched and she looked away. Rebecca sensed there was more to the story than Doris was letting on. But before she could ask anything further, Doris was stepping out the door. 'Well, I shall meet you at the post office in the morning,' she said. 'If there is anything else you need, please let me know.'

She watched Doris walk to the gate and turn for a last brief wave before heading down the hill. Rebecca was about to shut the door when she noticed her suitcase was still on the veranda where Ernie had left it. She brought it into the living room and undid the locks, rummaging through the silk underwear and nightgowns and uncovering the package wrapped several times in brown paper. She took it to the kitchen and unwound the paper to reveal a Vallauris vase enamelled in black and hand-painted with pink, yellow and blue flowers. She had bought it in Monaco one heady summer. She carried the vase to the kitchen and placed it on the table. She studied it from several angles before her hands clenched into fists. The vase was as out of place in the Formica kitchen as she was in Shipwreck Bay. This time Ned's voice sounded louder in her head: *It was good while it lasted, wasn't it, Becky?* Filled with a sudden rage, she swatted at the vase and sent it crashing to the floor. The shattered pieces scattered over the linoleum and some slid under the fridge and stove. Rebecca stared at the fragments for a good minute before she rushed out of the room.

'Go to hell, Ned!' she hissed, slamming the door behind her.

CHAPTER TWO

The back door to the post office wouldn't budge so Rebecca tried the front door. It swung open to reveal a polished wooden floor littered with postal forms and a long counter covered with dust. A set of cast-iron scales stood in the centre of it. She scanned the room and her eyes settled on a portrait of the young queen who had only recently ascended to the throne. It hung at an odd angle from the picture rail. Rebecca's nose twitched. The air was stagnant with the odours of an old public building: damp paper, aging leather and mould. The previous postmistress must have left weeks ago – and in a hurry too by the state of the place. Rebecca sighed and fingered the bow on the neckline of her blouse. She had dressed in her best for her first day at work. She hadn't expected that a major cleaning job would be required.

Beyond the counter were the sorting boxes and she was relieved to see that at least these had been emptied. Johnny must have been seeing to that. Perhaps he wasn't the 'dope' Ernie had suggested. She glanced at the clock on the wall. The hands hadn't moved since her arrival. They were stuck at half past eight. She reached into her handbag and took out her Bulova watch: fourteen-carat white gold with diamonds around the face. She hadn't been game to wear it – too expensive for a postmistress's salary. She would have to send away for a catalogue and get something simpler, something officious-looking, a watch that wouldn't invite questions.

She lifted the counter flap and stepped into the sorting room. The window blind was closed so she switched on the light. On a large square desk in the middle of the room sat a stamp cancelling machine, an accounting machine and a typewriter. Along one side of the wall was a bench with a telephone and a telegraph machine. On the opposite side was a miniature telephone exchange. She leaned towards the noticeboard and squinted at the numbers written there. There were only a handful of subscribers in the whole town! She recalled the busy exchange at the Sydney General Post Office where she had worked as a telegraphist during the war. The service was available twenty-four hours a day and the crew of telephonists worked in shifts. Marion had been employed there and Rebecca had enjoyed watching her friend handle one of the switchboards: bells ringing, plugs flying in all directions, and Marion as calm as a millpond in the centre of it all. 'What number please?'; 'Do you wish to extend your call for another three minutes?' Housed in a magnificent sandstone Italian Renaissance building, the General Post Office had been a town unto itself, with teams of deliverymen, clerks and telegram boys. Rebecca would probably still have been working there if it hadn't been for Ned.

Rebecca leaned her head against the doorframe. The post office had the same effect on her as her new rental house: she was awash with incredulous disbelief that she had ended up in this place at the end of the world. Part of her wanted to laugh and part of her wanted to cry. The stuffy air was oppressive and she strode to the window and rolled up the blind. She gasped when she realised she had uncovered an enormous picture window with a view straight out to the ocean. Was God punishing her? She turned the stiff latch and pushed open the window. A gust of wind sent papers and forms fluttering over the floor. She closed her eyes and inhaled the salty breeze. 'You won't beat me, you know,' she said to the almighty creator she only half-believed in. 'Nor will men, nor this town, nor memories!' At the sound of a boat's labouring engine she opened her eyes again. A long black vessel was motoring into the bay. At its bow stood a harpoon gun and fastened to either side of the boat were two whale carcasses. Their tail flukes had been hacked off and their bleeding bodies were bloated with air. One of the whale's tongues floated like a gigantic balloon in the water. The sight disturbed Rebecca. Only a few hours ago those majestic creatures had been living things, the royalty of their domain – and now they were lifeless and grotesque. She shivered.

'Well, good to see you again! I hope you had a peaceful night's rest?'

Rebecca turned to see Doris standing in the doorway. She was wearing a polka dot blouse with a full skirt, pearls and heels. For an elderly countrywoman she certainly knew how to dress.

'Have you looked in your office yet?' Doris asked. 'I made sure Johnny had at least left that in good order.'

Rebecca turned to the door at the end of the room marked 'Postmaster'. She bit down on a smile. This post office might be a small operation but she would be the queen of it. She liked that idea more than anything. Doris pushed open the door and Rebecca followed her inside. The room was tiny, with nothing more than a desk and a swivel chair. There were two windows: one large and one shaped like a ticket window at a train station. To Rebecca's relief neither of them faced the ocean. The large one looked over an unruly patch of garden while the other faced the street. The room stank of bleach. She wondered why special attention had been paid to cleaning it while the rest of the post office was filthy. Doris twisted the catch and opened the smaller window. 'In the old days the townspeople would ride up on their horses and collect their post here,' she said.

Rebecca moved around the desk and sat in the chair. The office would be quite nice with a painting – something formal like a landscape or still life – and a potted plant. As the postmistress of a small town with no bank she would be the representative of not only the Postmaster-General's Department but the Commonwealth Bank as well. She would be a respected government official. She swivelled in the chair and her foot kicked something. A box. She pulled it out and placed it on the desk. It was labelled: *Personal and Private. Property of Mabel Peberdy.*

'Oh that,' said Doris, glancing at the box. 'That's some of Mabel's personal correspondence and other things. We've been waiting for the family to come pick that up but nobody has yet. They live in Melbourne and I dare say they are too heartbroken to do it. Two tragic deaths in the family within a year would be too much for anybody.'

'Two?'

Doris stared a moment at Rebecca then shrugged. 'You're going to hear about it from somebody in the town, so I may as well be the one to tell you. Mabel hung herself here in this office.'

Rebecca followed Doris's gaze up to the ceiling. A single rafter stretched across the span of the roof. Had the previous postmistress really fastened a rope to it and killed herself? In a flash of imagination, she saw a woman hanging there, legs swinging, tongue bloated like the whale's. Suddenly being in this office by herself didn't seem so appealing. She turned to Doris, aghast. 'Why?'

Doris pursed her lips. 'Mabel went a bit funny in the head after the death of her daughter. The poor girl drowned. She was all Mabel had in the world. Her husband died young and, as I said, the rest of her family lives in Melbourne.'

Rebecca's throat constricted as if she was suffocating. She tore her eyes away from the ceiling and wondered if hanging was better than drowning. At least Mabel's demise had been quick and efficient and by her own choice.

Doris pressed her finger to the corner of her mouth. 'You seem like a sophisticated young woman, Miss Wood. I'm sure you will quickly put it out of your mind.' Her eyes narrowed and her voice took on a kind, soothing tone. 'I know it's not easy … Well, I know it's not easy to be alone. At least I had my Reggie for forty years. But your generation …' Doris shook her head. 'You lost so many young men, didn't you?'

Rebecca's jaw clenched. Doris was fishing. She imagined everybody in the town would probably wonder the same thing.

Why wasn't she married? She wanted to tell the old biddy to mind her own business, but instead she lowered her eyes. 'Yes, that's true,' she said quietly. 'Robert ... well, he was an aircrew navigator. He went down over the Arafura Sea.'

Doris sighed. 'Well, my dear, we women carry on, don't we? You're still young. A pretty thing like you won't be alone forever. Time heals all wounds, eventually.'

Robert had not been a straight-out lie. He and Rebecca had seen each other for six weeks before he had been posted to the RAAF. He had been nice to her, always picking her up on time and bringing her flowers from his mother's garden. She had been heavy-hearted when she had learned of his death. But that memory was not as painful as some of her others, so she felt safe to share it. From Doris's sympathetic expression it was clear that the story of Robert had created a kind of intimacy between them. Rebecca knew that when it came to women it was better to confide *something* rather than nothing at all. Mystique in a woman was alluring to men but it was throwing yourself to the dogs if you tried it with women. A woman who did not share her deepest, most painful secrets with other women was immediately under suspicion. Rebecca understood it would be better for the townspeople to view her as a heartbroken spinster rather than know the truth.

A foul fishy smell that she was beginning to recognise drifted in through the window. Rebecca flinched. 'They are boiling those whales they caught this morning, obviously,' she said, getting up to slam the window shut. 'It's like having day-old tuna and sweaty socks stuffed into your nostrils. I hope the town is not always going to smell this bad.'

Doris shot her a glance. 'Oh yes, it will … at least from now until November. Each of those whales represents a thousand pounds in oil. That money makes a lot of difference to families in this town.'

Rebecca stiffened, not liking the feeling of being chastised for something as reasonable as objecting to a putrid smell. She flashed a smile to hide her annoyance. 'Well, I shall try to bear it better then,' she said.

Doris didn't take her eyes from her face. 'That's the right attitude, Miss Wood. Because to us that *bad* smell is the smell of people's livelihoods. And it would do no good to let people here think that you disapproved of it.'

CHAPTER THREE

After Doris left, Rebecca returned to the office and sat down in the chair. Her hands formed into a steeple under her chin and she listened. The post office itself was silent but the boughs of the fig tree outside were creaking in the sea breeze. She raised her eyes to the ceiling. Mabel's death had nothing to do with her so why should she spoil her peace of mind pondering it? But that noise ... At first Rebecca hoped she was imagining it. Could she bear it every day? The wind was making the sea choppy and her skin prickled with the sound of the waves rolling and crashing onto the sand. As a child she had loved that rumbling; now she dreaded it. For a moment she saw herself at ten years old on the long hot ride from Sydney to Whale Beach. The solid tyres of the motor bus made the shock of every stone and rut shudder through the vehicle. She pictured Debbie sitting next to her, her plump legs swinging from the seat. Their parents were sitting across the aisle: relaxed and sun-kissed, younger-looking than she would ever see them again. Debbie opened her mouth and let the bus's vibration hum through her body and out her lips. 'Ahhhhhh!' Rebecca wanted to laugh but took her responsibility as the older sibling seriously. 'Stop it!' she scolded. Debbie frowned and curled her lip. 'Make me!'

A loud *bang* came from the sorting room. Rebecca jumped. A young man in a delivery boy's uniform and cap had thrown a heavy-looking canvas bag onto the table and was now in the process of emptying it. He whistled 'Mockin' Bird Hill' out of tune as he did so. It was like nails on a chalkboard. She cleared her throat.

'You must be Johnny?'

The young man dropped a parcel and gaped at Rebecca. He couldn't have been more than seventeen but his freckled cheeks were gaunt and lined. His mouth twisted into a number of expressions ranging from surprise to puzzlement before settling into a lopsided smile. 'Stone the crows, Miss! You gave me a fright! I wasn't expecting anyone to be here today!'

Rebecca walked into the sorting room. 'I'm the new postmistress,' she told him, reaching out her hand. 'Rebecca Wood.'

Awe flashed across the young man's face. He wiped his hand on his trousers before taking hers. His skin was cold and clammy and his palm was rough. The sight of his nails, black with what she hoped was bicycle grease, made Rebecca withdraw her hand as quickly as she had offered it. Although Johnny stared directly into her face it wasn't with lasciviousness. His eyes danced with a kind of silly innocence as if he were regarding his schoolmistress rather than a woman. He was more twelve than seventeen.

'I'm glad that you're here, Miss Wood,' he said. 'I've had a heck of a time trying to manage the post office on my own as well as keeping up the deliveries. I've had nothing but complaints.'

Rebecca eyed the envelopes and parcels strewn across the table. 'Did you pick these up from the train station this morning?'

'Yes, on the nine o'clock. I can sort them now or do you want me to chop the wood for the fire first?'

The question stopped Rebecca short. 'Fire? It's not cold enough for a fire.'

Johnny blinked at her. 'Not now, but later in the afternoon the post office can get pretty chilly. The last postmistress – the young lady from Wollongong – always complained of it.'

Rebecca rarely felt the cold. Even on brisk winter days in Sydney she hadn't worn a coat or scarf. Ned liked to joke that Rebecca could always raise the temperature of a room and he didn't need a blanket when she slept beside him. She was about to tell Johnny not to bother, but when he turned back to the post and began his tuneless whistling again, she thought she might bite through her own lip if he didn't stop that irritating sound.

'Yes, wood for the fire is a good idea,' she said, giving him a tight smile.

Johnny nodded. He whistled while he took off his jacket and hung it on a hook, and whistled while he rolled up his sleeves. He continued to whistle as he walked to the back door, found it stiff and squeaky and went looking under the sink in the tearoom for some grease which he used to lubricate the hinges. When he finally left, Rebecca returned to her office with her temples throbbing. The delivery boy seemed amiable enough, but he was the kind of happy simpleton that often got on her nerves. She'd have to make sure to keep him busy and not under her feet.

While the rhythmical thwack of Johnny chopping wood came from outside, Rebecca sorted the day's post by street name and then by house number. Those in town would have their mail delivered once a day, while those who lived on the outskirts or further afield would have to come to the post office to collect theirs or else wait for the contractor who would deliver twice a week. Rebecca studied the family names as she worked, memorising them: Dolan, Ludlow, Ryan … The Pike family, at 4 Ocean Road, seemed to receive the most mail of all. Mrs Pike subscribed to a number of periodicals ranging from the dull *Home Journal* to the audacious *Harper's Bazaar*. She also received *The Home Detective*, a tamer spin-off of the American periodical *True Detective*, which was banned in Australia due to its sensationalistic depiction of real crimes. Her husband was more prosaic in his tastes, subscribing to the major newspapers from Sydney, Melbourne and Canberra. Rebecca's stomach knotted when she saw the front page of *The Sydney Morning Herald*: 'Mystery Woman at Centre of McKell Scandal Remains Elusive'. She held her breath, barely able to move, as her eyes raced over the article:

> The latest revelation in the many-sided life of the Minister for External Affairs, Ned McKell, appears to be a long-standing relationship with a woman who was neither his wife nor his personal secretary. It is believed the relationship commenced some time before his appointment to the cabinet and ended earlier this year. After the scandal broke out last month when

it was revealed that Minister McKell had taken Miss Thelma Marr to a Surfer's Paradise motel, the theatre actress was quick to dispel rumours that she was a homewrecker. 'I am not the first mistress he has had in his life!' she exclaimed. 'There was another woman before me.' While Minister McKell has not been returning telephone calls, and his wife of 20 years, Cynthia, has declined to comment, the prime minister has been quick to defend one of his favourite cabinet members. 'He has made extraordinary achievements at an important time in Australia's post-war development and was key in the official peace treaty with Japan. I do not believe a man's personal affairs should be aired in the press.'

While those in high places may be unwilling to criticise Minister McKell's behaviour, the identity of his previous mistress is the subject of conjecture in pubs, hairdressers and parlours everywhere. It seems everyone knows someone who believes they know who she is and there is hardly a glamorous woman in Australia who isn't currently under suspicion …

Rebecca felt the burn of bile in her chest. Damn you, Ned! She cursed under her breath and then glanced out the window to check Johnny was still outside. At the sight of the young man swinging an axe to split a log she turned back to the newspaper. Although the journalist seemed to be hinting at actresses and singers, all it would take would be one dogged reporter to catch a scent leading directly to her.

Rebecca squeezed her eyes shut. The sounds of whistles and cheers intermingled with jazz music filled her head. V-J Day 1945. There had never been so many people gathered in Martin

Place. The news of the Japanese surrender had sent Sydney into a frenzy of gaiety. Everyone was celebrating, waving streamers and flags, and dancing in the crowded streets. Her mind travelled to that party in Rose Bay, when she had first spotted Ned McKell eyeing her across the room. He'd approached her with a seductive smile on his square-jawed face. 'The one thing your eyes haven't told me yet is your name ...'

Seven years! For seven years, Rebecca had been discreet while Ned had squired her to the most fashionable nightspots – not just Sydney, but also London, Paris and New York. She had sat up with him for hours after their lovemaking, listening to his political ambitions and suggesting campaign strategies. She had hosted parties for high-profile men in the apartment Ned had rented for her and garnered support for him. She had spoken with the skill of a press secretary to the political reporters who in turn never once breathed a word of the affair in their articles. Rebecca had been not only well-liked but also respected and listened to by the party's inner circle, including the prime minister himself. Marion, who was in a similar relationship at the time with the attorney-general, compared their roles to those of women like Cleopatra and Diane de Poitiers: women who held influence over powerful men. In that whole time Rebecca had never revealed her relationship with Ned to anyone outside the inner circle. She had never even made him promise to leave Cynthia, so assured was she that they were meant to be together forever. A wedding ring would make no difference. Then Ned let his vanity get the better of him and fell for the charms of nineteen-year-old Thelma Marr, oozing with sex appeal but not possessing one ounce of common sense –

or loyalty, it seemed. Even when Ned had dumped Rebecca and she was turned out of her apartment because he was no longer paying the rent, she had not betrayed him. She'd slipped away and nursed her wounded heart in a bedsitter in Neutral Bay. She'd been shocked enough by his fickleness then. Now this? To leave her potentially exposed to the press was unfaithfulness of the worst kind! The prime minister was right when he said that the personal lives of his ministers were off limits to public scrutiny. That had been the case until stupid Thelma Marr. Thanks to the starlet's desire for notoriety the newspapers now saw the scandal as an opportunity to increase their circulations. Thelma may not have been aware that Rebecca had been Ned's previous mistress, but the gossip columnists were now after her like hounds after a fox. If they found her she would be torn to shreds as a paramour, a seductress, a femme fatale. It wasn't lost on her that the word for female fox was 'vixen'.

She studied the photograph below the article and cringed at the caption: 'McKell leaves The Celebrity Club with the striking blonde mystery woman'

In the picture Rebecca had her hand wrapped around Ned's arm but her face was hidden in the shadows. Blonde was the hair colour she had been born with. When Doris had mistakenly thought her flame-red hair was natural it had only testified to her skill with Du Barry's Color Glo in Tiger Lily.

She folded the newspaper and placed it in the Pikes' pigeon hole. Whether her disguise was going to give her the anonymity she longed for, only time would tell. She hoped she was a good enough actress to avert suspicion – and that there wasn't anybody in town who would ask too many questions.

CHAPTER FOUR

After Johnny left on his first mail run for the day, Rebecca searched the cupboards in the tearoom and found an apron, a broom and a bottle of glass cleaner. She bustled about cleaning the main area of the post office. A sheen of perspiration dampened her forehead as she swept the floor and swiped at cobwebs. The windows were sticky with salt spray and she washed them before vigorously applying the glass cleaner. The GPO had a team of cleaners and Rebecca had employed her own maid when she lived in Potts Point. Here in Shipwreck Bay, however, she and Johnny would be responsible for the presentation of the post office. From the current state of the place she figured the delivery boy wasn't going to be of much help. Still, Rebecca relished order and cleanliness and as she dusted and polished her pulse steadied and she began to think more clearly. If any member of the Sydney press should walk in now and see her at work, she doubted that she would be recognised as Ned McKell's mysterious mistress. Ned might know the ins and outs of de-escalating the arms race but he wouldn't have a clue how to make his own pot of tea, let alone lower himself to scrubbing a toilet. A glamorous mistress would be assumed to be as clueless to domestic life as her lover. The efficient running of a home was the domain of a wife. She managed the social calendar, took care of the children and organised the meals. A mistress, on the other hand, was a man's idealised companion: his equal in drive and desire for independence. To Rebecca, Ned had been her entree into a world of power she could never have moved into as a woman on her own.

Her eyes began to burn and she told herself it was the dust. She would not cry over him or let herself be defeated. What sort of woman cried over a man who couldn't care less if she was alive or dead after seven years together? Even when the tears began to fall she wiped them away with the corner of her apron and re-powdered her face. She caught sight of the lines around her eyes and snapped the compact mirror shut.

She mopped the floors and threw the dirty water out on the unkempt garden. Then, after combing her hair and reapplying her lipstick, she sat down at the front counter, sorting out the drawers. She arranged the stamps into denominations and straightened the forms for registered letters and telegrams. With her love of order she wondered how she'd ever got into such a mess with Ned. But then she'd never had much luck with men. How could she? Her father had walked out on her mother when Rebecca was twelve years old and had never been heard from again. She'd never been given a role model for a man who could be relied upon. Things would be different next time. She would choose an entirely different sort of man: somebody steady, a man she could view as her rock. Passion would play no part in it. Letting her feelings run away with her had brought her nothing but grief. She would never make that mistake again.

'Good morning! You must be the new postmistress?'

Rebecca looked up to see a dark-haired woman staring at her over the counter. She had been so lost in thought she hadn't heard her enter. The woman's grey woollen dress was form-fitting over her trim figure. She had accessorised it with mustard-coloured shoes, bag and belt. With her straight nose and arched eyebrows the customer had a perfectly symmetrical face, like a doll's. But she wore the pinched, unhappy expression of a pretty woman whose beauty was fading. Her pale lipstick and the heavy layer of pancake make-up on her skin couldn't soften the bitterness that emanated from her eyes.

'I'd like to place a money order, please.'

'Yes, certainly,' Rebecca replied, looking through the drawers for the money order forms. She hadn't seen any when she had tidied the drawers earlier and felt herself growing hot under the woman's scrutiny. 'If you would give me a minute …'

'Mabel kept them over there, under the sorting shelves.' The woman pointed to the cupboard.

Rebecca opened the cupboard and found the forms. 'Who should I make it out to?' she asked, searching for a pen. The woman reached into her purse and took out a silver-plated fountain pen and handed it to her.

Rebecca paused before taking it, inwardly berating Johnny for putting her in such an embarrassing position. What sort of post office counter didn't have a drawer full of pens?

'I believe you only started today?' The woman's lips formed into a tight grin.

Marion used to say that sort of smile was 'as fake as a bullet bra'. The lips moved but the eyes stayed frozen. Rebecca didn't smile back. She knew when she was being patronised.

'It's never easy to take up a new position, is it?' The woman spoke in a condescending manner but Rebecca recognised the unhappiness in her tone. Women like that were a dime a dozen in Sydney society: women who had been told from a young age that their good looks would make life easy for them. They would collect corsages and hearts from dozens of ardent admirers and live out the rest of their lives like Greek goddesses. The idea that beauty would buy her enduring love had been shattered for Rebecca from an early age, when her parents rejected her, so she hadn't given it much weight. But for other women, possibly like the one standing before her, it seemed they couldn't get over their shock. It must have been a disappointment for this particular woman to find herself in a place like Shipwreck Bay at thirty-something years of age.

Rebecca noticed something else about her. Behind her carefully powdered façade she was examining her like a hawk. Rebecca knew that look too. Did the woman see her as competition for something? The most desirable man in Shipwreck Bay perhaps? But a glance at the woman's left hand revealed a glittering gold and diamond wedding ring, designed in the shape of a glitzy ribbon-wrapped bouquet. Whoever this woman's husband was, he spent money on her.

'Who should I make the money order out to?' Rebecca asked.

'Beril Jents haute couture.' The woman lifted her chin in the air.

Rebecca made no comment and wrote the order out. What does she want me to do? she thought. Gasp in awe? Ned had bought her a gold lamé dress from Beril Jents before they had set sail for Monaco two years ago. Where did this woman wear her couture clothes anyway? To church? To the local dance?

'I'll withdraw the money from my husband's account. He's the shire secretary,' the woman continued.

Rebecca was sorry for thinking unkind thoughts about Johnny. He wasn't half as irritating as this woman. She spoke to Rebecca as if she was some country hick who'd never worn silk underwear.

'And what is your husband's name?' she asked.

'George Pike.'

Rebecca's muscles twitched along her jawline. She realised who the woman was: the subscriber to all the magazines including *The Home Detective*. Her husband received the metropolitan newspapers. She reappraised Mrs Pike, wary that before her stood the kind of person who might take a keen interest in the identity of Ned McKell's mystery woman.

At that moment Johnny returned and rushed into the post office to grab his second bag, trailing mud from his shoes over the freshly mopped floor as he went. He stopped short when he saw Mrs Pike and hovered between the sorting room and main office, looking very much like he wanted to avoid her. But it was too late.

'Well, there you are, Johnny,' said Mrs Pike.

Johnny cowered. 'Hello, Mrs Pike.'

'Did you find my copy of the *Vogue* pattern book that went missing?'

Johnny shook his head ruefully.

'Well, keep looking,' said Mrs Pike tersely. 'I want my tennis dress ready for summer.'

Rebecca completed the money order and handed Mrs Pike her receipt.

'Thank you,' the woman said, practically snatching it from her. 'I will have to invite you to one of my bridge nights.'

'That would be lovely,' replied Rebecca, although she couldn't imagine anything worse.

'I'm Nancy, by the way,' the woman said. 'I believe you are Rebecca Wood. You worked at the GPO in Sydney, didn't you? In the telegraph department, during the war?'

Rebecca nodded. It didn't bode well that she already knew so much about her. She must have got that information from Doris. Or perhaps they'd pored over her references together when she'd applied to rent the house. She wouldn't be able to trust anyone. This was a small town. People talked. They talked in Sydney too. But this was different. Here there was no place to hide.

After Nancy left, Johnny hoisted his restocked mailbag onto his shoulder. 'Watch out for Mrs Pike,' he warned Rebecca. 'She's a dragon. If I don't whistle at every single house on Ocean Road she has her husband write an official complaint about me to the Postmaster-General's Department. What do you think about that?'

Rebecca eyed the muddy footprints Johnny had left on her clean floor, and then looked back to the street where she caught a glimpse of Nancy entering the greengrocer's. The woman picked up an orange, sniffed it and then promptly put it down again. Rebecca thought back to her life in Sydney: the clothes, the jewellery, the parties. That was all done now. Gone! Ned had been her benefactor for that lifestyle, but now she was paying for every last penny of it on her own. Not with money, but with her dreams. They were unravelling before her eyes. She turned to Johnny. 'I think you had better blow your whistle at every house,' she told him.

★

Rebecca let out a breath as quiet descended on the post office again. She was determined to get the place in order before she had any more customers like Nancy Pike. She knew little about country life. She had grown up in North Sydney. But from the Minister of Commerce and Agriculture she had gleaned that society in country towns was as hierarchical as it was in the city, but much more suspicious of newcomers. It was important to ingratiate herself quickly, even with someone as aggravating as Nancy Pike. After all, she would be privy to everyone's personal details: everything from how much money they had in their bank accounts to how often they wrote to their mothers. They had to trust her. If they didn't, someone might feel compelled to investigate her past.

She mopped Johnny's muddy footprints from the floor then set to work tidying the banking forms, placing fresh withdrawal and deposit slips on the courtesy desk. Neither of the chained pens worked and Rebecca searched around the cupboards for replacements. When she couldn't find any, she searched for a stationery order form instead. The rumble of a farm truck pulling up outside followed by a second one caught her attention. A truck door creaked open and slammed again. The driver of one of the vehicles called out to the other: 'Good day, Gav, I haven't seen you in a while!'

'No, I haven't been to town lately,' answered the other driver. 'Thank God the dry spell has come to an end, heh?'

'Too right. I'm hoping for a better summer pasture than last year – and no bushfires either.'

'I don't know about that. Barney Higgins reckons we're in for a tough one.'

The men burst through the post office door. The first man was short and stocky. His shirt buttons strained over his generous gut. The other man was tall and lanky. Their eyes nearly popped out of their sunburnt faces when they spotted Rebecca. 'Crikey!' said the short man, nudging his friend. 'I'll have to come into town more often!'

The tall man smiled shyly at Rebecca and took off his hat but the other man couldn't contain himself. 'I'm Bob Hill,' he said, stepping towards the counter and grinning with a mouthful of large square teeth. 'And this is my mate, Gavin Young. He's from Billabong Station and I'm the owner of Toggalong Creek Farm.'

Rebecca gave her most winsome smile. 'Good morning, gentlemen.' She turned to the postal slots to retrieve the men's mail. She found a note from Johnny that there was more mail than could fit in the slots and to check a box in the sorting room. While there, Rebecca glanced at the map on the wall. Both properties were about twenty miles out of town, in opposite directions. She overheard Bob tell Gavin that he had forty-four milking cows now and wanted to improve the carrying capacity of his pastures. Those details seemed like some strange pieces of a puzzle to Rebecca but she quickly jotted them down in her notebook. When she'd met Ned she didn't know a thing about government but she had been an astute learner. In the end, the prime minister had referred to her as 'the best-informed woman in politics'. She would apply the same approach to Shipwreck Bay.

After bundling the packages and tying them with string to make them easy to carry, she returned to the counter. 'It looks like neither of you has been to town in a while,' she said, handing the bundles to the men.

Gavin rubbed his neck. 'No, my wife usually picks up the mail when she comes in, but I needed to get fertiliser today.'

Bob nodded towards the fig tree outside the post office. 'You see that tree? Everyone around here calls that the Tree of Knowledge. You want to know why?'

Rebecca could guess but she lifted her brow with feigned curiosity.

'Because those of us on the land get our news there when we pass each other on our way to the post office or to the pub.'

Rebecca laughed and Bob's eyes gleamed. 'Well, it's been a pleasure to meet you …'

'Rebecca Wood.'

At that moment she noticed a blonde woman peer through the glass of the post office door then quickly move away. Was it another person from the town curious to learn more about her? She thought of the article in *The Sydney Morning Herald* and her stomach dipped. Maybe she had made a mistake coming to such a small place. Perhaps she should have gone somewhere bigger like Melbourne or even more remote like Alice Springs. But four hours away from her beloved Sydney had been as much as she could bear. It was exile enough.

'Oh, that's one of the Norwegian women,' Gavin said, noticing where Rebecca was looking. 'They're a funny lot. Courteous enough but they stick to themselves.'

Gavin seemed innocuous but Bob's eyes were roaming over Rebecca's womanly contours as if he were picking a prize heifer. Her curves and her husky voice didn't impress women. She could not afford that the first thing the wives of the town heard from their husbands about the new postmistress was that she was attractive.

'It must get lonely out there on the farms,' she said. 'Tell your wives I look forward to meeting them and everyone else from around the town.'

Bob's face slackened at the mention of his wife, but Gavin seemed touched by Rebecca's geniality. He cleared his throat. 'Thank you very much, Miss Wood. I'm sure Iris would appreciate that.'

Rebecca waited until the two men were back in their trucks and had taken off before she turned back to her work again. The wind had calmed and she could no longer hear the sea. She glanced at the clock that was still telling the wrong time and was about to adjust it when the blonde woman she had seen earlier rushed through the door, bumping her shoulder roughly against the doorjamb in her hurry. Rebecca flinched, imagining how much that would have hurt, but the woman herself seemed to barely notice.

'You are the new postmistress.' It wasn't a question but the woman's sing-song accent made it sound as if it was. She was young, maybe no more than twenty but her pale eyes and the frown lines on her forehead made her look older.

'Yes, how may I help you?'

The woman placed a passbook on the counter and a grimy-looking money bag. 'I want to deposit this. I do the banking for the whaling station.'

Rebecca gingerly opened the bag. Inside were pound notes neatly divided into denominations and fastened with a clip. The woman passed her a piece of paper with the accounting written out. Her hands were smooth and tanned but the fingernails were bitten to the quick and the cuticles were ragged and raw-looking.

Rebecca counted out the money and felt the woman's eyes on her. Her addition and the woman's matched. She put the coins and notes in the drawer, filled out the woman's passbook and stamped it before handing it back to her. She expected the woman would leave then but she went on watching her. It was the kind of staring someone did when they thought they recognised you from somewhere.

'Is that all I can help you with today?' Rebecca asked.

'You smell it, don't you?' The woman's eyes were steady on her.

Rebecca frowned and shook her head, not understanding.

'The stink. The whale flesh. It's on everything. The money. The passbook. My clothes.'

Involuntarily Rebecca sniffed the air. She shrugged. 'I smelt it blowing in on the breeze a few times. But not on you. I can't smell it on you.'

The woman's eyes crinkled into a smile. She looked prettier then. 'I can even taste it in my coffee in the morning. I scrub it every day out of my clothes and hair. When my husband leaves for the station I start baking. Bread, *solskinnskringle*, *krumkake* – it doesn't matter. I always have something baking so the house smells like hot pastry, cinnamon, butter, vanilla … anything rather than that stench. We can't eat everything I bake ourselves so I give it to the other women. "Why do you bake so much?" they ask me. "You don't have any children." They think I do it because I like it. They think I do it as charity because my husband makes more money than theirs and they have so many children to feed. I don't tell them I bake to get rid of the stink. They would take it as an insult because that stench is what they rely on. But I don't associate the smell with money. I associate it with my husband.'

The woman gave Rebecca the impression of a fly that was beating itself against the glass again and again, trying to find a way out. It stirred a sense of sympathy in her.

'I'm Rebecca Wood,' she said. 'I'm renting a house on Mountain Road.'

The woman stared hard at her. It was impossible to read the thoughts behind those pale eyes. Then her shoulders relaxed a little. 'I'm Berit Olsen,' she replied. 'I knew the former postmistress well. Mabel was kind.'

Rebecca pursed her lips. 'I am sorry. It must have been a distressing way to lose her.'

Berit paused as if she was on the verge of saying something but then thought better of it. She put the passbook in her handbag and folded the cloth bag. Before she left she looked at Rebecca again. 'You have nice clothes.'

Rebecca brushed her sleeve self-consciously. She did have nice clothes. That fact might give her away. But still she wouldn't be able to give them up. They were the last thing she had left now that love, dignity and a front-row seat to world politics were gone. She was tempted to say that she made them herself but that would be a lie she couldn't carry off. She couldn't thread a needle let alone sew a hem. 'Thank you,' was all she managed.

She watched Berit scurry down the street, head down and eyes averted from anyone who passed her. Something told her that she didn't have to worry about that young woman snooping into her affairs. It was clear that she had trouble in her own life, perhaps much worse than her own.

CHAPTER FIVE

At the end of the day, Rebecca locked up the post office and turned the sign on the front door to 'Closed'. She left via the back door, averting her eyes from the view of the ocean as she locked the door and placed the key in her purse. The steep hill to her house caused her to shorten her steps and to lean slightly forward. Her breathing quickened and her skin grew hot but the walk up was not as arduous as Ernie had made it out to be. She felt invigorated rather than weary when she reached the gate to her garden. But the feeling evaporated the moment she stepped into her house. The pink and cream décor looked sickly sweet in the late afternoon light, like the icing on a wedding cake. 'God!' she cursed under her breath as she stepped out of her shoes and placed them in the cupboard near the front door. After undoing the bow and the buttons of her blouse, she hung it in the wardrobe along with her skirt. She dropped her hose and slip into a basket to wash later, before returning to the living room wearing only her bra and panties. Sinking onto the sofa with a sigh, she scanned the room. Her gazed moved from the milk glass table lamps to the needlepoint cushions before settling on the nodding-donkey figurines on the windowsill. After spending the day tidying the post office she had started to feel it was a place where she could belong. It appealed to her sense of orderliness and her desire to be mistress over her environment. But here in the cottage she felt even more like an actress who had stepped into a play. For a moment she considered collecting the figurines and cushions and hiding them away in the wardrobe in the second bedroom, but then decided against it. It was better that she felt out of place. Cursed would be the day when she began to see this quirky cottage as her home.

'I need a drink,' she said, rising to her feet. She was halfway to the kitchen when she realised that there wasn't any alcohol in the house. She found herself mentally walking through the routine she had kept whenever she returned to her Potts Point apartment. She had performed it so often it had been automatic. She would close the door behind her as if shutting out the world. Then she would put down her purse and gloves and head straight to the cocktail cabinet where she would pour herself a gin and tonic. She could taste the sharp effervescent sensation of the drink on her tongue. The memory sent her into the kitchen searching in the cupboards for anything that might resemble the ingredients of a cocktail but all she found were cans of tuna and cream of mushroom soup along with a packet of dried pasta. Doris had tacked a recipe for a tuna and macaroni casserole on the back of the cupboard door. Thank goodness for her landlady! Rebecca hadn't even thought to go grocery shopping. Organising the post office had kept her fully occupied and she hadn't stopped for lunch. Now she realised she was hungry. She buttered a slice of bread and returned to the living room with it, switching on the radio as she passed by. *The Mayfields* serial was coming to an end and everything was being tied up neatly as it always was: Carol and Jack were back together again after all the trials and tribulations of young love. Rebecca chewed the bread, only half-listening to the news report that followed the play, giving the details about the riots at the Bonegilla migrant camp. Some European refugees were protesting about the living conditions, complaining about the monotonous meals of mutton and rabbit and that the few vegetables they got had been boiled to death. She threw back her head and switched the radio off with her toe, relishing the silence again. When did she get so used to quiet? When did she get so used to living alone? Her mind drifted to Marion. Her friend was a social butterfly who never stayed at home long enough to notice the décor. Rebecca had told her that she was leaving Sydney but not where she was going. She couldn't risk Marion writing to her or sending her elaborate gifts as she was prone to do. She couldn't afford her doing anything that might lead the press straight to her. For the first time since leaving Sydney, Rebecca realised how utterly alone in the world she was. She'd been that way most of her life so what had prevented her from noticing it so keenly until now? A calendar filled with fascinating and glamorous people who had already forgotten her? She pursed her lips and loosened the pins in her hair. Her mother had been diagnosed with lung cancer at the start of the war and was dead by its conclusion. In between her job at the GPO, Rebecca had nursed her: draining her pleural effusions, cleaning up her vomit and faeces, and holding her mother's hand when the pain increased in severity and she could barely breathe. But at the end of it all, it wasn't Rebecca's name her mother had whispered in her final moments. Her daughter was attractive, intelligent and loyal – and yet she couldn't say one kind word about her, even then. Rebecca rose to her feet at that revelation. She thought of the dried-up beauty she had met at the post office that day, Nancy Pike. She mustn't allow herself to be bitter. Did she want to end up like her?

An idea seized her and she got up and flung aside the curtains on the far side of the room to reveal the view of the ocean. 'You can't punish me forever!' she told it under her breath. She went to her wardrobe and took out a cotton plisse dress and tied a scarf over her head, fastening it under her chin. Before she knew it, she found herself marching down the hill towards the beach. The sun was beginning its descent into evening, sending beams of spectacular mauve and tangerine light across the sky. The time just before day slipped into evening had special meaning for Rebecca. It was the time she felt closest to Debbie, although decades separated them now.

Rebecca made her way down a narrow track through scrubland before coming upon the stretch of beach. The warmth of the soft sand rose through the thin soles of her shoes. At the northern tip, a flat rock platform protruded into the silvery ocean. Above it loomed a lushly forested headland. At the southern end, a smaller headland separated the beach from the bay. Rebecca was alone. There was nobody walking at the water's edge or swimming. Not even a single fisherman was casting a line from the rocks. Did the population of Shipwreck Bay prefer to tuck themselves away in their homes rather than enjoy the splendour of their natural surroundings? Rebecca squinted at the ruffled waves like a matador staring down a bull. She could not deny the beauty of the ocean but she was aware that it was a mysterious world full of currents. After a few minutes she turned away from it and began walking north. Crabs scurried from clumps of kelp as she approached, while the seagulls standing on the shoreline sized her up as potential competition for fish. Her eye followed the graceful arc of an albatross as it flew from the rocks and soared high into the air before coming to land on the water. The consul-general of Sweden had once told her that according to Scandinavian folklore albatrosses carried the souls of drowned sailors.

'Debbie?' Rebecca whispered to the wind. But only silence answered her.

Before coming to Shipwreck Bay, Rebecca had tried to learn as much about the township as she could but had found nothing about it at the State Library except a brief mention in a book on shipping disasters. The area's greatest claim to fame seemed to be that so many vessels, having made their way far from the other side of the world, met their watery end outside the bay. The story that had most stayed in Rebecca's mind was that of the sinking of the *Durham* migrant ship in 1864. Gale-force winds had created waves up to fifteen feet high and driven the ship onto the rocks. The passengers who had managed to leave their cabins were washed from the decks by the waves before they could reach the lifeboats. Those who had remained below drowned when the ship broke apart. Out of the 463 people on board only one survived: a fourteen-year-old girl who had clung to a piece of wreckage and miraculously washed up on the beach. She went on to marry the lighthouse keeper at Twin

Falls and had twelve children before accidentally choking on a chicken bone just before her thirty-fifth birthday. According to the book, night fishermen sometimes claimed to have seen the ship's spectral form on moonlit nights and heard the screams of its ghostly passengers.

A glint from the headland caught her eye and she moved towards it. Carved into the sandstone rock was a steep staircase. On the sandy bottom step was the distinct outline of a large bare footprint. Curious, Rebecca climbed the stairs and soon found herself on a winding track bordered by pines and palm trees interspersed with coastal banksia. The sky darkened a shade and the screeching of cockatoos and lorikeets roosting for the night was deafening. She knew it would be wiser to turn back. She didn't know where the track led and soon it would be too dark to see her way safely down the staircase again. Yet she felt compelled forward. The glint flashed again and she saw that it was the sun reflecting off a stained-glass window set in a white tower. She thought she might be looking at a lighthouse. A few yards further on, though, the trees parted and before her rose an Italianate mansion. The brilliant white walls stood out against the sky. The plasterwork was richly decorated with cherub and flower motifs. The upper level had a veranda with filigree panels. The views from the house must have been magnificent. Momentarily forgetting that she was trespassing, Rebecca walked down a gravel path towards the hidden treasure. Who could possibly own a house as splendid as this one when all the other homes in Shipwreck Bay were so modest? The garden was beautifully kept too, with neat hedges and garden beds planted with magnolias, lilies, fan flowers and ferns. Under a large native fig tree sat a cast iron table and chairs.

The beauty of the grounds thrilled her, but as the daylight was fading by the minute she had to find her way to the main road and use that to return to town. Then something made her stop in her tracks. To her right, under a jacaranda tree, was a single tall tombstone surrounded by an iron fence. Her discovery was accompanied by an uncomfortable feeling of being watched. She glanced over her shoulder but there was no one behind her. Then she slowly raised her eyes to the first-floor window above her. A dark figure moved behind it before disappearing. Rebecca did not want to get off on a bad foot with the mansion's owner, so she quickly walked around to the front of the house, where she was relieved to see a long driveway. She hurried down it and was glad to find that it connected with the main road as she had hoped. Down in the bay a few lights flickered and she walked quickly in the direction of them. A wallaby gave her a fright when it bounded out of the bush that bordered one side of the road. She prayed she wouldn't step on a snake. The sound of birds stopped and the night became unnaturally quiet except for the rolling of the ocean waves. Rebecca would have given anything for a torch. The rumble of a motor car approaching from behind made her stop and turn. She saw its lights first but couldn't make out the driver until he came to a stop beside her and rolled down the passenger window.

'Goodness! What are you doing all the way out here on your own?' It was Ernie, the stationmaster. He pushed open the door for her. 'I've just dropped off some chicks to Mick Dolan and was about to come see you,' he said. 'Your luggage arrived this evening.'

Ernie was leering at her again, but what choice did she have other than to accept a lift from him? A sleazy man was something she could handle; a venomous snake soaking up the day's warmth from the road was something she could not. She climbed into the car and glanced at the back seat to see her pearl-blue Starline suitcases and hat boxes. When she had bought that luggage she had been travelling with Ned to places like London and Paris. Never in her life would she have thought she'd be hauling those stylish pieces to anywhere as dull as Shipwreck Bay!

'I was exploring the beach and got lost,' Rebecca said. She considered asking Ernie who owned the mansion on the headland but an instinct stopped her. 'I forgot how quickly the sunset fades even at this time of year.'

When they arrived at Rebecca's house, Ernie dropped the bags next to the mat and leaned against the doorframe making eye contact with her as if he expected she might invite him inside for a drink – and maybe more! Why was it if a man did her a favour he seemed to expect something sexual in return? It would have been irksome enough in someone she found attractive, let alone in Ernie Mullens. She didn't take her key from her pocket but held his gaze square on. 'I can't thank you enough for your kindness,' she told him, smiling sweetly. 'I'm going to bake you some of my digestive biscuits. I'll get Johnny to deliver them to you when he picks up the mail. Everyone says they are delicious!'

Ernie's come-hither gaze wavered. He looked perplexed, not sure whether to be encouraged or disappointed. 'Ah, thank you,' he said, tugging on his bottom lip. 'My grandmother used to make those.'

Rebecca turned from him to his car and waited for him to take the hint. To her relief he did.

'I'll send them soon,' she said, watching him shuffle down the path and ease himself into the driver's seat. She carried her bags inside to her bedroom and opened straight away. Out of them billowed a fantastic array of silk, taffeta, damask and lace. She unfolded a steel-blue sheath dress and held it up. 'Oh, how I've missed you!' she said with all the aplomb of a society hostess welcoming an old friend at the door. Rebecca continued going through the bags and holding up her collection of cocktail and day dresses. She admired each one before putting it on a padded coat hanger and storing it away in the wardrobe. It was only when she'd finished and shoved the suitcases under the bed that she reminded herself that her role as the town's postmistress required a more restrained look and that she was probably never going to wear those dresses again.

CHAPTER SIX

Doris arrived at the post office the following morning with a plate of jam drop biscuits. She was accompanied by a woman with permed grey curls and a lace blouse that was so stiff with starch it lifted at her shoulders.

'This is my friend Mrs Marge Mullens,' Doris said. 'You've met her husband already. Ernie, the stationmaster.'

Marge's eyes were enormous behind her horn-rimmed glasses. She studied Rebecca with such intensity that she felt poked and prodded by the woman's gaze. Had Ernie said anything to his wife that had put Rebecca in a bad light? 'Your husband is a lecher,' she wanted to tell Marge. But instead she said, 'Of course, he was so kind to give me a lift home last night.'

'Where's Johnny?' asked Doris, carrying the biscuits to the tearoom. 'These are his favourites.'

Doris filled the kettle with water and lit the gas stove. Rebecca frowned. She was working and still had so much to do to get the post office in order. She couldn't have people dropping in at any time on social visits. Then she noticed Marge's magnified gaze travelling from her kitten heel pumps to her pink pearl earrings and dreaded what conclusions she might be drawing.

'Mrs Mullens,' she said, taking the woman's arm, 'do come through to the tearoom.' She pulled out a chair for her and then took some cups and saucers out of the cupboard. 'Johnny's out on his delivery at the moment, but I'll put some aside for him.'

To her relief Marge stopped staring at her clothes and looked around the tearoom instead. 'I've never been back here before,' she said. 'I've lived in Shipwreck Bay all my life and I've never been in this room.'

Rebecca's mouth curved into a smile but if she had been a child she would have crossed her fingers behind her back. 'Well, let's hope it's not the last time.'

For the next hour Rebecca had to stop her eyes drifting to the wall clock as the women filled her in on the politics of the local women's bowling association, of which Doris was president and Marge was secretary. For something that was supposed to be a hobby, there seemed to be more rules, by-laws and resolutions than there was legislation being put before parliament. But her skin prickled when it became clear that they were intent on stopping one member from being given lifetime status despite the fact she had twice been runner-up in the district championships.

'Gladys is a fine woman,' declared Marge. 'But they say that daughter of hers is getting up to all sorts of mischief with the local football team. We can't let the good name of the Shipwreck Bay Women's Bowling Association be muddied.'

'Indeed,' said Doris, shaking her head with an air of regret. 'Indeed.'

Bollocks, you can't! thought Rebecca. Malicious gossip was nothing new to her: Sydney had been full of it. The advantage of a city with a large population was that there were so many victims to choose from, and so many distractions, that the sheer exhaustion of it often led to people turning a blind eye. But in a town as small as Shipwreck Bay, being singled out could be fatal. Gladys was a scapegoat for something. Boredom? Self-loathing? Petty jealousy? She probably had tea and jam drops with Marge and Doris at the bowling club all the time, unaware that they were plotting her downfall. Rebecca couldn't afford for these two prattlers to start undermining her.

'Mrs Campbell,' she said, taking a nibble of one of the biscuits. 'These are the most delicious jam drops I've ever eaten. Do you make the filling yourself?'

A satisfied smile rose on Doris's face. 'Yes, I do. I use the oranges from my own trees.'

'She is the queen of conserves,' piped in Marge, with a high-pitched laugh. 'Her strawberry jam is famous. She always wins first prize at the Twin Falls Fair.'

Doris patted her friend's wrist. 'Marge is being modest. Her chutneys and relishes can't be beaten.'

Rebecca raised her eyebrows as she looked from one woman to the other, then glanced at the plate in front of her. 'Oh dear,' she said. 'I'm afraid, Mrs Mullens, I offered your husband some digestive biscuits in return for his kindness in dropping off my luggage. I had no idea he was married to such a good cook! He must have baulked at something so plain! Although I must say he was very gallant about it.'

'Digestive biscuits can be quite delicious if you dunk them in sweet tea,' replied Marge, looking uncertainly at Doris.

'I coat mine in chocolate,' Doris said. 'And the next batch I'm thinking of trying *mint chocolate* or a layer of caramel.'

'Oh, that sounds very decadent!' chimed Marge.

Rebecca blew out a long breath and shook her head. 'I could do with some cooking lessons. It sounds like the both of you know what you're talking about when it comes to digestive biscuits.'

Doris and Marge shared a look then Doris winked at her friend. 'Well, it would be a pleasure to teach you how to bake,' said Doris. 'But I wouldn't bother with digestive biscuits when there are so many others to try. We could start with some ginger nuts and honey jumbles.'

Rebecca felt like an archer who had hit the bullseye. There was nothing more these two old biddies would enjoy than 'a project' and as long as she was that to them they would defend her against gossip. Making sure that Rebecca was seen in the best light would become a matter of personal pride.

*

After the women left, Rebecca turned her attention to the accounts books. The telephone rang, giving her a start. She went to the sorting room and picked up the receiver.

'Shipwreck Bay Post Office, Postmistress Wood speaking.'

It was the first time Rebecca had used her official title and she stood taller as she did so. She'd never had a title before, only a position. It didn't matter that her domain was a small town and she was in charge of only one person. The title was a marker of status and something she had achieved on her own. It gave her hope that perhaps it was not all going to be downhill after Ned.

'Byron Bay Post Office, Postmaster Jenkins. Are you ready to take a telegram?' a gruff voice on the end of the line answered her.

Rebecca replied that she was and wrote down the message: *McEwen willing to consider. Meet Tuesday, September 18th, 10 o'clock.* She double-checked the address before ringing off.

It wasn't as exciting as being a telegraphist during the war but, still, it was a start to official business. She typed up the message, addressing it to Mr Stefan Otto of 144 Ocean Road, Shipwreck Bay. Most migrants anglicised their names but for some reason Mr Otto had kept his German spelling. The name sounded vaguely familiar. She checked the telephone subscribers' list. Stefan Otto was one of the names along with George Pike and a Dr T. Litchfield. She glanced at the map, surprised to discover that the address was for the house on the headland she had seen the previous evening. She recalled its grandeur and the figure she had seen pass the window. Who exactly was Stefan Otto then? He was certainly very rich. She was tempted to take the telegram herself in order to find out, but before she could give the matter any more thought, Johnny returned.

She handed the telegram to him. 'Deliver this when you go out on your second route.'

Johnny glanced at the address. 'Oh, so he's back! The Pikes won't be at all pleased.'

Rebecca raised an eyebrow, her curiosity piqued.

Johnny grinned as if excited to have a titbit that interested her. 'Old Stefan Otto used to be an important man in this town. Now he lives in Europe somewhere. He only comes back every so often to check on his house and business and … to cause trouble.'

'What sort of trouble?'

'He doesn't agree with the whaling station. But my mother says that's just because he wants revenge on the town.'

The delivery boy pursed his lips. At first Rebecca thought it was because he was holding something back, but then she suspected it was because he didn't have much more to offer. She had thought she had come to a quiet, sleepy town. It didn't bode well that someone who lived in Europe most of the time, and obviously had a lot of money, wanted to settle a score with Shipwreck Bay. 'Revenge for what?' she asked.

He shook his head. 'Something happened during the war. I was too young to understand but I hear he was some sort of spy.'

Dear God! thought Rebecca. With all the paranoia over Soviet spies in Australia, Shipwreck Bay would be a light bulb flashing on the surveillance map of ASIO if they thought there was a spy in their midst.

'Take the telegram to Mr Otto's place but don't linger there,' she told Johnny sternly. 'Don't start a conversation with him.'

'Not much chance of that,' replied Johnny. 'Mr Otto keeps to himself. The maid and gardener don't speak a word of English and the butler will only talk to me out near the gate. It's as if he doesn't want me near the house.'

'Then keep it that way,' Rebecca warned him.

She watched Johnny pedal off on his bicycle then went to the tearoom and poured herself a glass of water. During the war the Department of External Affairs had been a hotbed of spies. Ned had been given the minister's role with the expectation of a post-war clean-up. What if the press got wind there was a suspected spy in Shipwreck Bay and they started swarming all over the town? What if one of them recognised her from Sydney and made something out of it? Rebecca's imagination grew wild with scenarios. She saw herself on *Movietone News* being pushed and shoved by government agents towards a car while the press chased after them, their camera bulbs flashing. 'I'm innocent,' she'd protest. 'I'm not a spy!'

'You were Ned McKell's mistress!' they'd cry. 'Nobody can believe anything you say!'

The bell on the post office counter rang. Rebecca put the glass down and patted her face with her handkerchief before walking out the front. A middle-aged couple were waiting there. The woman's dress was clean but worn. The man leaned on the counter to support himself and Rebecca noticed the sleeves of his suit were patched. Her stomach flipped when he glanced at her. Her mother had that look on her face when she had been put on oxygen during her last days. It was the expression of someone who was exhausted by life and wanted to give up, but some power outside of themselves forced them to keep going.

'I'd like to ... send a registered letter ... to Judge Rainbow ... in Wollongong,' the man panted.

His wheezing sent Rebecca into a panic. But she calmed herself by a sheer force of will, remembering that in the telegraph office she had always been admired for her sangfroid.

'I can organise that for you.' She indicated a chair at the side of the waiting area. 'Why don't you take a seat while I get the form.'

The woman leaned across the counter and patted Rebecca's hand. 'He insists on sending the letters to the judge himself,' she whispered. 'Although it nearly kills him to walk up the hill to get here. I can't believe that for thirty years I watched him leave at four every morning and walk all the way to the coal mines at the top of the mountain.' Her eyes teared up.

Rebecca quickly looked away and reached for the registered mail documents. A dull thud had them both turn in the direction of the man. He was on his knees, clutching at his throat.

'Corman!' the woman cried.

She rushed towards her husband, who was now on his back and gasping for air.

Air-raid drills and first-aid training flashed before Rebecca's eyes. The voice of the medical officer who had been in charge of instructing the post office staff boomed in her ears: *If someone is having difficulty breathing, loosen any tight clothing, check for wounds …*

Rebecca swung open the counter door and hurried towards the couple. She loosened the man's collar and belt. He was sucking in air but not breathing it out. He reminded her of a fish fighting for breath after it had been pulled out of water. Rebecca could never stand the sight of that and as a consequence never ate fish.

She tugged off her cardigan and rolled it before placing it behind the man's neck to keep his airway straight. 'Stay calm. Stay calm. Panicking won't help,' she told him, speaking as much to herself as she was to the man. She remembered the telephone subscribers' list. 'I'll call the doctor.'

She dialled the number and the line was answered by a nurse. Rebecca described the man's condition. 'I'll speak to Doctor Litchfield immediately,' the nurse told her. She must have put her hand over the receiver because all Rebecca could hear after that was a muffled conversation. The nurse came back on the line. 'The doctor is on his way.'

Rebecca returned to the couple, relieved to see that the man had improved slightly. The colour had come back to his face but he was still straining to breathe.

His wife glanced at Rebecca. 'What's on your face you can wash off. What's in your lungs you can't.'

Rebecca was about to ask the woman what she'd meant, but the sound of a motor car stopping outside the post office turned her attention to the street. A man in a grey suit was stepping out of a Holden sedan. He walked around it, opened the passenger side door and grabbed a leather bag.

'The doctor is here,' Rebecca told the couple.

Doctor Litchfield took off his hat as he stepped into the post office. He was younger than she had expected: in his late thirties and trim-looking with brown hair cut short but left wavy on top.

'Well, Mr Ryan,' he said, kneeling beside the older man, 'it looks like you've taken a bit of a turn.'

He opened his bag, took out a stethoscope and listened to Mr Ryan's chest. His brow wrinkled. The doctor didn't like what he was hearing.

'He's able to do less and less these days, Doctor Litchfield,' the woman said.

The doctor nodded. 'Let's get him comfortable at my surgery, shall we? I'll fetch the stretcher from my car. Do you think you ladies will be able to help me? I don't want to put him over my shoulder in his condition.'

He looked up at Rebecca for the first time. Doctor Litchfield had pale English skin with high colour in his cheeks. The slight downward slope of his blue eyes gave him the appearance of someone who was kind. The impression was strengthened when he beamed Rebecca a self-deprecating smile. Dozens of laugh lines fanned from around his eyes and she wondered if he was the sort of person who laughed a lot, when he wasn't worrying about one of his patients.

'I'm sorry,' he said, rising to his feet. 'We haven't been introduced. I'm Doctor Timothy Litchfield. And you must be our new postmistress?'

'Rebecca Wood,' she said, taking the hand he offered her. Unlike most men, Doctor Litchfield looked straight into her face and nowhere else.

He turned back to his patient. 'Right, let's get Mr Ryan into the car.'

After they had moved Mr Ryan onto the stretcher, Doctor Litchfield picked up one end while the two women lifted the other. Once they had eased the patient into the back seat of the car, Doctor Litchfield folded the stretcher and then opened the passenger side door for Mrs Ryan. He gave a nod to Rebecca. 'I'm sure our paths will cross again soon, Miss Wood.'

Rebecca watched the car take off then returned to the post office. For a second she thought she herself might faint and had to grip onto the counter until the blood returned to her head. What a morning! At least Corman Ryan's collapse had taken her mind off spies, and the town's doctor seemed like a decent person. She went to the tearoom, intending to make a strong cup of tea but her hand trembled and she dropped the kettle. The sea was roaring turbulently, pounding onto the beach – or was it her imagination? She clamped her hands over her ears. Her mother's panicked screams rose above the sound of the waves. Rebecca felt herself being sucked back into her ten-year-old's body, the salt stinging her sunburnt skin and her throat so dry she couldn't swallow. She saw them: the bathers forming a human chain to keep back the curious crowds. Her father on his knees, his face in his hands. A woman she had never seen before was putting a towel around his shoulders. Rebecca stood at the edge of it all, a silent witness. She had known it then and she knew it now: she had been forsaken.

CHAPTER SEVEN

Rebecca spent the rest of the afternoon in her office, combing through the accounts books and files. Mabel had been a meticulous bookkeeper. Income and expenses were neatly recorded in the ledger with nothing crossed out or bleeding over the columns. In the files, related documents were grouped together and bound with a clip so that there was nothing out of place and no unnecessary clutter. It seemed that Mabel was the type of person who kept on top of things. Rebecca glanced at the box containing the deceased postmistress's personal items. So how to explain her dramatic end? Rebecca understood grief and how it could twist the mind out of shape, but to her it was like a dark shadow that followed you. Sometimes it engulfed you, but you had to be strong and pull yourself out of it. Losing a child was a tragedy, although many women lost children and went on living. A heavy sensation gripped her heart and she rubbed at her chest. Perhaps some women had a stronger will to live than others?

She picked up Mabel's box and carried it to the sorting room where she placed it in the bottom of the cupboard. Her hand lingered over it for a moment. She was tempted to open it and learn something about her predecessor. But there was a danger in stepping into the minefield of someone's private thoughts, the ones every person keeps hidden behind their public mask. Rebecca had learned that when she was an adolescent after sneaking a look at her mother's diary. The first words she'd laid eyes on had shocked her: *Rebecca is a cold, selfish girl. I feel nothing for her at all.* She'd put the diary straight back and never dared to venture into her mother's secret confessions again. She could have guessed her mother's opinion of her from the way she ignored her, but to see it there in that erratic, jagged handwriting had been like having a nine-inch nail twisted into her heart. She sometimes wondered if those damning words in her mother's diary had become a self-fulfilling prophecy, because other women often described her as aloof and self-contained. But the words of a perfect stranger, someone who had nothing to do with her, what could be the harm …?

'Knock! Knock!' a man's voice called cheerily.

She went out to the counter to find Doctor Litchfield standing there. The knot in his tie had slipped an inch and he had the slightest shadow on his upper lip, yet he still managed to maintain a prim and proper air.

'I thought I'd better inform you of Mr Ryan's progress, Miss Wood,' he said. 'It must have been an awful shock to have him collapse on you like that. Although Mrs Ryan tells me that you handled the situation with great composure. Level-headedness is a wonderful quality in any sort of emergency.'

Doctor Litchfield had an expressive face. He wrinkled his brow, lifted his eyebrows and blinked as if to emphasise each point as he made it.

'What is wrong with Mr Ryan, exactly?' she asked.

'Pneumoconiosis – dust on the lung,' replied Doctor Litchfield, patting his chest. 'It occurs when miners regularly inhale coal dust. The disease is a terrible one that develops slowly over many years and results in the scarring of the lungs and breathing difficulties.' He grimaced. 'It will kill him eventually.'

Rebecca had never heard of pneumoconiosis. She hadn't known any men who performed manual work. Her own father had been a bank clerk. 'Is it a common disease?'

'Unfortunately so,' he answered, frowning. 'I see it more than I'd like, Miss Wood. *Far more* than I'd like.' He stared off into space for a moment before rousing himself again. 'Mechanisation of the mines is increasing productivity but unfortunately it's also increasing coal dust. The high mortality rate is entirely preventable, of course, which is the tragedy. If the coal companies would agree to their men having regular X-rays we could catch it early and so slow its progress. But sadly profit often trumps morals. Even many of the miners resist the idea, frightened of losing their jobs.'

Doctor Litchfield looked towards the post office door as if he was thinking about leaving but then he turned back to Rebecca. 'So how are you finding Shipwreck Bay? You probably haven't had much of a chance to get to know it yet as you only arrived on Sunday evening, is that right?'

Rebecca wondered if someone had told him that or whether the whole town had been watching her arrive at the station, peering from behind their lace curtains and venetian blinds.

'The beach is very pretty,' she replied, diplomatically. 'Apart from that I haven't seen much else.'

Doctor Litchfield rubbed his chin. 'You are from Sydney, aren't you?'

'Yes, that's right.'

'Whereabouts did you live?'

'Potts Point.'

Doctor Litchfield's eyes lit up. 'Oh really! That's a jolly part of the city, isn't it? All those nightspots. Did you live there long?'

Rebecca hesitated. She was not used to a man asking her so many questions. In her experience men liked to talk about themselves.

'A few years.'

'And before that? Were you born in Sydney?'

There was nothing in Doctor Litchfield's kind and animated face to suggest he was scrutinising her the way Nancy Pike had, but she had to be cautious not to reveal something she might later regret. She suspected the only way she was going to put a stop to his stream of inquiries was to ask him about himself.

'Yes, I was. And you? Were you born in Shipwreck Bay?'

The smile froze on Doctor Litchfield's face. He lowered his eyes. 'My father was the local doctor here. I studied in Sydney and returned there after my war service. I enjoyed city life very much but after my father died, my mother suffered a stroke and I came back here.'

Rebecca winced. Apart from the fact that she was hiding her past, she had never been fond of asking too many personal questions of someone she didn't know well. There was always the risk of trespassing on a sensitive topic. 'I'm sorry to hear that. Is your mother all right now?'

Doctor Litchfield shook his head. 'I'm afraid not. There is little she can do for herself and she isn't able to speak more than the occasional muffled word or two.' He seemed to reflect on his mother's state a moment before looking up and smiling again. 'Some things can't be helped. Still, I must say that I'm glad to be here. It's a wonderful town with wonderful people.'

Rebecca felt her face involuntarily twitch and Doctor Litchfield noticed. He clapped his hands together. 'You don't quite think so, do you, Miss Wood?' he said with a hearty laugh. 'Never mind. At first, people here can be downright odd towards newcomers. That's not unusual in small towns. They will warm to you soon enough!'

'Thank you,' Rebecca replied. She could see from his lively manner that Doctor Litchfield was not duplicitous or cunning. But that meant she would have to be extra careful around him. She could not afford for his affability to cause her to drop her guard. She was quite certain she would only be welcome in Shipwreck Bay as long as her secret remained just that – a secret.

He wandered towards the window and looked out. 'It's a shame the garden has been let go. Mabel was so proud of it.' He glanced back at Rebecca. 'I suppose you saw the flowers at the station? All her work. She had such tremendous civic pride.'

Rebecca glanced at the garden. It was very untidy. The rose stems were woody, the English ivy had grown rampant and cotoneaster seedlings had sprung up in the beds. It spoiled the presentation of the post office and she didn't want to be seen as an inferior postmistress to Mabel. But she didn't like any activity that involved dirt and she was certain Johnny wouldn't be much help. The expense for a gardener was not in the post office budget – nor her private one.

'I don't have a green thumb, unfortunately,' she said.

Doctor Litchfield raised an eyebrow and smiled at her. 'Don't you? I'm very fond of gardening. I got that from my mother. She created the most spectacular garden at our home. You must come and see it sometime.'

Rebecca couldn't miss the sparkle in Doctor Litchfield's eyes nor the delighted smile on his face. 'A flower to the bees,' Marion had often said to describe Rebecca's uncanny allure to men. But what caught her off-guard now was that Doctor Litchfield wasn't the usual sort of 'bee' that honed in on her. Rebecca's type was self-absorbed, cocksure and highly ambitious. Doctor Litchfield didn't display any of those characteristics. He was so … *nice*. Robert had been nice too. But theirs had been a wartime affair, an affection borne from the heightened awareness of the fragility of life. It would not have lasted in peacetime.

She smiled but did not accept Doctor Litchfield's invitation. She had not come to Shipwreck Bay seeking a romance. Her plan was to stay until all the fuss about Ned McKell's 'Mystery Woman' died down and then move back to Sydney.

The door to the post office swung open and Berit Olsen hurried inside, glancing over her shoulder as if she was afraid of being followed. But there was no one else out on the street.

'Hello, Mrs Olsen,' said Doctor Litchfield. 'I hope you are keeping well?'

Berit started in surprise. Her eyes were faraway and unfocused. Then she seemed to recognise the doctor and nodded shyly. 'Yes, well, thank you, doctor.'

'Good!' said Doctor Litchfield. Then turning to Rebecca again he said, 'Well, I mustn't keep you. I hope you shall be very happy here, Miss Wood. Please let me know if there is anything I can do to help you.'

After Doctor Litchfield left, Berit turned to Rebecca. 'He is a nice man. *Too nice* for Shipwreck Bay.'

Rebecca didn't confess that she had been thinking the same thing. She took the passbook and money bag Berit handed her and filled out the deposit slip. There was a pound note and a few coins in the bag, far less than the sum Berit had brought her the previous day. She wondered why she didn't save up her banking and do it once a week like the other businesses did, according to the accounts books she had checked that morning.

'You said that you knew Mabel Peberdy well?' Rebecca asked. 'There's a box of her things here that her family hasn't collected. I wondered if we have the right address?'

Berit flinched and glanced over her shoulder again. 'I knew her but not her family. Well, except her daughter, Anne. I often saw the young woman walking along the beach. She was, you know ...' Berit struggled with the translation of the word. '*Evneveik.*'

Rebecca shook her head and Berit tried again. 'Simple ... slow.'

'You mean she was mentally retarded?'

Berit nodded. 'Pretty and sweet but yes ...'

Rebecca turned back to the banking. The idea that Mabel's daughter had been retarded made the whole tragedy seem worse. She imagined the girl must have wandered too close to the waves and been washed away. She shouldn't have been left to walk on the beach alone. *Never turn your back on the ocean* was a warning Rebecca's father had often given. She froze, her hand clenched tight around the handle of the rubber stamp. She hadn't obeyed that warning, had she? And she had paid for it. She was still paying for it.

'Are you all right?' Berit asked.

Rebecca released her grip on the stamp and put it back in the drawer. 'Yes, I just remembered something that I have to do later this afternoon.'

She meant to slide the passbook back to Berit, but she pushed it too hard and it tumbled to the floor. 'I'm sorry ...'

Berit bent down to pick it up and the collar of her blouse gaped open. In the middle of Berit's chest, just below the collarbone, was a bruise the size of a grapefruit or, more precisely, from the four-knuckle bruises above it, the size of a man's fist. Berit straightened and realised that Rebecca had seen the injury. Neither woman said anything for a few moments.

'If he hits you, it's not going to get better,' Rebecca finally offered.

Berit glanced at her hands.

'He might kill you.'

'I know.'

Now Rebecca understood why Berit had come to do the banking on a day when she didn't have much money to deposit. This is the point I should stop saying anything, she thought. I don't want to know. I don't want to get involved. I can't. I have enough trouble of my own.

'There's no smell today,' she said, hoping to change the subject.

'The men are still out on the boat. They haven't found anything.' The pleading look on Berit's face was palpable.

Of course Berit would come for help when her husband was out at sea. Rebecca felt like she was wandering dangerously close to a cliff edge. Wisdom was telling her to step back yet by some odd impulse she floundered forwards.

'Do you want me to do something for you?'

Berit's eyes flashed. 'On the days when I would bring a lot of money, Mabel used to put some of it aside, in the safe. It should still be there in an envelope with "B. Johnson" written on it. Johansen was my maiden name.'

Rebecca knew that she should not get involved in something like this, especially now. She wavered a moment and then almost kicked herself when she heard herself saying, 'I see no reason why we can't continue to do that.' Was it the memory of what her mother had written about her in her diary all those years ago that was goading her to act unselfishly?

She checked the safe and nodded to the young woman to assure her the envelope was still there.

Berit smiled with relief. For the first time she looked as if her spirit had not been completely broken.

CHAPTER EIGHT

A great bellowing broke the dawn silence. Rebecca opened her eyes. The sound had been mournful, desolate. She was filled with sadness and a sense of hopelessness. When Ned had unceremoniously dumped her she'd gone into survival mode, salvaging what she could of her dignity and the last seven years of her life, without ever questioning if there was any point to it all. Now, in the grey light of morning, that was all she could think about. Her hand slipped to her stomach. In Monaco Ned had told her that he loved her as they walked through the beautiful Jardin Exotique. His declaration had taken her by surprise because he was not usually a sentimental man. But nobody can be trusted completely, regardless of what they say. She'd dared to think that he might be happy when two months later she told him she was pregnant. She'd hoped he'd put his arms around her and tell her that he was thrilled. Instead he had turned grim and started pacing. Then the next day he handed her a piece of paper with the address of a Macquarie Street specialist; he'd paid a hefty sum so she would be diagnosed as mentally unfit to have a child. 'It's the only way to do it legally, otherwise you could go to jail,' he told her, pleased with himself for finding such a clever solution to 'her dilemma'. Rebecca cried and then he did put his arms around her. 'There is nothing else to do in this situation,' he said. 'I already have two children with Cynthia. It would ruin me. You ought to think about the kind of life that an *illegitimate* child would have, Rebecca. Think of it!' She did think of it as she stared at his gold wedding ring. She'd gone to the appointment the following day and they never spoke of the matter again.

Why had she fallen so hard for a man who was bad for her? And why did she keep loving him long after he had shamelessly discarded her? She clenched her fists. No matter how lousy Ned had been to her, no matter all the pain he had put her through, she missed him. She hated herself for that.

The bellow came again, this time full of agony. It was a whale in its death throes. The harpooner had failed to kill it quickly. Every muscle in Rebecca's body tensed. She sat up and strained her ears, but no other sound followed it. Tears filled her eyes. It was as if that cry had contained not only all her sorrows, but all the sorrows of the world: the failure of the human race to ever overcome its wickedness.

*

The foul smell from the whaling station assaulted Rebecca's nostrils as she made her way to the post office. The wind was blowing in from the sea and bringing the stink with it. She took her handkerchief from her purse to cover her nose but then noticed the grocer and two women watching her. She tucked it away again and nodded as she passed them.

When she reached the post office she gave a start. The garden beds that surrounded it on two sides had been transformed. The weeds and the overgrown vines had been cleared and the soil had been tilled. Was this Doctor Litchfield's doing? Her question was answered when she opened the post office and found a note from him slipped under the doorway.

Dear Miss Wood,

I hope you don't mind my garden handiwork. I have some seedlings and bulbs in my greenhouse that I thought we could plant together.

A beautiful garden is a delightful thing to look at and I hope it will remind you how very much the people of Shipwreck Bay appreciate you taking on the role of postmistress in our little town.

Yours truly,
Timothy Litchfield (Dr)

Rebecca bristled. While she was sure Doctor Litchfield had made the gesture with the best of intentions, she did not like the presumptuousness of it. It was one thing to be in agreement that the garden was in need of attention and quite another to go ahead and fix it without asking her. Perhaps he'd seen it as some sort of courting gesture. But if Doctor Litchfield knew about her past would he still be so keen?

'What's happened out there?' asked Doris, striding in the door.

Rebecca looked up. She was relieved to see that her landlady was carrying a couple of parcels for posting and not a plate of biscuits. She showed her the note from Doctor Litchfield.

'Well, you've certainly made an impression,' said Doris, lifting her eyebrows. 'Ernie told me Doctor Litchfield was praising your composure over what happened with poor Corman Ryan yesterday. It seems to me that you have already caught the eye of the town's most eligible man.'

Rebecca weighed the parcels Doris was posting and dampened stamps for them in the sponge on the counter. 'Why isn't he married?'

Doris raised her eyebrows and Rebecca felt rebuked. She was expressing the same curiosity about Doctor Litchfield's marital status as people usually did about hers. *If she's such a catch, why isn't she married? Was she a late bloomer? Too selfish to share her life with another? A sexual deviant – or, at the other end of the spectrum, completely frigid?* Despite what others might assume, she was alone due to bad choices. She couldn't fathom anyone intentionally choosing to live in solitude unless they were a priest or a nun.

'He *was* married,' said Doris, picking through her coin purse to pay for the stamps. 'In Sydney, when he came back from his war service. But she took off without a word one day. She broke his heart, that's for sure. Some women can't appreciate an honest, hardworking man who treats them well. He hasn't looked at another woman since.' Doris placed her money on the counter and grinned. 'Not until now at least.'

Rebecca was ashamed of herself. Having a broken heart was the stuff of love songs and poems, but there was nothing romantic about it. It was like existing in a deep well of sadness. She cleared her throat and gathered Doris's parcels.

'So these are going to Canberra? Johnny will put them on the train first thing in the morning.'

'My daughter lives there with her husband and my two grandchildren.'

From the whimsical smile that came to Doris's face, Rebecca assumed the relationship was a good one. She couldn't understand why, if someone was blessed with good family relations, they would live apart from them. 'You don't want to move there to live with them?' she asked.

Doris's face flushed and she lowered her eyes. 'The younger generation is different. They want their independence and freedom. They don't want their mother – or grandmother – hanging around and doling out old-fashioned advice.' Doris's gaze drifted towards the street. 'Besides I've lived in this town all my life. I can't imagine living anywhere else.'

Despite her distrust of the woman, Rebecca felt sorry for her. It wasn't a good feeling to be unwanted. Her own mother barely acknowledged her and yet they remained bound together until her death by a silence heavy with guilt, shame and bitterness. She gave Doris her receipt and change. 'Well, at least you have all your friends here,' she said. 'Marge and the women from the bowling club.'

Doris's hand flew to her chin. 'Oh, I almost forgot – speaking of friends, Nancy Pike asked me to invite you along to her bridge game this Friday night.'

Rebecca had intended to spend Friday night with her feet up drinking wine and reading a book. The last thing she wanted was to end the week with a bunch of gossiping women.

She stalled for time. 'Oh ... but Saturday will be busy here at the post office. I was planning on getting an early night.'

Doris met Rebecca's gaze. 'Nancy's husband, George, is the shire secretary. He is the most powerful man in town. Nothing happens without his seal of approval. Nancy is an important woman to have on your side.'

Rebecca couldn't imagine Nancy ever being on her side, but she got the message. 'All right, I'll be there.'

*

Rebecca hesitated in front of Nancy's house holding a box of Cadbury's Milk Tray chocolates that she'd bought at the general store. Unlike the humble weatherboard cottages around it, the house was new. She cast her eye over the skillion roof and hopper windows, then took in a breath before making her way down the crazy paving pathway. A man in his early forties wearing a check shirt and pleated trousers opened the front door before she even had a chance to knock. He'd been frowning but smiled as soon as he saw her. 'Well, hello,' he said. 'You must be our new postmistress. Come inside, the other girls have all arrived. I'm George Pike, Nancy's husband.'

His sunken eyes and prominent underbite gave George Pike the appearance of a piranha. He was certainly no match for Nancy in terms of beauty. Rebecca shook his hand and tried not to stare at the lacework of red veins that covered his nose and cheeks. He smelt vinegary. Shire secretary or not, he was a drinker. George guided Rebecca down a corridor reeking of tobacco smoke and Glamorene carpet cleaner, and then into a sunroom with wood-panelled walls covered in sporting ribbons. Card tables had been set up and a group of women were gathered around them, drinking sherry and picking from platters of devilled eggs and crackers topped with cheese and tomato. Their chatter sounded like a flock of barnyard chickens. They fell silent when Rebecca entered behind George.

'Miss Wood is here,' he announced.

Doris beamed at her, but the others squinted as if they were sizing her up. Rebecca had thought of dressing down to avoid scrutiny but couldn't bring herself to do it. She knew she hadn't been invited to be made welcome; she'd been invited so she could be appraised. Clothes had always been her armour. Now it seemed that the women were scrutinising her emerald green dress as if searching for a chink in it.

'Oh, Rebecca, how nice of you to come,' said Nancy, ignoring the formal way George had introduced her and thrusting a glass of sherry into her hand. 'Lyn has a cold and couldn't make it so I'm glad you could take her place.' Nancy seemed to want to give the impression that she and Rebecca were on intimate terms, but the chill in her voice belied any semblance of friendship.

Nancy guided Rebecca towards a woman with olive skin and bleached hair. 'This is Elaine. She's my bridge partner.' Elaine was slightly older than Nancy and Rebecca while the other women were in their fifties and sixties. Apart from Doris and Marge, they were dressed plainly in shirtwaist dresses and flat shoes. As Nancy introduced them Rebecca memorised the women's names by associating them with their physical appearance. There was Carmel, who was as big as a house;

Sue, who was rake thin; and Joy, who had a mole the size of a marble smack in the middle of her forehead.

From the way the women looked at Nancy to take their cues, it was clear that she was the town's female leader. Only Doris seemed able to hold her own in Nancy's presence. 'Rebecca can partner with me tonight,' she said, placing her arm possessively around Rebecca's shoulders, as if the novelty of pairing with the newcomer was her right because she was her landlady.

'You have played before, haven't you?' Elaine asked Rebecca.

'A few times,' she answered, although she was an expert card player. Ned had admired her ability to concentrate. Even if her emotions were in turmoil, Rebecca usually remained outwardly cool. When it came to cards, she was all logic and strategy and not a trace of passion; entirely a different woman to the one she was when she was in love.

'Right, I'll be off to the pub then,' said George, 'I'll leave you girls to it.'

He and Nancy made as if to peck each other on the cheek but stopped half an inch from each other's flesh. The farce gave Rebecca the impression they couldn't get away from each other fast enough. She scanned the room. As well as the sporting ribbons there were two large display cabinets jammed with trophies. In one were prizes for boxing, darts, football and fishing. In the other stood gleaming cups for dancing, gymnastics and badminton. His and her display cabinets?

The tables were cleared of food and Nancy placed a deck of cards on each one along with a packet of cigarettes and an ashtray. She, Elaine, Doris and Rebecca sat at one table while the other women occupied the other. Nancy took out a cigarette and so did all the other women, except for Rebecca.

'Where's Earl?' Doris asked Nancy.

'He's in his room,' she replied, shuffling the cards. 'He knows it's ladies' night and not to disturb us.'

Rebecca assumed 'Earl' was a child. She glanced at the trophies and ribbons but couldn't see any for a junior. Either Earl was an underachiever or his awards were kept elsewhere.

'George looked out of sorts tonight,' said Elaine. 'Is he all right?'

'It's blasted Stefan Otto, isn't it?' said Doris. 'George has spent months lobbying for Sanders Olsen and his men to be given a factory ship so they can catch more whales and process them faster, and Otto keeps putting a stop on it. It seems he's got enough Nazi friends in high places to side with him.'

Nancy took a drag of her cigarette and said nothing, but Rebecca's ears pricked up at the mention of the town's spy. Although she feared the implications of having someone so dangerous in close proximity, she couldn't help being fascinated. It was a much more intriguing aspect to the town than bowling clubs.

'He did enough damage lobbying for that quota on the humpback whales. He has no loyalty to this town,' said Joy, scowling.

'But the price of whale oil is dropping,' ventured Carmel, pursing her lips as she shuffled the cards for her table. 'There are other things this town needs now. Like a hospital, for instance.'

A glance from Nancy censured her and Carmel fell quiet. It was clear that having an opinion that contradicted their queen bee wasn't to be tolerated. Rebecca couldn't resist the temptation to poke at the hive.

'Is Stefan Otto's house the one on the headland? I saw it the other evening. It's rather beautiful.'

The look Nancy shot her could have struck Rebecca dead. Her eyes turned black and the veins on her neck popped out. Rebecca had only meant to tease her hostess. The reaction was far more than she'd anticipated. What was it about that house that had got her back up?

'Of course he's got a fancy house,' growled Sue. 'It was built on the backs of the miners. Then when he was bored with that source of income he withdrew his investments and poured his money into shipping and the steelworks at Port Kembla.'

Elaine huffed. 'He's a traitor in more ways than one. Everyone knows he was the one who sent the signal out to those enemy submarines during the war. If George hadn't intervened we'd all be speaking German.'

It was obvious from the women's reaction that Rebecca had stepped on an old wound in the town. Still, a Nazi spy who wanted to stop whaling was an interesting combination. She was about to ask how that was possible when Doris shook her head subtly, warning her to stay off the subject. Whoever Stefan Otto was, he'd managed to get himself ostracised by the people around him. Rebecca would have to be careful if she didn't want to end up in the same position.

'Well, let's play bridge, shall we?' said Elaine, dealing the cards.

It was a relief when the game finally got started. Ned had once remarked that someone's true personality was revealed in two environments: in the sack and at the card table. Rebecca kept her eyes fixed on her hand, careful not to give any secrets away. She knew the best card players were able to pick up the slightest cues from their opponents in order to construct what cards they were holding. After the first couple of tricks it was clear this was a game Nancy took seriously. Anybody who thought bridge was just for fun and a social activity wouldn't have lasted long against her. She played smoothly and deliberately and with no hesitation. Rebecca relaxed her own competitive nature. She'd pushed her hostess far enough and when it was Nancy and Elaine who won she took it gracefully.

'You didn't play too badly at all *for a beginner*,' Elaine told her, with a touch of sarcasm. 'Doris might consider replacing Lyn with you.'

But cards were not the only thing Nancy played with uncanny precision. When the decks were put away, she laid out a supper of Swedish meatballs and ham roll-ups and a bowl of rum punch before beginning a tricky line of questioning that would have put any police detective to shame.

'So which church service will you be attending this Sunday?' she asked Rebecca, passing around a plate of cheese cubes on toothpicks.

Religion was a topic Rebecca preferred to stay clear of with people she didn't know. Nancy's question had been posed to set her up in some way. How she answered it would give a myriad of information about her – from her morals to her social background. She had been brought up Anglican, but didn't go to church now. Fortunately, spending time with politicians had taught her how to be politely evasive. 'I was planning to go with Doris this Sunday. Why do you ask?'

She had no idea what religion Doris was, but she remembered her landlady mentioning to Ernie something about organising the flowers with Marge for the Sunday service. She assumed from the lack of religious paraphernalia in the house that the Pikes weren't Catholic and the free serving of alcohol made them unlikely to be Methodists. But whatever church service Doris and Marge attended must have been acceptable to Nancy, otherwise she wouldn't have them in her house. She just hoped it was not something as fervorous as the Salvation Army.

Nancy's eyes narrowed to slits. 'Oh, so you are Anglican then?'

Rebecca nodded, biting down on a cracker smeared with processed cheese. She hadn't eaten the gooey stuff since she was a child and ran her tongue around her mouth to dislodge it from between her teeth.

Her inquisitor wasn't about to be deflected easily. 'Whereabouts did you worship in Sydney?'

Rebecca had to be careful. For all she knew, Nancy could originally be from Sydney and have friends all over the city.

'In the northern suburbs,' she replied, giving a wide area in order to be as vague as possible.

The other women were riveted by the exchange. From the way she pinched her lips, Nancy wasn't satisfied with Rebecca's answers to her questions. She changed tack. 'I'm pleased to hear you are a believer. Since the war a lot of people have given up churchgoing, but the practice of religion is what keeps families together and men faithful. Don't you agree?'

Now Rebecca was sure this curiosity had as much to do with her being unmarried as it did with her being new to the town. Did Nancy think she was going to try to steal her husband? She pictured George Pike's red face and piranha mouth and almost laughed. She remembered how Ned handled situations where reporters asked uncomfortable questions. His favourite response was to give the answer to a question he had wanted to be asked instead.

'It certainly seems since the war that people have been very concerned with peace. That's why our relationships with Britain and the United States are so important.'

Marge let out a sharp laugh. 'Well, tell that to the Minister for External Affairs,' she said. 'Ned McKell has us kowtowing to Asia.'

Rebecca squirmed at the mention of her former lover's name. Ned was an important cabinet minister, so it shouldn't have surprised her that he'd come up in a discussion about post-war diplomacy. Nevertheless, the reference to him reminded her that somewhere on this earth he still existed, still had a life and a position, but was completely out of reach to her.

'The Japanese were our enemy. They nearly invaded Australia,' said Joy, 'so pandering to them makes no sense at all.'

Rebecca itched to correct their statements. Her mind flew back to those late-night discussions with Ned, draped over a double bed at the Wentworth Hotel, with Billie Holiday on the record player and glasses of Cognac in their hands. While he did believe that Asia was as important as Europe or the United States to Australia, Ned hated relying on alliance diplomacy. He had wanted the country to develop greater self-sufficiency.

But right now Rebecca wasn't naked with the Minister of External Affairs in a luxurious suite at the Wentworth. She was in a twee sunroom in an obscure South Coast town holding a cheese cube on a toothpick in her fingers. She wasn't going to draw away from one dangerous topic only to take up another one, so she remained silent.

'That's not all he is pandering to,' said Elaine, with a bawdy glint in her eye. 'He doesn't seem to be able to keep his hands off anything in a skirt. That Thelma Marr is half his age.'

Rebecca swallowed the cheese cube and it stuck like a lump in her throat. She glanced at Doris but she was busy downing her second glass of rum punch, lost in her own thoughts. The subject of a sexual scandal enlivened the conversation.

'Ooh,' said Sue, rubbing her hands together. 'But wouldn't you like to know who that mystery woman is? The girls down at the bowling club say it's Miss Australia. What's her name again?'

Nancy reached for a cigarette and lit it. 'Whoever she is, she's a first-class whore. That Cynthia McKell comes across as a fine woman. Why would a man chase after some minx when he's got a woman worth her weight in gold at home?'

'Don't ask me,' said Elaine, crossing her arms. 'They used to shave the heads of women like that and run them out of town. They should still do that, if you ask me.'

Rebecca flinched. That's what people did to mistresses around the globe, didn't they? Stoned them, gouged their eyes out, set them on fire. She should consider herself lucky if her only consequence was to be humiliated in the press. She was relieved when she saw Doris gathering up her things and getting ready to leave.

'I'll have to get going too,' she said, standing. 'It will be busy at the post office tomorrow.'

Nancy saw them to the door. 'Well, it's been nice getting to know you,' she told Rebecca with a forced smile. Rebecca could feel Nancy's gaze burning into her back as she walked down the path with Doris. The older woman was unsteady on her feet. When they were a block away, Doris stopped and grabbed Rebecca's arm, staring into her eyes.

'They always despise the other woman, but she is a human being too.' Rebecca's muscles tensed. For one disconcerting moment she thought Doris had guessed that she was Ned McKell's mystery woman. But then Doris looked off into the distance as she dredged up a memory of her own. 'I was in love with a married man once,' she said. 'It was during the Great War. Things happen. Life is not perfect. Nancy should understand that better than anyone.'

CHAPTER NINE

Rebecca would have preferred to have spent her Sunday morning as she had in Sydney, lying in bed with a cup of tea and the papers. Instead she donned a demure checked dress with a pillbox hat and strolled to the Anglican church which was located further down the hill towards Ocean Road. The Catholic church was directly across the street from it, as if the two religious houses were engaged in a duel. Rebecca wished she had been born a Catholic. She fancied the Renaissance-style pomp and lavishness of the ceremonies, the images of the Virgin Mary, and the reverence for relics. Religion for the Catholics seemed to be about spectacle. The services were a feast for the senses. The Anglican service on the other hand was staid and conservative; spiritualism with all the magic taken out of it.

She took a place at the end of the pew next to Doris and nodded to the familiar faces of people she had seen come into the post office that week. Nancy was there with George in the front row. Between them sat a pasty-complexioned boy of about twelve who she assumed was Earl, their son. Her mind drifted back to Sunday school at the church in North Sydney, which she would walk to on Sunday mornings with

Debbie. While Rebecca and the older children studied Bible stories, the younger children would be involved in activities like making necklaces from dried macaroni or biblical figures from sections of egg cartons. Although those activities seemed like fun, Debbie would invariably come down with a feigned stomach-ache or some other malady so that Rebecca would have to take her home. 'I want to be with you,' Debbie would tell her. Then the two of them would spend the rest of the morning looking at tadpoles in the creek that ran behind their home or climbing trees.

Doris nudged her and nodded with her head towards the church door. Rebecca turned to see Doctor Litchfield coming up the aisle, pushing an elderly woman in a wheelchair. She was thin and slumped heavily to one side. Doctor Litchfield smiled at Rebecca as they passed and she responded in kind. Doris noticed the exchange and whispered, 'That's Doctor Litchfield's mother, Gillian. She was such a beautiful woman in her time. The stroke she had was devastating. He dotes on her. I'm sure part of the reason he never remarried was so that he could take care of her. There isn't a mother anywhere who could claim to have a more devoted son.'

The pair stopped at the front pew and Doctor Litchfield parked his mother in her wheelchair beside it. He rearranged the shawl that had fallen from her shoulders and placed the prayer book in her lap, opening it at the first page. Rebecca knew she shouldn't stare but she was fascinated. Mrs Litchfield tried to say something but only muffled sounds came out. Rebecca bowed her head. She wished her own mother had understood how deeply she had cared. She had been helpless in the face of her mother's illness. She'd done everything in her power to make her mother comfortable but she had always looked past Rebecca, as if she was hoping for someone better than her daughter to appear.

The priest was a crusty old man with pouches under his eyes and floppy jowls that wobbled when he spoke. His sermon was centred around 1 Kings 16:31 and Jezebel who was, according to him, 'worse in her wickedness than Cleopatra, Mary Queen of Scots and Madame Pompadour combined'. They were women Rebecca admired. As she listened, she noticed the similarity between the 'preacher's voice' the priest was using and how Ned had sounded whenever he'd had to give a political speech. In some cases, the changes in Ned's voice had been so startling that she couldn't believe it was the same man she shared a bed with. When the spotlight was turned on him he became the caricature of a politician, with a voice that was loud, dramatic, authoritative and as resonant as a Shakespearean actor. She wondered what he was doing now. She doubted he would still be with Thelma after she'd spilled the beans not only on her affair with him but also his affair with Rebecca. It irked her to think that he might be in church at this very moment, holding a prayer book and singing louder than the rest of the congregation. If that was the case, Cynthia would be staunchly by his side, helping him redeem himself as a credible politician. Rebecca admired Cynthia, who she was sure didn't love Ned any more than he loved her but who played the dutiful wife in order to wield a power of her own in social circles. The woman had even had a few dalliances of her own – but she was better than Ned at being discreet.

Rebecca shifted in her seat when she found herself thinking about Ned again. While the priest droned on, she mentally made a list of the things she disliked about him: his egotism, his lack of sensitivity, the fact that he was a tad premature in bed – she made a list whenever she thought she was in danger of going mad from pining. But then the priest looked at her and frowned, and she wondered if she had been scowling.

Holy Communion was administered to Gillian Litchfield first and then the rest of the congregation was called up. Doctor Litchfield knelt next to Rebecca at the altar but kept his eyes straight ahead of him. She bowed her head with the others and detected the clean lemon-scented smell of the doctor's clothes. It stood out against the mustiness of the church and the unpleasant whiff of the priest's stale breath as he placed the wafer in her cupped hands and promised her everlasting life. Doctor Litchfield was a nice-looking man and, from the way Doris spoke about him, he was a sincere and caring person. As she made her way back to the pew, Rebecca wondered what it would be like to be with someone like him. Someone solid; a man you could trust. She tried to envisage a life she had never known: Sunday mornings in church, lunch afterwards with another charming married couple, evenings spent reading together by the fire. A man like Doctor Litchfield would never have persuaded her to have an abortion. And if he was so loyal to his ailing mother, he was probably not the type of man to cheat on his wife either. But try as she might she could not picture it. He was simply not her type. She rose with the rest of the congregation for the recessional hymn 'Glorious Things of Thee Are Spoken'.

Morning tea was served from a trestle table outside the church. Rebecca felt the eyes of the congregation firmly on her, curious and intrigued. She did her best to hold a pleasant, unassuming expression as she surveyed the spread of lamingtons and shortbread biscuits. But she could feel Doctor Litchfield's attention on her the whole time. He was deep in conversation with a grey-haired man and his plump wife but his body was turned in her direction. Rebecca could tell a man was interested at twenty paces.

'I am surprised to see you here, Miss Wood!'

Rebecca spun around to see Ernie Mullens leering at her. The man didn't wear his Sunday suit any better than he wore his uniform. The fabric stretched and puckered, emphasising his flabby chest and rotund stomach. He'd greased down some wisps of hair across his scalp in an attempt to disguise his baldness. Rebecca cringed as he leaned closer, eyeing her up and down as if they were sharing an intimate secret. 'I didn't think you looked like the churchgoing type,' he said in an overly familiar tone. 'But don't worry, I'm not either. It's Marge who insists I come.'

He grabbed one of the lamingtons and turned his head sideways to bite it. The filling oozed out over his fingers and he licked them, looking at her in an amused way. 'Still, it's a good way to meet the locals,' he continued. 'It puts on a good show.'

If a dolt like Ernie Mullens could see her churchgoing was false, what was everyone else thinking? She didn't belong in a town like Shipwreck Bay. She stood out like a sore thumb. But if she left abruptly that would only raise more suspicion.

'I'm the postmistress now,' she told him, with a light-hearted air she hoped would throw him off the subject of faith. 'I've got an important role in the town, just like you.'

Ernie licked his lips, about to make some smart alec remark but Doctor Litchfield approached, leaving his mother for a moment in the care of Doris.

'Good morning, Miss Wood! Isn't the weather glorious?' he said, placing himself between her and Ernie. 'Though I do say we might get some rain this evening.'

He nodded to Ernie and guided Rebecca to the other side of the table. 'Well, look at what we have here,' he said, indicating the morning tea spread. 'Have you made your selection? I'm sure all the ladies are watching you, wondering whose contribution you will try first.'

Rebecca grimaced. She seemed to have stumbled from one awkward situation straight into another. Doctor Litchfield obviously thought he had rescued her but she didn't need rescuing, not by anyone. She would have preferred to have handled Ernie herself.

He poured out two cups of tea. 'Ernie oversteps his mark sometimes but he is harmless. Such a sophisticated lady in our midst would have quite turned his head. All you have to do is threaten to report his behaviour to Marge and he'll never bother you again.' He added milk to the tea and then lifted the sugar bowl in a manner of asking Rebecca if she was taking any.

'Yes, just one,' she said.

He handed her the cup and his gaze lingered on her face. She assumed he was expecting her to say something about the garden. He'd 'overstepped his mark', but she could hardly rebuke him for what was essentially an act of kindness. 'You must have got up very early to clear the garden beds. It was as if elves had got to work overnight.'

Doctor Litchfield laughed. 'I've always been an early riser. Early to bed and early to rise and all that.'

Rebecca didn't subscribe to that theory. If she had her way she would live like a Spaniard, taking a siesta in the afternoon and staying out until late in the night. But life as a postmistress in a small town put a stop to that idea. She would have to do what the locals did, including keeping normal business hours.

Doctor Litchfield sipped his tea. 'I was going to suggest that if you are free this afternoon, we might plant some of the seedlings I've put aside for the post office garden.'

It was bad enough that she'd had to sacrifice her Sunday morning for church. Kneeling in dirt on her afternoon off didn't appeal to her either, especially if Doctor Litchfield was going to read something more into it. She glanced around and saw that Nancy's friends, Carmel and Sue, as well as Doris and Marge were all looking in their direction. It wouldn't do for her to be ungenerous to the town favourite.

'Yes, let's finish the job,' she said, hoping to keep things sounding professional. 'What time should I meet you there?'

*

Rebecca borrowed a gardening apron and gloves from Doris and waited outside the post office at three o'clock for Doctor Litchfield to arrive. It was a perfect afternoon to be outside, warm but not too hot. The soil smelt rich and loamy. She closed her eyes and breathed in the fresh air. The breeze was invigorating without the stink of whale flesh polluting it. Shipwreck Bay could be a pleasant little town for a holiday if it wasn't for that smell and, perhaps, for its parochial inhabitants. At the sound of a car approaching she opened her eyes. Doctor Litchfield pulled up in front of the post office and climbed out. His blue checked shirt and tan pants flattered his skin and brought out the brightness of his eyes. He looked like a model in an advertisement for Mark Foy's menswear.

'Hello, Miss Wood! I am here at your service!' he said, grinning and flashing his straight white teeth.

If Marion had been with her she would have nudged Rebecca in the ribs and said, 'Go on. The best way to forget one man is in the arms of another.' Marion had sashayed through two serious relationships, including the one with the attorney-general, which had ended amicably, and several flings in the ten years that Rebecca had known her. But she'd never had her life turned upside down or had to go into hiding because of any of them. Rebecca would not be dallying with handsome Doctor Litchfield's heart. She didn't need the wrath of Shipwreck Bay's female community coming down on her.

Doctor Litchfield opened the boot and lifted out trays of seedlings. He passed her some trowels and took out a spade and watering can before closing the boot again. She followed him to the garden beds where he surveyed the soil.

'I raised all these myself,' he said, placing the trays of seedlings and the spade on the ground. 'But I have to confess that in my mother's garden it isn't a hard thing to do. The self-sowers grow like crazy in the spring and the perennials seem to divide and multiply on their own.'

'I hope I will be able to keep the garden up,' Rebecca told him. 'I've never had a garden to care for before.'

Doctor Litchfield smiled. 'It will be easy. I've planned it so that all you will have to do is deadhead any blooms past their prime and give the garden a water when it's dry. Anything more complicated than that I'm happy to attend to myself. It will be wonderful to see the post office looking spruce again.'

While Doctor Litchfield turned over the soil, Rebecca set out the plants according to the plan he had drawn: hydrangeas and gardenias in the part-shade and roses and cottage flowers in the sun.

'I like to plant the seedlings in groups,' he told her. 'So everything doesn't become a jumble, one must give careful consideration to the plants being in harmony in regards to size and colour when they bloom. My mother was an expert gardener. She was very particular about the different heights, forms and textures of plants and the variety of effects they created.'

Rebecca patted the soil around a peony rose. The only men she had known who had paid that much attention to aesthetical detail were either painters or homosexuals. Doctor Litchfield seemed neither.

Seeing he wasn't engaging her with horticulture, he tried a different tack. 'And what about your family?' he asked. 'They can't be too happy to have you so far away from them?'

Rebecca paused and wiped her hands on her apron.

'Unfortunately, I've lost both my parents. My mother just

after the war and my father ... well, my father a few years before that.'

'And no brothers or sisters?'

Rebecca hesitated. 'No.'

She looked up to see Doctor Litchfield watching her, with something she took for sympathy in his eyes. She thought of the way he had handled the collapse of Corman Ryan, so kindly, so compassionately. She didn't like compassion. It made her feel like a charity case.

'So you are an only child like me?' he said, adjusting his gloves. Then, as if sensing her resistance to consolation, he added, 'They say we are self-possessed and focused. Content in our own company and rich in imagination.'

Rebecca wasn't an only child. She didn't even feel duplicitous for pretending that she didn't have a sister. It was what she had always done. Her past wasn't a scab for every man and his dog to pick at as a way of casual conversation.

'A small compensation for being utterly alone once your parents have died,' she said.

They continued on planting in silence. As they worked, some of the townspeople passed them by. The men tipped their hats and the women wished them 'Good afternoon'. The elderly couple Rebecca had seen Doctor Litchfield talking with at church that morning stopped to admire their work. He introduced them as Maeve and Cecil Barney.

'What are you planting there?' Maeve asked.

'Mostly roses, geraniums and gardenias,' Doctor Litchfield replied. 'It will be a pretty and fragrant garden when we have finished.'

'Oh, that sounds splendid!' she said, clapping her hands. 'People will come to the post office just to admire the garden!'

Maeve hadn't acknowledged Rebecca at church but she beamed a warm smile at her now. What a difference being seen with Doctor Litchfield made. It was as if she was now wearing a sign that read 'certified and trustworthy'.

*

'Did you know many of the towns along the coast have been named after ships in honour of vessels that met their tragic ends off their shores?' Doctor Litchfield asked her when they were alone again. 'Shipwreck Bay claimed more than its fair share. I have some coins from the *Durham* in my study at home.'

Rebecca hadn't accepted his invitation to see his mother's garden and she wasn't going to jump at the chance to view his coin collection either. 'That's interesting,' she said, never taking her eyes from the pansies she was planting around the borders of the beds.

As the sun began to set, they swept the paths then watered the plants before washing their hands and putting the tools back in Doctor Litchfield's car. 'Well, I think we have done a splendid job here,' he said, placing his hands on his hips and looking over the beds. 'It will look spectacular when everything blooms.'

Even in its nascent state, the garden gave the post office a quaint charm that it hadn't had before. They could have been in the South of France, rather than on the coast of New South Wales. It was difficult to maintain her ire at Doctor Litchfield when he had improved the appearance of the building she was in charge of.

'Thank you, Doctor Litchfield,' she told him. 'I wouldn't have known how to tackle the garden without you.'

He smiled at the softening of her attitude. 'I think now we have planted a garden together we can go by first names, don't you? Please call me Timothy.'

'Rebecca,' she said with a degree of firmness, so he couldn't interpret anything but friendship in the intimacy. 'Please call me Rebecca.'

Timothy gave her a lift up the hill in his car. When he stopped in front of her house he turned the motor off and opened the car door for her. 'Well,' he said, glancing at the car as if he meant to leave but making no move to do so. Then patting the back of his head in a way that made him seem nervous, he asked, 'Do you like to dance, Rebecca? The surf club at Twin Falls puts on a dance one Saturday night a month. It's not the Trocadero or anything fancy like that. But it's a nice night and the band is good. A lot of the local people go. I can take you next Saturday if you like.'

Doctor Litchfield was dangling candy in front of her. She did not like church, gardening or coin collections, but she did like to dance. An evening at the surf club was probably going to be ham sandwiches and pineapple upside-down cake served for supper, and fruit punch instead of champagne, but at least it would be a night out. Still, she couldn't accept, not without the risk of leading him on.

'Well, hello, you two! How did your gardening project progress?'

Rebecca turned to see Doris standing at her gate, a bunch of freshly cut marigolds in one hand and a pair of secateurs in the other. 'Splendidly, Mrs Campbell!' Doctor Litchfield replied. 'I was just telling Rebecca about the dance they have at Twin Falls Surf Club.'

Doris smiled at Timothy's use of Rebecca's Christian name. She stepped out of her gate and towards them. 'Oh, you must go,' she said to Rebecca with a dreamy look on her face. 'It's always such a nice evening and Doctor Litchfield is a very good dancer.'

Put on the spot like that, Rebecca had no choice but to accept. 'Thank you,' she told him. 'That would be very nice.'

He blushed like a ten-year-old boy. 'I'll pick you up at six o'clock.'

The two women watched Doctor Litchfield get back in his car and take off down the road. Doris leaned into Rebecca's side. 'I dare say there will be some nurses from Twin Falls Hospital who will be very jealous of you.'

Rebecca walked down the path to her front door, feeling as though in accepting the invitation to the dance she had stepped into a potential minefield. It was going to be a delicate operation to let down the town's most popular man.

CHAPTER TEN

The following Saturday Timothy picked up Rebecca to take her to the dance in Twin Falls, one and a half hours away. His eyes ran over her midnight-blue satin dress and her hair, which she wore rolled and swept to the side. He smiled but said nothing.

It was early evening and still warm, but Timothy wound his window up. 'I don't want to make a mess of your hair,' he explained. 'You must have taken some time with it. It looks very elegant.'

Rebecca lightly stroked her forehead. 'The humid weather makes it difficult to keep tidy. I try to wear it off my face when I go dancing.'

'Do you like dancing?' he asked, starting the car engine and heading in the direction of Ocean Road.

'Yes.'

'And parties? You look like someone who enjoys dressing up.'

Rebecca averted her eyes from the sea as they came parallel to it. It was rippling and turbulent and made her apprehensive.

'Yes, I like to dress up.'

It was getting hot inside the car. She took out her handkerchief and patted her neck. The breeze outside looked refreshing. She wanted to wind down her window and let it blow over her face no matter what it did to her hair. But she was conscious that Timothy was sneaking glances at her.

'Did you go to a lot of parties in Sydney?'

'A few.'

'That's interesting.' He changed the gears to take a hill and didn't say anything further.

'Why is that interesting?' she asked.

Timothy placed one hand on top of the other on the wheel in a casual manner. 'Well, Shipwreck Bay is so quiet. You must have got tired of parties – like I did. Otherwise why would you have taken a position here?'

Rebecca glanced at her lap. She'd got herself cornered, although she doubted that was Timothy's intention. Ned had a trick when a reporter trapped him. There were many different explanations for anything, but instead of giving the main one you offered one of lesser importance and emphasised it so that it sounded true. 'There weren't many positions where I could be a postmistress. I'd had a responsible job in the telegraph office at the GPO but after the war the men didn't want women to work there anymore. They wanted us all to go home, but I didn't have a home to go to. I haven't been able to find any positions as challenging as the one I had to leave. Being a secretary and taking dictation doesn't satisfy me.'

Timothy glanced at her. 'Doris told me about your fiancé. The man who died in the war.'

Rebecca sat back further in her seat. Well, at least if Doris was going to spread gossip it was the type Rebecca had wanted her to spread. If everyone in the town thought she had lost a fiancé, at least that might stop them all wondering why she had never married.

'I don't like to talk about it,' she said.

Timothy turned his eyes back to the road. The view to the ocean was blocked by trees and Rebecca clasped her hands and looked at the scenery. It was the first time she had seen the farms on the outskirts of town, the ones served by the mail contractor. The open skies and the roads with no other traffic on them were a novelty to her. Cows and crows were the only living things to be seen. There wasn't another human being anywhere.

'I'm divorced, Rebecca,' Timothy said, negotiating a sharp bend in the road.

She nodded. 'Yes, I know.'

'I hate saying the word. *Divorced.* When I got married, I thought it would be for life. When I promised "for better, for worse and in sickness and health", I meant it. My wife, unfortunately, had other ideas.'

'I'm sorry.'

'Arabella … she wanted to get married. I thought she was perhaps too young and after the war there were so many veterans I had to help. I worked long hours. She … well, she got bored.'

Rebecca fiddled with her bracelet. 'You really don't have to explain it to me. I understand. It hurts to be betrayed.'

'It sure does,' he agreed, blowing out a deep breath. 'It's terrible you lost your fiancé, Rebecca, but at least he was a hero. My wife was a —'

For one surreal moment Rebecca thought Timothy was going to say 'slut'. She recoiled.

Timothy licked his lips. 'I'm sorry. I'm talking too much. You don't want to know all of this. My wife was a very shallow person. A party girl. She broke my heart. That's about the sum of it.'

Rebecca understood better than he knew about getting your heart broken. She, too, had wanted someone she could rely on, somebody to be her port in a storm, and she too had been betrayed. But was he still so upset over something that had finished years ago? Was she still going to feel damaged by Ned for as long as that? Or maybe that's what happened to you when you lived in Shipwreck Bay. Maybe all you had to think about was your heartache.

'You don't want to leave here one day?' she asked. 'Get out and go to a big city again?'

Timothy's face turned dark. 'You mean leave my mother?'

'You could take her with you, couldn't you?'

He placed his hands more firmly on the wheel and his jaw tightened. Rebecca flinched. Was he upset by her question? She had not expected such a reaction from the affable doctor. The temperature in the car seemed to rise another few degrees. Hairstyle or not, she wound down her window. 'I'm sorry. I spoke out of turn. I don't know your exact circumstances. All I know is that things can change so rapidly, and life is so short … We could all have the rug pulled out from under us at any time. Like that patient of yours, Corman Ryan. When he and Mrs Corman got married they never expected he would get so sick.'

The frown on Timothy's face softened. He shook his head. 'No, it is me who should apologise, Rebecca. We all have our Achilles heel and mine happens to be my mother. She didn't deserve what happened to her.' He let out a breath and turned to her, smiling again.

'Let's change the subject, shall we? You seem to have made yourself indispensable here. A number of my patients have commented that you have got the post office shipshape and the mail is running smoothly for the first time in months.'

The knot in Rebecca's stomach dissipated. She was relieved they were on good terms again. 'Well, as a credit to you, I've had nothing but compliments about the garden,' she replied. 'The roses are already producing buds.'

Her comment elicited a curious grin from Timothy. 'Good soil is the key to a healthy and abundant garden. A good foundation is important; with it you can achieve anything.'

*

Twin Falls was a much larger town than Shipwreck Bay. They drove by a bowling green, a hospital and a gasworks. There was a sawmill further up the mountain and dozens of holiday cabins along the beach. The town probably attracted the tourists who bypassed Shipwreck Bay. Apart from the lack of facilities, the reek that the whaling station emitted would be enough to turn anybody away.

The surf club was located at the end of the main street in a fibro-cement building. They entered a foyer decorated with balloons and streamers. In the hall, a dance orchestra was playing 'Rambling Rose'. Timothy paid for their tickets and led Rebecca around the outskirts of the crowded dance floor to a table near the stage. 'People come from all around for this dance,' he said, raising his voice to be heard over the music. 'As far as Penguin Bay and Bottle Mountain.'

He waved to someone and Rebecca turned to see who it was. She cringed when she discovered George and Nancy Pike looking in their direction. Against the lavenders, pinks and yellows of the other women's frocks, Nancy stood out as sophisticated in her dress of pearl-white slipper satin. She ran her eyes appraisingly over Rebecca's dress but her expression didn't show any improvement in her feelings towards her. Obviously the bridge night had not been the social lubricant Rebecca had hoped it would be.

She swallowed when George and Nancy headed towards them.

'Hello, Doctor Litchfield. Hello, Rebecca,' said Nancy, smiling at Timothy and looking over Rebecca's head. 'I hope you won't monopolise our good doctor, Rebecca. There's always a measure of single *young* women here waiting for the chance to take a turn on the floor. Doctor Litchfield is a much-desired partner!'

'So your husband must have his pick of young women too!' Rebecca replied, smiling at George as if she was making a joke. The annoyance that flashed across Nancy's face was risky but worth it. 'I do agree we older women should not monopolise the men.'

George's eyes glinted. He sized Rebecca up as if she was a bottle of cool, refreshing beer. He certainly reeked of the stuff. But his gaze lingered over her longer than she had anticipated for something that had been only said in jest. Does the piranha think I'm flirting with him? she wondered. She turned away and squeezed Timothy's arm. 'They're playing a rhumba,' she said. 'It's my favourite dance.'

'Don't worry about Mrs Pike,' Timothy told her once they were on the dance floor. 'Jealousy sometimes gets the better of her. She was Miss South Coast in 1938 and prides herself on being the most fashionable woman in town. She actually has a heart of gold and will warm to you soon enough.'

But it wasn't Nancy that was bothering her. It was George and that look he'd given her. It wasn't the same as Ernie's drooling over her. Ernie was like a teenager ogling girlie magazines. George's glance had something malevolent in it that made her skin feel like it had spiders crawling over it.

*

In the break between sets, Timothy led Rebecca back to their table then went to get some fruit punch. Rebecca felt a tap on her shoulder and turned to see Elaine, Nancy's bridge partner, standing behind her along with a man whose jet-black hair was greased into a quiff. 'Hello Rebecca, I wanted to introduce you to my husband, Frank,' Elaine said.

Rebecca took the hand Frank offered her but was uncertain, as if she was one of those characters in a cartoon who'd been asked to sniff a boutonniere and would get a squirt of water in the eye for their troubles. But there was nothing unpleasant in Frank's manner. 'Compliments to you on the garden,' he said. 'Everyone in town is talking about it.'

'And that's not all,' added Elaine, nodding in the direction of Timothy who was engaged in conversation with the matronly woman who was passing out the drinks through the servery window. 'You have caught the eye of our most eligible man.'

Rebecca forced a smile. Wasn't Elaine the same woman who had exuded if not outright hostility, then at least coolness towards her at Nancy's card party? It was obvious what had brought about the change in her demeanour.

As the evening went on, it became even clearer that Timothy was Rebecca's entree into regional society. As he twirled her around the dance floor in a swing waltz she noticed the admiring glances and smiles the other dancers sent their way. 'You are the belle of the ball,' Timothy whispered in her ear during a foxtrot. 'Everyone is looking at you.'

With songs like 'I'm Sailing on a Sunbeam' and 'My Fate is in Your Hands' and a finishing time of midnight, it was a more homespun evening than dancing at the Coconut Grove or the Tropicana with diplomats and movie stars, but Rebecca found herself enjoying the evening. When an elderly gentleman tapped Timothy on the shoulder and indicated he'd like to dance with her, she would have been more than happy to accept. But Timothy stiffened. 'Not tonight, Charlie. She's all mine.'

The old man looked taken aback but wandered off without protest. Rebecca frowned. Nancy hadn't been entirely wrong in suggesting it was courteous to share partners. The old man was probably a widower and this was his night out. Was Timothy so easily made jealous?

'I'm not a possession, Timothy.'

His eyes opened wide in surprise. 'No, you are certainly not.'

Rebecca nodded to the old man who was sitting on the side watching the other dancers and looking dejected. 'Then why didn't you let that man dance with me?'

Timothy's eyes settled on her face. 'Because if I'm going to bring the most attractive woman in town to a dance, then I intend to hold on to her.' He squeezed her hand tighter and smiled. 'Let's not make a scene. You're a good dancer, you know. You must have done a lot of dancing in Sydney.'

A couple sat down next to the man and they started chatting. Rebecca decided to let the moment go and not spoil the evening. 'My parents were good dancers,' she told Timothy. 'When I was a young child they would move the furniture in the living room aside and dance after dinner.'

'Only when you were a child? Why did they stop?'

It was the second time he had caught her out. As a doctor he was probably used to listening for the things that patients omitted telling him: little facts that would be important to a proper diagnosis. She was spared answering the question by the master of ceremonies calling for a 'Monte Carlo'. A flurry of excitement ran through the room as the dancers arranged themselves into groups in each corner of the hall. The master of ceremonies shuffled the cards and blindly picked one with the corner written on it, eliminating the contestants in corner number three. The dancers spread out again over all four corners and the game continued until the only couples remaining were Rebecca and Timothy in one corner and George and Nancy in the other. Nancy's mouth set into a grim line and Rebecca recalled all the trophies and ribbons in the sunroom of their house. Of all the couples to end up in competition with that evening, it had to be them!

The master of ceremonies called out George and Nancy's corner, and Timothy and Rebecca were announced triumphant. The other dancers clapped while Nancy shot Rebecca a look that would give her nightmares. But she forgot her vexation when several people made a point of shaking her hand and introducing themselves. 'Thank you very much,' she said when she was handed the prize of a box of chocolates and a ticket for the Sydney lottery. 'I have truly enjoyed tonight.'

'Well, I think that was a successful evening,' Timothy said to her when they got in the car for the drive home. 'Everyone admired you and envied me, and if that ticket comes through we shall both be rich.'

'But what will we do with all that money?' Rebecca asked, stifling a yawn. 'Shall we build a park for the town and fill it with flowers from your mother's garden.'

Rebecca had been joking but Timothy sent her an astonished glance. 'That's a thought. This town doesn't have a proper memorial to the fallen. It's generous of you to think of something like that!'

Rebecca paused, unsure whether to correct him or not. If she won the Sydney lottery she would be on the first boat to Europe where she would live out her days in sartorial elegance. She would not be funding a park for Shipwreck Bay. She glanced out the window. The ocean was dark now. Only the white caps of foam were visible in the moonlight. A shiver ran through her as she recalled the way he had sneered when he'd described his former wife as shallow and a party girl. Although she managed to keep up polite chit-chat with Timothy during the rest of the drive, she was acutely aware that there was a lot about her that he probably wouldn't like if he knew the truth.

★

On Monday morning, while Johnny was out on his deliveries, Berit arrived with a bag of coins to deposit into her secret account. She was wearing a long scarf tied over her head and neck, and sunglasses, but they didn't completely hide the bruises under her eyes. The tremble in her hands was so pitiable that Rebecca had to resist trembling herself, as if Berit's fear was contagious. But too much empathy was useless and could even be dangerous. One of them had to keep a clear head.

'Does anybody else know he hits you?' she asked.

Maeve Barney walked by the window and glanced inside. Her husband, Cecil, and another man were chatting together under the Tree of Knowledge.

Berit's mouth twitched. 'Everybody knows. How could they not? Look at me! It's not the first time he's gone this far. Doctor Litchfield is the only one who has tried to help me.

He spoke to Sanders after he broke my arm once. A real man doesn't hit a woman, and all of that. Of course, it didn't stop Sanders but at least Doctor Litchfield tried.'

Rebecca chewed her lip. Poor broken-hearted Timothy. Yes, he was decent enough to have tried to intervene.

Berit noticed the others outside the window too. 'They close ranks in this town,' she said. 'It doesn't matter what one of the men does, they will protect him. They make excuses for Sanders even though everyone knows he's a monster. Mabel's daughter, Anne, was molested. The police sergeant claims it was someone out of town but I don't think so. I'm sure it was someone she knew and that's why she wouldn't tell her mother. She was afraid, so she drowned herself.'

A shudder ran through Rebecca. If she was Catholic she would have crossed herself. 'It was suicide? It wasn't an accident?'

The door swung open and Joy, Nancy's friend, blundered in holding two string bags of groceries in her hands. She stood in line behind Berit.

Rebecca and Berit exchanged a glance. Rebecca took a lost parcel form from the drawer and handed it to Berit. 'Do you mind filling this in while I serve Mrs Flick here?' she asked in an authoritative voice.

Berit stepped aside and Rebecca nodded to Joy to come forward. 'How can I help you, Joy?'

Joy glimpsed the bruises on Berit's face when the young woman went to the courtesy desk to fill in the form. She rolled her eyes at Rebecca. 'They are drinkers that lot,' she whispered. 'The wives give too much mouth. They keep spick and span houses but then their morals are highly questionable.

My husband has seen them more than once bathing down at the waterhole. *Naked*.'

Rebecca wanted to grab Joy's pug nose and twist it but she resisted the urge. 'Now, what is it you were after?' she asked.

'The Pan Pacific Scout Jamboree commemorative stamp collection, please. It's for my nephew's birthday. He's a collector.'

Rebecca opened the stamp book and glanced in Berit's direction. She tried to hurry Joy up so they could continue their conversation.

'Will that be all?' Rebecca asked, passing the stamps and collecting the pennies Joy meticulously counted out and placed on the counter.

'The whole town is talking about the garden you and Doctor Litchfield planted. You should see the glorious grounds at the Litchfields' home. They are simply lovely! I used to think Gillian was unlucky not having a daughter, but her son does a fine job of keeping them.'

'He is a very talented horticulturist, that's for sure,' agreed Rebecca, deliberately looking past Joy and signalling to Berit to return to the counter.

Joy leaned in closer. 'And there's talk of a romance. Elaine says you and the doctor made a very handsome couple on the dance floor.'

Berit had bruises all over her and Rebecca had just learned that Anne Peberdy had been molested and then drowned herself. She wasn't in the mood for a tête-à-tête with Joy.

'He was just making me feel welcome,' she told Joy. 'Haven't you heard that there is a nurse at Twin Falls Hospital he is quite enamoured with?'

Joy's eyes grew wide. Then she grinned like a child who had been given a lolly. 'No! I haven't heard that from anybody!'

Rebecca winked and clucked her tongue. 'That's right. Apparently he's been seeing her in secret for some time.'

Joy's mouth dropped open. She reminded Rebecca of a laughing clown at a fair. 'Well ... I best be getting on,' Joy said, grabbing her groceries and rushing towards the door.

There you go, thought Rebecca, watching Joy's girdled hips wobble as she hurried straight towards the general store, get out there and spread that juicy gossip.

Berit passed Rebecca the form.

'Do you think your husband molested Anne?' Rebecca asked her, ripping up the form and throwing it in the wastepaper basket.

Berit shook her head. 'No, he is only interested in harming me ... and the whales. Some of the whaling wives are convinced it was the shire secretary. There was a problem between him and some girl guides a few years ago.'

Rebecca remembered the creepy look George had given her at the dance. 'But you don't think so?'

'The fact that Anne refused to name the man is what puzzles me. I can't see why she wouldn't name George Pike.'

'Perhaps she was afraid her mother would lose her position at the post office?'

Berit shrugged. 'It's possible he threatened her with that, but I'm not sure she had the intellectual capacity to understand.'

Rebecca pondered what Berit had said. If it was a local who had molested Anne, then there was an evildoer among the townspeople. She might have even passed him in the street, whirled past him on the dance floor on Saturday night or sold him stamps.

'I live by myself,' she said, trying to act as normal as possible in case anyone else came inside. 'If there is anything you want to leave with me … something you might need, you can store it at my house.'

Berit's eyes filled with tears. 'Everyone liked my husband back in Sandefjord,' she said. 'My father and brothers even thought he was a good man. But he is vile … he does things … I never know what is going to set him off.'

'Well, if it gets any worse, come to me.'

Berit shook her head. 'I'm not getting you in trouble too.'

'Then go to Doctor Litchfield. You've got to get away from your husband when he's violent.'

After Berit left, Rebecca returned to her office and stared out the window at the garden. A woman should be safe in her home. She should be able to trust her husband. God, any woman in a small town like Shipwreck Bay should be free from danger, especially one as vulnerable as Anne Peberdy. She thought of Berit's battered face and promised herself that if any man did that to her, she'd kill him.

★

At six o'clock, Rebecca went to Doris's house for dinner and a cooking lesson. Doris seemed to have forgotten that she had revealed a past affair to Rebecca and she set the table with a freshly ironed cloth and a posy of zinnias with the prim and proper air of a model homemaker. Rebecca chopped the lettuce and tomatoes for the salad while Doris lifted a tray of buttered potatoes and slid it into the oven.

'Now those are in we can start on the crust for the apple pie,' she said, wiping her hands on a tea towel. 'I can't believe you've never made your own crust before. Did your mother never let you in the kitchen?'

'I've never had a pie that didn't come from the cake shop before. My mother wasn't a very adventurous cook.'

Dinner in Rebecca's home had invariably been meatloaf, mashed potatoes and gravy with overcooked peas or butter beans. But her lack of home-making skills was not entirely her mother's fault. Rebecca had never had a great interest in domestic life. When she wasn't at school, she had spent most of her adolescence in her room reading Romantic novels or practising ballet, the one outside-of-school activity her mother had allowed her.

'Don't you know the way to a man's heart is through his stomach,' said Doris, taking a canister of flour from a cupboard.

'That must be where I'm going wrong,' Rebecca replied, with a wry smile.

When the meal was ready they sat down in Doris's dining room. The furniture was polished mahogany and Rebecca's gaze drifted to the china cabinet. In among the wedding silver were photographs: Doris in her French tambour lace wedding dress; a young man with light eyes and batwing ears in an ANZAC uniform; a child with short blonde hair cut straight across her forehead. She wondered how many family meals had been shared at this table and if Doris minded eating alone at it most nights now. Her landlady handed her the butter for the bread and Rebecca was relieved that Doris didn't insist they say grace. Perhaps her churchgoing was as token as her own.

'Well, you certainly have the town all aflutter, Rebecca,' Doris said, cutting a slice of her pork chop. 'You've arrived out of nowhere, like Mary Poppins, and got the post office all sorted out. Then, if that wasn't enough, you've stolen the heart of our beloved doctor.'

Rebecca squirmed. Obviously the false gossip she had given to Joy about Timothy's relationship with a nurse had not been strong enough to deflect attention from her.

'Stealing Doctor Litchfield's heart might be a bit of an exaggeration,' said Rebecca. 'We only went to a dance.'

Doris cocked an eyebrow. 'That might have been true of another man, but Doctor Litchfield didn't show any interest in anybody until you came along. It upset everyone that he married someone who treated him so callously. You can see how devoted he is to his mother. A man like that is worth his weight in gold.'

Rebecca looked at her plate. Perhaps Doris was right about Timothy and her real problem was that she always chose the wrong sort of man.

'What was Doctor Litchfield's wife like?' she asked.

Doris shrugged. 'I never met her. They didn't come back here for the wedding. It was a bit of a whirlwind romance, I hear.'

Rebecca tried to imagine Timothy's wife for herself. He was a good-looking man and Arabella was such an exotic sounding name that she pictured someone tall and elegant with ballerina bone structure. She'd met a 'party girl' at

Marion's apartment once who had been named Anastasia, so Rebecca visualised someone like that: mysterious, reserved, seductive. But if she had really been a party girl, why hadn't Timothy seen trouble coming?

After the apple pie and a cup of tea, Doris's head began to droop, so Rebecca got up to leave. 'Thank you for a delicious dinner,' she said to her, as they made their way to the front door.

'You're welcome!' Doris stood in the doorway and pulled the front of her cardigan tighter against the fresh breeze that was blowing in from the ocean. 'I like you, Rebecca. Most people in the town seem to as well, but just be careful of Nancy. She gets involved in everybody's business.'

'What has Nancy been saying?'

Doris's eyes searched Rebecca's face. 'She says that there is something suspicious about you. That you are far too glamorous to have come to a place like Shipwreck Bay without an underhand reason, especially as you don't have a husband or a family.'

Rebecca crossed her arms. Did Nancy really say that or was it Doris who was trying to probe her for a reaction? Had tonight's dinner been to make Rebecca feel welcome or to examine her more closely?

'It's never easy to be a newcomer,' Rebecca replied, with a measure of diplomacy that would have made Ned proud. 'People make up all sorts of things about you based on their own prejudices. All you can do is work hard to prove your worth.'

'That's the right attitude,' Doris said in a tone that sounded reassuring but in which Rebecca sensed a hint of falseness. 'That is really all you can do.'

The women wished each other good night. As Rebecca walked up the hill to her home she thought over her conversation with Doris. I should be a politician, she mused, with my ability to deflect questions. She smiled at her own cleverness but inwardly she sensed that life in Shipwreck Bay was not going to be that simple, especially where her relationship with Timothy was concerned. He was premium husband material, but women like her, and probably Arabella, were beyond appreciating that. They chased glamour and excitement. They seemed to want men who were just that little bit out of reach.

*

The wind whistled at the windows of the post office and rain lashed against the glass. It was the kind of coastal storm Rebecca had heard about but hadn't yet seen. Out on the ocean, great daggers of lightning burst over the waves and thunder reverberated in the sky. Rebecca watched the streams of water gush down the street and hoped the garden she and Timothy had planted would not be swept away.

Johnny crammed the mail into his postbag then donned a raincoat and gumboots.

'You're not going out in this weather!' she told him.

He slung the bag over his shoulder. 'But Mrs Pike will complain if the post is late.'

'I'm not having you struck by lightning or crushed under a fallen tree just so she can receive Vogue on time. The post can wait.'

Johnny let out a breath and hung the bag back on its hook. Then he set about placing buckets under the leaks that were dripping through the roof in the sorting room. At first the splashing noises irritated Rebecca but soon the rain on the tin roof was so loud that nothing else could be heard. She picked up the telegram she had received for Stefan Otto an hour earlier: *Rumour of reshuffle. New minister for primary industries to be announced today.*

She hadn't read anything about a cabinet reshuffle when skimming through the metropolitan newspapers before putting them into the Pikes' mail slot. She wondered why the prime minister was reshuffling his cabinet before announcing the new election date. Would it affect Ned? Was it anything to do with the scandal? The role of Minister for External Affairs might be considered too risky for a known philanderer: all that travel to foreign places with exotic women! But Ned was a skilled survivor, with a knack of making sure wherever he ended up was to his advantage. It was herself she had to worry about. Would a cabinet reshuffle settle down the interest of the press in her identity – or heat it up? She glanced at the telephone and was tempted to ring the telegram through to Stefan Otto rather than have it delivered. She might inadvertently get more information about the reshuffle and at the same time satisfy her curiosity about the man the whole town seemed to hate. Had he really been a spy? She sighed. But that would be against regulations, so old Stefan Otto would have to wait along with the rest of the town to receive his communication. She folded the telegram and slipped it in an envelope to be delivered when the storm cleared, and settled down at the counter.

She was absorbed in sorting cheques when the front door to the post office slammed. She felt the man's presence before she looked up: it was as malevolent and menacing as the tempest outside. He glared at her with cold eyes. The man's features were fine but his skin was tanned like leather and his beard was sun-bleached. He could have been thirty years of age – or forty or fifty. It was impossible to tell. The rain outside hadn't managed to penetrate his heavyweight coat and jumper and the water ran off him onto the floor. He strode towards her and thumped both his palms down on the counter. She didn't have to ask who he was. She could smell it on him. The storm must have kept Sanders Olsen from his murderous work at sea.

'What the hell is my wife up to?' he yelled, banging his gnarled hands on the counter again. The middle finger of his right hand was missing. It gave his hand a strange, claw-like appearance. 'Why is she coming here so often?'

Sanders was clearly a man who used his size to intimidate and Rebecca wasn't about to be bullied. She met his gaze steadily as if waiting for him to say something else.

Sanders tugged his ear. His bluff charge had failed. He glanced around him then growled, 'Do you know who my wife is?'

'I don't know who you are,' she lied. 'So how could I possibly guess which of the dozens of women who come here is your wife?'

His eyes narrowed. 'Berit Olsen. She was seen coming here yesterday and the day before that. What was she doing?'

Unlike whoever it was who had seen Berit and told her husband, Rebecca was aware that a woman's life was in danger. The worst thing she could do would be to start making denials.

'What do most people do at the post office?' she replied, meeting his gaze. 'Whatever that is, I assume it's what she was doing. I'm not running any other sort of business here, you know.'

Sanders touched the base of his throat and squinted. Predators like him went for the weak or the injured but didn't like to get hurt themselves. She'd proved to not be as easy a target as he'd first assumed, like a whale that rams its tormentor's boat rather than tries to flee.

Sanders backed away a step from the counter. 'If she's up to no good I'll throttle her,' he said.

Rebecca was a woman holding an important government position and she wasn't going to let him forget it. He might have brute force but she had authority that was bestowed on her by the Crown.

'Well, that will be a matter for the police then,' she replied. 'I'll be writing a report on our conversation today for the Postmaster-General's Department.'

He eyed her up and down. 'Write your report if you want but if you and my wife are up to something you will both regret it!' With that, he rushed back out into the storm, leaving a trail of mud and the stink of rotten fish behind him.

Rebecca turned to see a stricken Johnny standing in the doorway of the sorting room. His legs were trembling. Rebecca had heard the phrase 'he was so scared his knees were knocking' many times but she had never seen anyone actually in that state.

'Are you all right, Miss Wood?' he asked. 'Do you want me to fetch the police sergeant?'

Berit had already hinted that the local police sergeant was ineffectual at protecting women. Most likely he would only make things worse for Berit. 'Sanders Olsen doesn't scare me,' she told him. 'He's nothing more than a stupid thug.'

'You should be scared of him,' Johnny said. 'I've seen what he does to seals – and their pups.'

'Enough!' Rebecca scolded him. 'The storm has eased off now. You can go and deliver the mail.'

She watched Johnny pick up his bag and head out the door. He would be gone for a couple of hours and she was glad for the quiet. She turned back to the cheques but could no longer sort them. Her hands were shaking so violently she had to tuck them under her armpits to still them. Berit was as alone as she was: another doe on the run. Where was she intending to go? Rebecca hoped it was somewhere her husband would never find her.

CHAPTER ELEVEN

The following evening, Rebecca walked down to the beach, lured to it like a detective to the scene of a crime. A flock of gulls flew overhead. Their sad guttural cries added to her melancholic mood. She didn't know why she couldn't stay away from the ocean, seeing that it held such unhappy memories. She took off her sandals and dug her toes into the wet sand and let a foamy wave wash over her feet. Perhaps she was drawn to the sea because she shared its restlessness. Like her, it never seemed to be satisfied, never still. The wave rolled back, sending seaweed and shells spinning in its wake. She thought of Berit and wondered if one floundering swimmer was really in a position to help another. Perhaps she would speak to Timothy and ask him for his assistance. Since Berit had told her that he'd already tried to help her, Rebecca's respect for him had grown and her distrust of the other townspeople had increased. Doris and Marge should spend less time trying to bring down the woman at the bowling club and put their efforts into helping someone in need of a friend. And what about poor Anne Peberdy? Was it really someone from the town who had molested her?

She stepped onto the rock platform. It was still warm from the day's sun and rough under her feet. Dozens of rock pools glittered in the fading light. She bent over a deep one, blinking at the life that was gathered there: sea anemones, limpets, starfish and even a couple of pulsating jellyfish. It was a miniature township of its own. Look, there's Nancy and her friends, she thought, eyeing the cluster of barnacles. And that chiton crawling out from under a rock is Ernie Mullens and those sea snails are the Sunday congregation. She assigned the whelk boring a hole in a mollusc to George Pike and a purple sponge to Doris.

Surely in a small town like Shipwreck Bay it was impossible for the identity of the person who had molested Anne to remain a secret. Somebody had to have noticed something. Then she thought of her own private life and wondered if perhaps secrets were possible anywhere. Sometimes a thing could be happening right under your nose and still you failed to see it. Ned's affair with Thelma Marr had blindsided her. Affairs didn't just happen. They took planning and subterfuge, walking into another room to take a call, and hushed conversations. She should know. Yet, she had perceived none of those things. One day your life was a certain way, the next you were on your knees and wondering what had happened to you.

A wave crashed over the rocks, splashing her with its spray. *Never turn your back on the ocean*, her father had warned her. She spun around and faced it. Something moved beneath the water at the edge of the platform. She squinted, wondering if it was a seal or a dolphin. The creature broke the surface and Rebecca blinked. A rubber eye-mask and snorkel emerged from the water.

A man in a wetsuit lifted himself onto the rocks. He removed his respirator and fins and, leaning against a boulder, stood up. Her eyes ran over the tall figure with his broad shoulders and long, muscular legs. She was transfixed, not quite able to comprehend that another human being had appeared out of the sea. The man removed his mask and, as he did so, caught sight of Rebecca. He too seemed surprised to find someone watching him. They stood frozen for a few seconds, like two beasts of the forest sensing each other, before the man made some decision in his mind and moved towards her.

'The visibility is quite good,' he said, answering a question Rebecca hadn't asked. 'I was surprised to see it so after the storm.'

His voice was deep and resonant and yet somehow quiet and considered at the same time. It might be described as softly spoken, but it was too rich and authoritative for that. It was an educated accent with a touch of something else in it. The man stopped before her, water dripping from his thick dark hair and settling as droplets on his square face. A handsome face, Rebecca noticed, with a fine nose and thick, full lips. He seemed somehow familiar, although they had never met before. His brow was brooding and his brown eyes looked at her as if he was expecting her to come out with some equally thoughtful revelation of her own.

'I've been admiring the rock pools,' she said. 'When I was young I was fascinated by the life in the rock pools around Sydney.'

The man nodded as if Rebecca had given an answer to a question he'd been asking himself about her. He crouched to his haunches and slipped off his tank. It must have been heavy but it didn't seem to bother him. He bent over the pool and peered into it. 'Life came from the sea. These sponges and starfish are our ancestors.'

'I thought we came from apes,' she said. 'At least that's what I was taught at school.'

The man put his mask on the surface of the water to better watch the graceful movement of a starfish propelling itself across a rock. 'The sea was brimming with life long before the land was,' he said. 'Somewhere in the vast mass of water something moved from non-living to living. We carry in our veins a salty stream of sodium, potassium and calcium: the same composition as sea water.'

The man exuded intellect and sophistication. Was he a marine scientist? She wondered if he was from Sydney or Melbourne. He must have come to the South Coast to explore its pristine ocean, still unspoilt by industrial activity.

She nodded out to the sea, which was becoming rougher by the minute. 'Aren't you afraid to dive out there all by yourself? Something could happen to you and nobody would know.'

The man stood upright again. 'I don't fear the sea any more than I fear God.'

Rebecca gave a start and almost laughed at his declaration. Then she wondered what it would be like to not be afraid. To not open her eyes in the morning and worry about how she was going to get through the day, to not be constantly looking over her shoulder, to not be circumspect about everything she said so that her secret wouldn't be discovered. It was a long time since she had felt unafraid. From the age of ten she'd known that terrible things do happen. Even before the debacle with Ned, some part of her had always been on tenterhooks, waiting for disaster.

'I fear God,' Rebecca told him. 'He does random, cruel things, just like the sea.'

A trace of a line formed between the man's eyebrows. 'We only fear what we don't understand.' He looked out to the waves. 'I suggest you conquer your fear of both God and the ocean. The sea is our home. It is seven tenths of the earth's surface and is inhabited by an abundance of life. In the end it will creep up on us and the whole world will be under water again.'

'What about the sharks and other monsters? Aren't you even frightened of them?'

His focus narrowed on her face; his mouth was set into a serious line but amusement shone in his eyes. 'The *monsters* are less interested in us than our egos allow us to believe. The truly dangerous beasts are the ones we carry around in our minds.'

Rebecca thought she had never heard anything truer. 'You seem to know a lot about the ocean. Do you dive here often?'

'As often as I can. The sea life is magnificent and the water is clean.'

He gathered his gear. Rebecca thought he was getting ready to leave and somehow that disappointed her. She would have liked to talk to him more. She missed the intellectual conversations she used to have in Sydney.

'It's getting dark, we best get off these rocks,' he told her. 'Let me escort you back to the beach track.'

He reached out his hand to help her onto the sand. Rebecca liked how firm yet gentle his grip was. Then he sat down on the rock ledge and put his tank on his back and she marvelled at how strong he must be to carry such heavy equipment with apparent ease. They walked along the water's edge, Rebecca dwarfed by the tall man.

'So, you're from Sydney, are you?' he asked. 'What brings you here? Are you on holidays?'

'No, I'm the new postmistress.'

The man stopped and frowned. Perhaps, like the others, he didn't think she looked very 'official'. But then she saw it was something else altogether. 'What happened to Mabel was dreadful,' he said. 'I can't understand it.'

'Did you know her well?'

The man looked down. 'Mabel was the postmistress here for twenty years. She was the only decent person in the whole town. A tiny woman with a gigantic heart and soul. She lost her daughter, tragically.' He turned to the ocean. 'Poor Mabel. Her heart was broken.'

When they reached the track the sky was black and the stars were out shining. The man watched Rebecca dust the sand from her feet with her handkerchief and put her sandals back on.

'I'll walk you to the road,' he said.

Rebecca wondered where he was staying. The pub had rooms, so probably there. But when they reached the intersection of Ocean Road and Mountain Road, he turned to her. 'Are you all right from here? It's too dark for me to walk back along the beach so I'll head in that direction.'

He glanced towards the hill that led north out of Shipwreck Bay. Was he staying with a farmer or camping somewhere in the bush? It was a long way to carry his gear, even for someone as fit as he obviously was.

'Where are you staying?' she asked him.

'I live here in Shipwreck Bay.'

'You do?' The man did not seem at all like someone who would live in the town. His whole manner spoke of a deeper mind, a broader world of experience. But perhaps like her, he'd been 'shipwrecked'? Her heart lifted at the idea that she might see him again and hear more of his interesting conversation.

'Where?' she asked.

'There.' He pointed in the direction of Stefan Otto's house on the headland.

'There?' Rebecca's thoughts were muddled. She looked at the man uncertainly. 'Do you work for Stefan Otto?'

The line between his brows deepened. 'I *am* Stefan Otto.'

Rebecca had the sensation that the road was tilting under her feet. This was Stefan Otto? He wasn't at all like she had imagined. She wasn't able to reconcile that the most intelligent person she had met since coming to Shipwreck Bay was also the town pariah.

The lights were on at the Pikes' house and the curtains were still open. Nancy could glance out the window at any moment and see them. But it wasn't the persistent rumour-mongering that bothered Rebecca now. It was the impression of standing in the centre of a brewing storm of feelings that made her uneasy. Her heart was beating faster than normal and her cheeks felt hot. She took a breath to calm herself and said diplomatically, 'Well, good evening, Mr Otto. Thank you for the chat. It has been most interesting.'

'Wait a minute. I think we may have …'

But Rebecca pretended not to hear him and turned and walked quickly in the direction of Mountain Road. What on earth had suddenly made her so afraid of the man who had escorted her like a gentleman from the beach? Surely not the idea that Doris might accuse of her of fraternising with foreign agents and sending Morse code messages from her pink and cream cottage? What then? Feeling foolish, she turned, hoping to redeem her dignity with a brief wave or a slight nod of the head. But Stefan Otto was nowhere in sight. He had vanished into the darkness as mysteriously as he had emerged from the ocean.

CHAPTER TWELVE

Rebecca stared out of the sorting room's picture window, straining to see beyond the bay to the headland where Stefan Otto's house stood. But she could only catch a glimpse of the square cupola of its roof. The rest remained hidden among the trees. When the locals had spoken about him she had pictured someone old with white hair and a cruel mouth. She had not imagined an attractive man with whom she would enjoy having a conversation.

The back door slammed and Johnny scuttled into the sorting room, the mailbag from the train slung over his shoulder.

'Good morning, Miss Wood,' he said, emptying the bag on the table.

Rebecca cast her eye over the letters and packages. She reached for an envelope addressed to Stefan Otto and flipped it over. The sender was an R.H. Bidwell in Byron Bay – the same person who had been sending telegrams to him. The hand was masculine and, to her surprise, she found herself pleased that the correspondent was not a woman.

'Why did you tell me Stefan Otto was an *old* man?' she asked Johnny.

The delivery boy jerked his head back and regarded her with wide, open eyes. 'Because he is! The man must be at least forty or more!'

A realisation dawned on her and she shook her head. Compared to Johnny, any man over thirty would appear old.

Johnny began sorting the mail into the slots. The photograph on the front page of the copy of *The Canberra Times* destined for the Pike household gave her a jolt. It was a picture of Ned standing outside Parliament House with a group of jostling reporters in front of him. She was about to reach for it when Johnny grabbed it and placed it in the slot.

'Anyway, it doesn't matter how old he is,' he said, continuing to put the mail in order. 'What he's doing isn't right. This town needs the whaling station as much as it needs the mine.'

But Rebecca was no longer thinking about the mysterious Stefan Otto. What was Ned doing on the cover of *The Canberra Times*? A sense of panic ran through her. Did it have anything to do with the scandal? There was nowhere in town she could get a copy of the newspaper, but it wouldn't be good form for Johnny to see her reading a paper that had been paid for by the Pikes. He might be friendly but she knew he could talk.

'Before you take the mail I need you to unblock the drainpipe out the back,' she told him. 'We are in for another storm this afternoon.'

Johnny squinted outside at the clear, cloudless sky. 'Really? I didn't hear anything about that.'

'And if the wood is dry, I need you to get the fire going,' Rebecca added, pushing him towards the door. 'If it rains, it will get cold here this afternoon.'

With Johnny out of the way, Rebecca slipped *The Canberra Times* from the Pikes' slot and read the headline: 'Extensive Reshuffle to Reassure Anxious Voters'.

She quickly scanned the article and discovered that Ned had been made the Minister for Commerce and Agriculture: 'The prime minister felt that any step that would lead to a restoration of confidence should be taken.' It was an extraordinary appointment as that role had been traditionally filled by a member of the Country Party. It looked like a ploy to keep Ned at home, but his new position was a side-step not a demotion. The new role was equally as prestigious and important, if not as glamorous. Rebecca tried to imagine Ned slapping a cow on the rump or talking to farmers about their crops. Knowing him, he would pass those duties on to a junior minister and stick to commerce. He certainly knew how to land on his feet.

The sound of splashing water alerted her that Johnny had managed to unblock the drainpipe. She quickly read the rest of the article. The prime minister described Ned as having a 'sterling career ahead of him'. Rebecca pursed her lips; perhaps the scandal could finally be put behind them? She flicked through the rest of the newspaper. Her throat contracted when she reached the women's pages and she saw a picture of stony-faced women standing outside a church under a headline that read: 'Australian Women's National League Demands That McKell's Mystery Mistress Be Identified'. In the article, the president, Mrs Ivy Crankshaw, was quoted as saying, 'No family is safe while that woman remains at large.'

Rebecca's stomach pitched. The women seemed to view her as some sort of dangerous criminal. How was it that the scandal had barely been a blip in Ned's 'sterling career' while it had blighted her life? What would they say if they knew that Ned's wife, Cynthia, had known all about her – and that even from a distance there had been a degree of respect? Rebecca had always been discreet. But a mob would never understand something like that. Like Nancy and her friends, they were after blood.

'Knock! Knock!'

Rebecca spun around to see Timothy standing at the counter. His clean-shaven face had a glow to it.

'Goodness me, are you all right, Rebecca?' he asked. 'You are very pale!'

'You gave me a surprise, that's all!' she answered breathlessly.

Timothy laughed and glimpsed the newspaper Rebecca was holding. She didn't want him to think that she was going through the Pikes' personal mail. She casually folded it and put it down on the counter as if it was hers. But Timothy took it and studied the front page. 'Yes, the cabinet reshuffle seems very mysterious,' he said. 'What do you think of a banana farmer being appointed Postmaster-General?'

Rebecca shrugged, relieved that Timothy had not made any association between her and Ned. 'Oh well, we all have to make the best of things,' she said.

Timothy nodded towards the garden. 'It took a bit of a beating during the storm. Still, the soil held and that's the main thing. The flowers will spring back.'

Rebecca thought Timothy was like those plants, buoyant and optimistic, at least when he wasn't talking about his mother. With Johnny still outside, she wanted to take the opportunity to ask him about Berit. She was on the verge of mentioning the situation when he blurted out the purpose of his visit.

'I wondered if you would give me the pleasure of joining my mother and me for lunch this Sunday, after church?'

Rebecca choked on her answer. A dance was one thing, an intimate lunch with Timothy and his mother quite another. She was about to turn him down when Maeve and Carmel came into the post office. She changed her mind. At least it would be an opportunity to talk to him confidentially about Berit.

'All right, that sounds very nice,' she told him.

'Wonderful!' he said, grinning from ear to ear.

He beamed at Maeve and Carmel on his way out. 'Good morning, ladies!'

Maeve raised her eyebrows. 'Oh, you've made someone a very happy man!' she said to Rebecca.

Carmel clapped her hands together like a delighted child. 'I do hope we will have another wedding soon. This town could do with a lift.'

Rebecca ignored their comments and put *The Canberra Times* back in the Pikes' postal slot.

'How can I help you ladies today?' she asked, hiding her true feelings behind a mask of efficiency.

She was living two parallel lives – one as a postmistress gradually finding her place in the town, and the other as a hunted animal that was about to be devoured by the beast of the press.

★

The house Timothy shared with his mother was tucked away down a long laneway that ran off Ocean Road. Timothy drove his car down the winding gravel drive, bordered by hoop pines and Chinese elms. The sandstone house that came into view was in the colonial style, with French doors and windows framed by green shutters. A stone fountain stood in the middle of what would have once been a carriage loop, giving the house a genteel elegance. The garden was every bit as magnificent as Joy had indicated. The bowling-green perfect lawn was edged with garden beds teeming with early spring flowers in full bloom: purple snapdragons, scarlet salvia and coral-pink azaleas. Butterflies and bees abounded in it and a pair of colourful rainbow lorikeets feasted on the dark purple fruits of an umbrella tree. Timothy helped Rebecca from the car. Then he took a folding-frame wheelchair from the boot and eased his mother into it. Mrs Litchfield's right arm was in a sling and Rebecca wondered if she had injured it. He pushed her down the stone path towards the house with Rebecca following behind. The front wheel of the chair squeaked.

'Goodness,' said Timothy. 'That's a rather unpleasant sound. We will have to give that some oil, won't we, Mum?'

Rebecca liked the way Timothy called his mother 'Mum'. He was normally so proper in his speech that the intimate way he addressed his mother touched her. She had noticed that when he spoke to Mrs Litchfield, it was not in the patronising tone people often used with invalids, but with warmth and affection. He had described the situation of his mother's affliction as his 'Achilles heel'. Timothy was jolly and sociable with everyone but she was beginning to understand how much secret pain he felt but didn't show.

The inside of the house was as charming as its exterior. The floorboards were wide and the dark teak furniture was complemented by the cream walls and the high white ceilings. The seafoam green of the soft furnishings gave the house a sense of airy lightness. Everything was fresh, as if it had been recently redecorated.

'It's beautiful!' she said. 'The colour scheme is perfect for a coastal setting.'

He watched her with eager eyes. 'I'm glad you like it. Mum's favourite colour is green.'

Timothy led his mother out onto a veranda decorated with potted ferns and palms. He placed her at the head of a table that had been laid with chartreuse green china and sparkling silverware.

'Please sit down and make yourself comfortable,' he said, pulling out a chair for Rebecca. 'Our maid, Shirley, has Sundays off so you will have to put up with my attempt at cooking, I'm afraid.'

'So you cook as well as garden?' Rebecca raised her eyebrows in admiration. Timothy was certainly a most unusual man. Her father had never entered the kitchen to do anything other than to fix the sink. Ned wouldn't have had the slightest idea of how to cook an egg. All the other men she had known had shared a similar aversion to anything domestic.

'Of course,' Timothy answered, with a pleasant smile. 'We Litchfields have always prided ourselves on being self-sufficient.'

After Timothy left to prepare lunch, Rebecca turned to Mrs Litchfield. 'You have a marvellous son,' she said.

Mrs Litchfield watched her silently, with eyes that were startlingly clear and beautiful. She moved her mouth as if she wanted to say something.

Rebecca leaned in closer and placed her hand over the old woman's and immediately regretted it. Her flesh felt cold and stiff, not at all like that of a living person. It sent a shiver through her. What would it be like to be trapped in your own body – alive on the inside but not able to communicate with anybody or do anything for yourself?

'Nnnn,' Mrs Litchfield said, shaking her head. 'Nnnn.'

At a loss about what to do, Rebecca poured her a glass of water and then realised that with one hand strapped and the other limp Mrs Litchfield wouldn't be able to drink it on her own. She lifted it to Mrs Litchfield's lips, but the woman shook her head violently.

'Nnnn!' She turned her chin to her strapped hand.

'Do you want me to untie the sling?' Rebecca asked. 'Is it uncomfortable?'

Mrs Litchfield stared at her and said nothing. What on earth is wrong? thought Rebecca.

How was it that Timothy was able to cope with his mother's impairment so cheerfully day after day while she was exhausted after only five minutes? She thought of her own mother. Perhaps love – and other complicated emotions – gave you the strength?

Mrs Litchfield turned her chin to her strapped arm again and nodded. Not knowing what else to do, Rebecca loosened the knot and slid the sling down. Then gave a start. The old woman's arm was covered in bruises.

'Oh, don't do that,' said Timothy, putting the baked ham he was carrying down on the centre of the table and rushing to his mother's side. He tied the sling again and tucked his mother's bound arm against her chest. 'She doesn't feel it,' he explained. 'Sometimes she throws it around and bangs into things. I have to stop her from hurting herself.'

'Oh, I'm sorry,' said Rebecca, 'I thought she was uncomfortable.'

'That's very kind of you, Rebecca. But unfortunately no matter what I do for her there is going to be some degree of discomfort.'

Tears sprang in his eyes and Rebecca glanced away so as not to embarrass him. He kissed his mother on the cheek and she stared at him with suffering eyes.

'Now, Mum, we have a lovely visitor today. Aren't we lucky?'

Mrs Litchfield looked from her son to Rebecca and the hostile expression returned to her face. She doesn't like me, Rebecca thought. She doesn't like me at all. Rebecca studied the surroundings instead. The house and garden were quiet, with only the whisper of the sea in the background. Everything was graceful and understated. It created a different atmosphere to the excitement and glamour that had so often filled her life in Sydney. 'Rebecca likes the house,' Timothy told his mother, tucking a serviette into the collar of her dress and placing another on her lap. 'She said it's beautiful!'

'Has it been in your family a while?' Rebecca asked.

'It was built by my great-grandfather. My forebears were dairy farmers and speculators. It was my grandfather who became the first of the family to study medicine. It was necessary then as there were no medical men for miles around.'

Timothy went to the kitchen again, and Rebecca pretended not to see that his mother was squinting at her. He had inadvertently answered another question she had wondered about. The house was far grander than she had expected for a doctor in a remote town, so it was clear that the Litchfields had other money besides Timothy's income. Perhaps that was why Mrs Litchfield had taken a dislike to her. Rebecca wore good clothes and tasteful jewellery but there was no mistaking that she had a lust for life and a desire for beautiful things that women of the upper classes took for granted. You couldn't fake that inborn class, that complete self-assuredness that came with family money. Mrs Litchfield, no doubt, thought Rebecca was some gold digger after her son's inheritance. Perhaps she even reminded her of Arabella.

'You don't have to worry, Mrs Litchfield, I'm not here to steal your son from you.'

Mrs Litchfield grimaced and shook her head. She leaned over towards Rebecca and nearly toppled from her chair. Rebecca gingerly righted her before Timothy returned with a tray of crusty bread, potato salad and tomato aspic.

'What did you think of Father Rob's sermon this morning?' he asked, sitting down.

Rebecca cut into her ham. She hadn't liked the message at all and had done what she always did when she was bored: she tuned out. But she had caught enough of the sermon to know it was fire-and-brimstone preaching. The idea that a kind and loving God sent people to hell was anathema to Rebecca. Her mind had drifted to Stefan Otto, who feared neither God nor the sea. She had gone to the rock platform the evening before, hoping for another encounter. But she'd only stayed for ten minutes and quickly returned home. It was a foolish idea to have dallied with, she knew. She'd always been one to play with fire.

'Father Rob was certainly passionate about the subject,' she said. 'What did you think?'

Timothy cut up his mother's food into tiny pieces before poking them on a fork and helping her to eat them. There was something pitiful about a grown woman being fed like a baby. She'd had to do that for her own mother in her dying days, and it made the inevitability of deterioration and death too real for Rebecca.

Timothy waited for his mother to chew and wiped some dribble from her chin. 'I thought it was hopeful for everybody,' he replied. 'Repentance means that you have sinned against God, but if you are willing to repent, then God can forgive you.'

Rebecca found it difficult to watch Timothy feed his mother. She chewed with her mouth open and when she didn't like something she simply let it drop from her lips into her lap. All the time, Timothy managed to keep up a pleasant conversation about his plans to build a bigger greenhouse and the challenges of creating a garden in a coastal climate. He certainly was an extraordinary human being, able to remain patient and charming under difficult circumstances.

Rebecca waited for him to pause for a moment before asking the favour she had in mind. 'Timothy, I wanted to ask you about Berit Olsen. Her husband beats her.'

He grimaced and nodded. 'I've spoken to Mr Olsen about the matter.'

'With all respect, I don't think he listened. She came into the post office the other day covered in bruises.'

Timothy stopped feeding his mother and turned to Rebecca. 'The wise doctor who trained me at Sydney Hospital gave me a sage bit of advice. "Speak to the husband once, offer the wife help to leave once, but if nothing changes then leave the matter alone."'

Rebecca bristled. 'What does that mean?'

'It means that if neither is willing to change, then on some level they must like things as they are. Any local doctor in any town in Australia will tell you that they have had wives scream blue murder against their husbands and yet return to them again and again.'

Rebecca's hands twitched. She had the unsettling feeling of having been put in her place. 'What a thing to say! Berit doesn't like being hit. She is terrified of her husband and, after meeting him, I can understand why.'

Timothy's mouth pursed and he glanced at his mother. 'Rebecca, all I can tell you is to not get in Sanders Olsen's way … and don't assume everything Berit tells you is true.'

'Why do you say that? I've seen her bruises!'

But Timothy was already standing and gathering the plates, clearly a sign he didn't intend to discuss the subject further. 'I'll go get us dessert, shall I?'

Rebecca sat back in her chair and crossed her arms. What was that all about? Mrs Litchfield was glaring at her again. Obviously she didn't approve of Rebecca creating tension over lunch. Perhaps Timothy hadn't been willing to discuss Berit's dilemma in front of his mother.

'Nnn, nnn,' the old woman said, shaking her head and trying to lift her strapped arm. 'Nnnn … nnnn … you. Nnnn … you.'

'Oh, shut up!' Rebecca hissed under her breath.

*

Just as they finished their dessert of custard and stewed apples, a trim woman in a tweed suit by the name of Mrs Todd arrived. Timothy introduced her as his mother's nurse. Together they settled Mrs Litchfield into an armchair in the sitting room, propping her up with cushions and covering her legs with a checked blanket. Mrs Litchfield's head drooped as if she was exhausted by all the fuss – or exhausted with life. 'I'm just taking Rebecca for a walk around the garden,' Timothy said directly into her ear. 'Then we can have a slice of apple spice cake. That's always been your favourite cake, hasn't it, Mum?'

Mrs Litchfield's eyes moved from Timothy to Rebecca blankly. Rebecca was losing patience with both of them. She did not feel like walking around the garden or spending another minute in their company. She certainly wouldn't mention Berit to Timothy again; she would try to help the young woman herself. But her own precarious position in the town gave her no other choice than to maintain a polite charade with the Litchfields. She couldn't afford to be rude.

On the way to the garden, they walked down a corridor lined with family photographs in silver frames. 'These are pictures of Mum,' said Timothy, stopping in front of some photographs of a young woman dressed for a ball and for tennis; in another she was picnicking with friends. Mrs Litchfield had certainly been beautiful when she was young, with her raven hair and swan-like neck. She looked so alive, so charming, so brimming with energy. So very different from the woman she was now.

Timothy led Rebecca out into the garden and pointed to the beds of fragrant English roses planted along with sweet alyssum and geraniums. 'Mum called this part of the garden her Pink Palace,' he said. 'She thought a great garden should be beautiful in every season, which is why she has bordered everything with neat box hedges, so the garden would still look elegant and formal even in the cold months.'

Although Rebecca was not a gardener, she did appreciate beauty when she saw it. All the flowers were in shades of pink ranging from magenta to peach to the palest ballet slipper.

'It's lovely,' she said. 'It's so feminine.'

Timothy nodded, pleased that she appreciated it. 'I see a lot of similarities between you and my mother. You both like order and beauty. You are both very particular about your dress.'

Rebecca understood he'd meant it as the highest compliment but she did not want to be compared with the paralysed Mrs Litchfield: trapped, helpless and frail.

Rebecca was surrounded by beauty but she was on the verge of tears. Mrs Litchfield hadn't always been an elderly invalid. But her days as a great beauty and a creator of it were gone forever. To the end of her life Mrs Litchfield would rely on her son and a nurse for everything. Rebecca caught sight of her reflection in one of the downstairs windows. What did the future hold for her, the hounded, scandalous woman? Would she die like so many other mistresses when the men they loved had no further use for them – poor, forgotten and old in some rat-infested hovel?

'You look very thoughtful, Rebecca,' Timothy said, coming to a stop.

She faced him. As a doctor he must have seen many terrible things: the results of shocking accidents, children with incurable diseases, wounds with maggots in them. In his own personal life, his bride had deserted him and his mother was paralysed. Life held such beauty and *such horror*! Her mind drifted to whoever had molested Anne. What kind of person could have done that to a vulnerable, innocent girl?

'Do you really think everyone can be redeemed?' she asked him. 'What about child murderers? Or Hitler? I don't believe evil people can change and so trying to help them is meaningless.'

Timothy tilted his head, puzzled. 'Redemption is freedom by payment of a price. So, yes, I believe anyone can be redeemed if they are willing to pay the price. They have to atone for their sins and be willing to change their entire life.'

Her mind drifted back to the women standing in front of the church in *The Canberra Times*: *No family is safe while that woman remains at large*.

Clearly not everyone shared his opinion. And women like her were considered irredeemable, perhaps even among the worst of the evildoers.

CHAPTER THIRTEEN

It seemed everyone who came to the post office on Monday morning had a special smile or a wink for Rebecca. Word must have spread that Timothy had invited her to lunch with his mother after church. Now the townspeople who had once regarded her suspiciously were beaming as if they shared an agreeable sense of history with her. Which, of course, they did not.

'I guess this means we will lose another postmistress,' said Marge, biting her lip as she passed her mail over the counter for Rebecca to weigh. 'Just when everything has started running so smoothly again.'

Rebecca dampened the stamps before pasting them on the envelopes. She could imagine how the rumours were being tossed about by the women of the town. The story would be growing with each telling. Yes, she had lunched and gone dancing with Timothy but that didn't automatically make them engaged.

'That will be ten pence, Marge.'

Marge doled out her coins. 'We'll have to have that baking lesson soon,' she said with a wink. 'Can't have the good doctor starving to death.'

'He's not likely to starve,' Rebecca replied. 'He's a very good cook.'

Doris floated into the post office wearing a buttercup yellow sundress and carrying a posy of flowers.

'Well, who's got the whole town talking?' she said, striding to the tearoom and returning with a glass filled with water. 'I hope you will let me make your bridal bouquet.'

Doris arranged the posy on the counter. Rebecca would move it as soon as she left. It wasn't in keeping with the official atmosphere of the post office, and everyone would assume Timothy had given the flowers to her.

Doris glanced sideways at her. 'What's that sour face for? You can't stay melancholy forever. You and Doctor Litchfield are a good-looking couple.' Her gaze dropped to Rebecca's stomach. 'And you can't leave things too much longer, you know. Time doesn't wait for us women.'

Something that felt like lightning snapped inside Rebecca's head. Two hundred million volts of pain shot through her. Her Achilles heel, Timothy would have called it. She saw herself lying on the operating table in the rooms of the doctor Ned had sent her to in order to abort their baby. Afterwards the doctor had given her his hand to help her sit upright. 'You'll be able to get on with things now,' he'd told her. 'Forget about all this.'

But Rebecca had never forgotten. She'd buried it, but she'd never forgotten.

'When someone is right for you, you don't need to dither,' Doris continued, oblivious to the blow she had inflicted on Rebecca. 'I knew Reggie was the one for me the day I saw him.

My mother used to sell produce from her garden at the Twin Falls Fair. Reggie came to show off some prize cows from the dairy farm he was managing. I was immediately struck by his rugged good looks and cocky confidence.'

Carmel and Joy walked into the post office, talking with each other. Rebecca blinked at them, still reeling from the memory of what had happened to her baby. The women greeted Doris and Marge and admired the flowers Doris had placed on the counter. 'Oh, so pretty,' said Joy. 'Spring is my favourite time of year.' Rebecca wanted to cover her ears and shut out the din of female chatter. She wanted to throw that annoying posy against the wall.

'Excuse me a moment,' she said to the women. She went through the tearoom and out the back door. She stood on the steps, taking great gulps of air. The day after the abortion she had held her stomach and cried, begging the dead child to forgive her. By sheer force of will she had convinced herself that the pregnancy had never happened, that she'd never had an abortion, but she realised now that all she had done was to numb a part of herself. To hell with those women, she thought. How dare they force their ideas of happiness upon her! Marge's husband was fat and lecherous. Why were women with the worst husbands so determined to see other women married off?

The bell on the post office door tinkled and the chatter of the women abruptly ceased. Rebecca straightened, puzzled by the sudden silence. She returned to the post office and froze. Stefan Otto was standing in the doorway, two large bundles of envelopes under each arm. He was wearing tailored trousers, a white shirt and a navy-blue blazer. Contrary to the wild Neptunian image of him that she had been carrying around in her head, he looked sharp.

Doris and the other women stared at him with stupefied expressions. He didn't acknowledge them. They parted like the sea before Moses when he stepped towards Rebecca and placed the bundles on the counter.

'Good morning. I'd like to send these,' he said. 'Registered mail.'

His eyes settled on Rebecca's face but his expression was deadpan and gave her no clue as to what he was thinking. Did he even remember they had met on the beach?

'All of them?' she asked. 'I mean, all of them registered mail?'

He nodded.

Rebecca pulled the stacks towards her and began weighing and calculating the costs by destination on a piece of paper. The letters were going to different universities around the world, including the Department of Zoology at London University. Her fingers itched with curiosity as she touched them. What fascinating correspondence did they contain? When she was an adolescent she'd harboured a desire to go to university to study languages. She'd taught herself to speak and write French in preparation. But when she'd turned sixteen her mother had told her to leave school and get a job, so her language skills became just another charm she used to impress the European dignitaries Ned was required to entertain.

She was aware that Doris and the others were watching her. The degree of hostility they directed at Stefan Otto through their glares, and the disdain he showed by completely ignoring them, was so thick in the air she nearly choked on it. She passed the registered mail forms to him to sign, hoping he would not mention the other evening on the beach. Their fingers touched. Warmth tingled over her skin and she blushed. It was the same sensation she'd felt when he had taken her hand to help her onto the sand, but she hadn't known who he was then. Any sign of flirtation now and she would find herself shunned too.

'I knew I'd seen you somewhere before,' he said, glancing at the white gold and onyx ring on her finger. 'You looked familiar to me.'

Rebecca raised her eyes to his. She felt her brow wrinkle as if she was sending him a plea to not mention their meeting. 'I don't think so,' she said, with a nervous smile. 'I've only been here a short while.'

'Not here. In Sydney. I recognise you from Sydney.'

Her mind raced. She could not have met Stefan in Sydney. She had no recollection of it – and he was not a man you would forget. The women in the post office turned from Stefan to Rebecca as if they were watching a tennis match. Heat burned Rebecca's skin. Her bra and slip seemed to have shrunk. Every part of her felt tight.

She took the money Stefan handed her. 'Perhaps at the GPO,' she said, keeping her voice steady. 'It was a very busy place. You must have seen me working there.'

He glanced at her hand again. Rebecca looked at the ring too and then it dawned on her. She had seen him before! It was at an antiques auction she'd gone to with Ned soon after they had met. Ned's eye had been on a fifteenth-century Portuguese suit of armour he'd wanted for the hall of his Sydney home. It was a ridiculous, impractical thing but Ned never deprived himself of anything he wanted. He'd purchased it for an excessive sum. Among the collection there had been a piece of jewellery that had caught Rebecca's eye: the white gold and onyx cocktail ring she was now wearing. Marquise cut with a decorative scalloped border, it was both striking and unique. Ned told her he would get it for her. Not since she was ten years old had Rebecca been given a gift, so the idea of a present of any sort thrilled her. For most of the auction, Ned was the highest bidder but just when it looked like the ring was theirs, another bid had come from the back of the room. Rebecca wasn't able to see the man bidding against them clearly, as he was obscured by a woman with a broad hat. But she could see enough to ascertain that he was dark-haired and tall. While Ned grew increasingly flustered and bothered, determined not to be outdone, his opponent kept coolly raising his offer. Then just when Ned was on the verge of giving up, the other man stopped bidding. After the auction, as Rebecca and Ned were leaving, the man who had been bidding against them stood up too and smiled at Rebecca. She'd realised from his expression that he hadn't really wanted the ring; he had merely taken pleasure in making Ned pay a lot of money for it. That was seven years ago, and he'd had very short hair then and been thinner about the face, but she was certain now that the man was Stefan Otto.

Rebecca brought her hand to her mouth, and then caught herself when she remembered the presence of the other women.

'No,' she said, doing her best to suppress a smile. 'I am sure you are mistaken.'

Stefan raised his eyebrows and took the receipt from Rebecca. 'Perhaps I am,' he replied, tucking it into the inner pocket of his blazer. 'My apologies.'

He was turning to go when Nancy rushed in the door with her son. Her eyes opened wide and her face blanched when she recognised Stefan. Rebecca couldn't see Stefan's face but it seemed to her that his whole back stiffened.

'Good morning, Mrs Pike,' he said, before brushing past her and out the door.

Nancy stood on the spot, wavering as if she had seen a ghost. Her reaction wasn't one Rebecca would have expected from someone who had just faced their foe. Something had flickered in her face that Rebecca recognised. It was the same thing she'd felt every time someone had mentioned Ned after he'd betrayed her: a bitter concoction of pain, self-doubt and deep regret.

'The hide of the man!' said Doris, with a hiss. 'The absolute hide!'

'He struts around like he owns the town – owns us!' said Elaine, crossing her arms. 'Well, he doesn't! We'll show him he doesn't!'

Nancy shook herself as if gathering her wits. 'It's all right,' she said. 'George will deal with him. He can't stop the whaling. He can't stop anything.'

But the other women wouldn't leave the subject alone. They gathered around Nancy like yapping chihuahuas. 'But you should have seen all the letters he came to post,' cried Carmel. 'More than I send in a month!'

'He only comes back to Shipwreck Bay when he wants to cause trouble,' Joy added.

Nancy looked pale and a little shaken. 'I told you not to worry. George will handle it.'

Marge adjusted her glasses and set her jaw. 'I'm sure George will show him what's what,' she said. Then she nodded in Rebecca's direction. 'You should have seen the way he eyed our new postmistress. Looked her up and down like a delicious piece of candy. Disgusting!'

Nancy turned in Rebecca's direction. Her eyes focused not on her face but on her throat. Rebecca swallowed and fiddled with the cocktail ring. 'Well, I doubt that,' Nancy said. 'Stefan Otto has very particular taste.'

Rebecca suspected Nancy was bluffing. She could see it in her pinched expression. If envy were a weapon, Nancy would have shot Rebecca dead.

*

The flow of people coming to the post office stopped after lunchtime. Johnny had a telegram to deliver and Rebecca was glad to have the post office to herself for a while. She lingered at the picture window and stared in the direction of the beach again, hoping for a glimpse of Stefan, although from the way he had been dressed he hadn't looked like he was headed for the water. What did he do with himself all day, apart from write letters to universities and go diving?

Rebecca curled a strand of her hair around her finger. Doris and the other women weren't wrong to point her in the direction of Timothy. There could be no more pretending. If she wanted to make something of her life, she had to choose differently. Yet there was a force in her as relentless as the tide that seemed to be forever carrying her to self-destruction. From the moment she'd met him, Rebecca had known that Ned was conceited and self-centred and she'd still fallen for him. Now that same current was pulling her in the direction of a man with the kind of magnetism that could only spell trouble.

She was startled from her thoughts by the wail of an alarm. She squinted to the horizon and saw the whalers' chaser boat speeding up in pursuit of something in the direction of the headland. She hoped that the whale would lead Sanders Olsen and his men onto the rocks. If that beast of a man drowned, it could only be a good thing.

'They'll be gone for a while.'

Rebecca turned to see Berit standing at the counter.

'You have to be careful,' Rebecca said to her. 'Somebody told your husband that you were coming here often. He interrogated me.'

Berit's mouth set into a grim line. 'But you didn't tell him anything. Thank you.'

'People are intrigued by the suffering of others,' Rebecca told her. 'For them it's just entertainment, something to be discussed over the back fence. But for you their loose tongues could be deadly.'

Rebecca noticed for the first time that Berit's eyes were the most beautiful shade of delphinium blue. Why had fate matched her with such a terrible husband? Why not somebody better? Somebody kinder? Rebecca rarely felt empathy for others, but she did for Berit.

'For a long time, I tried to guess what set Sanders off,' Berit said. 'I thought it was some fault in me and if I could just do this or that differently then things would return to how they were before we got married. It took me a while to understand that what he does is deliberate and that he keeps control by constantly changing the rules. Once I understood that, I learned to play on his arrogance by acting meeker than I am. That's how I convinced him that I should do the bookkeeping and banking for the whaling station: to save him precious time. He might be cruel but he is also stupid. He thinks that he has broken me and that I am too scared to ever do anything against him.'

Rebecca grimaced. 'But he suspects something now. You have to be careful.'

The sound of an explosion made both women jump. 'It's the harpoon gun,' said Berit, with a shiver. 'They've got something.'

Rebecca didn't like the omen. She took the whaling station passbook from Berit and banked the money she had brought, subtracting part of it to add to Berit's secret stash. She handed the passbook back to Berit, but the young woman was in no hurry to leave. 'In Norway they view men like my husband as heroic. Songs and poems about the so-called brave whalers abound. But I believe there is nothing heroic about those brutes. It's the whales that are noble. Did you know that the bull will not desert a cow? If she is harpooned he will not leave her, although he will be shot too.' Berit shivered. 'I've grown to hate the clanking of chains when they haul up a whale carcass onto the flensing deck.

They hack into the flesh and peel back the blubber like the skin on a banana. I watch them and think that my husband and his men are like dirty thieves. I don't think they have a right to do it. The whales don't belong to them.'

*

When Rebecca left the post office for the day the air was thick with the stink of boiling whale flesh. A coastal shower was beginning to blow in. The droplets were light at first but increased in intensity. She was soaked by the time she got home. She hurriedly opened the gate and ran down the path towards the veranda. The rain was cold and she was rummaging in her handbag for her key when something on the doormat caught her eye: it was an envelope with her name on it. The stationery was ivory linen. A drop of water dripped from her hair onto the writing and the ink ran so that her name became a black smudge. Rebecca opened the door and placed her bag and the letter on the coffee table before racing to her bedroom to take off her wet clothes and stockings and hang them in the bathroom.

She wrapped herself in a robe then returned to the living room and picked up the envelope. She hadn't heard from Timothy since the previous day and assumed the letter was from him. Intrigued, she opened it. A single line was all the note contained: *Will you come and see me?* But the message wasn't from Timothy. A surge of adrenaline flashed through her body when she saw the signature at the bottom of it: Stefan Otto.

CHAPTER FOURTEEN

The next morning, Rebecca waited at the post office for Johnny to arrive with the mail from the train. Her mind kept drifting to the note Stefan Otto had left for her. Had he delivered it personally or had one of his servants left it? Had anybody seen him? She twisted the cocktail ring around her finger. They'd been at the same auction together years ago bidding for the same ring. And now they were here together in Shipwreck Bay. Perhaps some things were fated.

When Johnny didn't appear by half past nine she assumed that the train must have been late. But when another hour passed she sensed there was something wrong. She had just closed the post office door and tacked a note on it, intending to walk to the station herself, when Timothy appeared.

'Rebecca!' he called, striding towards her. There were dark circles under his eyes. 'I'm sorry I didn't call you yesterday but Mrs Jones went into a long labour. It was touch and go.'

She could hear in his tone how worried he had been about the mother and baby. 'I hope everything is all right now,' she said.

'As good as gold! Both Mrs Jones and the baby are doing well,' he replied, scratching the back of his head. 'But, unfortunately, I can't say as much for your delivery boy.'

He turned towards his car. Johnny's bicycle was tied to the roof.

'What's happened?' Rebecca asked. 'I was on my way to look for him!'

'Johnny hit a rock and came off his bicycle. He dislocated his shoulder. I managed to set it again, but he will be sore and swollen for a few days. He probably shouldn't lift anything heavy for a few weeks.'

Rebecca let out a breath. 'Did he damage the bicycle as well?' Then, thinking she might have sounded callous, she added, 'He should rest as much as possible, so I will have to deliver the mail.'

Timothy brushed his fingers over his mouth to hide his smile. 'I am sure that will make more than a few people's day. You will be the prettiest delivery boy this town has ever seen.'

He untied the bicycle and lifted it from the roof. 'It looks all right to me,' he said, resting it against the fig tree. 'But give it a test run before you go too far.' He returned to the car and pulled the mailbag out of the back seat. Rebecca tried to take it from him, but he shook his head and nodded towards the post office. 'I'll carry it in for you.'

It was then that Rebecca noticed the grocer and his wife were watching the exchange, as were the owners of the general store. Nancy Pike drove past in a beige Cadillac but made a point of looking away, while Elaine and Frank waved enthusiastically from their truck as they drove past.

'It seems we have the whole town talking,' Timothy said, smiling. He placed the bag on the sorting table and looked around as if searching for something else he might help with. 'I hope you don't mind.'

Rebecca did mind. The pleased look on his face gave her the impression he was enjoying the townspeople speculating about their relationship. From the time she and Timothy had planted the garden together she felt he had been staking a claim on her.

'Timothy, I think you should be aware ...' She stopped when she realised he was staring at something. His smile had vanished and his expression was grim.

The door to her office was open, giving a clear view to her desk and chair. Then she remembered the awful thing that had happened there and realised that, as well as the police sergeant, Timothy would probably have been called to the scene to declare Mabel deceased. How terrible it would have been to have found someone you knew in that condition. He was not only the person who saw the town's babies come into the world but was also present when one of the townspeople departed it.

'It's very sad what happened to Mabel,' she said. 'It must have been a terrible shock.'

Timothy flinched. 'Yes ... especially Mabel. She was a town fixture. She was liked by everyone.'

Rebecca did not want to be reminded of what had happened in the room where she spent so much time. She guided Timothy's attention to the picture window by standing before it. But the sea evoked as painful a memory for him as it did for her.

'Her daughter had drowned herself a few months before,' he said, his shoulders slumped. 'I had to identify her. It was terrible. The crabs had already got to her face.'

Rebecca let out a gasp. Death was such an ignoble thing. If she'd had a choice, she would like to go as Cleopatra did: on a stage set by her servants for maximum glamour.

'Anne was partially deaf and a loner,' Timothy continued, rubbing his neck. 'A delightful girl by nature but her condition meant she had a lot of health concerns over the years. I got to know both mother and daughter very well. It's been a terrible tragedy for all concerned.'

'Berit said the girl had been molested and that's why she took her life.'

Timothy squinted at the sea, pain etched on his normally jovial face. 'Indeed, that appears to have been the case. I suspected it from her injuries. Poor child.'

Rebecca's stomach turned queasy. 'Do you think it was someone local?' she ventured.

At first she thought Timothy hadn't heard her because he continued to stare at the sea, but then he shook his head. 'No one from Shipwreck Bay would have hurt Anne – or Mabel – that way. We get all sorts of people coming through town. The area is a renowned fishing spot. And Anne ... well, I had warned Mabel ...'

'Warned her about what?'

Timothy bit his lip and looked around the room. He seemed flustered. 'It's indelicate to say ... but I guess you will understand. As Anne got older she grew ... well, let's be frank, *promiscuous*. Not her fault, of course; it was a lack of inhibition brought on by her deficiency. But I always feared that if she wasn't supervised, she could come to harm if she happened upon the wrong sort of person.'

'Mabel must have felt horribly guilty.'

Timothy shrugged in sad resignation. 'I'm sure that was the case.'

Rebecca could see how upset Timothy was getting and let the story alone. Instead she asked him about something that held much more interest for her.

'What do you know about Stefan Otto? Was he really a spy during the war?'

Timothy flashed a look at Rebecca. 'I heard he came in here yesterday,' he said, straightening. 'I don't know if he did any spying. I was away at the time doing medical service in Greece, but there was some suspicion, I believe. His parents were well regarded in town, but I've always found Stefan rather extreme. At school he often expressed radical ideas about society and now of course he espouses the belief that whales are intelligent animals with feelings and therefore we shouldn't hunt them.'

'You went to school together?'

'Yes, boarding school in Sydney. But Stefan was a few years above me.'

Rebecca tried to feign ambivalence, but every new fact she learned about Stefan filled her with eagerness to know more.

'Which school did you go to?'

Timothy's face pinched. He turned to her. 'I don't need to tell you this, Rebecca, you are a grown woman. But Stefan Otto has some notoriety. He doesn't spend a lot of time in Shipwreck Bay, but each time he comes I hear stories all the way from Wollongong to Penguin Bay of broken hearts and sullied reputations.'

Realising that she wasn't going to get anything more out of Timothy, she saw him out to his car and thanked him again for bringing the bicycle and telling her about Johnny. She waved to him as he drove away. Stefan Otto was notorious? A man who also had interesting and radical views? She had almost snickered when Timothy used the words *broken hearts and sullied reputations*. He was a nice, caring doctor, to be sure – but so old-fashioned! She returned to her office and opened her desk drawer. The card Stefan had left for her lay there facing upwards.

Will you come and see me?

Timothy had meant to warn Rebecca about Stefan, but instead he'd waved a red flag at a bull. She was more intrigued than ever.

CHAPTER FIFTEEN

Johnny's accident was a fortuitous thing. If one of the town gossips saw Rebecca paying a visit to Stefan Otto, that would get tongues wagging. But going there on official duty to deliver his mail … She clenched her fists. Temptation was taking her down a dangerous road. It was bad enough she was being watched because of her supposed romance with the popular doctor. What would happen should her name be associated with someone everyone in town hated?

The day was overcast as she set out on her route. The sea was grey and foreboding. Great rollers swept into the bay and washed over the rocks with a thunderous pounding. One thing she could be sure of was that Stefan Otto was unlikely to be out diving that day.

'Good morning, Miss Wood,' said George Pike, as he waited by his letterbox. 'Anything important from Canberra today?'

The Pikes received more mail than anybody else in town and she had been too distracted that morning to notice if there were official letters from anywhere. She handed George his mail, but he was determined to impress her.

'I've demanded a special inquiry into whaling in Shipwreck Bay,' he said, his little piranha mouth moving up and down. 'We are far behind the rest of the world in exploiting our ocean resources.'

Rebecca nodded, not willing to express an opinion on the subject. She was inclined to agree with Berit that shooting grenades into whales to blow up their insides was not a particularly humane way to kill anything. But, in reality, her main objection to whaling was the terrible stench it brought to the town.

'Are you finding Shipwreck Bay to your liking, Miss Wood?' he asked, no doubt to delay her. She didn't like the way he was looking at her again. Berit said there had been some trouble with George and girl guides, and Rebecca could believe it.

'I'd better get on my way,' she said, securing the mailbag more tightly on her bicycle.

He placed a clammy hand on her wrist. 'It's my plan to create more jobs and growth for Shipwreck Bay,' he said, his breath smelling like sour milk. 'I've got big plans for this town! You could be part of it. I could do a lot for you.'

Rebecca pulled back and George's grip grew tighter. For a moment she saw a vision of a frightened Anne Peberdy wrestling with George as he kissed her with his disgusting lips and left his musty smell all over her. Did he do that to the poor girl? Was George her molester?

'Let go of me,' she told him firmly.

Nancy's voice called from somewhere in the house. 'George, where are you? You need to sign these certificates for the football team.'

George released Rebecca and straightened himself. 'I'm coming,' he called back to Nancy. Then turning to Rebecca as if nothing unpleasant had happened, he smiled and said, 'Well, all the best to you, Miss Wood. I'm sorry to hear about Johnny. I've seen him speed down the hill towards the station and have warned him several times. Still, he's young and strong. He'll mend quickly enough.'

Rebecca worked the rest of the run feeling like she wanted a bath after her encounter with George Pike. She was no stranger to nasty, brutish men who didn't feel any compunction to control their hideous impulses. Her first boss used to press his fat belly against the back of her chair when he gave her instructions, and once at a Christmas party one of Ned's aides had told her that she would 'look good on her knees' and was then surprised that she didn't take it as a compliment. But what baffled her most about George Pike was Nancy. How had the former beauty queen ended up married to him?

It was just after one o'clock when Rebecca finished delivering the mail around town. She was glad she had kept up her morning calisthenics exercises and her legs were strong enough to cope with the hills. The sky had cleared and a bright, hot sun shone across the water. She gazed in the direction of the headland, took a breath and pedalled towards Stefan Otto's house.

The last time she had gone down Stefan Otto's driveway she had been panicked in her desire to get back to the main road and hadn't paid much attention to her surroundings. Now she saw that the drive was bordered by thick plantings of clivias. The vibrant orange blooms gave her the impression that she was riding through a ring of fire. Dozens of tiny birds – wrens, finches and robins – darted in and out of the scrub. Her mailbag was almost empty and she cruised along with a thrill of childish ease. She reached the front gate and found that it was secured by a chain and lock. A sense of disappointment swept over her. There was a brass bell on the gatepost and Rebecca rang it. A moment later, an elderly man in a butler's uniform came out of the front door and walked towards her. When he reached the gate, he regarded Rebecca with large protruding eyes.

'I have Mr Otto's mail,' she told him. 'I am the new postmistress.'

The butler said nothing and his dour expression didn't change. He didn't open the gate and invite her inside as she expected. He simply lifted his hands towards her to take the letters.

'I have a request from Mr Otto to see him,' she said.

The butler shook his head. 'Mr Otto has no visitors,' he replied in a thick German accent.

'But I received a note from him yesterday. Perhaps you left it for me? On my doormat?'

'No,' he said, again shaking his head.

Rebecca was annoyed by his obstinacy. 'I didn't bring the note with me but I most certainly received one.'

The butler stared at her incredulously. 'Mr Otto sees no one!'

The statement was delivered with such conviction that Rebecca began to wonder if perhaps she was indeed mistaken. Had it been a prank by somebody else in the town? Someone who had seen her encounter with Stefan Otto on the beach and wished to trap her in some way?

As curious as she had been to meet Stefan Otto again, Rebecca wasn't about to be treated like a begging tramp. If Stefan Otto had written the note, and he'd expected her to come, then surely he would have advised his servant. She handed the mail to the butler and stepped back on the bicycle, riding back into town with as much dignity as she could muster but feeling like a dog with its tail between its legs. She would never make a fool of herself like that again!

CHAPTER SIXTEEN

Johnny lived with his parents and older brothers on a dairy farm on the outskirts of Shipwreck Bay. It was the last house on the second mail route and rather than leave the mail in the letterbox at the gate, as she had the previous two days, Rebecca decided to pay her recuperating delivery boy a visit. She closed the gate after herself and pedalled down the long drive towards the homestead, which was barely visible behind a shelterbelt of pine trees. Rebecca had never been on a working farm before. The closest she had come to agricultural activity was the market gardens in Marsfield where she had gone with her parents when she was a child. Those had been intensively farmed plots with glass houses and rows of tomatoes, cauliflowers and lettuce surrounded by hedges of olive trees.

The Turners' farm was made up of open paddocks dotted with black and white cows. The afternoon was hot and the grassy smell of hay and steaming manure was overpowering. Rebecca wrinkled her nose. Shipwreck Bay was full of unpleasant smells. If not the whaling station, then the caustic rock dust smell that occasionally wafted from the mine – and now this. If it were not for the regular sea breezes, Rebecca wondered if she might suffocate.

The homestead was a rambling house with a sagging wraparound veranda and a rusted corrugated-iron roof. The outbuildings were also corrugated iron. Poking up from the long grass that surrounded them were piles of wood, rusted old machinery and kerosene drums. Rebecca was filled with an urge to tidy things up, to beautify them and put everything in order. But as she dismounted and wheeled her bicycle to the front step she saw that a woman's touch had already been applied to the homestead garden. Poppies, peonies and daisies sprouted from the raised garden beds and a yellow rose bush flourished near the front step. Johnny was sitting on the veranda with his arm in a sling. He was absorbed in a Superman comic and almost jumped out of his skin when Rebecca greeted him.

'Miss Wood!' he said, rising to his feet.

Rebecca was about to ask him how he was feeling when the screen door slammed and a plump woman with prematurely grey hair stepped out of the house. She blinked at Rebecca with an air of wonder.

'Mum, this is Miss Wood,' Johnny told the woman, an unmistakeable note of pride in his voice.

Mrs Turner wiped her fingers on her apron before taking Rebecca's hand in hers. 'It's a pleasure to meet you, Miss Wood. Johnny has told us so much about you. In fact, you are all we hear about these days. "Miss Wood did this; Miss Wood thinks that." She paused and peered at Rebecca uncertainly. 'Is everything all right? It must be difficult for you to manage the post office as well as the deliveries on your own.'

'I'm managing,' Rebecca answered, handing Mrs Turner her mail. 'I came to see how Johnny was getting along.'

Relief flooded over Mrs Turner's ruddy face. 'Well, come inside,' she said, laughing. 'Let me put the kettle on. I baked some biscuits this morning.' Then turning to Johnny she said, 'Go fetch your father. He's in the milking shed.'

'Oh no, please don't disturb your husband,' Rebecca said. 'I can only stay a short while. I've got to get back to the post office.'

Mrs Turner shook her head and ushered Rebecca inside. 'Roy would be upset if he missed meeting you. He only goes to town for the stock sales and it's unlikely he'd run into you there.'

She led Rebecca down a narrow hallway with walls hung with photographs of people who, from the muttonbird sleeves of the women's blouses and the handlebar moustaches on the men, belonged to the last century. The frames were dusty and Rebecca wondered if anybody noticed the photographs anymore or whether the aunt who had given birth to thirteen children or the grandfather who had drowned in a swollen river were as forgotten as the old machinery left to rust in the paddocks outside.

The hallway ended with an olive-green kitchen. On one side of it were the sink and cupboards, and on the other were shelves of saucepans along with canisters of flour and other household supplies.

'Please sit down,' said Mrs Turner, indicating a long wooden table that looked like it could seat twenty people. She set about making Rebecca a cup of tea, sneaking glances of reverence at her as if the postmistress was a member of the royal family who had suddenly dropped in. Rebecca got the impression Mrs Turner was mentally saving up details about her to share at the next Country Women's Association meeting. 'You'll never believe who came by to visit Johnny ...'

Mrs Turner placed a teacup and a plate of digestive biscuits in front of Rebecca before taking a seat herself. 'Johnny certainly didn't exaggerate how pretty you are!' she said, admiring Rebecca's crisp linen dress.

Rebecca nodded, embarrassed by Mrs Turner's deferential attitude towards her. She picked up one of the biscuits. 'Marge Mullens told me these are particularly good when dunked in tea.'

Mrs Turner was looking at Rebecca's face so intensely that she took a moment to register what Rebecca had said. 'Oh no,' she said. 'I don't think that's good at all. You end up with crumbs in your tea.' She pushed a melamine dish towards Rebecca on which sat a lump of bright yellow butter. 'I eat mine with butter. They taste delicious that way.'

Rebecca took Mrs Turner's advice and smeared butter over the digestive biscuit before biting into it. 'Hmm, yes, very nice,' she said, thinking the sweet, creamy butter would improve the taste of an old boot.

'I churned the butter this morning,' Mrs Turner said, taking a sip of tea. 'It's come straight from the cow to the kitchen. That's the advantage of living on a farm.'

The sound of male voices approaching had Mrs Turner glancing out the window. She leaned in closer to Rebecca and said hurriedly, 'I want to thank you for keeping Johnny on. Mabel was a dear to take him under her wing. I was a bit worried about the lass from Wollongong. She didn't seem to like Johnny at all. The boy is no use to us on the farm and I couldn't imagine sending him off to the mines. He's so happy these days too. He is always saying what a kind person you are.'

Rebecca shrank inwardly. Johnny was as irritating to have around as a dripping tap. It was awkward to be so highly regarded by someone who tested your patience. But she would never consider dismissing him. That would be like kicking a puppy and she wasn't as callous as that.

Johnny burst into the kitchen followed by three men who seemed to have all been cast from the same mould: tall and lanky with tanned faces. The most weather-beaten of them was Johnny's father. He nodded at Rebecca while his two elder sons, Fred and Bill, simply gaped.

'It's very nice to meet you, Miss Wood,' said Mr Turner. 'Johnny took quite a tumble but he'll be back at the post office as soon as Doctor Litchfield allows it. We can't have him shirking his duties.'

'I don't think he'll want to stay away,' said Fred.

A smile came to Bill's face. 'No, I don't think so either.'

Rebecca was aware that everyone's eyes were on her, expecting her to take the lead in the conversation. She had no idea what she could say or comment on with any intelligence. She was considering a question about herd size or milk when she was saved from being out of her depth by the sound of a motor car pulling up outside.

Johnny looked out the window. 'It's the Doc!' he cried.

Timothy's arrival caused the same level of excitement as her visit had. Everybody piled out the door to greet him. Rebecca followed behind.

'Well, Johnny, you are looking brighter,' said Timothy, reaching into his car for his bag. His smile broadened when he turned and saw Rebecca standing with the others. 'Miss Wood, this is a nice surprise!'

She smiled back with a new-found respect for him. After the embarrassment of being turned away by Stefan Otto's butler, she was more endeared to a man who had good manners.

'It's kind of you to visit Johnny,' he whispered to her, as the gathering returned to the house. 'The people on the land always appreciate those small courtesies.'

'I'd better head back now. I'll leave you to your examination.'

'No, wait!' he told her, touching her arm. 'I won't be long and then I can drive you back.'

While Timothy examined Johnny, Mr Turner and his two sons excused themselves to get back to work. Mrs Turner treated Rebecca to more tea and digestive biscuits. 'Doctor Litchfield is a wonderful man,' she said, in a lowered voice. 'You heard about poor Corman Ryan, I suppose? Dead at only forty-two years of age! It's a hard life, mining. Harder than farming, I think, because at least we have fresh air and food on the table every night, regardless of what nature throws at us. Life will be tough for Colleen with little ones to feed. Doctor Litchfield visited her husband twice a day and refused to accept any money for his care.'

Rebecca turned to the sitting room where Timothy was examining Johnny. She caught a glimpse of him, holding

Johnny's shoulder. The sunlight was streaming through a window and lighting his hair like an angel's halo. Was it possible for any man to be that saintly?

★

Timothy dropped Rebecca back at the post office. 'I'll see you later,' he said, untying her bicycle from the roof and standing it upright for her. He looked in the direction of the post office and nodded to Rebecca. Nancy Pike was pacing in front of the door, holding a large bag. Rebecca didn't like the fervid look in her eyes. She was on a mission, and a woman like Nancy on a mission was a dangerous thing.

'I'd better go,' she said. 'Thank you for driving me back.'

Nancy clucked her tongue when Rebecca approached the post office and leaned her bicycle against the veranda rail. 'Where have you been?' she asked. 'I've been waiting for you for over an hour! You can't just shut up the post office during business hours for a rendezvous with your boyfriend!'

Rebecca's skin prickled. She did not like Nancy telling her what she could or couldn't do. 'I was on the delivery run and checked on Johnny. Doctor Litchfield happened to be there at the same time.' She rummaged around the bottom of the mailbag for the post office key. 'You might be aware that Johnny fell off his bicycle and I have to do the delivery runs now.'

Nancy's haughty air wavered but she made no apology. Instead she changed tack. 'Well, how kind of you! I'm sure Doctor Litchfield appreciated you checking on his patient. The welfare of the people of this town is very important to *him*.'

Nancy was clearly worked up about something. Rebecca vowed to keep quiet if it might make Nancy go away faster. She unlocked the door and Nancy followed her inside, heading straight for the community noticeboard. 'These have just been printed,' she said, reaching into her bag and pulling out a rolled-up poster.

Normally it was the postmistress who decided what went on the board, but Rebecca left Nancy to do what she wanted. The woman was like a runaway train, but sooner or later she would have to come to a stop. Rebecca only wanted to make sure she wasn't in her way when she did. She tidied the counter and disappeared into the tearoom to remoisten the stamp sponge. When she returned to the main area, Nancy was arranging a pile of pamphlets on the counter. Rebecca picked one up.

Public Meeting this Thursday
The Future of Whaling in Shipwreck Bay
Memorial Hall
7.00 pm

She sensed trouble brewing. 'What is this meeting about exactly?'

'The factory ship, of course,' said Nancy, a triumphant look in her eye. 'You might be aware that the Commonwealth Government has brought over a Norwegian captain to advise them on modernising the Australian whaling industry. But we have our own capable Norwegian captain right here in Shipwreck Bay. All Sanders Olsen needs is a factory ship and then the whaling station will be able to increase their catch a hundredfold.' She lifted her chin. 'It was a good decision the day they elected George the shire secretary. He's always had great ambitions for this town!'

Rebecca wanted to poke Nancy in the eye. Her husband had great ambitions to get into women's panties, more likely! Apart from the jewellery, nice home and clothes that he provided for her, what on earth did Nancy see in him? Rebecca re-read the flyer. As much as Nancy's haughty manner irked her, she took some pleasure at how angry Stefan Otto would be about the proposal. Perhaps he'd come out of that big white castle of his to attend the meeting. Then she could have the satisfaction of ignoring him.

'You'll be coming to the meeting of course, Rebecca.'

'Of course. I wouldn't miss it.'

'Good!' said Nancy, brushing down her sleeve with an air of triumph. 'We have a very important minister coming especially to speak to us.'

Rebecca put down the flyer. Pins and needles prickled her arms. 'Who? The Minister for Fisheries?'

Nancy's eyes lit up. 'No, someone higher than that! The Minister for Commerce and Agriculture!'

Rebecca's mouth fell open.

'Yes!' said Nancy. 'Ned McKell himself! What do you think of that?'

Rebecca stared at Nancy, stunned. Ned coming to Shipwreck Bay was probably her worst nightmare. She would have nowhere to hide then.

CHAPTER SEVENTEEN

·

Rebecca walked to the meeting at the memorial hall with her eyes cast down. The evening was warm but her hands were freezing cold. A nagging pain ached in her temple. Timothy strolled beside her, humming a cheerful rendition of 'Near You' and sending her a smile every so often, as if encouraging her to join in too. She did her best to smile back and not give away the sense of dread that was weighing on her. She had hoped she'd be able to invent some last-minute ailment that would prevent her from going, but when Timothy insisted on coming by her house so they could go together, she realised she wouldn't be able to fool a doctor. If she could have disguised herself in some way she would have. But it was too late in the day to be wearing sunglasses and a hat. Perhaps Ned would not recognise her with red hair? She scoffed at herself for clinging to that. Even someone as self-absorbed as Ned would recognise the woman who had been his mistress, red hair or not. The best she could hope for was that he wouldn't give anything away. After all, hadn't their life together been clandestine? There had been many occasions when either Cynthia was present or some gossip columnist had got his or her name onto the guest list and she and Ned had walked past each other like ships in the night, without even a glance or the slightest smile to give themselves away. Rebecca bit her lip. Even if he pretended not to notice her, that wouldn't stop the pain of seeing him again. All those stolen moments with Ned had amounted to nothing except her ruin.

'Hello you two,' said Elaine, as she and Frank fell into step beside them. 'It looks like everyone is coming tonight!'

People were heading from all directions towards the red brick hall. Carmel, Sue and Joy were striding along with their husbands. The Turners were there along with Bob Hill and Gavin Young, the farmers Rebecca had met at the post office. Both men shook Timothy's hand and introduced Rebecca to their wives, Beverley and Iris, who was pregnant. 'You must join us for the Country Women's Association meetings,' Beverley said to her. 'It's always a nice chance for women from the township and the countryside to mix.'

Nancy was standing at the door to the hall, dressed to the nines in a frock of organza lace with a flared skirt and tight bodice.

'So glad you could come,' she said, thrusting the night's agenda into Rebecca's hand.

Half the seats in the hall were already occupied. People were chatting excitedly to each other but Rebecca felt like a patient about to undergo a dangerous procedure, the outcome of which she couldn't be sure. She caught sight of Father Rob signalling them to join him in the front row. She pretended not to notice and steered Timothy to some seats at the back near the door. A table and chairs had been set up on the low podium at the front of the room. Rebecca hoped she'd have phenomenal good luck and somebody very tall would sit in front of her, so that Ned might not see her from that position. Sanders and his whalemen were seated in the left-hand front corner. Like Sanders, they were all rough weather-beaten men. Their wives sat in the seats behind them. Berit glanced at Rebecca and gave her a discreet nod. Rebecca returned the greeting with a quick blink of her eyes, careful that nobody caught a hint of their alliance.

At seven o'clock George Pike appeared at the entrance door. Everyone turned to look at the two men with him, except for Rebecca, whose breath had caught in her throat. It stayed trapped there as Ned passed her on his way down the aisle. An ache of inexpressible sadness pulsed in her chest. The square head, broad shoulders and confident gait that she had once known so well seemed to belong to a ghost now. She didn't even know who the weedy aide with him was. His life had moved on and so had hers. They had parted only a few months ago, but there was a great distance between them now.

'Are you all right, Rebecca?' Timothy whispered to her.

'There isn't enough air in the room. The stuffiness is getting to me.'

The sympathetic glance he gave her sent a pang of guilt through her.

'We'll leave as soon as it's over,' he reassured her.

George Pike stood up and, after a few attempts to adjust a squealing microphone, addressed the meeting. 'Ladies and gentlemen of Shipwreck Bay, thank you very much for coming along tonight. As you know, the future of our town and the welfare of its citizens is my greatest concern. Tonight it is my immense pleasure to introduce the Minister for Commerce and Agriculture, Mr Ned McKell.'

The woman next to Rebecca nudged her companion. 'Isn't he the one who's been in trouble over that mystery woman? The mistress who has gone into hiding?'

'Oh yes,' the man answered. 'The press are still looking for her. A thoroughly despicable woman with an utter indifference to morals.'

'No doubt she has gone back to whatever hole she crawled out of,' the woman agreed.

Rebecca lowered her eyes.

Ned's voice sounded through the microphone. 'Thank you, Mr Pike,' he said, 'I am very pleased to have been invited to address the good ladies and gentlemen of Shipwreck Bay.' He was using the politician's voice that Rebecca had heard so many times, espousing flattery but reeking of condescension. 'I have always been concerned for our regional towns and their industries. It is the little people who make this country great.'

Rebecca's head shot up. In all the years she had known him, Ned couldn't have cared less about the 'little people'. He was a snob who drank French wines and bought his suits in London. He wouldn't have lasted a minute in Mrs Turner's olive-green kitchen, discussing the best way to eat digestive biscuits and complimenting her freshly churned butter. What a fake, sanctimonious chump! Rebecca squinted, noticing for the first time the unattractive furrow of wrinkles on his forehead and the beginnings of a double chin. Even the clean lines of his silk suit couldn't hide the emerging bulge of his belly. He was eighteen years older than her but when they were together she'd thought that had only added to his sophistication. It was common lore that men improved with age while women simply got old. But he was the one falling to pieces now, not her. She rubbed her forehead and recalled all the nights she had lain in her bed weeping – over him! She had completely wasted seven years of her life. The realisation hit her so violently that at first she thought she had shouted the words out loud. She glanced around, and let out a breath when she realised she hadn't. She raised her hand to her throat as if trying to quell an actual outburst.

'Australia has fallen behind,' Ned droned on, 'while Britain, the Soviet Union, Japan and other nations have been reaping the economic benefits of the recommencement of whaling after the war.' He nodded to his aide, who stood and moved towards a slide projector. 'While the British have been using aeroplanes and radar equipment to hunt down whales, Australia is still restricted to sea-based spotting and onshore processing stations. It is my plan to change that and to invest in Shipwreck Bay's whaling station by procuring a factory ship.'

George Pike flicked the lights off. Ned's aide pushed the projector button and an image appeared on the screen of a massive ship, the size of a steamer, with a large square opening in its stern and a sloping ramp. A dead whale was being hauled up through it. Ned nodded at the slide. 'The rear slipway on this Dutch factory ship allows the whalers to winch the entire beast by the tail flukes onto a flensing deck the size of a football field.'

Sanders Olsen and his men grinned at each other, pleased by the proposal. The aide clicked to the next slide of a group of men covered in gore standing around a whale carcass from which the flesh had been hacked away. Blood, oil and entrails covered the deck. Steam wafted overhead and added to the macabre atmosphere of the scene.

'After the whale is flensed, the strips of blubber are deposited down manholes and into revolving choppers. The blubber passes through these before sliding into cookers, which extract the oil. Processing the whales like this is extremely effective. It means they can be processed wherever they are caught.'

Sanders stood up and addressed the meeting. 'It will greatly increase the number of whales we can kill and process.'

'Not to mention reducing the bad smells of onshore processing,' added the aide. The remark was met with silence. Obviously the young man hadn't been briefed that the odorous slaughterhouse stench that came from the whaling station was something nobody in the town would admit to.

'And how will this investment help the farmers or those in the mines?' asked Bob Hill. 'What about us?'

Ned nodded with the smugness of someone who had anticipated the question. 'Such a large operation requires the labour of five hundred men. It will bring employment to Shipwreck Bay. And as the workers will be accompanied by their wives and children, the population of the town will grow quickly, thus increasing the demand for food and services.'

Excited chatter broke out among the gathering. There were possibilities for nearly everyone in the town, including Timothy whose services would be in demand. He turned to Rebecca.

'This could mean a hospital for Shipwreck Bay,' he said. 'Men from the mines won't have to go all the way to Wollongong for specialist treatment, as poor Corman Ryan had to do.'

The woman next to Rebecca didn't like the idea at all. She folded her arms across her chest. 'They'll employ migrants, no doubt,' she muttered. 'The town will be overrun by dagos.'

'And thanks to these floating factories, the blue whale is on the verge of extinction and the humpback and other species are sure to follow.'

Everyone's heads swivelled to see Stefan Otto standing at the back of the room. George turned the lights back on.

'The blue whale is the largest animal to have ever lived on our planet,' Stefan continued. 'That one in the photograph has been torn to shreds for products that can easily be replaced by other ones. What a great testament to man's ability to destroy all that is most majestic in nature.'

Rebecca forgot her intention to ignore Stefan and gaped along with the others. There was something about him that simply couldn't be resisted. Then she remembered what Timothy had told her about Stefan's notoriety with women. Her mind conjured up an image of frilly panties dropping to ankles all the way from Wollongong to Penguin Bay. Part of her hated the idea that Stefan might have so many lovers, but part of her completely understood. Some people were simply born for passion.

Ned was flustered by the appearance of Stefan. He was never at his best when confronted by a person of intellect. He paused uncertainly, and then the smarmy politician's smile returned to his face. 'It sounds like your allegiance is to the whale, an oversized fish!' he said, with a gruff laugh. 'My allegiance is to the people of Shipwreck Bay and to securing a future for them.'

Rebecca cringed. Whales are mammals, Ned, she reproached him inside her head. Every ten-year-old kid knew that. He was clearly out of his depth in his new role. She wondered if he would even be able to tell the difference between a sheep and a goat.

'The Norwegians and the British along with the Dutch and others have destroyed stocks in their own waters so they have come south to plunder the Antarctic region,' Stefan replied, pointing to the picture on the screen. 'But that's the story of whaling, isn't it? Destroy one species, so move onto another. Decimate one hunting ground then seek out another.' His eyes scanned the audience. 'What will you do when there are no whales left and the ocean is forever thrown out of balance?'

George Pike's mouth twitched. 'The whales are like kangaroos. If you cull kangaroos, that means that there is more food for the remaining kangaroos and so their population increases.'

'By that reasoning the sea should be brimming with whales, but clearly it is not,' Stefan replied, coolly. 'The whalers' own logbooks reflect that. They have to go further and further out to find anything. All this ship will do is finally destroy an already depleted population. It seems to me it would be wiser for Australia to develop cheaper oils for lubricants, soaps and margarine such as cotton, rapeseed and flax. We could lead the world instead of following it. And that way you actually would be supporting farmers and developing a strong, independent nation.'

The gathering broke into a dozen animated discussions. Ned tried to speak above the crowd but he was drowned out. It wasn't lost on Rebecca that Stefan was once again making him look silly, as he had at that long-ago auction. Ned had always espoused that Australia should be self-reliant, but it was Stefan who had actually suggested a way for the country to do it.

Nancy brought the meeting back to order. 'Be quiet, please!' she told the gathering. The look she flashed Stefan was lethal. 'Please be quiet and let Mr McKell speak!' she said, although Rebecca got the impression she was more worried about George being made a fool of by Stefan than any discourtesy to Ned.

Ned straightened his collar. 'Besides, the International Whaling Commission has recommended quotas for the humpbacks —'

'Quotas that members can decide whether to adhere to or not,' Stefan countered. 'Which makes them ineffectual. The whaling station here is not supposed to kill a female with a calf, but they clearly did earlier this week, leaving the young whale to the sharks.'

Sanders Olsen jumped to his feet, ready to brawl with Stefan, but was held back by a burly man next to him, who whispered something in his ear. Bob Hill stood up to speak. 'Mr McKell, it's sounding to me like you want to spend millions of pounds on something that will not help us farmers in the long run. We would benefit more from growing the crops Mr Otto has mentioned.'

Having successfully thrown the meeting into disarray and made fools of Ned and George, Stefan turned to leave but then saw Rebecca and smiled. Timothy grabbed her hand and held it. Stefan raised his eyebrows and cocked his head at Rebecca who wanted to shake off Timothy's grip but he held on to her too tightly, as if Stefan was some sort of marauding barbarian about to snatch her away. Out of the corner of her eye, she saw Ned rise from his seat on the podium. He had recognised her at last.

She turned to him. Don't, for god's sake, Ned, don't, she urged him silently. She watched in horror as his lips moved. But just as he said 'Becky?', George took the microphone from him and the ensuing squeal masked the utterance.

'Well, moving right along, do we have any more questions for the minister?' he asked.

Ned recovered himself and sat down again. Stefan left and Timothy released his grasp on Rebecca's hand and the circulation returned to it.

'I don't like the way Stefan Otto looked at you, Rebecca,' Timothy told her. 'I've got a good mind to go to his house right now and tell him to stay away.'

'You'll do nothing of the sort!' Rebecca said, in a hushed but angry tone. 'I'm not some possession to be fought over!'

She stood up to leave. Thank God everyone had been so distracted by Stefan Otto that they hadn't noticed what had happened with Ned. Then she glanced in Nancy's direction. The shire secretary's wife squinted at her in a way that made Rebecca fear that she had seen the whole thing – and hadn't been fooled one bit.

CHAPTER EIGHTEEN

The following morning, after collecting the mail, Rebecca pedalled uphill from the station. Her legs pumped hard with the effort. There was no tree cover and the sun was bright. Perspiration prickled her brow and she stopped to pat her face with her handkerchief before continuing. She hated sweat and was glad that she'd had the foresight to keep a fresh blouse in the staff cupboard. The sound of a car rumbled behind her and she swerved over to the side of the road to let it pass. Instead it slowed down alongside her.

'I'd recognise that pretty derrière anywhere!'

She stopped and turned to see Ned grinning at her from the passenger window of the car. His aide was at the wheel and brought the vehicle to a halt. He kept his eyes on the road ahead of him and didn't look at Rebecca but she was sure his mouth twitched as if he was trying not to smile.

'What are you doing here, Becky?' Ned asked, glancing at the mailbag attached to the back of her bicycle. 'Why are you in Shipwreck Bay?'

His sardonic smile used to be something that amused her. Now it was infuriating. How did they both end up in Shipwreck

Bay? It was a place that until a few months ago she had never even heard of. But she was trapped here while Ned was free to saunter off anywhere he liked.

'For God's sake, Ned!' she hissed. 'What if someone sees us talking?'

He shrugged. 'Relax. They'll think I'm asking for directions.'

Ned's head looked even bigger framed by the car window. Why had she never noticed quite how big it was before? She'd lain next to it enough times, sharing the same pillow. But now she found that the size and shape of his head provoked her in a way that made no logical sense. 'I had to get out of Sydney because of you – and Thelma Marr and her mouth,' she spat. 'I had to flee the press. This isn't a joke for me, you know.'

'You should have come to me,' he said, as if Rebecca's predicament was news to him. 'I would have done something for you.'

Rebecca's head spun. 'I had to get out of the apartment because you stopped paying the rent without telling me!'

The accusation of his self-centredness didn't even make Ned squirm. It confirmed to Rebecca just how little he had thought of her when he was with Thelma. She put her feet back on the pedals and continued up the hill. The aide pressed the accelerator and kept the car parallel to her. It irritated her even more. Who was this new aide of Ned's anyway? How could she know he was to be trusted when Ned himself was being so careless? For all she knew, the aide would telephone the press as soon as he and Ned got back to Canberra.

They approached the town and she saw Nancy's car parked outside the general store. Whatever Nancy had suspected the previous night, the picture of Ned's official car stalking Rebecca would only confirm it. Suddenly, it didn't matter that Ned McKell, the man she had once loved, was trying to talk to her. All she could think about was how to get rid of him.

She stopped her bicycle and the aide braked. 'For God's sake! Leave me alone, Ned!' she said. 'I don't need you to make things worse! I'm here because the gossip columnists are out to crucify me!'

Ned raised his eyebrows. 'Listen, Becky, I've acted terribly and I feel awful. Let me fix things for you. You don't have to stay in this godforsaken town and work at the post office!'

He opened the car door to get out but Rebecca slammed it shut with her foot. 'You'll *fix* things will you, Ned? Like you fixed our baby!'

Ned's face froze. His aide, perhaps sensing the conversation was heading towards perilous ground, got out of the car and stood on the other side of the road. He took out a notebook from his pocket and flipped through it as if he was oblivious to the argument between Rebecca and his superior.

'That man who was sitting next to you at the meeting, Becky. Are you seeing him?' Ned asked.

Rebecca bristled. When Ned had free access to her, he'd stopped wanting her. Now someone else was interested, he was jealous.

'He's the local doctor, Ned. One of your little people.'

Ned flinched. He tried to open the car door once more but Rebecca pushed it closed with her foot again. 'Get lost, Ned. Don't you get it? Things are over between us.'

From the dumbfounded expression on Ned's face, he didn't get it at all. Instead he sent her an awkward smile. 'You look very pretty with red hair, you know. I liked your blonde hair but red suits you even better.'

'I mean it, Ned!'

He threw up his hands. 'Oh, come on, Becky!' He reached to unlock the rear passenger door. 'I'll take you back to Sydney and get you an even better apartment. We can be as we were before. We were happy, weren't we? That thing with Thelma is well and truly over.'

'What about that thing with Cynthia? You are married, remember.'

Ned slid over to the driver's side and got out. 'Enough of this,' he said, walking towards her. 'Come on! Get in!'

Rebecca's blood boiled. Ned was one of those people who didn't change. He was the sort of person who did the same thing over and over again. That's why he couldn't accept that she had changed. If she went back to Sydney with him, he would treat her well until he found somebody else and then he'd abandon her again.

'Come on, Becky,' Ned repeated, lowering his voice as if he was trying to calm a nervous horse. 'We can sort this out.'

She made as if she was about to get in the car but when Ned leaned in to kiss her she stamped hard on his foot with the heel of her shoe. He winced in pain. 'Christ!' he swore.

'Go to hell, Ned!' she told him, before remounting her bicycle and pedalling away.

★

When Rebecca returned to the post office, Berit was pacing outside the door, her face tense. Rebecca ushered her inside then shut the door again, leaving the 'Closed' sign in place. She led her to the tearoom, where nobody would see them from the street. 'What is it?' she asked. 'What's happened?'

Berit's eyes were aflame. 'I'm ready to make that withdrawal,' she said.

'Are you sure?' Rebecca was still agitated after her encounter with Ned. It was not a moment to be careless.

Berit nodded solemnly. 'Sanders and the men are distracted by the idea of the factory ship,' she said. 'It's now or never for me. I'm going to catch the late train out of here when Sanders is asleep and Ernie Mullens is off duty.'

Rebecca's hands were shaking when she reached into the safe to get Berit's passbook. She couldn't forget the threats Sanders had made to her. She handed Berit the money along with a letter she had written a few days before.

'What's this?' Berit asked, holding up the envelope.

'It's a letter for you to give to my friend, Marion Bedford. She's in Sydney. I've included the address. It's best you go to a big city, where your husband is unlikely to find you. Marion will help you.'

Berit held Rebecca's gaze. Her lips trembled. 'Thank you,' she said. 'When Mabel died, I didn't think there would be anybody else I could turn to.'

Against all instinct, Rebecca embraced Berit. The young woman was bony, like a bird. 'You take care of yourself,' she told her. 'And have fun in Sydney for me!'

Berit nodded. 'Perhaps I'll find a new – and kinder – husband there.'

After her encounter with Ned, Rebecca wasn't in the mood to discuss the finer merits of men. 'Berit,' she said, lowering her voice gravely. 'Men are predators and we are the prey! Don't be naïve when it comes to them! They study us much more closely than we realise. They watch for our weaknesses and then they pounce! Don't trust any man until he proves himself!'

Berit's eyes grew round at the vehemence in Rebecca's voice. Rebecca herself was surprised by it. She felt like she was talking to her younger self, trying to stop her from making the mistakes that she had. Ned had made her feel so special, so unique, so irreplaceable. But she had been replaceable, hadn't she? Now the relationship she had thought of as the love of a lifetime had come to a tawdry end with that stupid encounter on the road. She placed her hand on Berit's arm. 'Promise me that you won't let the next man you meet beguile you … that you won't fall for being told that he loves you without proof of it, or give yourself away because you have stars in your eyes. Choose someone solid. Someone who will respect you and take care of you.'

Berit smiled. 'Like Doctor Litchfield, you mean?'

Rebecca straightened, surprised at the mention of Timothy.

Berit grabbed her hand and squeezed it. 'I saw the way he was looking at you last night. He is nice, Rebecca. He's not a predator.'

Rebecca relaxed and shrugged. 'No, a little pushy perhaps but definitely not a predator.'

'Do you like him as much as he likes you?'

Rebecca realised how young Berit looked with her smooth skin and big eyes. She was glad that Berit would have someone as worldly as Marion to guide her when she got to Sydney.

'I do like him,' she said. 'But I think we are better suited to friendship than romance.'

Berit thanked her with a fierce embrace.

'Goodbye and all the best,' Rebecca said. 'Don't tell Marion where I am. Just that I'm all right.'

'Did you run away from something too?' Berit asked, frowning. 'Shipwreck Bay is a place you escape from, not *to*.'

'You'd better get going,' Rebecca told her, guiding her towards the door. 'Before your husband gets back.'

She watched Berit walk down the hill towards the whaling station. *Men are predators and we are the prey! Don't be naïve when it comes to them!* She leaned against the doorpost and sighed. Had she really been talking to Berit when she had said that – or to herself?

CHAPTER NINETEEN

When Rebecca arrived at Stefan Otto's house to deliver the mail, she expected his morose butler would collect it from her as usual. She rang the bell on the gatepost and gave a start when Stefan came out instead. A few days ago she would have been delighted, but the morning's events had dampened her enthusiasm for flirtations and dangerous liaisons. She took the letters from her mailbag but didn't dismount her bicycle.

'There seems to have been some misunderstanding,' Stefan said when he reached the gate. 'You'll have to excuse Albrecht. He is not used to visitors. You got my note?'

Rebecca shuffled through the letters although she had already sorted them into bundles at the post office. 'I'm here to deliver the mail not because of your note. As you live so far out of town you might do me the courtesy of coming to collect your mail yourself. My delivery boy has injured his shoulder.'

She handed Stefan the letters. Despite her resolve she couldn't get her feet back up onto the pedals. It was as though the soles of her shoes were stuck on the tar.

'You seem angrier than last time we met,' he said studying her. 'I don't think you have a strong opinion on whaling, so perhaps it's the company you keep. You have strange taste in gentlemen friends.'

Rebecca refused to let herself blush. What a debacle the previous evening had been! Ned, Timothy and Stefan all in the same room! 'Which gentleman are you referring to?'

He raised an eyebrow. 'Are there so many conquests?'

'Not as many as yours, from what I hear,' she retorted.

His lips curved into a smile. 'I'm sure you've heard a lot of things about me from the good people of Shipwreck Bay. It's unfair because I know so little about you, and yet I'm fascinated. Won't you join me for a cup of tea?'

'No, thank you, I have to get back to the post office. It's Christmas in a few months. People will be writing away for their catalogues.'

'They can wait.'

Rebecca managed to get her left foot back on the pedal. 'I'm not a conquest, Mr Otto. You can't charm me into your lair.'

'I know. I was hoping you might charm me into yours. Won't you call me Stefan?'

Rebecca glared at him. 'You've got some nerve.'

'I do.'

Her right foot found the pedal. 'Good afternoon, Mr Otto. Once again it's been delightful chatting with you.' She wobbled then got her balance and turned back in the direction of the road. The last thing she needed was some conceited, egotistical man in her head, heart – or bed.

'Wait!'

Rebecca stopped and put her feet on the ground. She didn't turn around but she could hear Stefan running towards her. She clenched her eyes shut for a moment to muster as much fury at him as she could. She'd just warned Berit against foolishly following her desires and now she was at risk of doing that very thing.

'That was rude of me,' he said, looking at her with contrition. 'I'm sorry. I'm rather stuck for interesting conversation and I do find myself fascinated by you. What on earth is a woman like you doing in a town like Shipwreck Bay? Is it something to do with Ned McKell? Is it something to do with that scandal in Sydney?'

'I don't need to explain anything to you,' she said.

'No, you don't. It's obvious to me that Ned McKell is an idiot.'

Despite herself, a laugh escaped from Rebecca's lips. The afternoon sun through the trees sent dappled light shimmering over the spot where they stood contemplating each other. The women of the town had said that Stefan had been a spy during the war. That seemed like a dubious accusation. He didn't have a German accent, so she gathered he'd been born in Australia, and if he'd been found guilty of spying he would be in jail. He wouldn't be freely travelling between Europe and Australia. She felt something in her soften and hated herself for it. Laughter always lowered her defences. Be curious, she told herself, but keep up a wall, don't give in to your feelings.

She played with the cocktail ring on her finger. It was bold and elegant. Although it had been given to her by Ned she continued to wear it every day because she had chosen it. 'Why did you bid against Ned at that auction?' she asked. 'Because he was a politician?'

'No, I didn't know him from a bar of soap … then.'

'Then why?'

'Because I watched the two of you together. He bought the suit of armour of a minor aristocrat for a stupid sum, while you selected something far more beautiful and valuable. A man like him could never appreciate a woman like you. You have a passion for life. I can see it in your eyes.'

Rebecca sensed cracks forming in the wall she was trying to build. His derision of Ned comforted her bruised pride. Perhaps that was what he intended. Flattery! she tried to tell herself. But flatterers were spineless men who got what they wanted by manipulation. Like Ned. There was nothing about Stefan that suggested weakness or that he couldn't obtain what he wanted simply by asking for it.

He looked in the direction of the house then back at Rebecca. 'Come inside for a while,' he said. 'You seemed captivated by the rock pools at the beach. I'll show you my aquariums.'

At that moment the butler came out of the house and, seeing Stefan talking with Rebecca, opened and closed his mouth as if he'd been taken by surprise.

'Albrecht!' Stefan called to him. 'Miss Wood is staying for a cup of tea. Bring it to us in the library.'

The butler roused himself. He turned towards the house, and then stopped a moment to look back at Rebecca again. He shook his head as if he was befuddled by what this sudden turn of events might mean.

★

From the ornate exterior of the house, Rebecca was expecting an interior filled with European Renaissance furniture. But instead of family crests and heavy furniture, she was surprised to find that the house contained barely any furniture at all. A few wicker chairs, a navy-blue canvas sofa and a side table stacked with books were all that occupied the drawing room that she and Stefan passed on their way to the grand marble staircase. The entrance hall itself was devoid of clutter and the bare polished floorboards and bisque walls created a suitable backdrop for the sculpture of a whale and an upright rowboat that had been turned into a display shelf for shells and coral.

Stefan guided her ahead of him up the stairs and then into a large room on the first floor. The space was lined with ceiling-to-floor shelves that were crammed with reference books. Full-length windows gave a panoramic view out to sea. Any other visitor would have had their breath taken away by the spectacular sight of nothing but blue water as far as the horizon, but the endless sea viewed from the height of the headland had a terrifying effect on Rebecca. It sent her heart racing and made her disorientated and dizzy. She looked away from the windows and turned her attention to the array of aquariums that were set up around the room. The colourful fish gave the impression that Stefan had brought miniature oceans into his home. From the great care that had been taken with the arrangement of the rocks, coral and seaweed, the tanks had not been set up for scientific observation alone.

She peered into a tall tank with seahorses floating gracefully in and out of a clump of kelp. Their dorsal fins fluttered like angels' wings. 'They are moving pictures,' she said.

Stefan stood so close to her she could feel the warmth of his arm against hers. 'Seahorses have an elaborate courtship ritual. The male will spend days enchanting his beloved. Then they will swim tail in tail, synchronising their movements with each other. Unlike any other species we know of, it's the male seahorse that becomes pregnant, carrying the young through gestation and delivery. During that time, the female will greet him each day and the two will dance alongside one another, reaffirming their coupling.'

A wiser woman would go now, she thought. A wiser woman would not let herself be seduced like this. This was all going in one direction and one direction only, and the longer she stayed in Stefan's company the harder it would be to resist.

She moved away to the next tank where an octopus was hiding under a rock. Stefan dipped his hand in the water and wiggled his fingers. The octopus reached out its tentacles and attached himself to Stefan's palm, gazing up at him with its large round eyes. 'Some people have a kitten or a puppy,' he said. 'I have Dunkel here. He is a highly intelligent creature with his own affectionate personality. I've taught him to open jars.'

'No!' Rebecca had heard octopuses referred to as 'the intelligent aliens of the sea' but she never knew they could be trained.

Stefan widened his eyes to match Rebecca's incredulous expression. 'Yes, seriously. If I put a tasty morsel of food in a jar and place it in the aquarium he will unscrew the lid.'

A knock sounded at the door and Albrecht came in with a tray of tea things, which he placed on a steamer trunk that was being used as a coffee table. He laid out the cups and saucers noisily and set down the teapot. He said something in German to Stefan, who nodded. Then before he left the room he glanced at Rebecca as if he still couldn't believe what he was seeing.

'What did he say?' Rebecca asked.

'We don't have any cakes in the house, it seems, so Hilda is making lemon biscuits for us. She'll bring them up shortly.'

Stefan touched the teapot then quickly removed his hand and shook it. 'It's scorching hot,' he said. 'While it's cooling let me show you the view from the balcony.'

Before she could think of an excuse not to go outside, Stefan swung open the glass doors and guided her onto the balcony. The sea breeze was strong and she had to hold onto her skirt with one hand and keep her hair out of her face with the other. Stefan gripped the balustrade and stared out at the ocean like a ship's captain surveying the sea. Rebecca gingerly sidled up to him but kept her eyes fixed on the garden below. A small boat lay propped up on trestles while its motor lay in parts on a blanket beside it. He must be working on it, she thought.

'Look there!' said Stefan. 'It's a humpback!'

Rebecca gathered her courage and lifted her eyes to where Stefan was pointing in time to catch a spume of mist rising from the ocean and a giant, graceful shape moving just below the surface.

'During summer, humpbacks spend their time feeding in the cold water of the Antarctic,' Stefan explained. 'In late autumn, they move north to warmer waters for mating and calving. Now they are on their way back to the Antarctic.' A broad smile came to his face. 'Look, she has a calf.'

Rebecca peered at the spot where the whale was swimming and noticed a small replica swimming beside it. She could feel Stefan's excitement ripple through him. His love of sea creatures might see him ostracised from the town, but she admired his conviction.

'Ned doesn't have a clue about anything natural,' Rebecca told him. 'He's terrified of ants. I'm sure he was only made Minister of Commerce and Agriculture because of the scandal. You made him look like a fool.'

Stefan's gaze stayed on the whale and her calf. 'Leave it to humans to destroy the most magnificent animals that ever lived. The whales have been here longer than us. They are mammals that have made their journey back to the ocean. You'd think it would be wiser to study them than to kill them. But no, they are pursued until they are exhausted, stabbed and blown up. They are sentient beings that see their family groups slaughtered and their children murdered before their eyes. Nearly all the species are now near extinction. And what for? Greed? Ignorance? All for an industry that doesn't even make economic sense.'

'How did you become so passionate about the ocean? Is it something from your childhood?'

'I was born here in Shipwreck Bay. In this house, in fact. I've grown up with the smell of salt in my nostrils and the sound of waves crashing in my ears.'

'Is that why you oppose the whaling station?' Rebecca asked. 'Because you love the sea creatures so much? The townspeople gave me the impression that you were doing it to spite them.'

Stefan huffed. 'The people of Shipwreck Bay like to think they are important. They mean nothing to me.'

The vehemence in his voice startled Rebecca. She knew there was animosity between Stefan and the townspeople but this was more than that.

'Something happened during the war, didn't it?' she asked.

Albrecht knocked loudly on the glass door, giving both of them a start. 'Biscuits!' he said, pointing to a plate.

Stefan looked from Albrecht to Rebecca. 'Let's go inside and have that tea, shall we? What happened during the war is a conversation for another time.'

Back in the calm of Stefan's library, Rebecca tried to slow her heartbeat. Stefan was intriguing and she was in danger of falling into that exhilarating state that had caused her nothing but grief. Her friend Marion hopped in and out of men's beds and thought nothing of it. Rebecca wasn't like that. She craved love. She had yearned for it from her parents, she had yearned for it from Ned. But she hadn't truly received it from anyone. This man was a stranger. She knew nothing about him. What gave her the idea that he might hold the key to what she longed for?

'Does the ocean really terrify you so much?' he asked her.

Suddenly she was conscious that while she had been thinking, he had been watching her. She took a breath. It was better for him to believe it was the ocean that was bothering her than her thoughts about him.

'I've travelled to Europe on liners, which was rather difficult for me,' she said. 'I spent most of those trips inside. But I can't imagine the courage of the people who came here all the way from England in wooden vessels not much bigger than fishing boats.' She quickly glanced at the view then back again. 'I can't imagine the terror of going down *out there*.'

Stefan took a sip of tea. 'There are hundreds of wrecks beyond the headland. *The Durham* is broken up, but there is an old schooner not far from it with its figurehead intact. It looks as complete as the day it set sail. It does have an eerie feeling to it, though, with that I have to agree. Going down in a shipwreck would not be pleasant at all.'

No, going down in a shipwreck would not be pleasant, and neither would having her heart broken again. A wiser woman would learn from her mistakes, wouldn't she? She would not be here in this quiet library, drinking tea with a man who made all her nerve endings tingle. Hadn't losing all she had built during her years with Ned taught her anything? You cannot construct a solid house on sand. Rebecca felt the pain of Ned's betrayal again and drew her willpower from it.

'I'd better get going,' she said, standing up. 'The factory ship proposal has caused a stir in the town and I'm sure all the gossips will be gathered around the Tree of Knowledge to talk about it. They will wonder why the post office has been closed most of the afternoon.'

Stefan met her gaze and held it. 'Let them wonder.'

But Rebecca was resolute. 'That's easy for a man to say. Gossip can kill a woman.'

Stefan didn't protest further and walked with her to the gate. 'Come again, Rebecca. Perhaps then you will tell me the truth about what scares you so much about the ocean.'

Rebecca mounted her bicycle and headed back towards the town. She couldn't see herself sharing with Stefan something she had not confided in any other human being. Not even Ned or Marion or any of the headmistresses who had expelled her for 'unruly behaviour' from the many schools she had attended. Tragedy, she had observed, was something people exclaimed over or pried open for its gory details. What Rebecca feared more than no sympathy was false sympathy: the kind words that would be uttered only to be forgotten two minutes later. She stopped and turned back towards the gate. Stefan was still standing there watching her. I don't need to explain anything to him, she thought, he seems to understand me without me uttering a word.

CHAPTER TWENTY

Rebecca stepped out of the shower the following morning and stopped short. Stefan was in her house? She could hear him talking, although his exact words weren't clear. A thrill ran through her. She rubbed herself down with a towel, wrapped her robe around her and peered out of the bathroom door. The bedrooms were empty and he wasn't in the living room. She glanced out the window but he wasn't in the garden or on the street. Where was he? Then she heard his voice again, coming from the kitchen. He had come to see her? She stepped into the room expecting to catch him but it was empty. Her gaze dropped to the radio on the bench. That's where the sound of his voice was coming from. She had forgotten to turn the radio off when she had finished her breakfast.

'The whales were driven to near extinction when they were being hunted by rowing boats and had harpoons flung at them,' he was saying. 'Now the British are hurling the full force of post-war weaponry against them, including submarine detection devices that mean even a submerged whale cannot hide. The expansion of factory ships in our waters will wipe them out completely.'

'So you claim that Australia will be wasting the investment?' the radio interviewer asked him. 'That we have already missed the boat, so to speak?'

'I'm saying that Australia should take a leading role in conservation, rather than destruction. Our oceans might become the only place left for anybody to see a whale.'

Rebecca recognised the interviewer as Ian Browne, a popular ABC regional radio personality, who she had met on many occasions when he had interviewed Ned. Her mind travelled back to the meeting at the memorial hall. If Stefan's disruption of that hadn't been enough to have him driven out of town, then surely speaking on a popular program to discredit Ned's plan would be.

Although it would make her late for work, Rebecca brewed a cup of tea and listened to the rest of the interview.

'The International Whaling Commission simply cannot control an industry that has no concern for the health of our oceans nor sees any value in taking care of its life forms. Instead it encourages slaughter for profit,' Stefan argued. 'It is up to us as citizens of this country to decide that for ourselves and then put pressure on the government by demanding alternative products.'

Rebecca had heard economic arguments against whaling before but, as far as she knew, Stefan was the only person opposing it on the grounds of conservation and of valuing something as inherently precious simply because it existed.

The interview concluded and Rebecca returned to the bathroom to apply her make-up. She wiped the steam from the mirror and noticed that the blonde roots of her hair were starting to show around her temples. She'd have to dye it again soon, she thought, brushing rouge over the tell-tale roots as a temporary measure. Would she have to keep this disguise up forever?

She jabbed the brush back into its holder and gripped the sink. Hadn't what had occurred with Ned taught her anything? What else had to happen to her before she finally woke up? Stefan was an outsider, like herself. What good would they do each other? They'd both attract negative press. Then she would be hounded again, fleeing like a hunted animal, and his cause would be discredited. He was better off with fleeting conquests and she needed to settle down. Perhaps some girls got better instruction about life from their mothers. Hers had barely spoken to her about anything. Maybe she had to train herself to appreciate a kind and honest man. Why couldn't she fall head over heels for a sensible choice? Why not Timothy? He was intelligent, he was good-looking, he was nice. He could offer her stability and a beautiful home. Timothy obviously wanted her. She'd be a fool to throw a chance like that away. She put on her dress and slipped on her shoes, before heading to the front door. Before she shut it behind her she glanced at her doll's house of a living room. She yanked the door closed, hoping that this time she wouldn't be such an idiot.

★

On her way down the hill towards the post office, Rebecca noticed the local police sergeant's car parked outside the whaling station. She stopped, a prickle running down her spine. There was no activity outside the station and no smell of whale flesh. From that distance all was silent. She squinted, not sure what to make of the sergeant's presence. Did it have something to do with Berit? Had Sanders reported his wife missing? Surely even he would have realised she'd fled of her own volition. Or had he thought he'd broken her down so much that she would remain his victim forever?

That monster wouldn't find her now. It made her smile to imagine that Berit had already arrived in Sydney and was at that moment on her way to Marion's chic apartment. She laughed out loud as she thought about the life her friend would reveal to the young woman. It would be glamour morning, noon and night as they drifted from high-society dinners to gatherings of artists in bohemian coffee houses. Rebecca pursed her lips, half-jealous of the young woman's chance to live a life completely different from the one she had known in this godforsaken town. And I'm stuck here, she thought, because of my stupid mistakes.

Johnny was due back at work, and Rebecca soaked up her last chance for peace and quiet in the post office before the blustery boy arrived from the station with the mail. She was at her desk reconciling the accounts when she heard the bell on the front door ring. She stepped out to find herself face-to-face with Nancy. They held each other's gaze. Rebecca had been waiting for this moment, sure that Nancy had made the connection between her and Ned at the meeting. Only she had expected that the confrontation would come sooner than this.

'Good morning, Nancy,' she said. 'How can I help you?'

Nancy's eyebrows puckered into a frown. 'Did you know Stefan Otto was coming to the meeting?'

It was not the question Rebecca had been expecting. 'No.'

Nancy scrutinised her suspiciously. 'He embarrassed George but that was his intention, no doubt.'

Rebecca's mind was ticking over so fast that it resulted in an awkward silence. Where was this conversation going?

Nancy gave a snort. 'If he thinks he can get at me by humiliating my husband, he's wrong.'

Rebecca's apprehension gave way to curiosity. 'Get at you? Why would he be trying to get at you?'

Nancy tossed her head and ignored the question. 'We'll get that factory ship for Shipwreck Bay,' she said, a pinched look on her face. 'Nothing Stefan Otto can do will stop it.'

A thought popped into Rebecca's head, but she caught herself before she voiced it. Nancy was one of Stefan's conquests! She was sure of it! There was more to Nancy's anger than Stefan opposing the factory ship and making a fool of George. Hell hath no fury like a woman scorned and all that. She tried to imagine them coupling but couldn't. Nancy was beautiful, no doubt, but not at all the kind of woman she thought Stefan would be attracted to. But then how well did she really know him?

'I don't understand much about the town's politics,' Rebecca said, playing coy. 'Why did you ask whether I knew if Mr Otto was going to the meeting or not?'

Nancy's eyes glinted. 'Because you are the postmistress, aren't you? Haven't you listened in on his telephone conversations or conveyed telegrams to him from that dreadful Professor Bidwell?'

Rebecca realised Nancy was the worst kind of snoop, but then she wondered if it was possible that she hadn't made the connection between her and Ned? Perhaps her obsession with Stefan had made her miss what had occurred entirely? Then she noticed the arch of Nancy's eyebrow; she was watching her like a cat about to pounce on its prey. She wanted something.

'I'm not going to spy on Stefan Otto for you, if that's what you are asking,' she said firmly. 'It's not only unprincipled but it's against regulations.'

Nancy's mouth twitched. 'That's a pity,' she said with a sigh. 'Especially as I thought you were intending to make a life in this town. If you won't do it for me, then you might do it for Doctor Litchfield's sake. He's been lobbying for a hospital for Shipwreck Bay for years.'

'I can't,' repeated Rebecca, glad to have such a bona fide excuse. 'Interfering with private correspondence is a criminal offence.'

'All right then,' Nancy said, shrugging her shoulders and turning towards the door. Rebecca exhaled, relieved that the tense discussion had passed and she seemed to have got away scot-free. But before Nancy reached the door she turned around. 'Ned McKell said your name the other night. He seemed to recognise you from somewhere. I've been racking my brain wondering how you two might know each other.' She adjusted the brooch on her lapel and then looked up at Rebecca. 'He didn't address you as Miss Wood or even Rebecca. 'Becky' is what he said.' A slow, treacherous smile crept over her face. 'Perhaps you two were friends – or a little more – when you lived in Sydney?'

A sour taste rose in Rebecca's mouth and she swallowed as she sized Nancy up anew. Now it was clear why she hadn't gone running around spreading gossip straight after the meeting. It was because she understood that knowledge is power, and the knowledge of someone's darkest secret is the greatest power of all.

'You're mistaken,' she replied, fixing her eyes on Nancy and hardening her voice deliberately. 'I've never met Ned McKell before.'

Nancy's jaw set into a firm line and she tossed her head. 'I don't believe you. But either way, I'm very good at finding out the truth.' Then she lowered her tone. 'Perhaps you'll rethink what I'm asking you now. You've got a lot riding on that little secret, haven't you?'

At that moment, Marge came into the post office, her arms full of packages to post. She glanced from Nancy to Rebecca, sensing the tension in the air. Nancy nodded to Marge but said nothing before striding out the door.

'What was that all about?' Marge asked Rebecca.

Rebecca couldn't let Marge know anything was wrong. 'Nothing. She's uptight about the meeting, that's all,' she replied. Then forcing a smile, she added, 'Could you excuse me one minute?'

She went to the sorting room and tried to think of some way she could counter Nancy's plot, but whichever way she looked at it she had been checkmated. She felt sick with the thought of what Nancy could do to her if she decided to go to the press with her suspicions. Her head became light and she pressed her hand against the wall for support. 'Damn!' she swore, under her breath. If she could have strangled Ned at that moment, she would have.

★

After she had taken care of Marge, Rebecca paced back and forth in her office. What would she do if Nancy started telling people that she was Ned McKell's former mistress? Nancy was the type of woman who could raise hell. Her mind struggled to come up with counterarguments. Ned's stupid blunder hadn't been noticed by anybody else; Rebecca could simply deny it. What evidence could Nancy really obtain other than malicious hearsay? Rebecca bit her thumbnail and considered the options. It wasn't the townspeople she had to fear so much, it was the press. They'd be down here in a flash to rip her to shreds.

'Miss Wood!'

Johnny rushed through the back door. He was breathless and pale.

Her skin bristled. 'What's wrong, Johnny? Did you hurt yourself carrying the mailbag?'

He shook his head. 'Did you hear about what happened? Down at the whaling station? Mrs Olsen! They found her dead this morning!'

Rebecca frowned, not taking in his words immediately. Mrs Olsen? Berit was in Sydney with Marion. They would be getting to know each other over a coffee at Rosetti's in the Cross. Who was this Mrs Olsen?

'Miss Wood?'

Then slowly, like water seeping into the crevices of a rock, Rebecca began to comprehend. Berit had not got away. She had tried to, but her husband had killed her for the audacity of trying to escape his violence. She remembered what Johnny had said about Sanders killing seals and their pups. 'The monster murdered her, didn't he?' she said.

'She'd hung herself, Miss Wood.'

Johnny's words hit her like a punch. 'What?'

He nodded and looked up to the beam where Mabel had done the same thing a few months before. 'She hung herself … up on the winch they use to hoist the whales onto the flensing deck.'

*

Rebecca legs were shaking as she ran towards Timothy's surgery. Nancy's threat was forgotten as she tried to make sense of the horrific news. Johnny had told her that Berit's body was being taken to the hospital in Twin Falls and Timothy was going to perform the autopsy there. The pulse in her head was deafening. She couldn't get her thoughts together. How could Berit have gone from hopeful to suicidal? She turned over their last conversation in her mind. Was Berit thinking about taking her own life even as she was talking to her?

Timothy's nurse was not at her desk but Timothy was in his office, packing his medical bag. He glanced up at Rebecca when she knocked on his door. His face looked grim and tired.

'Is it true?' she asked, her gaze dropping to the pair of forceps in Timothy's hand. 'About Berit Olsen?'

He nodded, placing the instrument in his bag. 'I'm on my way to Twin Falls now. I prefer to take care of the people from Shipwreck Bay myself rather than leave it to strangers.'

Rebecca tried to imagine Berit's last moments. She'd hung herself from the winch on the flensing deck? That was too grotesque, too dramatic for Berit. Rebecca simply could not believe it. Then she thought of Sanders Olsen's large, muscular hands, capable of doing inhumane things. Wasn't the most dangerous time for a woman when she tried to leave her abuser?

'I think her husband strangled her and then tried to make it look like she had killed herself.'

Timothy's face turned ashen. He moved towards her, knocking the sweets bowl off the corner of his desk and scattering Fruit Tingles and Fantales across the floor. 'Rebecca!' he said, frowning. 'Have you taken leave of your senses?'

His alarm at her accusation made Rebecca wonder if she had been too reckless. But he was the one who was going to perform the autopsy and she couldn't stop herself now.

'You know he was violent. Berit was planning to leave him.'

Timothy leaned against his desk, his arms folded. 'Did you encourage her in any way?'

She flinched. Was he going to blame her for this?

'Berit came to the post office almost daily and we chatted. I saw her yesterday. She seemed happy and excited about the future: not at all like a woman planning to kill herself.'

It was impossible to tell what Timothy was thinking. He was usually so animated with gestures and facial expressions that it was difficult to read him while he looked so deadly serious. 'And she told you that she was planning to leave her husband?'

'What else could she do? He was beating her black and blue. It was only a matter of time before he killed her.'

Timothy reached into his bag and pulled out an envelope. Rebecca's stomach turned when she saw it. It was the letter she had given Berit the previous day, introducing her to Marion. Berit had been so close, thought Rebecca, so close to getting away and starting a new life.

'Luckily, I saw this before Sanders Olsen did,' he said. 'I told you not to interfere and you wouldn't listen. Mrs Olsen was mentally unstable. She made up stories all the time. I believed her husband had broken her arm until I learned that she'd done it herself when she tripped down some stairs. She could go from elated one moment to melancholy the next. Do you know how Sanders Olsen lost his finger? His wife attacked him with a meat cleaver!'

Rebecca stopped short. 'The girl was terrified, and who wouldn't be in her situation?'

'She was lying to you. I told you not to believe everything she said.'

Rebecca recoiled. 'Are you blaming me for this? It seems to me a lot of women commit suicide in this town, Timothy!'

He kept a steady gaze on her and then blinked. His expression softened. 'I'm sorry, Rebecca. I'm shocked too. This is not something I enjoy. But all the women involved were close to each other and it's not unusual for one suicide to trigger another. Mrs Olsen probably got very excited that someone as glamorous as you took an interest in her and even wanted to send her to a friend in Sydney, but when she realised that she just wasn't up to that sort of life, she fell back into despair again.'

Rebecca followed him out to his car. 'I'm sure that's not what happened,' she said. 'I'm convinced her husband was beating her.' She glanced towards the bay and saw that the whaling chaser boat was heading towards the horizon. 'Look! He's going back to work straight after his wife has been found dead. Isn't there something callous about that?'

'The Norwegians hide their feelings, Rebecca. They are a quiet race who don't make a fuss about things.' He put his hand on her shoulder. 'Please don't go around saying anything about this. You must know that I'm fond of you and hope that you will stay. The people of Shipwreck Bay won't take kindly to you accusing the whaling captain of murdering his wife. You don't know these people as I do. Please trust me.'

Rebecca watched him drive away. Her mind raced to recall her conversations with Berit. Could what Timothy had told her possibly be true? Had Berit deceived her? No, Timothy was mistaken. Perhaps in his great desire to see the best in people he was blind to reality. Rebecca looked out to the chaser boat disappearing into the distance in search of a whale to kill. If Sanders Olsen had not murdered his wife with his own bare hands then his violence had driven her to it – a perfect murder. Rebecca would somehow get to the truth. Then Timothy would have to believe her.

CHAPTER TWENTY-ONE

Berit's funeral was a pauper's affair with a graveside service and a cheap pine coffin. The prayers were conducted by a Lutheran priest from Wollongong whom Timothy had contacted after the local priest refused to perform rites for someone who had committed the 'sin of suicide'. Rebecca, Timothy, Doris, Marge and Ernie stood on one side of the grave in the headland cemetery and Sanders Olsen with some of the whalers and their wives on the other. The mourners' clothes flapped like sails in the strong wind and Rebecca needed both hands to hold on to her skirt. Sanders didn't meet Rebecca's eye once, but she observed him. He didn't appear grief-stricken or remorseful. He rolled back and forth on his feet as if he was more annoyed by his wife's death than he was upset. He kept glancing at the whaling station at the bottom of the cliff, giving the impression that the service was an inconvenience to him and that he was itching to get back to work. Rebecca gritted her teeth. The bastard wasn't poor. He could have done better by Berit than disposing of her like a vagrant. Timothy's fingers brushed her arm. Although she was grateful he had come, she didn't lean against him for support.

'There was absolutely nothing to indicate foul play,' Timothy had assured her when he'd called her from Twin Falls after completing the autopsy. He'd been discreet, not wishing to upset her, but when she pressed him for details he'd reluctantly given them to her. 'No sign of a struggle. No scratches or bruises on her body. No skin under her nails. No clumps of hair missing from her head.'

Rebecca wondered how a battered woman couldn't have residual bruising, but Timothy wouldn't lie, so that fact had only added to her confusion.

While the priest said the final prayers, the stench of boiling whale flesh wafted from the whaling station. Everyone tried to ignore it but it was overpowering. Even Doris, a firm supporter of the stink's association with prosperity, couldn't stop her nose from twitching. Rebecca scowled, wondering if Sanders Olsen had gone out on his chaser boat to kill a whale the morning of his wife's funeral. The mourners took turns dropping a trowel of dirt into Berit's grave. Ernie sidled up to Rebecca when he handed the trowel to her, too close for decency. She could smell the scent of mothballs on his suit. 'It's always the young and beautiful, isn't it?' he whispered. 'Such a waste.'

Rebecca grimaced and wished she could pinch him hard on the arm. The wind picked up and everyone seemed relieved when Doris suggested the mourners go back to her place for a cup of tea. Sanders Olsen declined and made his way with the other Norwegians down the cliff towards the whaling station. Rebecca watched them then looked back to Berit's grave, stuck out of the way of the others and not buried in the Lutheran section. She was in death as she had been in life, isolated and alone.

★

Rebecca didn't go home after she finished work that day. She walked to the beach and stared out at the ocean. She couldn't bear the idea that she might have let Berit down. Perhaps if she hadn't been so preoccupied with her own dilemma she could have done more to help her.

She turned to a group of rocks poking up from the sand. Somebody had left their beach towel on one of them. They must have draped it over the rock to dry and then forgotten about it. Now it lay there limply, covered in sand and seagull droppings. Lost property disturbed Rebecca. She'd avoided the lost and found department when she had worked at the GPO. The sight of piles of mislaid umbrellas, scarves, books, glasses, bags and shoes made her uneasy. What had caused their owners to forget them? Rebecca never overlooked any item. She didn't leave her possessions in places she couldn't find them nor did she ever get up from a seat or a table without checking behind her. She couldn't endure the panicky feeling that came with realising you had lost something. An image flashed into her mind. She tried to push it away but it rose clearly before her: her mother kneeling on a beach blanket, the tie on her knitted swimsuit coming undone as she rifled through an overstuffed picnic hamper. She was pulling out plates and forks and knives, setting them up on the blanket. Stop! Rebecca told the image. Stop now! Don't let it happen! But her mother paid no heed to her and the memory kept rolling. Her fingers clenched at the sound of Debbie squealing. She shut her eyes and opened them again. Rebecca's father was propelling Debbie into the air and catching her again with his muscular, tanned arms. Her sister's face was red with delight. She wriggled her chubby legs and cried, 'Do it again, Daddy! Do it again!' Suddenly Rebecca was there with them. Gone were the hips and breasts men gawked at. She was ten years old again, her body boy-like in its leanness, her hair as blonde as a Swede's.

'I'm going for another swim,' she told her mother.

'Don't be too long,' her mother replied, taking a cake tin from the bag and opening it to inspect a vanilla sponge decorated with pink icing. 'Or this will melt completely.'

Debbie started chanting, 'It's Becky's birthday today! It's Becky's birthday today!'

Her father lowered Debbie to the ground and handed Rebecca her sister's plastic bucket and spade. 'Take your sister with you,' he said. 'So your mother and I can get lunch ready.'

Rebecca loved her sister and was happy to do almost anything with her. But swimming was an activity she enjoyed on her own. Still, she took Debbie's hand and together they headed towards the water.

'Watch out for Debbie, Rebecca!' her father called out after them. 'Don't let her out of your sight!'

It was December and the beach was crowded with people who had come up on the bus from Sydney. The inspector was blowing his whistle, making sure that swimmers stayed between the flags. Rebecca glanced at the ruched swimsuits of two older girls, leaning back on their elbows and surveying the world around them with a nonchalant air. They seemed impossibly glamorous to her with their red lipstick and waved hair. One day I will be like that too, she thought. She set Debbie up where the sand was still dry, a safe distance from the water. An elderly couple sitting in sling-back chairs were deep in conversation nearby but stopped for a moment to smile at the two girls. Debbie will be all right here, Rebecca thought. She made several trips to the water's edge and back, filling up the bucket with water and moistening the sand around Debbie.

'You build a castle while I go for a swim,' she told her. 'When I come back we'll decorate it together.'

Rebecca turned to the ocean like a priestess worshipping her god. She had loved the sea since the first time her father had dipped her into it, holding her by her hands and dangling her legs in and out of the waves. She stopped to watch two women walk into the surf backwards, flapping their arms and giggling. Some swimmers had a theory that it was easier to enter the water that way. Even in December the Pacific Ocean was cold. But that was what Rebecca loved most – the invigorating shock of it. It made her feel alive as nothing else did. She dived under a wave, relishing the feeling of gliding through the salt water. She shot up to the surface and checked on Debbie, smiling at the sight of her sister, her brow furrowed in concentration and her tiny hands moulding the base of her castle. Rebecca swam out further and dived down again, moving gracefully through the water like a mermaid. She touched the sand at the bottom and floated for a few moments. The sunbeams in the water danced around her and her hair waved like seaweed. A school of silver fish swam towards her then reeled away. She held her breath for as long as she could, weightless and hypnotised by the magical world around her before propelling herself up to the surface. She blinked the water from her eyes and squinted at the beach. Debbie's spade was still at the spot where she had left her, but her sister was gone. Rebecca pushed her hair away from her face and looked left and right. The beach scene was exactly the same as it had been a few minutes earlier: the elderly couple were still talking, the glamorous girls were still lying on their beach mats.

She swam back to shore and scrambled from the surf, her legs trembling beneath her. Where was Debbie? Had she gone back to their parents? A sense of panic overtook her. 'Did you see where my sister went?' she asked the elderly couple. 'The little girl who was playing here?' The couple turned to her, their faces blank for a moment before concern came to their eyes. A woman's shrill scream made Rebecca's heart stop. People were gathering around the edge of the surf. A small object was bobbing in the shallow waves. At first Rebecca thought it was a towel or a shirt. Then she saw Debbie's pink bucket floating nearby. She lunged towards the water, her legs almost giving way. But a lifeguard reached Debbie before she did. He scooped her up in his arms and laid her on the dry sand, placing her legs higher than her head. He pressed her abdomen. Debbie was grey like an old marble statue and her eyes were glassy. The lifeguard pressed on but when he saw that his efforts at resuscitation were futile, he shook his head and closed Debbie's eyes. Rebecca's throat was seared by a silent scream. This isn't how it happens! Little girls don't drown in minutes without anybody noticing! The other lifeguards formed a human chain to keep back the crowd who were trying to see what was happening. But then two people were let through. Rebecca felt as if she had left her body when she saw her mother throw herself down next to Debbie. 'No!' her mother screamed, trying to shake the little girl back to life. 'No!' Rebecca's father looked from Debbie to Rebecca. The commotion and chaos around them muted to silence as a question formed on his lips. At that moment she knew that everything had changed between them.

Rebecca stared at the forgotten towel on the rock, caught in the grip of her most painful recollection. After Debbie's death, it was Rebecca who became the ghost in the family while her sister was remembered in framed pictures on every cupboard and shelf. Debbie's milestones – her birth, the day she started walking, her first word – were commemorated with candles and flowers while Rebecca's birthday became nothing more than an anniversary of Debbie's death. Rebecca was fed and clothed and taken to school and ballet lessons but she was invisible. How could it have been any other way? She had been responsible for watching Debbie, but she had taken her eyes off her. Her sister had died because she'd wanted to go swimming by herself.

The sound of a speedboat cutting through the waves brought her back to her senses. Rebecca turned to see the slim craft travelling at high speed, its bow lifted and a wash of white foam spewing out from behind it. Despite his dark glasses, she recognised the driver immediately: Stefan. She ran to the water's edge and called out but he didn't hear her. He was travelling towards the bay and Rebecca wondered what was so urgent.

She hurried along the beach and scrambled up the low grassy headland between the beach and Shipwreck Bay.

When she reached the top she saw immediately what had caught Stefan's attention. A massive whale had swum into the bay. She could see its grey body twirling just under the surface. It made horse-like snorts when it surfaced to breathe. People had come out of their houses to watch it, but from that distance Rebecca couldn't recognise any of them.

Stefan revved his motor and drove at high speed between the whale and the land. The whale disappeared and the surface calmed again. Stefan cut his motor, looking in the direction of the headland, perhaps assuming that would be where the whale would head. But the next moment the whale propelled itself out of the water only a couple of yards from his boat. Rebecca gasped at the size of it. It must have weighed over thirty tons. Rebecca clutched her throat, afraid to keep looking. Surely Stefan and his boat were about to be crushed. But the whale spun onto its back away from the boat, hitting the water with a giant splash that washed over the vessel and sent it bobbing in the swell. His clothes saturated, Stefan wiped the water from his face and pushed back his dripping hair. He scanned the bay trying to see where the whale would next breach.

More people appeared on Ocean Road to see what was going on. The sea remained still and so did the spectators, wondering what would happen next. A glint from the water off the opposite headland caught Rebecca's eye and her jaw clenched. The whale chaser boat was cruising towards the bay, grim as a military ship. The whalers should have finished hunting for the day but somebody must have alerted them. A humpback in the bay was an easy catch.

Stefan saw the chaser too and started his motor again, travelling in a straight line between the boat and the bay. Now Rebecca understood that he had been trying to save the whale, to drive it back out to the open ocean. The chaser was bearing down on Stefan's position. The harpooner stood at the gun with Sanders behind him. The whale sent up a spume of spray. It was closer to the headland now but still in imminent danger. The harpooner slammed the charge of gunpowder into the harpoon gun and Rebecca tensed, waiting for the horrific sound of the explosion that would follow. But then he swivelled his gun in the direction of Stefan and his boat. A scream tore itself from her throat. He was going to kill Stefan!

Stefan realised it too and zigzagged the speedboat while the chaser pursued him. The speedboat was no match for the large vessel bearing down on it, but Stefan continued his desperate manoeuvres. When he was in the sights of the harpooner, the man pulled the trigger. The harpoon shot from the gun but Stefan swerved at the last moment and it missed his boat by a yard. The line spooled from the chaser boat and disappeared impotently into the waves. Stefan turned his boat for one last glimpse of the bay, but the whale didn't reappear; it must have moved on. He stuck his middle finger up to the chaser boat then sped out of the bay and in the direction of his home on the beach headland.

Rebecca bent over and clutched her knees, the pain in her chest was as sharp as a knife as she tried to get air in and out of her lungs. She glanced at the people on Ocean Road.

Surely someone was going to report the actions of the whalers to the police sergeant? Then she looked across the bay to the opposite headland and the cemetery where Berit had been laid to rest only that morning. She remembered what Berit had told her about the town closing ranks and felt a surge of anger burn through her. 'I'll get you, Sanders Olsen,' she said. 'You wait and see. I'll get you.'

CHAPTER TWENTY-TWO

Rebecca climbed the cliff staircase and found Stefan standing in his garden, bare-chested and wringing out his shirt. Her ribs hurt. She had to catch her breath before she could speak. 'Sanders Olsen tried to kill you with a harpoon gun! I saw the whole thing!'

Stefan used his shirt like a towel and wiped the water off his face and torso. His jaw was set and the line between his brows had grown deeper.

'I'm sure he killed Berit because she tried to leave him,' Rebecca continued. 'Although Doctor Litchfield found nothing that could prove it in the autopsy report.'

Stefan rubbed his shoulder. 'I believe you are right. Sanders Olsen is capable of anything if someone crosses him.'

Rebecca had seen shirtless men before but Stefan's chest and shoulders were those of an athlete and she averted her eyes. For different reasons they were both in danger, and she couldn't let her attention stray. She sat down in a garden chair. 'We must to go to the police. If the police sergeant here won't do anything, then we need to go somewhere else. Twin Falls. Wollongong.'

'We can't. *You* can't. If the local sergeant hasn't arrested

Sanders Olsen then the police outside the town aren't going to interfere.'

Rebecca pressed her hands together. He was right. If she went to the police there would be questions about her and who knew where that would lead. She had trouble enough with Nancy. But she couldn't abandon Berit. She couldn't let Sanders treat her like a piece of rubbish and get away with it.

'People from the town saw it all too,' she said. 'They stood on Ocean Road and watched. I don't believe any of them will go to the police and report what they saw.'

Stefan sat down next to her. 'Oh, they will report what they saw. Only it won't be the same thing that you and I saw.'

Rebecca studied his face: so calm and yet so passionate and full of purpose. He had almost been killed trying to save a whale. She wasn't prepared to die for anything.

'They also stood in their doorways and watched when I was arrested on those trumped-up charges of spying,' Stefan said. 'I was marched to the train station like a criminal, my widowed mother weeping. After all my father had done for this town! If there was a fire or a flood he didn't send the servants: he went himself. When I was older I went with him too. George Pike's father abandoned his mother when George was a small boy. My father bought her a house and sent George with me to school in Sydney. He was given the best of everything, as if he was my father's own son. I thought of him like a brother. Then he turned on me like that.'

Rebecca folded her arms. 'There's something dodgy about George Pike. Something off. Why would he have done that to you, especially as your father had been so generous to him?'

'Because I had something he wanted, and George doesn't let morals or a sense of obligation get in the way. He's corrupt. How do you think he affords all that jewellery for his wife? He's got his fingers in extortion, gambling rackets and pornography up and down the coast. His role as shire secretary is just a respectable front for who he really is.'

Rebecca thought of the trophies in the Pikes' sunroom and George's unpleasant behaviour. She had suspected there was something shady about him but she hadn't imagined something quite as underhand as Stefan had described.

'What did you have that he wanted?' she asked.

'I was engaged to Nancy.'

Rebecca sat back, her mouth open. She had surmised that Stefan and Nancy might have had a fling once but never anything as serious as an engagement. 'You will have to explain that to me,' she said. 'The woman has threatened to expose my affair with Ned McKell because I told her I wouldn't spy on you. She's malicious!'

'I will,' he said, standing. 'But first let's go inside. I need to change into dry clothes and we both need a drink.'

★

Rebecca waited in the library for Stefan as the last glow of sunset shone over the ocean. He returned in dry clothes with his hair combed away from his face and turned on the table lamp next to her before taking a seat in the armchair opposite. Albrecht arrived with a decanter of whisky and two glasses. He poured the drinks and then left.

'So,' said Stefan, raising his glass before taking a sip, 'let me explain the situation that you find so unlikely. Nancy then was not the woman you know today. I can't recognise her myself. She was vivacious, open-minded and good at everything she tried.' He stopped a moment and raised his eyebrows. 'You find this unbelievable, don't you?'

The whisky tasted smoky. It was like having a roaring fire in her mouth. Rebecca guessed it was Scottish. Ned had preferred sweet whiskies, almost like liqueurs. It pleased her that Stefan's and Ned's tastes were different.

'The "good at everything she tried" part I can believe,' she said. 'She's very determined. But I can't imagine you with her any more than I can imagine why she would choose George Pike over you.'

'I can't imagine you with Ned McKell either.'

Rebecca grimaced. 'Touché! A psychologist once told me I was attracted to Ned because he filled the place of my absent father. Did Nancy remind you of your mother?'

Stefan swirled his whisky thoughtfully. 'No, they could not have been more different. My mother was homely and humble and didn't have Nancy's need to be admired. When I was arrested, I believe George frightened Nancy into marrying him. Her grandparents were German. He promised to protect her from being sent to a camp too. George is a good talker and Nancy was always ambitious – and I suspect from the age of their son he got her pregnant.'

'But she acts like she hates you. She was the one who broke your engagement.'

Stefan shrugged. 'She's bitter and angry at everybody. She thought she was marrying the future prime minister. What she got was a corrupt petty official who keeps her like a trophy in a locked cabinet. She'll never get out of this town now and she knows it.'

Rebecca ran her eyes over Stefan's linen shirt and the Rolex watch on his wrist. He possessed that European mystique that she found so alluring. Being with him stirred up memories of her trips with Ned to the Continent: the smell of strong coffee in the cafés, the layers of history in the buildings, the sophisticated dinner party conversations. He reminded her of a thrilling place that was as far away from Shipwreck Bay as anything she could imagine. Nancy was a fool. But Rebecca was a fool too, for ever believing things would last with Ned. He'd been a gateway for her to the wider world she craved. In that regard, she and Nancy had more in common than she cared to admit. They had both had men wave the possibility of the fulfilment of their desires for a grand life before them, only to snatch it away from them again.

'You're right that we can't go to the police about Sanders Olsen. But I'd like to finish him off just the same. George Pike too. I think that there is something I can assist you with. Would it help your cause to stop the factory ship if I arranged a meeting with the prime minister?'

Stefan's eyebrows lifted. 'You'll be able to do that? It could make all the difference.'

A slow smile came to Rebecca's face. 'I know just the person to speak to.'

★

Rebecca waited until Johnny had left for the mail run before she put the 'Closed' sign on the front door and sat down at the exchange. The telephone rang a few times before Marion's voice came on the line.

'Becky! Darling!' she cried. 'I've been so worried about you! You disappeared off the face of the earth!'

Rebecca imagined her sophisticated friend standing by her hall table, her long red fingernails wrapped around the telephone cord, her jet-black hair impeccably set. At this time of the day she would be getting ready for a luncheon and she pictured Marion wearing something bold and well-cut. Perhaps the red brocade pencil dress Rebecca had always admired.

'I had to, Marion. The press have been terrible.'

'I know, darling. They are brutes. I suppose you saw that vicious article by Heather Crow?'

Rebecca's stomach rolled. Heather Crow was Sydney's most famous social columnist. She saw herself as the arbiter of Sydney society; politicians and their wives, along with actors, artists and social climbers, feared her more than they feared organised crime.

'No, what did she write?'

'Just the usual nastiness. Your name's not mentioned, thank God! I'll send you the clipping if you like.'

Rebecca gave her the address of the post office, though she dreaded to think what Heather Crow might have to say.

'Shipwreck Bay? Where on earth is that?' Marion asked.

'I'm not in Shipwreck Bay,' Rebecca fibbed. 'I'm further down the coast. In a secret location. Don't tell anyone, Marion.'

'Hmmm,' said her friend. 'It sounds to me like some millionaire playboy has you tucked away at his holiday villa. Come on, spill the beans.'

Marion had a take on the world that was hard to resist. Life was one big party to her. Rebecca felt a twinge of envy as she pictured Marion's social calendar over the summer – the glamorous New Year's Eve party at the McGrath's mansion in Double Bay and dinners on yachts. She sighed and decided to play along with her. 'Something like that, but I promise I'll tell you all about it later. For now I'm wondering if you can get me a meeting with the prime minister?'

Marion clucked her tongue and laughed. 'Now, you're aiming high! But you know he is faithful to that old frump of a wife of his. Nobody has cracked that nut yet.'

'Not for me, Marion. A meeting for a friend of mine. Have you heard about Ned's proposal for a factory whaling ship?'

Marion paused before answering. 'No, I can't recall that one. But since he was given his new role he's been making proposals left, right and centre. It makes my head spin. To tell you the truth, I think he's utterly lost without you to steady him.'

Rebecca wouldn't allow her mind to go in the direction of her former lover. 'This isn't to spite Ned. Apparently the proposal doesn't make any economic sense and could do irreparable damage to the whale populations. I need you to get a meeting with him for a friend of mine, Mr Stefan Otto.'

'Is this your millionaire playboy?'

Despite the gravity of the situation Rebecca almost laughed. She looked around the shabby sorting room then out to the headland where she could just make out the cupola of Stefan's mansion poking out above the trees. 'Yes, I guess you could call him that.'

★

Rebecca found it difficult to concentrate for the rest of the day. The scene she had witnessed in the bay had disturbed her. She thought of the people she had seen on Ocean Road, witnesses to a near-murder, and strained to think who those small figures had resembled. Timothy, she was quite sure, was not among them. But what about Doris and Marge? George and Nancy? All the people she saw at church every Sunday? She eyed the customers as they came into the post office, wondering if they had been there. She had thought Shipwreck Bay was simply a remote town where people were bored senseless with their little lives. Now she saw that its virtuous façade hid something darker, more sinister.

Marion called back with a time for Stefan to see the prime minister. 'The prime minister sends his regards to you,' she told Rebecca. 'Everybody here misses you and hopes to see you again soon.'

After Rebecca put down the receiver she thought about what Marion had said. It was nice that she was well thought of in her old circle, but there was no way back to her past. Time went forward and only forward. She had no choice but to go in that direction too, although what lay ahead of her was far from certain.

Rebecca waited until the sun was on the verge of setting before walking along the beach and up the cliff staircase to

Stefan's house. She rang the bell on the door and waited. The light was mellow and soft. The trees were giving off a damp, earthy aroma. From somewhere in the scrub came the song of one whipbird calling to another. The male bird made a 'whip-crack' cry that was answered by the female's demure 'choo-choo'. Although she had grown up in a leafy part of Sydney, she had never actually seen a whipbird, which made these creatures all the more mysterious. Albrecht answered the door and squinted at her. From the blank expression on his face, she was afraid she'd have to go through the 'Mr Otto has no visitors' scenario with him all over again. But this time Albrecht nodded a silent greeting and ushered her inside.

'Mr Otto is in the library,' he said.

Albrecht walked up the stairs and Rebecca hesitated, not sure if she was supposed to follow him or wait. Halfway up the staircase he turned and glared at her. 'Mr Otto is in the library, madam.'

Rebecca nodded and followed him up to the first floor. He opened the door to the library and directed Rebecca inside before shutting it behind her.

Stefan was sitting on the sofa, browsing through a volume on marine biology. He was wearing a casual button-down shirt and tan slacks, and looked relaxed for someone who had almost been blown to smithereens. At the sound of the door clicking shut he looked up. His eyes opened wide when he saw Rebecca standing there.

'I'm sorry,' she said, shrugging awkwardly. 'I expected Albrecht to announce me.'

An amused smile came to his face. He rose to his feet and indicated for her to take a seat on the sofa opposite him. 'Sadly, Albrecht's skills have been sliding with age. He gets confused when anything puts him out of his routine. When my mother was alive we only received visitors in the afternoons between two o'clock and five.'

Rebecca thought of the lonely grave in the garden. 'It's your mother's grave out there, isn't it? That's why you come back. That's why you keep this house. To visit her.'

The muscles in Stefan's neck tightened. 'She died when I was in the camp. I never saw her again after I left here. They wouldn't bury her in the town cemetery with my father. A god-fearing woman full of Christian charity and the bastards wouldn't even let her be buried in sacred ground. Now I can't get the Shire Council to consent to exhume my father and have him buried here with her, so my parents are separated in death when they never spent a day apart in their whole married life.'

Behind the anger she could hear the sadness in his voice. 'I'm sorry. It's awful. I'm sorry about the camps too. I remember how they rounded up everyone of German, Japanese or Italian descent during the war. Were the conditions terrible?'

Stefan shrugged. 'The camps were basic. But I can live with that. Being put on trial and treated like a criminal is what I can't forgive.'

Rebecca took the slip of paper from her pocket and passed the details of the arranged meeting with the prime minster to him. 'Ned is all about his ego and impressing people. The prime minister will be concerned about the figures. If you can prove to him the factory ship is not economically viable, he will put a stop to the plans.'

Stefan glanced over her. 'You are very impressive.'

'I'd better get going,' she said, rising from her chair. 'It won't do either of us any good to be seen in collusion with each other. I hope in some way I've helped you. I wish you the best of luck.'

She headed towards the door but Stefan reached it before she did. She thought he was going to open it for her but instead he stood in front of it.

'I'm going to Jasper Rocks tomorrow. I want to do some diving and now I'm going to meet with the prime minister it would be especially useful for me to see what's happening out there in ocean. Will you come?'

'Jasper Rocks? What's at Jasper Rocks?'

Stefan smiled. 'A fisherman's shack I use when I want to be alone. A scenic cove. It's tucked away and very private.'

Rebecca held his gaze, uncertain, then looked away. 'No.'

'No? I thought perhaps you wanted to be with me as much as I want to be with you.'

The bubbling of the aquarium aerators suddenly seemed very loud. Rebecca noticed Stefan's pet octopus eyeing her from his tank. He extended one of his suckered arms and wiggled it as if waving to her. She swallowed. 'I can't just leave the post office. Everyone will think that's suspicious.'

'So you want to, Rebecca, but you think you can't?' He placed his fingers under her chin so she had to meet his eyes. 'Can't you invent a sick relative? The station is Angelcliffe. It's on the Sydney line. If you get the late morning train the day after tomorrow, I can meet you at eleven o'clock. That should give you enough time to come up with something plausible.'

This was Adam and Eve in reverse. Stefan was tempting her in a way that was proving hard to resist. It made Rebecca wonder if deep down she really had changed at all.

'I have to go,' she said, stepping back to create distance between them. He moved out of the way and said nothing until she was out the door and halfway down the stairs.

'Rebecca!' he called out after her. 'What are you so afraid of?'

She walked on out the front door and hurried towards the gate, which Albrecht was holding open for her. Her heart was pounding as she headed in the direction of the town, bathed in the silver of twilight. Out on the ocean, waves were rolling in from the deep and she stopped a moment to watch their dark shapes rising, curling and breaking. The sound was like thunder. Dear God, what am I doing? she thought. But this time it wasn't the ocean that was frightening her.

CHAPTER TWENTY-THREE

Rebecca's excuse that her great-aunt had suddenly fallen ill caused her more complications than she had anticipated.

'I would be happy to drive you all the way,' Timothy told her when they arrived at the station in his car. 'I don't like the idea of you travelling to Sydney by yourself, feeling alone and distressed. I could come with you to the hospital and give a second opinion on your great-aunt, if you like. I am familiar with geriatric patients.'

Rebecca's conscience dug into her like a termite boring into wood. It had been bad enough that Timothy had insisted on driving her to the station when she only had one small suitcase to carry. But now all this fussing over her?

'Please, we'd better hurry,' she told him, pulling at the lace of her collar. 'The train is due in a few minutes.'

If she missed the train, he would certainly insist on driving her to Sydney and then everything would unravel. He reluctantly stepped out of the car and took his time to walk around to her side and open the passenger door for her. Then he paused for a moment before taking her suitcase from the back seat. She breathed in and out slowly, careful not to give her impatience away.

When he finally got her bag out she smiled, but it wasn't the expression of affection he took it for. She needed him to get a move on. 'It's very nice of you to offer to take me,' she told him as they walked together up the ramp to the platform, 'but you can't leave your patients.'

'There isn't anyone who needs me as much as you, right now,' he said.

Rebecca wanted to scream. From the moment she had arrived in Shipwreck Bay he had been making presumptions. But she kept her expression – and her voice – sweet.

'What about your mother?' she asked him. 'Mrs Todd might be there to look after her, but she will fret without you.'

Timothy looked thoughtful and then squeezed her arm. 'Very well. But you'll call me when you get to Sydney, won't you?'

She nodded and gave him a strained smile, wondering what excuse she was going to have to come up with when she failed to do so. She wanted to ask him if he had heard about Sanders Olsen's attempt to kill Stefan and whether that had changed his mind about Berit's death. But she didn't want to risk starting a conversation that would make her miss the train.

Her jaw clenched when she saw Elaine, standing at the ticket office window. She was wearing a pea-green travelling dress and holding a crocodile-skin overnight bag in her hand. For an excruciating moment Rebecca was certain Elaine must also be travelling to Sydney. She would have no choice then but to continue the ruse and go all the way to the city too and bypass Angelcliffe altogether.

'Hello, Mrs Fryer!' Timothy called out to Elaine. 'Where are you off to?'

Elaine smiled broadly when she saw them. 'Penguin Bay,' she replied, tucking her ticket into her purse. 'I'm going to see my sister's new baby.'

Rebecca's shoulders relaxed. Elaine was heading south.

'Oh, what a pity,' said Timothy. 'I was hoping you might be headed for Sydney. Rebecca's great-aunt is terribly ill and she is hurrying to see her. I'm sure she could have done with the company.'

'Oh, I'm sorry to hear that,' said Elaine, giving Rebecca a sympathetic nod. Rebecca could barely bring herself to be civil. Berit was dead, probably murdered, and Stefan had nearly been killed too and everybody was smiling at her as if they were the best of friends.

She bought her ticket from Ernie who, conscious of Timothy's presence, refrained from saying anything more than 'Good morning' to her.

The train bound for Sydney appeared round the bend of the bay. She stared at it, willing it to come faster. Timothy stepped into her line of vision. 'We'll have something to discuss when you get back,' he said, staring into her eyes.

The besotted look on his face made Rebecca's stomach plunge. She was sure what he meant by 'something to discuss' was a marriage proposal. She was saved from having to reply by the train coming to a squealing halt.

She took her seat and waved to Timothy from the window as the train pulled out of the station. It gathered speed and she moved to the other side of the carriage. She lifted her gaze and stared up at the green mountains, unable to bear looking at the sea.

The station at Angelcliffe could have been missed in the blink of an eye. Rebecca had forewarned the conductor that she wished to get off there and as they approached he directed her to the front carriage. The station was one carriage length and bore only its sign. There was no seat or awning and certainly no stationmaster or ticket office. It was just as well. The last thing Rebecca wanted was to be seen.

'Are you sure this is where you are meant to get off?' the conductor asked, glancing at Rebecca's smart pinched-waist suit dress. She'd had to wear city clothes to make her story of going to Sydney believable.

'Yes, it is,' she replied, uncertainly. There was nothing around the station but bushland and a dirt road. 'My brother and his wife will pick me up here.'

For a moment, she hesitated about getting off the train: one of her Roger Vivier–shod feet hovered over the platform while the other one remained firmly on the train. But then, impelled by some force she didn't fully understand, she committed herself to a forward course of action and placed both feet on the platform. 'Thank you,' she said to the conductor, reaching out to take her suitcase from him. She watched the train pull away then looked around her. There was no sign of Stefan. She strained her ears, thinking that she may have heard the hum of a car approaching. But then she realised it was only the complex song of a lyrebird strutting in the undergrowth. The bird, she knew, composed its mating song by copying the noises it heard around it. She spotted it perched on the piece of ground it had cleared, with its plumes fanned out behind it and its little beak trilling with the sounds of water drops, kookaburra laughs, frog croaks and even wood being chopped.

'Rebecca.'

She turned to see Stefan standing behind her. The top buttons of his blue polo shirt were unbuttoned, giving her a glimpse of his tanned chest. The bottoms of the casual trousers he was wearing were rolled up above a pair of sandals. His gaze travelled over her suit dress and down to her expensive shoes. 'You overdressed for the occasion,' he said, with a smile. 'We have to trek through the bush to get to the shack.'

Rebecca's stomach fluttered at the sight of him. 'I had to pretend I was going to Sydney,' she told him. She pointed to her suitcase. 'I brought a change of clothes with me.'

Stefan averted his eyes but didn't completely turn away when she went behind a tree to change into a white cotton frock and flat shoes. She caught him grinning and she smiled too. After she had finished changing, he picked up her suitcase and took her hand in his free one. As soon as their skin touched, Rebecca knew they had crossed a line from which there was no turning back. They would be lovers.

The bush track Stefan led her along had a downward slope and became narrower and more overgrown the further they walked. The rainforest around them felt primeval, with its lush understorey of tree ferns, tropical orchids and strangler figs. It was alive with birdsong, from the whistling of the brightly coloured king parrots to the cooing of the brown cuckoo-doves. They passed a satin bowerbird perched on the branch of a tree. In the dappled light his plumage showed up as a brilliant cobalt blue. Rebecca stopped a moment to admire him and became aware of the sound of running water. A little further down the track, they came across a cascade and waterhole. A water dragon scurried off the rock where it had been sunbaking and plopped into the water. This is paradise, Rebecca thought. As they continued on, she caught glimpses of the ocean through the trees. Then the track came to a sudden end at a small, crescent-shaped beach. To the right, tucked away in an inlet, Stefan's speedboat was tied to a wooden jetty. The headlands were steep and topped by deep green scrubland. The place was as secluded as anything Rebecca could have imagined.

'The shack is this way,' said Stefan, leading Rebecca along the beach.

Set back from the sand and tucked away in a grove of palm trees was a wooden fishing shack mounted on pillars of stone. The roof was corrugated iron and a rainwater tank sat on one side of it and an open-air kitchen on the other. It couldn't have been more different from Stefan's elegant home in Shipwreck Bay. She followed him up the rickety wooden stairs to the front door and caught a glimpse of an outdoor toilet and shower at the rear of the shack. She feared the interior was going to be equally primitive and was surprised when Stefan opened the door and she found herself walking into a sparsely decorated but comfortable living area. A large double bed, covered in white linen, dominated the room. On one side hung a hammock and on the other a large pine bookshelf housed novels and a collection of seashells. The air was thick with the smell of salt. Rebecca could hear the sea too, rolling onto the shore and breaking around the headland rocks. She wouldn't have been able to stand the sound if Stefan hadn't been there with her.

Stefan placed her suitcase at the foot of the bed and stood near her. 'It's my hideaway,' he said. 'The water is crystal clear and abundant with sea life. There is no one else around for miles.' He took her shoulders and turned her to face him. 'Except for you, Rebecca. You are the only person I've ever brought here.'

She scrutinised his face and wondered if he was telling her the truth.

'Am I really the only other person you have brought here? No other woman?'

Stefan took her hand. 'No other woman, Rebecca. I promise you that.'

'Why?' she asked him. 'You hardly know me.'

His eyes settled on her face. 'Because I sense a deep sadness in you and this is a place I come to when I want to forget my troubles.'

'I'd give anything to be able to forget my troubles,' she said. 'But they follow me wherever I go. I'm not sure how I thought I'd escape them simply by moving to Shipwreck Bay.'

'Well then,' he said, 'come with me and I'll show you how easy it is to forget them.'

*

Rebecca stood on the jetty and bit at her nail. She watched Stefan step into his speedboat. It was a fine looking craft with sleek lines, but still Rebecca felt it was far too small to imagine herself going out to the open sea in it. It had been bad enough when Ned used to insist she go with him on the prime minister's private yacht on Sydney Harbour. She spent those trips staring at her martini in the bar below the deck.

Stefan held the boat steady and reached his other hand towards Rebecca with the intention of helping her into it.

'What are you doing?' she asked him.

'We're going to find ourselves a whale.'

'Can't we see one from the headland?' she asked, watching the boat rise and fall in the gentle waves. 'I saw the whale you rescued from Shipwreck Bay and the water here is much clearer.'

'No,' he replied, 'it's not the same thing. I want to show you one up close.'

Rebecca froze. She couldn't have moved even if she had wanted to. 'I can't, Stefan,' she said, breathlessly.

She supposed that she was not really in any danger. Stefan was an experienced sailor and the sea was calm. But there was a difference between staring at the ocean from the beach and going out on it. The thought of getting in the boat and moving away from land and into the open ocean seized her with such bone-chilling terror she thought she might pass out. She wanted to run away and hide in the shack or go all the way back to Shipwreck Bay, anything but get in the boat. But she knew that it was foolish, all in her head, and she did not want to look ridiculous in front of Stefan.

'My sister … she drowned,' she managed to say.

Stefan's face turned serious and he fixed his eyes on her. 'I'm sorry, I didn't know that.'

Rebecca looked away, embarrassed. She knew the fear inside of her made no logical sense, but she could no sooner get in that boat than she could leap off a tall building.

'All right, Rebecca,' Stefan said, climbing back on the jetty and taking her hand, which even to her own senses had turned as cold as ice. 'Let's go back.'

*

Rebecca watched Stefan put the kettle on the gas stove and slice some bread for sandwiches. She was shivering despite the warmth of the day and the blanket that Stefan had wrapped around her shoulders. Although she felt foolish, she was relieved that she was not on the boat.

'I'm sorry,' she said.

Stefan placed a mug of tea in front of her. 'No, I'm sorry. I did not realise that your fear was so bad. When we first met, you were staring into rock pools and you have walked along the beach many times.'

'I used to love the ocean more than anything. I used to fantasise about being a mermaid.'

He finished making the asparagus and cheese sandwiches and sat down at the cane table opposite her. 'How did your sister drown exactly?' he asked.

Rebecca paused. It was a dreadful secret to share. The thought that she was responsible for her sister's death filled her with more remorse and self-loathing than she could bear. What if it made Stefan despise her as much as she despised herself?

She curled her toes as if she were standing on the edge of a cliff. 'All right, I'll tell you what happened ...'

*

'That's a terrible story,' Stefan said, when Rebecca had finished describing Debbie's death. 'That would be distressing for anyone to have experienced. But it wasn't your fault.'

Rebecca winced. 'My sister drowned because of me. I was careless. I can never forgive myself for that.'

'You were a child yourself, Rebecca. Far too young to understand that life can change in a second.' He rubbed her hand then entwined his fingers with hers. 'Do you think perhaps that it's not so much the sea that you fear, but that you feel guilty about taking any pleasure from it?'

The warmth of his touch was comforting and Rebecca relaxed. 'When I think about doing things I want to, things that might make me happy, I become apprehensive,' she told him. 'I feel like I'm tempting fate.'

'It's unforgivable that your parents made you shoulder the blame. My guess is that they could not bear to take it on themselves. You were their scapegoat, Rebecca. If you don't allow yourself to enjoy what you love, then you always will be.'

She looked out at the ocean. 'I've been afraid of the sea for so long, I don't know who I would be without the fear. How could I change it now?'

Stefan squeezed her hand tighter. 'I think you know how, don't you?'

Rebecca bit her lip and nodded. 'All right.'

★

Rebecca tried not to stumble as Stefan helped her into the speedboat.

'Stay seated and hold on,' he told her. 'It will be a little rough until we get out past the breakers.'

Although the waves were small, Rebecca felt every bump as Stefan accelerated towards them, backing off the speed slightly a moment before they crossed each one. Despite her apprehension, a childish sense of adventure rose inside of her. She watched the beach disappear in the wake behind them then turned her gaze out to the open ocean. To her amazement, instead of panic at the sight of the endless expanse of blue, she felt a sense of freedom.

'There, up ahead!' said Stefan, cutting the motor and pointing to a spot twenty yards in front of them.

Rebecca looked to where he was indicating but couldn't see anything. Then the surface of the water swirled and churned. Several spurts of mist rose up into the air.

'It's a pod,' cried Stefan. 'There are three ... no, four of them out there!'

Rebecca had never seen whales up close. She watched as their dark grey backs rose in a curve before sinking below the surface again in a graceful movement. Their blowholes resembled large human nostrils. Then the whales disappeared and the ocean was still again.

At first Rebecca thought that was going to be the end of the sighting and the whales must have moved on or gone down deeper, but then Stefan leaned over the side and peered into the water.

'Look, look!' he said, gesturing to Rebecca. She squinted and saw a massive grey shadow move underneath them. Then suddenly a dark gleaming head, bumpy with knobs like a pickle, burst through the surface next to her. She found herself inches away from the barnacled chin and wide mouth of the creature. It turned slightly, and she and the whale looked into each other's eyes. It stirred in her a sense of the ancient and the mysterious. Then the whale propelled itself higher. For a brief moment her heart stopped as she feared that the whale was about to upend the boat. But it rolled on its side, missing the boat and smacking the surface of the water with its flipper. Rebecca watched it glide down deeper into the blue, awestruck by its majesty.

The pod swam about them for several minutes more, plunging beneath the waves then rising to the surface again. It was as if they were playing with Stefan and Rebecca while being mindful that the two humans were in a fragile position. Then, as quickly as the whales had appeared, they vanished.

'They were so close,' said Rebecca, pushing her damp hair out of her eyes. 'I thought they would flee the boat, but they were so close and curious about us.'

'They haven't learned fear,' Stefan said.

Rebecca sat quietly for a moment. After the encounter she could better understand Stefan's fascination with whales and his fierce determination to protect them. She looked out to the horizon. Once, she had felt a strong connection to the sea but that had been broken by Debbie's death. In some way she couldn't explain, she thought the sight of the whales may have restored it.

When he was sure the whales were gone, Stefan restarted the motor. 'When we get back, I'll take you snorkelling. We won't go deep, just around the headland.'

It had been enough of a trial for Rebecca to get on a small boat, let alone take the step of plunging into the sea. She waited for her stomach to tighten and for the urge to flee to once again overtake her. Those had been her usual responses to the ocean since losing her sister. But she felt strangely calm. She was ready to face the sea again.

CHAPTER TWENTY-FOUR

Back at the cabin, Rebecca changed into a gold halter-necked swimsuit that she had worn for pool parties. She realised she looked more like she was going to participate in an Esther Williams extravaganza than go snorkelling at a remote and wild beach. She wondered why she had thought to bring the costume in the first place. Had she always known that she would end up swimming with Stefan – or had she thought she might be lounging around in it, tanning herself on the beach?

Stefan was down at the water's edge when she stepped out of the cabin. He was rinsing out two sets of snorkels, fins and masks and turned when he heard the cabin door squeak. A smile curled the corners of his mouth when he saw her.

'Do you overdress for everything?' he asked.

'There is a wardrobe for every occasion,' she quipped back.

'Thank God you're not swimming in a wardrobe, at least.'

Rebecca laughed. Despite the fact he'd made fun of her costume, she had caught him admiring her figure. She liked it much better than when Ernie Mullens did it. She shamelessly ogled him too. He was wearing short Jantzen swimming trunks and no shirt, but this time she didn't turn away from the view of his taut body, from his broad shoulders to his muscly legs.

He strapped a knife to his calf.

'What's that for?' she asked. 'Do you expect to fend off a shark?'

'Nothing as dramatic as that,' he said, with a smile. 'People are careless with their fishing nets and lines. When they lose them, they can float for miles. It's not just turtles that get caught and drown in them.'

He handed her a mask and she slipped it on before following him into the water. The rippling waves in the shallows were refreshing. She sank down and dipped her face in the water to make sure the mask was airtight. Stefan passed her a pair of fins, and she tugged them onto her feet.

'Stay by me,' he said, attaching his snorkel to his mask. 'We are not going to go too far but if you panic, tug my leg.'

He pushed off and headed towards the rocks. If Rebecca hesitated she would lose him. She pushed off too, kicking her legs slowly to propel herself and surrendering to the weightlessness of the sea. At first she hadn't realised that she'd closed her eyes, but as soon as she opened them she felt the thrill of a different world opening up before her. Sun rays glowed and danced over an underwater garden of blue, red and green seaweed. Her heart rate slowed while every other sense in her body sprang to life. She was aware of the silkiness of the water against her skin, the warm sun on her back and the rasping sound of her own breathing. As she followed Stefan around the edge of the headland, brightly coloured fish darted in and out of hidden caves. A moray eel swam quickly away, weaving through the water like a long green ribbon, before disappearing into a crevice. Stefan dived down deeper to observe a wobbegong resting on the sea floor. Stefan moved gracefully, like a fish. He belongs to the sea, Rebecca thought. This is truly his home. He returned to the surface and Rebecca continued to glide after him. Everything was so quiet and peaceful, yet also dazzling and brilliant. She was a child again, fulfilling her dream of being a mermaid. Even when a grey nurse shark darted past them, uninterested in the two humans and going about its business, she did not feel afraid, only fascinated.

They snorkelled for another twenty minutes before returning to the beach where they lay back on a blanket and dried themselves in the sun. Stefan gazed at the ocean while Rebecca's mind raced. Why had she not returned to the sea long before this day? She thought of all the other enjoyable things she had missed out on because she had been too frightened or too guilty to experience them. Perhaps she had stayed with Ned longer than she should have because she didn't believe she deserved someone who was hers, completely and fully. She glanced at Stefan. He was an unusually attractive man. She imagined smart women in London, Paris and Rome, women who shared his passions as well as his bed.

She brushed his cheek with her fingers. His skin had the heat of the sun on it and was smooth, except for the light stubble on his jawline. He took her hand and kissed the palm; the sensation of his lips on her skin sent tingles down her arm. She shifted her body, filled with desire. He sensed the change in her and moved his lips to her mouth. She kissed him back, tasting the saltiness on his skin. His hand moved to her breast and traced the outline of it in slow circles. A pleasurable ache throbbed between her thighs. He loosened the tie of her swimsuit and peeled it down and off her body. His strong hands stroked her from her breasts to her stomach and hips and back again. Everywhere he touched her, the flesh seemed to catch fire. Her back arched and he paused a moment, before lowering his lips to the blonde hair between her legs. Her splayed fingers dug into the sand as sweet spasm after spasm overcame her like tiny shockwaves. When he leaned over her, his tanned body silhouetted against the blue sky, she wondered if she should tell him to stop. But when he pressed down on her and she felt the hardness of him inside her, she didn't care. She lost control of her senses and pleasure seemed to pulse in all her nerve endings. She felt herself tighten around him and a burst of euphoria rushed between them, as if they had both been lifted by a wave.

*

Afterwards, they took another swim in the waves then lay on the bed in the shack. Stefan leaned on his elbow and brushed a strand of hair away from her forehead.

'Do you want a husband and family, Rebecca?'

'Of course,' she answered. 'Isn't that what every woman wants?'

Stefan raised an eyebrow. 'I didn't ask you what women want. I asked you what *you* want. Because if marriage and a family are what you really want, you are going an odd way about it. In fact, I would go so far as to say that you are deliberately avoiding it.'

Rebecca looked up at the ceiling. 'I'm not avoiding it,' she said. 'I've just made stupid choices. I thought Ned loved me. I thought I'd stay young forever.'

Stefan cupped her cheek and turned her face to his. 'Why did you come to Shipwreck Bay – when, until today, the sea terrified you? I don't understand.'

His question made her aware that so many of the decisions she made were irrational. She'd had no real purpose in coming to Shipwreck Bay, other than to escape Sydney and notoriety.

'It was the first post I was offered. I needed the money.'

'What if you never get married? What if you never have children? What kind of life would you live then?'

Rebecca's stomach tensed. She was thirty-two. Almost thirty-three. There was a good chance she might never marry or have children but she couldn't bear to think about it. 'I imagine that it would be a very lonely life.'

He looked at her and smiled. 'That's a limited view, isn't it? What if you were a great society hostess? What if the most brilliant artists, pioneers and statesmen of our time were guests at your dinner table? What if you travelled the world, read important books and filled your house with great works of art instead of children and toys? Would you still feel lonely then?'

Rebecca turned away and stared at the ceiling again. What if she did live like that? What if she was completely her own woman with nobody else's needs to attend to? She squeezed her eyes shut then opened them again. 'That life might be available to someone very rich. That's not a possibility for a woman alone in the world with nothing but clerical skills.'

'You underestimate yourself, Rebecca. You are far more resourceful than you let yourself believe.'

A slight feeling of panic stirred in her. There was some meaning behind Stefan's words. Why was he saying this to her now? 'You were engaged to Nancy. You must want marriage and children yourself.'

'I wanted them once,' he said, pulling the sheet down and circling her stomach with his fingers. 'But I've changed. Marriage can be a trap.'

'A trap?'

'Greatness and marriage rarely go together, especially for women. To be exceptional requires energy, sometimes solitude, sometimes the freedom to be utterly selfish. A woman can't be free if she has to spend all day pleasing a husband and taking care of children.'

Rebecca closed her eyes again, trying to find the part inside herself that was honest. The idea of being a society hostess had always appealed to her. She'd held that fantasy when she had been with Ned but it had proved to be based on a flimsy foundation. Marriage represented something to her that meant safety and security.

She glanced at Stefan and realised that he was sleeping. Untangling her limbs from his, she stood up, wrapped a towel around herself and walked out of the shack and down to the water. The day was beginning to fade and wisps of gold and pink were appearing in the sky. She remembered the first evening after Debbie's death, when the local police sergeant had driven her and her parents back to their home after her sister's lifeless body had been taken away in an ambulance. They had all been in too much shock to fully understand the void that from that day on would inhabit their lives. Rebecca never forgot the sunset that evening: a spectacular display of red and lavender beams of sunlight dancing on the surface of the ocean as the police car slowly wound down the road from the peninsula. Rebecca's eyes had followed the sun as it vanished below the horizon. She had imagined it rising again on the other side of the world and told herself that Debbie now existed there. It would forever be the moment of the day when she felt closest to her sister, when the two worlds that separated them briefly collided.

The frothy waves splashed over her feet. It had been an extraordinary day of self-revelation, both thrilling and vindicating. But now overwhelming doubts rose up from within her. Her hands clenched as she tried to stop the sensation from taking over her body. But the harder she resisted it, the more determinedly it stabbed at her mind and stole her peace from her. It's dangerous to be happy, she told herself. For whatever makes you happy can be easily snatched away.

CHAPTER TWENTY-FIVE

Stefan walked with Rebecca along the bush track to the station. The rainforest was quieter than it had been when she arrived, as if all the animals and birds were resting under a magician's spell. The scent of moist vegetation and damp wood settled on her skin and clothes.

So much can change in such a short time, she thought, reflecting on the week she had spent with Stefan. Every day they had swum, snorkelled and made love. Ned had been forgotten, she had reacquainted herself with the magnificence of the ocean and her worries about Nancy and the press had barely crossed her mind. Now she had to return to everything.

Before the train arrived she changed into her tailored dress, stockings and shoes and this time Stefan did not look away. 'Let's meet as soon as I get back from Canberra,' he said, cupping his hands around the base of her neck and kissing her. 'Until then just lie low and play along as innocently as you can with those people. When the factory ship plan is destroyed, we will both get away from Shipwreck Bay.'

Rebecca frowned. 'Where will we go?'

'Europe, of course,' he said, smiling. 'You'll be happy there, Rebecca. You can start a life of your own. I'll help you.'

Rebecca wondered at what point they had come to such an agreement? A life of her own, on her own, wasn't exactly what she was after. But she pushed the doubts from her mind as she got on the train. She had a task ahead of her to focus on if she was going to pretend all was normal in Shipwreck Bay.

*

When she arrived at the post office, one look at the way Johnny had left it was enough to make Rebecca want to walk straight out. Documents were scattered over every surface rather than organised into neat piles and the binder folders in her office were out of alphabetical order. But what irked her most was the abandoned teacup sitting in the middle of her desk. Two clumps of mud on either side of it indicated that Johnny had been sitting there with his feet up. She picked up the cup and grimaced. A colony of green mould was growing in the sludge at the bottom of it.

'Dammit!' she swore, carrying the cup to the tearoom and depositing it in the sink.

She dampened a washcloth and returned to her office to clean up her desk. The fig tree outside the window creaked. The sound made her shiver and she looked up to the beam where Mabel had hung herself. She sat down at her desk, convincing herself not to look up again. It was then she noticed the envelope in her in-tray. The handwriting was Marion's. Rebecca opened it and read the letter inside:

My darling Becky,

I'm sending you Heather Crow's column as promised and because I hope it will give you a good laugh. You know that everyone in our set has got a good trouncing at some time in their life, and you're more fortunate than most because it doesn't mention your name. In fact, there is no clue to your identity in it, which means one thing: you've outwitted 'The Crow'! Quite an achievement! I'm sure that irritates her more than anything and that's why she is being especially vicious.

Now write and tell me more about your millionaire playboy! I'm dying to know!

With all my love,
Marion

The Woman Who Hides in the Shadows

As the weeks turn into months and the identity of Minister McKell's mystery woman still eludes us, the public's curiosity about her has not died down. We want to see the face of the type of woman who flouts Christian morals and pursues a man already committed to a wife. Her lover never respected her because a man who respects a woman will always propose marriage. What she thought was love was merely a fleeting dalliance because she made herself so available. Like so many of her kind, she has been discarded to fend for herself. No decent man will want her now and the fate that lies before her is tragic. Disillusioned by love, her good looks gone, she'll end her days as a pathetic figure in some cheap boarding house. Yet we can never feel sorry for her. She is a vixen who sold her soul for a fur coat and a diamond bracelet.

Rebecca dropped the article as if it was burning her fingertips. Her head throbbed. Is that how people saw her? Ned had made her feel so sophisticated, so worldly, so exceptional. That is what she had truly craved, not diamonds and minks! She swept up the article, took it to the tearoom and threw it in the sink before tipping the gunk from the teacup over it. Then she turned the tap on and saturated the paper until the ink smeared and it turned to pulp. 'I'm not what you think,' she said under her breath. 'You don't even know who I am!' She gathered the mess up, squashed it together and flung it out the window like a spit ball.

'Oh, Miss Wood, I'm so glad to see you!'

Rebecca turned to see Timothy's nurse standing in the doorway.

'Doctor Litchfield's mother has taken a turn for the worse. I've been trying to call you in Sydney but he must have taken your number down incorrectly. The operator could only connect me to a home furnishings store.'

Rebecca was too upset by Heather Crow's column to register what Nurse Gibbons was telling her at first. From the earnest expression on her plump, middle-aged face she was casting Rebecca into the part of a concerned soon-to-be fiancée.

'Doctor Litchfield thinks it is pneumonia. He's with her at Twin Falls Hospital now. I can drive you there if you like.'

Rebecca hesitated but saw there was no way to refuse without appearing callous. She composed herself and nodded. 'Yes, I would appreciate that,' she replied, picking up her purse and gloves. 'That's very kind of you.'

★

Twin Falls Hospital was a small twenty-bed operation housed
in a red brick Federation building. The reception nurse
led Rebecca to the intensive care ward where the sight of
Timothy sitting forlornly by his mother's bed made Rebecca's
heart plummet. Mrs Litchfield was lying propped up with a
clear plastic oxygen tent covering the top half of her body.
She was such a ghastly shade of grey that Rebecca would have
already assumed she was dead if it wasn't for the wheezing
sound of her labouring breath. Rebecca had intended to set
things straight with Timothy on her return by telling him
she wasn't going to accept his marriage proposal. But under
the circumstances she felt it would be heartless to bring the
matter up.

'Rebecca,' he said, rising to greet her and taking her hand.
'How is your great-aunt? Is all well?'

Timothy was gaunt, but polite as always. She wondered how
he managed to maintain his self-composure even in these most
trying of conditions. Pneumonia killed healthy people all the
time. She couldn't see frail Mrs Litchfield making a recovery.

'She's improving,' Rebecca replied, barely able to remember
the story she had made up before she went to Jasper Rocks.

'I placed a call to you on the Sydney number to make sure
you arrived safely but I couldn't get through. Then all this
happened.' He turned to his mother and winced. 'With all your
worries about your great-aunt, I didn't want to trouble you
with my problems, but Nurse Gibbons insisted on trying to
reach you. I see she was successful.'

Rebecca had deliberately given him a wrong number, but she hadn't expected that he would actually try to call her. Her mind flashed to Heather Crow's column. Perhaps she was a terrible person after all.

'I'm so sorry. Is it really pneumonia?'

He nodded and indicated for her to follow him out onto the veranda. Two male patients were sitting there smoking. The men glanced at Rebecca and Timothy, smiled and then went back to their conversation.

'Mum is exhausted from fighting one infection after another. I don't know how much longer she can hold on,' Timothy said, his voice trembling. 'I don't want her to suffer but I can't bear to let her go.' He set his jaw and straightened himself. 'I'm sorry.'

Rebecca's mind was swimming. The complicated feelings she had experienced about her own mother's death gripped her. She had grieved her mother's passing deeply, even though they hadn't been close. How much worse would things be for Timothy? She was at a loss at what to say to console him. 'What's important now is to maintain her comfort and dignity,' she told him.

Timothy laid his hand on top of Rebecca's and squeezed it. At first she thought the gesture was made in gratitude, but when he turned a shade paler she worried he might be on the verge of collapsing from the strain.

'Let's go and get something to eat,' she said. 'You aren't looking well at all.'

The surf club's buffet lunch was coming to an end. All that was left for Rebecca and Timothy to choose from were some tired-looking sardine and bacon rolls, a wilted salad and rice with meatballs. They settled on the latter.

'There's always something sorrowful about endings, isn't there?' said Timothy, when they took a seat by the window. 'The end of school, the end of summer, the end of the day ... the end of a life.' He moved the food around on his plate with his fork. 'Even the end of a buffet lunch has something wretched about it.'

The antagonism she had felt towards him lately vanished and was replaced by not only pity but a sense of kinship. She understood the torment of grief.

'Maybe your mother will pull through,' she suggested, hopefully. 'She survived a major stroke. She's stronger than she looks.'

Timothy rubbed his temple as if trying to soothe a memory that was lodged there. 'The drive here was the worst. I had to go at eighteen miles per hour because every bump was agony to her. I almost didn't attempt it. But I don't have an oxygen tent and the other equipment needed to support her in my surgery. Mum's suffering could have been eased if we had a hospital at Shipwreck Bay.' He glanced out the window at the sea, which was flat and green under the early afternoon sun. 'Let's hope the whaling station gets that factory ship so nobody else has to suffer.'

Rebecca felt a pang of guilt. Stefan, with her help, would be on his way the following day to do everything he could to stop it. 'Isn't there another way the town could get a hospital without the factory ship?' she asked.

Timothy shook his head. 'There is nothing else that would increase the population fast enough to warrant it.' He cut up a meatball, put a piece into his mouth and chewed thoughtfully for a moment. 'Fortunately, Ned McKell seems like a determined fellow. I heard George Pike went to Sydney today to discuss the matter with him.'

Rebecca suddenly felt hot and wished she was back at Jasper Rocks in her plain white cotton dress and not here, trapped in both her tailored suit and this awkward situation. 'Do you think Ned McKell will get that factory ship proposal through? There is a question mark about its economic viability.'

'As long as Stefan Otto doesn't interfere, he most likely will.'

Rebecca squirmed inwardly but did her best to appear composed. 'I know that some people in town believe he was spying for the Nazis during the war. But I think that's unlikely, don't you? There was so much hysteria during that time, anyone of German descent could be accused of horrendous things.'

Timothy pushed his food away and folded his arms on the table. 'Spy or not, the man has a sinister side. That intellectual façade he puts on is only to hide what he is really up to. I hold him responsible for Mabel's and Anne Peberdy's deaths.'

Rebecca jolted as if his words had bitten her. 'Why on earth would you say that?'

Timothy eyed her. 'Anne Peberdy spent her time at the beach collecting shells. I happen to know that Stefan Otto often saw her there and befriended her. One day she disappeared. Her mother was frantic. Then Anne turned up the following morning on her mother's doorstep, changed.'

'Changed? How?' asked Rebecca.

'Nervous. Distressed. I was her doctor. As I told you before, she had been interfered with.'

'Are you accusing Stefan Otto of such a terrible thing?' she asked with barely disguised indignation. 'You told me it could have been anybody. A fisherman, an itinerant ... Sanders Olsen is a much more likely suspect. Why are you accusing Stefan Otto of this now?'

Timothy frowned and studied her carefully. 'I told you that Stefan Otto was a notorious womaniser. He's forty-two and has never married. Anne was always talking about the nice man from the big white house. The day she was molested she stopped talking altogether.'

Nausea rolled in Rebecca's stomach and she averted her eyes. 'That doesn't mean he molested her. You told me yourself not to jump to conclusions. Stefan Otto doesn't come across as someone who would harm anybody, considering he spends his time defending whales. It's the people in this town who are potentially dangerous. Sanders Olsen nearly put a harpoon through him and nobody has made a complaint about it.'

Timothy's gaze ran over her before settling back on her face, which she realised now was more tanned than when she had left. 'Rebecca,' he said, a note of hesitation in his voice. 'At the meeting about the factory ship Stefan Otto gave you a very pointed look. Do you know each other better than I have assumed?'

'I've spoken to him once or twice when I've delivered the mail,' she said, feeling all the muscles in her back tighten. 'He came across as courteous and thoughtful. The whole town might hate him but I prefer to make my own judgements about people.'

'I'm only trying to protect you. Men like Stefan Otto draw women in with their cosmopolitan airs. Nancy was one of them once. Her parents didn't trust him but she was set on marrying the man. He promised her the world. He was going to take her to Europe. She was going to live in a castle! Luckily George discovered that Stefan Otto was part of that Nazi group that used to meet secretly in Sydney.'

Rebecca didn't move. She heard a faint hum in her ears.

'That's all hearsay,' she replied. 'People get hysterical in wartime. Remember that poor little girl, Matilda Powell, who was mobbed by a crowd simply for walking her pet dachshund?'

'Sometimes men see other men as they are. Stefan Otto is a predator and a liar,' Timothy said, resolutely. Then his expression softened. He reached over and touched her hand. 'But you, fortunately, are far too sophisticated to be fooled by someone like him. Given more time you would have discerned his true nature quickly enough.'

She turned away from Timothy and looked out to the sea, which had turned grey. Clouds were gathering. A storm was on the horizon. She was filled with a sense of foreboding: a warning of some sort. A warning that, in the fury of passion, perhaps she had failed to heed.

★

Rebecca lay spread-eagled on her bed, her skin on fire with the unusual spring heat. A mosquito buzzed around the room. It flew close to her ear and she swatted at it. The sound stopped then started again. She turned on her bedside light and sat up. Her thoughts turned back to New Year's Eve, 1945. She was dancing on the balcony of a harbourside mansion with Ned. Cynthia was supposedly in bed nursing a fever, but in reality was between the sheets with a newspaper tycoon. Sydneysiders were still living in wartime-like austerity, but you wouldn't have known it from the abundance of glittering jewels worn by the female guests and the expensive cigars smoked by the men. 'Come to Rome with me, Becky,' Ned had whispered in her ear above the notes of Len Barker's Dixieland Jazz Band.

'Isn't the city in ruins?' she asked.

'Partly, but it is still beautiful. The country is set to become a republic. It will be the first free election since Mussolini came to power. You will be a firsthand witness to history.'

And so Rebecca's fantasy life of limousines, fine clothes and dancing on the balconies of the homes of consuls-general around the globe escalated to new heights. As important events happened in the world, she was there. But it didn't last. Now instead of a grand hotel she was lying in Doris Campbell's weatherboard rental. She slid down the pillow and lay on her back, staring at the pink enamel pendant light. From there, her eye travelled down the rose-patterned wallpaper. The mosquito buzzed near her ear, but this time she caught it and crushed it in her palm. She didn't believe Stefan had molested anybody. Timothy would always side with the people of the town, and if they pinned awful crimes on Stefan then he would go along with them. But that was the difference between a loyal golden retriever and a lone wolf, wasn't it? One was part of the community while the other was on the outside of it. What irked her even more was Timothy telling her that Stefan had promised that he would take Nancy to

Europe. He had promised Rebecca the same thing – but not marriage. Heather Crow's words burned into her: *A man who respects a woman will always propose marriage …* Maybe Stefan liked her a lot, maybe he thought she was attractive, but he hadn't given her any indication that he loved her, let alone that he was committed to her. Why did she compromise herself for the convenience of men? Did she hope that by doing so they might eventually love her? She had done that with Ned, but he never did.

She turned off the light, lay on her right side and told herself, I shouldn't have let Stefan seduce me. Then she rolled over onto her back again and thought, I shouldn't sleep with him anymore. She turned over on her left side and decided, I should be more assertive with him about what I want.

But as irritated and confused as she felt, she knew one thing. Somewhere between the first time she'd encountered Stefan on the rock platform and the time they had met at Jasper Rocks, she had fallen in love with him. Another mosquito found its way into the room. 'Goddammit!' she swore, flinging her pillow in the direction of the buzzing sound. It stopped, momentarily, before beginning again. A minute later Rebecca's ankle started to itch. She turned on the light and looked at her foot. The red welt of a mosquito bite was forming on the sensitive spot above her ankle. She scratched at it and the itching stopped. But a second later the discomfort returned. She stared at the light again. It was going to be a long night.

*

When Rebecca returned to her house from the post office the following afternoon she found a lavish bouquet of pink dahlias and peonies sitting in a jar of water on her doorstep. She stared at the flowers, her mind racing. Had Stefan returned from Canberra so quickly? She picked up the display. The petals were fresh and hadn't browned at the tips despite the warm weather. He must have only just delivered them. Where did he get such beautiful flowers? There wasn't a florist in Shipwreck Bay. Surely he hadn't brought them all the way from Canberra.

Timothy pulled up in his car and got out. For a moment she considered hiding the flowers.

'Do you like them?' he asked, coming down the path towards her. 'I dropped them off before paying a call on Mrs Dolan.'

Rebecca's heart sank but she was careful to hide her disappointment. 'They're from your mother's garden?'

'Indeed,' he said. 'Thank you for coming to see her at Twin Falls yesterday. It meant a lot to me – and to Mum.'

Rebecca doubted Gillian had been aware of her presence and, if she had, wouldn't have been so pleased at all. But she did believe Timothy appreciated it.

'I lost my mother after she suffered a long illness,' she told him. 'I know it's a lonely experience.'

He nodded and something glimmered in his eyes. 'Would you like to come with me to Twin Falls this evening? I've finished with my patients and I'm on my way now. We can have something to eat after we visit Mum. There's a Chinese restaurant in the town.' He smiled self-deprecatingly. 'Nothing fancy, mind you. But the chop suey is good.'

She hesitated but then saw something about him that she hadn't noticed before. When he smiled the right corner of his lip lifted slightly higher. It gave his expression an endearing lopsidedness. It seemed to her that she hadn't studied his face properly before. Now she noticed not only his smile but the slight deviation in his nose. Was it from rugby? Cricket? A fight in the schoolyard? She was suddenly curious to know.

'All right,' she said, locking eyes with him briefly before turning away. 'I'll just put the flowers in a vase.'

★

'Do you have relatives besides your great-aunt?' Timothy asked Rebecca. They'd been driving in silence until then, Rebecca's mind a million miles away. She'd been thinking about Stefan. How had his meeting with the prime minister gone? Had it been a success?

'I don't have any other family,' she said.

Timothy rubbed his jaw. 'All I have left in the world is Mum.' He smiled at her before turning back to the road. 'Life doesn't always turn out the way we would like it to, does it? I thought I'd be happily married to Arabella with a family. I never expected my life to be like this.'

'Like what, exactly?'

'Thirty-eight years of age and alone. No grandchildren for Mum.'

Rebecca rubbed at her neck. She often wondered how different her life would be if Debbie had lived. Perhaps her mother would have loved her better and her father might never have left. Perhaps she wouldn't have fallen for a man like Ned. She might be married with three children. In any case, she'd have had a sister and that would be something.

'I was instantly smitten with Arabella,' Timothy said, shaking his head. 'I was back from war service and she was working as a nurse at Sydney Hospital. She liked dancing and so did I. It felt like we were a perfect match, but that turned out to be far from the case.'

Rebecca hadn't wanted him to talk about his marriage before, but now she found she didn't so much mind hearing his story. 'Why do you say that?'

'My work at the hospital was demanding. We had a deluge of war veterans coming our way. Men whose bodies and minds had been shattered by fighting or from being interned in prisoner-of-war camps. I told Arabella that it wouldn't be that way forever, and that when order was restored and things were running smoothly I would take her away for a glorious holiday. But she wouldn't wait.' He glanced at Rebecca then back at the road. 'It's a shameful thing. I'm even ashamed to say it. I returned to our apartment one evening to find that she'd cleared everything out and run off with an American sailor.'

'Oh,' said Rebecca, remembering her own humiliating episode of being thrown out of the apartment in Potts Point when Ned stopped paying for it. 'For some reason I imagined your former wife as being someone sophisticated. Not the type of woman to run off with a sailor.'

Timothy glanced at her. 'God, what a fool I was falling for her,' he said. 'Love brought out the protector in me. I wanted to give her everything. I was working myself to the bone with the intention of providing for her and our future children.'

Rebecca wondered about that for a moment. Did he have some financial difficulties after the war? She could understand from his personality that he would work hard for others, but did he really need to do so to *provide* for a wife and children? From his rather grand home, she had the impression the Litchfields were well cashed up.

'Where is she now?'

Timothy gritted his teeth. 'Well, after the sailor took her for every penny she had, he left her floundering. Now she doesn't have a thing. No hospital would take her after she ruined her reputation. She's a live-in nurse for an elderly man. That can't be much of a life for her.'

Rebecca shuddered. 'Would you take her back? It sounds like you truly loved her?'

Something flashed in Timothy's eyes. 'Would you take back someone who had treated you like that? I hope not. Once trust is broken you can never fix it.'

That's true, she thought. Trust was like the child she had aborted. You couldn't bring it back to life. 'It's better to choose wisely from the beginning,' she said. 'And to make sure that you know someone very well. Sometimes I wonder if we fool ourselves about who people really are and view them only as we wish to see them.'

Timothy brought the car to a stop outside the hospital. He turned the engine off but made no move to get out. He looked at her steadily. 'Rebecca, you and I are mature and we have experienced life. I believe something happened to you in Sydney, something that made you want to leave.'

Rebecca tried to hold his gaze but lowered her eyes and stared at her lap. She had spent so many years concealing, repressing and closing off parts of herself that she couldn't imagine telling Timothy about Ned – let alone about Stefan! Marion was forthright and outspoken. She hid nothing from anyone. But she obviously hadn't thought through how much Heather Crow's article would hurt Rebecca. In Rebecca's view, being open would only lead to rejection and judgement.

'You know that you can talk to me any time you want to,' Timothy continued. 'Whatever you confide in me, I won't tell a soul.'

Rebecca nodded. 'I know you wouldn't.'

She pursed her lips and wondered what would it be like to have one person in the world who knew absolutely everything about her? How would it feel to be able to be completely herself?'

Timothy watched her, but when she didn't say anything further he got out of the car and opened the door for her. 'Come now, let's see how Mum is doing and then we will go get something to eat.'

Gillian was dozing in her oxygen tank but perked up the instant she saw her son. 'Hello Mum,' said Timothy, gripping her hand and squeezing it. 'How are you today? Rebecca's come with me. Doesn't she look lovely, as always?'

The old woman glanced in Rebecca's direction and frowned. Timothy adjusted his mother's pillows. Then after greeting the two elderly women in the beds on either side of her, he went looking for the doctor to discuss his mother's condition.

'You must be Doctor Litchfield's fiancée?' said one of the women to Rebecca.

'Not quite.'

The old woman didn't hear Rebecca's reply and nodded. 'He's a lovely man. Always so kind and thoughtful. He puts a smile on all our faces when we see him.'

The woman turned her attention back to her crochet, and Rebecca sat gingerly on the bed next to Gillian. 'I know you don't care for me, Mrs Litchfield,' she whispered. 'But I just want you to know that I think your son is a lovely man too.'

Gillian's eyes flashed with what looked like fury. Rebecca recoiled, stung, although she should have expected it. She turned away and looked out the window. It didn't matter what Gillian thought of her because she had made up her mind to view Timothy more generously. He had gone out of his way to be kind and helpful the moment she had arrived in Shipwreck Bay. Maybe it was time for her to stop running after what couldn't be hers, and to start appreciating what was right in front of her.

*

The first day of November was hot and still. The sky was azure blue without a cloud in it. Rebecca filled a watering can and wet the plants in the post office garden. It was the first time she had bothered doing it since she and Timothy had planted everything back in late August. There had been enough rain at first but the last month had been dry and unseasonably warm and there was talk of a possible drought. She tipped the last drops of water over a sweetheart rose. She had changed like the weather. Even now, she felt as if she was becoming someone else by the day, maybe even by the hour.

'Good morning, Miss Wood,' Maeve greeted her with a wave. 'The garden has really taken on, hasn't it?'

'It has.'

Maeve glanced up at the sky. 'They are predicting a hot one this summer. You'll be out daily then.'

'I suppose I will,' she agreed.

'George Pike is in Canberra this week,' Maeve said. 'He was invited by Minister McKell to address the cabinet. It sounds promising about the factory ship. Your Doctor Litchfield might get his hospital yet.'

Rebecca felt light-headed, but she knew it wasn't the heat. It was her duplicity. She was helping Stefan block the factory ship because she believed Sanders Olsen had killed Berit, and also because, after seeing them up close, she had sympathy for the whales. But she could be sabotaging something important to the town where she might end up staying.

She wished Maeve well and went inside the post office. From the sorting room window she stared at the sea. Little tufts of white foam poked up from the expanse of blue. Suddenly her body was racked with sobs. Everything seemed to be coming apart. She tried to calm herself, to tell herself that all would be fine in the end. She was making a good judgement for herself, at last, because she had decided that if Timothy asked her to marry him she would accept. Stefan would be back soon and she would have to tell him. She loved him, ached for him, but she saw no secure future with him. She was a ruined woman, and before she ruined herself any further she had better make the best of things even somewhere as insular as Shipwreck Bay.

'Hello! Hello!'

Rebecca recognised Doris's voice and patted her face with the tea towel before going out to the counter. But she wasn't fooling her shrewd landlady that she hadn't been crying.

'Oh, poor you!' said Doris, clucking her tongue. 'It's always everything at once, isn't it? Your dear great-aunt and now Doctor Litchfield's mother.'

The last thing Rebecca felt like was a conversation with Doris, but she had no choice but to grin and bear it.

'I've made a Hawaiian chicken casserole for him,' Doris said. 'Why don't you drop by my house and pick it up after you finish here? You can heat it up in his kitchen and share it together. Shirley is laid up in bed with a bad cold and poor Doctor Litchfield is probably too distracted to fend for himself. He's been looking awfully pale and thin.'

Rebecca nodded. The good thing about women who nattered was that you didn't have to say anything to keep the conversation going.

*

After Rebecca finished for the day, she went to Doris's house and found that her landlady had left a note on the door explaining that she was cleaning the church and that the casserole for Timothy was in the refrigerator. Rebecca rolled her eyes. Only in Shipwreck Bay did people leave their doors unlocked and advertise the fact. She took the casserole from the refrigerator and then walked down the hill in the direction of Timothy's house. The light was beginning to fade and the ocean had turned a gloomy shade of grey. She waved to Elaine as she drove past and then to Carmel and her husband. Two weeks ago she had been furious at them for watching Sanders Olsen nearly kill Stefan. Now, much to her dismay, her resentment was fading. It was hard to keep up a solo battle against a whole town.

By the time she arrived at Timothy's house, darkness was falling. The hoop pines lining the drive looked like tall soldiers against the moonlit sky. Her shoes crunched on the gravel and she stopped a moment when she reached the front veranda. The lights were on downstairs and she could see Timothy sitting in the parlour reading a book. He was in his work shirt and pants but had loosened his tie. He was engrossed in the book and gave a start when Rebecca knocked on the window. Then he recognised her and his face lit up.

'Hello,' he said, opening the front door. 'What do we have here?'

'Doris made a casserole for you. Hawaiian chicken.'

Timothy ushered Rebecca inside and led her to the kitchen. 'Hawaiian chicken, heh? That sounds exotic! That was thoughtful of Doris.'

He was in much better spirits than he had been the day Rebecca returned from Jasper Rocks. 'How is your mother?' she asked him.

'Improving. It's quite miraculous really. It looks like she might even be able to come home in a few weeks.'

Rebecca rotated the dial on the oven. 'Let's warm that up for a bit then we'll put the casserole in for half an hour.' She glanced around the kitchen with its jade green countertops and its checkerboard floor. It was homely yet elegant. A beautiful kitchen. Perfect for a doctor's wife but not Rebecca's style. Timothy was watching her. Not in the wide-eyed way he usually did but intensely. His head was cocked and he was squinting. It gave Rebecca the unsettling feeling of someone looking through the sights of a gun.

'Timothy?'

'Yes?'

'Why are you looking at me like that?'

He stepped closer to her, curling her hair behind her ear and studying her. 'You have blonde roots. You're not a natural redhead.'

Rebecca patted her hair back into place. Plenty of women dyed their hair, but not for the reasons she did. 'No, I'm not a natural redhead. I like to change my appearance now and again. Being blonde all the time is boring. Don't you like it?'

He smiled cryptically. 'Women and their artifice! It's really not necessary, you know. You also wear a bit too much make-up, Rebecca. Why don't you let your natural beauty shine through? I rather liked the scrubbed look.'

Rebecca cringed. She did not like 'the scrubbed look' at all. She liked her eyebrows to be visible and her blonde lashes darkened to make the most of her eyes. Her lipstick gave her confidence to take on the world. She'd been wearing make-up and perfume since she was sixteen. She didn't intend to change now.

'Shall we set the table?' she asked, changing the subject.

★

'Well,' said Timothy, dabbing at his lips with the serviette. 'That was a fine chicken and pineapple casserole. Doris's cooking is hard to beat.' Then, smiling at Rebecca, he added, 'She told me that you are taking lessons from her.'

Rebecca nibbled on a slice of carrot, wondering if she would ever appreciate home cooking the way he did. 'Yes. She's a good teacher.'

'Why didn't your mother teach you? Isn't that how mothers and daughters bond? Cooking, sewing and all that?'

She flinched at his question and stared at her plate. 'My mother wasn't very well. Unfortunately we didn't do many things together.'

'What was wrong with her?'

'Melancholy, I think. She grieved the loss of my younger sister.'

Timothy put down his knife and fork. 'Oh, I'm sorry to hear that. I thought you were an only child. What happened?'

Rebecca looked up. His gaze was sympathetic and kind. If she was intending to marry him, she would have to learn to confide in him. Perhaps doing so would be the beginning of honesty with him.

'We were on the beach together. She drowned when I wasn't looking.'

Timothy stared at her for a moment then turned back to his plate and didn't say anything. He poked at a piece of chicken while Rebecca watched him, wondering what he was thinking. When she had told Stefan the story of Debbie's death, he had been understanding. But Timothy's lack of reaction was unsettling. He was always so attentive. If she hadn't known better, she would have assumed he hadn't heard her. She picked up her own knife and fork and returned to the meal. They continued on in silence until Timothy looked up at her. 'Let's go out in the garden, shall we?'

He got up and pulled out Rebecca's chair for her. She followed him to the veranda and he turned on the lights. The garden, so pretty during the day, looked strangely menacing at night with the shadows that stretched out over the lawn. A large golden orb spider was making a web across the path with its spindly legs.

'Smell the air,' Timothy said, inhaling. 'You can smell the sea and you can smell the roses all at the same time. I love this time of the evening, don't you?'

Rebecca took in a breath. She couldn't smell anything. She gave a start when Timothy suddenly dropped to his knee.

He held out a ring in his fingers. 'Rebecca, will you marry me?'

The world pitched around her but she steadied herself. This was what she had been expecting, wasn't it? Yet, it felt so odd, so wrong. In a dreamlike trance, she held out her hand for him to place the ring on her finger. She couldn't see it well under the exterior lights, but it was certainly a large diamond.

Timothy stood up and took Rebecca in his arms. He pressed her to his chest and rested his chin on her head. 'Your heart is beating so fast,' he said, releasing her. 'Did I give you a surprise?'

She looked up at him. His eyes were coal black in the dark; she couldn't see his irises at all. He took her hand and touched the ring with his thumb. 'It was Mum's engagement ring. It's quite unique.'

Rebecca snatched her hand back. She wanted to pull the ring off and tried, but it was stuck at her knuckle. 'But ... I can't take your mother's engagement ring,' she said. 'Not while she is still alive.'

'Why not? She can't wear it and she would want you to have it.'

'But it would be bad luck, wouldn't it?'

Timothy laughed and kissed her. His lips still tasted of Doris's casserole. 'I didn't know you were superstitious! I think a lot of people in Shipwreck Bay are going to be very excited. I'll speak to Father Rob in the morning.'

Rebecca lifted her hand to the light to look more closely at the ring. A thick gold band with a pyramid of round cut diamonds. The apex was a large yellow-brown diamond. It flashed in the light like a strange animal's eye. Although it was probably worth thousands of pounds, that diamond in the centre of it made her shudder.

CHAPTER TWENTY-SIX

Rebecca was frying an egg for breakfast when the news came over the radio. She stood in the middle of the kitchen holding the fry pan as she followed every word of the newsreader:

A Federal Government proposal to establish the Australian whaling industry as a major concern by the purchase of factory ships for operations in Shark Bay, Western Australia and in Byron Bay and Shipwreck Bay in New South Wales has been scrapped. The Minister for Commerce and Agriculture, Mr Ned McKell, conceded that whaling would continue to be carried out from chaser boats because the Commonwealth could not obtain the three million pounds needed to construct each factory ship. He added that the whaling stations would receive funding for modernisation and that he intended to undertake research into Antarctic whaling as a possibility for the future. The Premier for New South Wales, Mr Robert Harrison, described the concession as a farce and of no value whatsoever. He claimed that the Australian whaling industry was doomed for failure without employing factory ships alongside chaser boats. 'Onshore whaling stations are practically obsolete because

there are simply not enough whales to be harvested close to
shore anymore due to depleting stocks,' he said. Mr Harrison
concluded that the whole exercise had been a distraction to divert
attention away from Mr McKell's private life by making the
minister appear to be a champion of country towns …

Rebecca slipped the egg onto a piece of toast and put the pan
in the sink. Then she sat down at the kitchen table and rested
her chin on her hand. It was impossible to be pleased without
being apprehensive. It was the news that she had most wanted
to hear, but the news she had most dreaded too. She glanced
out the window. The sky was clear and blue but she had a
prickly feeling that a storm was brewing.

★

Rebecca realised there would be trouble when she passed by
the Shipwreck Bay Hotel later that morning. Usually the pub
didn't fill until the afternoon, but men were already spilling
out of it onto the pavement. Their voices were loud and their
faces red with drink. She glimpsed Sanders Olsen and some
of his whalemen at the bar talking with George Pike. The
way the men were speaking to each other, leaning in like co-
conspirators, made her stomach pitch. She hurried on to the
post office with a foreboding sense that something was shifting
in the town.

George Pike called an emergency meeting at the memorial
hall. Rebecca went along with Timothy to gauge the
atmosphere and found the residents of Shipwreck Bay and its

outskirts packed inside shoulder to shoulder. As well as the familiar faces of the women of the town and their husbands, there were people she rarely saw, including the entire Turner family. The heat had made the space stifling. Doris was fanning herself furiously in the front row, sweat dripping down her temples. Rebecca herself felt clammy as she and Timothy squeezed themselves into a standing position near the wall. Then Gavin Young spotted her and offered her his seat.

'The Japs and Soviets will have rich pickings in the Antarctic – and Shipwreck Bay misses out on a hospital!' George told the gathering, spit exploding from his mouth as he spoke. 'Ned McKell did his best for us but couldn't get the funding. It's up to us to keep up our demands.'

Iris Young leaned towards Rebecca. 'This is Stefan Otto's doing,' she said. 'Everybody knows he's behind it.'

The corner of Rebecca's mouth twitched. She was behind it too.

*

Late that night, Rebecca crept through the dark streets towards Stefan's house, using a small torch to guide her. She guessed he must be back from Canberra by now but was wisely avoiding the town. The light was on in a downstairs window and the gate was open. Had he been expecting her? She worked the hideous engagement ring off her finger and dropped it in her pocket before walking up the steps and pounding the knocker.

Stefan opened the door. 'Rebecca!'

She hesitated on the doorstep, uncertain about going inside. Every part of her ached with the sadness of what she was going to tell him.

'I sent the servants to Melbourne,' he said, leading her into the drawing room. 'I'm expecting some sort of reprisal. I don't need poor Albrecht's head dented by a brick coming through the window.'

The table lamp set off just enough illumination for her to see a carving knife and a piece of driftwood on the coffee table. She remembered the diving knife Stefan had strapped to his calf the day they went snorkelling. They had been at Jasper Rocks only a short while ago and yet everything had changed dramatically.

She sat down on the edge of the sofa and Stefan sat next to her. He picked up the piece of driftwood and played with it in his hands. They were the same hands that had glided over her body when they had made love. The memory of it sent a tingle over her skin. It wasn't like that with Timothy. His kisses were pleasant enough but she felt absolutely nothing.

'The prime minster listened to your argument at least,' Rebecca said. 'The factory ships won't be going ahead.'

His brows drew together as if something in her manner perplexed him. 'I think you've placed too much faith in politicians, even the prime minister.'

'What do you mean?'

Stefan put the driftwood down and picked up the knife; he ran his thumb against the blade as if to test it. 'There was never going to be a factory ship,' he said. 'There was never enough money for one.'

For a moment Rebecca forgot the reason for her visit. 'What do you mean there was never going to be a factory ship? Ned McKell came here promising the town that there would be. He got people's hopes up about a hospital.'

Stefan tossed the knife back on the table and stood up. 'Politics is a dirty game, you know that,' he said. 'To make people forget Ned McKell's indiscretions, he was allowed to make some promises he never intended to keep. Now the factory ship won't eventuate, he can claim it was for reasons he had no control over and that he sincerely tried.'

Rebecca rubbed her hands over her knees. Ned had played the people of Shipwreck Bay as skilfully as he had played her. She could see what would happen now. The blame would fall entirely on Stefan.

'You were right to send your servants away,' she said. 'The town is in a state to lynch you. George Pike is stirring everyone up.'

Stefan sighed. He reached towards her and caressed her cheek. 'If a man is going to steal a woman from another man, he should be determined to make her happier,' he said. 'I have stolen you from the intentions of Timothy Litchfield, and I intend to make you very happy.'

She raised her hand to stop him but he continued. 'I can't do much more for the whales here, so I will return to Europe. While Australia flounders around like some backwater island, I'll look for like-minded individuals in Britain and Germany.' He smiled at her. 'You will be very happy in Europe, Rebecca. I can see you flourishing there.'

She braced herself to tell him the truth. 'Stefan—'

'You could go to university, Rebecca. You could study law and put that brain of yours to good use. Would you like that? What a team we will make.'

Yes, what a team they would make – but not as husband and wife. The recollection of Heather Crow's attack on her fortified her resolve not to follow unrealistic dreams anymore. 'Stefan, I'm engaged to Timothy Litchfield. I'm going to marry him.'

The smile on his face froze. He frowned, not understanding. 'At Jasper Rocks …'

Rebecca burned with shame. Yes, at Jasper Rocks they had been lovers. Now everything had changed. 'I need to stop living on dreams,' she said, her voice taking on a pleading tone. 'I'm no longer a young woman. I can't keep running after men and their ambitions. I need a home: somewhere to feel safe. I want marriage. I want children.'

The bewildered look on his face was unbearable. She stood up and moved towards the window. For a moment she thought she saw a figure in the garden but then she blinked and it disappeared. Stefan came up behind her, placing his hands on her shoulders to make her face him. 'For God's sake, don't make the same mistake Nancy did! Don't throw yourself away on that colourless man! Can't you see how unique you are? How different?'

Rebecca squeezed her hands. Leaving Stefan was like taking a bitter medicine for a disease, but it was an illness she had to treat. 'Unique and different are fine for men!' she said. 'When you live your lives how you want to, people applaud you. It's not like that for women. We are crucified for doing as we please.'

'You think it's so different for men?' asked Stefan. 'I've paid the price for being true to myself. Society won't change unless people like you and me change it.'

If she stayed a minute longer, she would let him persuade her, then around and around the cycle she would go again. Where would that lead? Would she wait till she was forty-two, fifty-two ... an old woman before she finally faced the truth? 'I'm going now, Stefan. I can't see you anymore.'

She fled from the room and out the front door. Stefan ran after her. She was halfway down the front steps when he grabbed her arm. 'Dammit, Rebecca! It's not going to work with Timothy Litchfield. He will destroy your spirit. Yes, he might offer you some comforts but is that seriously all you want? Think of Nancy! Her spirit and dreams all dried up. Do you want your life to turn out the same way?'

A figure stepped out from behind a tree and moved towards them. The light from the drawing room window shone on the person and Rebecca saw it was Nancy holding a torch.

'Nancy?' Stefan said.

She sent him a piercing look. Her mouth twisted like a wrung-out rag. Then she turned to Rebecca. 'You tramp!' she screamed, pulling out a revolver from the pocket of her dress and pointing it at Rebecca. Her finger twitched on the trigger.

Rebecca stared in mute horror. Her mind slipped between calm, logical thoughts and nightmarish scenarios. Where had Nancy got a gun? Then she remembered Stefan had told her about George's criminal connections. Her disbelief switched to cold, stark fear. She saw a vision of herself lying on the ground, her hand clutched to her chest with blood pulsing out between her fingers.

Stefan put the palms of his hands out. 'Nancy, calm down. Somebody could get hurt.'

Nancy's eyes darted from Rebecca to Stefan. 'I know what you two have done and you won't get away with it. Especially her!'

Stefan dared to take a step closer but Nancy turned and fled back into the bushes. Rebecca doubled over. Her breath stung in her chest as she sucked in air.

'She's gone mad!' Stefan said.

'She knows about me,' Rebecca told him, looking up. 'She's guessed about Ned McKell. She'll go to the press, won't she?'

Stefan clutched his hands to the sides of head, too shocked to answer her.

They both stared into the bushes where Nancy had disappeared. It was eerily quiet.

'I'm done for,' Rebecca said.

CHAPTER TWENTY-SEVEN

Rebecca woke with a jolt in the early hours of the morning. She had been in the midst of a nightmare in which she was being chased up a never-ending staircase by a mob of pressmen. 'Is it true you are Ned McKell's mystery woman?' they shouted at her. The pressmen gained on her and transformed into hounds, ripping and tearing at her flesh. She woke just as one chewed off her foot. It took a moment for her to catch her breath and realise she had been dreaming. The moon was in its last quarter and the room was dark, yet an eerie glow flickered on the walls. She closed her eyes again for a moment and then the acrid smell hit her. Are they boiling a whale? she wondered. Now? She leaped out of bed and tugged aside the curtains. At first she thought she must have been looking at the sunrise then she realised the sky was still inky black and what she had thought was the sun were flames and flying embers. Something was ablaze. A bushfire? With trembling hands she tugged on a dress and slipped on shoes before running out into the street. She scanned the sky, trying to ascertain the fire's exact location. She saw two cars speeding along Ocean Road towards the headland and hastened her steps towards the town. Doris came out on her veranda, her hair in rollers.

'Rebecca!' she called out. 'It's Stefan Otto's house! It's burning!'

Rebecca ran like a madwoman through the town centre. The town's pump truck sped by her with Frank, Elaine's husband, at the wheel and Ernie clinging to the back. By the time she reached the headland, she was gasping for air. She screamed when she saw what was happening to the house. The fire had taken hold and was spreading rapidly. One tongue travelled up a wall, pushing out fists of flame that ate up the shingled roof. Frank was aiming the pump hose at the flames but the water seemed to evaporate before it even reached the building. The sound of shattering glass and cracking tiles was frightening. Rebecca imagined Dunkel and the fish being boiled alive in their tanks.

'Stefan!' Rebecca shouted, running towards the house. She was pushed back by a blast of searing heat that seemed to singe all her nerve endings.

Strong arms grabbed her and threw her to the ground. She looked up to see someone she knew but took a moment to recognise. It was Timothy, his face blackened and streaked with sweat. He rolled her on the ground then pulled her away from the building. 'Stefan!' she tried to say. Then nausea swept over her and she was sick. When her vision cleared she saw Elaine and Marge stomping on embers to prevent the fire travelling to the bush. The rest of the townspeople, dressed in nighties and pyjamas, stared at the conflagration with expressions of horror and awe. George Pike and Sanders Olsen stood together, their arms folded and their faces smug like two men at a church picnic. Then she knew. The fire had been deliberately lit. She and Stefan had expected some sort of reprisal, but nothing like this. She managed to get up and stagger towards the men, not sure what she would do when she reached them but was stopped by a deafening crash that left her ears ringing. The whole front wall had toppled over. She screamed, imagining Stefan crushed to death. She dropped to her knees, her insides hollow. Then a black shadow appeared from the rear of the house, hunched over and holding something to its chest.

'Stefan!'

Rebecca ran towards him but Timothy reached him before she did. He threw a blanket over his shoulders and guided him towards his car. Stefan slumped against it as the roof of the house collapsed and the structure imploded into a pile of bricks and fiery embers. At that moment all hope seemed to vanish from Stefan's eyes.

'Rebecca,' said Timothy. 'Get my medical kit and the canteen from the rear seat.'

She did as instructed and Frank – only Frank – stepped forward to offer assistance. Timothy poured water into Stefan's eyes and down his throat. Then he looked over his body and stopped when he saw his leg. Rebecca looked too. Through Stefan's torn trouser leg the skin was bright red, with oozing blisters.

'I have to get him to the surgery quickly,' Timothy told her. 'Then to the hospital if I am going to save his leg.' He turned to Frank. 'Help me get him into the car.'

Both men took Stefan either side by the arm, but before they lifted him Stefan handed Rebecca the wet towel he had been clutching to his chest. 'Return him to the ocean,' he told her, his voice cracked. 'Set him free.'

Rebecca took the towel and watched with tears streaming down her face as the car pulled away with Stefan, Timothy and Frank inside it. Then she gently opened the towel. At first she thought she was looking at a piece of flesh or a heart and then she realised it was Dunkel. The octopus stared back at her with his old man's eyes, wise and sad. She knew that if she didn't quickly get him into salt water he would die. She ran as fast as she could to the beach. The dawn was breaking when she reached the rock platform. She knelt in the same place she had first seen Stefan emerge from the ocean, and lowered Dunkel into the water before loosening the towel and releasing him. The octopus floated for a moment before moving his limbs and swimming away.

Rebecca sank down on the rocks, hunched over and shivering uncontrollably. She thought of Stefan's beautiful mansion. Standing there one minute, and the next obliterated as if it had never existed.

★

After Timothy had performed basic first aid on Stefan at his surgery he had taken him to Twin Falls Hospital, where he received skin grafts to his leg. 'He won't regain full use of that leg,' Timothy told Rebecca. 'But we acted quickly enough to save it.'

Although it broke her heart, she was grateful to Timothy, more grateful than he could ever imagine, for showing Stefan compassion. While many people in the town were of the opinion that Stefan had got what he deserved, that didn't stop them singing Timothy's praises.

'Doctor Litchfield knew that some people wouldn't approve of him helping Otto,' she'd overheard Joy tell Carmel at the Country Women's Association afternoon tea. 'But he went and did it anyway in full view of the other men. *There* is a doctor who is true to his creed.'

The priest made a special sermon of it the following Sunday: *If thine enemy be hungry, give him bread to eat; and if he be thirsty, give him water to drink: For thou shalt heap coals of fire upon his head, and the Lord shall reward thee.*

What everybody was saying was true: Timothy's selfless behaviour bordered on saintly. How would she ever live up to being the wife of a hero?

Rebecca's gaze drifted to Nancy sitting with her eyes straight ahead in the front pew. What had she been doing at Stefan's house with a gun anyway? Had she followed her there? Then it dawned on her. She had gone to warn Stefan about George and Sanders's plan. Perhaps the gun had been protection and she had been intending to give it to Stefan? If that was so, it could only mean one thing: she still loved him. Rebecca sat back in her pew and remembered the pained expression on Nancy's face when she had encountered Stefan in the post office. They had both lost him now. It linked them in the strangest of ways. As far as she knew Nancy had not revealed her secret to anyone. Perhaps she never will, Rebecca thought hopefully. It was smallest skerrick of comfort in the whole terrible ordeal.

*

Rebecca worked in the post office, sorting the ever-increasing volume of mail and catalogues that heralded the coming of the Christmas season. She could not bring herself to look at the ocean; not because she still feared it but because she had learned to love it. It was a different suffering to the one she'd experienced when she had first come to Shipwreck Bay, but it was suffering just the same. Sometimes she turned towards the headland where Stefan's house had once stood. The cupola was gone now and the trees were scorched, but somehow it was easier to look at that empty space than think of him in hospital where she couldn't be with him. She often imagined that she was there by his bedside: reading to him, straightening the bedclothes, telling him the news of the day. But that was the role of a wife and she was not his wife. She was engaged to the man who had saved his leg.

Then one afternoon, Timothy called her at the post office. 'I'm going to Twin Falls Hospital to pick up Mum,' he told her. 'Would you like to come with me?'

Rebecca's heart jolted with excitement but not because of Timothy's mother.

The weather was sweltering but the wake of dust that plumed out from under the car wheels made it impossible to open the windows more than halfway. Rebecca had to keep shifting position to stop her back sticking to the seat. The dry spell everyone had been predicting seemed to be upon them and the countryside was a sea of brown grass. Even the leaves on the resilient gum trees were curling and falling. They passed a creek that was a mere ribbon of stagnant water. 'We'll have trouble with bushfires if this keeps up,' Timothy said.

Rebecca did not want to think about fires. They passed the whaling station, which was almost deserted now the hunting season was over. Most of the whalers had taken up work on nearby farms, slaughtering sheep and cattle in the off-seasons, but Sanders Olsen had stayed on. She could see him hosing down a small boat. She and Stefan had stopped the factory ship, but that did not seem enough to make up for Berit's death. Now she hated the man even more, sure that he had lit the fire at Stefan's house in collusion with George Pike.

'What do you say to getting married before Christmas?' Timothy asked. 'I don't see any reason to wait. It's not my first marriage. People don't expect a long engagement.'

Rebecca felt stung. Up until that point she hadn't thought of herself as a 'second wife'. But as Timothy hadn't said it maliciously, she pushed her hurt aside. 'All right,' she said. 'I don't have any family to inform, so I can't see any reason to wait either. I will only invite my best friend.'

'That's right, your great-aunt is too frail to come,' he said, keeping his eyes ahead of him. 'Why don't you send her a letter? We can pay her a visit sometime in the new year.'

Rebecca had been caught out. She fiddled with the clasp of her purse. Had he done it intentionally? Had he guessed there had never been a great-aunt and was testing her? Part of her wanted to confess her lie, but something stopped her like a brake on a car.

'All right. Aunty May would love that,' she said, hoping that the subject of Aunty May would somehow get forgotten when the new year came around.

Mrs Litchfield was already dressed and sitting in her wheelchair when Rebecca and Timothy arrived at the hospital. While Timothy was filling in the discharge paperwork, Rebecca excused herself to go to the ladies' room. She made her way down the corridor and towards the men's ward. But when she peered in through the round windows of the double-doors she couldn't see Stefan in any of the beds.

'May I help you?' a nurse asked Rebecca.

She shook her head and continued on down the corridor. Then she spotted him through the glass doors at the end of it, sitting in an armchair on the veranda and staring at the ocean, a walking stick by his side. She remembered the first time she had seen him emerging from the sea. The words he had said to her during the fire about Dunkel came back to her: *Return him to the ocean. Set him free.*

'Hello.'

Stefan turned to her. 'Rebecca.'

She glanced over her shoulder. 'I can't stay long. I'm here with Timothy to pick up his mother, but I wanted to say goodbye.'

Stefan winced and looked back out to the ocean. 'If you are sure that your decision is right for you, I won't argue with you.' Then taking her hand in his, he added, 'But if you need anything, you can always write to me.' He gave her the name of the Menzies Hotel in Melbourne. 'I'll be there for some months yet, until my leg has completely healed. Then I'll be sailing to London.'

London, thought Rebecca. The largest city in the world. She imagined all the sights she had loved so much when she had visited with Ned: the shows in the West End, shopping on Bond Street, the Thames by night. She'd heard that coffee and espresso bars were springing up everywhere, filled with poets, philosophers, actors and writers.

'I'd better go.' She turned towards the door but hesitated, looking over her shoulder for one last glimpse of him. 'We'll always be friends,' she told Stefan. 'In our hearts, I mean.'

He smiled sadly. 'We will always be friends in our heads, Rebecca. In our hearts we will always be more than that.'

★

Rebecca kept the loss she felt over Stefan hidden and made plans for the wedding, which was to take place the Saturday after her birthday. After she and Timothy had made the official announcement of their engagement in *The Twin Falls Advocate*, the town was aflutter with the news. Timothy told everyone the story of how he had surprised her with his mother's engagement ring. It would not be fair to him if she didn't play the part of the excited bride.

Rebecca called Marion. 'I want to warn you it's not a rich playboy I'm marrying,' she told her. 'It's the town doctor.'

'Good Lord! The town doctor!' replied Marion, with a whimsical note in her voice. 'I had a physician lover once. He certainly knew his anatomy!'

Rebecca smiled, thankful that the whaling season would not be in swing when Marion came to stay. As adaptable as she was, she could not see Marion abiding the stink. 'Can you get me a dress?' she asked her. 'Something simple and *modest*.'

'Of course I can, darling. Leave it with me.'

Rebecca put the receiver down and stared at the ring on her finger. She was going to get married. She was going to be someone's wife and have her own home. She was even going to be taken to the restaurant at Twin Falls by Timothy for her birthday instead of feeling she couldn't do anything pleasurable on that day out of respect for Debbie. She would always love Debbie, but she couldn't mourn her sister – or punish herself – any longer. Life was changing rapidly. It all seemed like some strange fantasy she had cooked up in her head. When she had arrived in Shipwreck Bay she would have thought it was the last place she was going to find a husband.

A chill ran down her spine and she sensed someone behind her. She turned to see Nancy standing in the doorway of the sorting room, a bulging spiral-bound scrapbook tucked under her arm. The cover was navy blue and gilt-edged. It looked official, like the kind of scrapbook a police detective or lawyer might carry.

'*Something simple and modest*,' Nancy said, her eyes burning into Rebecca's face. 'Oh *please*! Ring your friend back and tell her not to waste the money.'

The tone of her voice was enough to convey that any hope Rebecca had held of a truce between them was gone.

Nancy threw the scrapbook on the table and flicked through it. Rebecca recoiled when she saw it was filled with newspaper cuttings, all of them about Ned McKell's 'Mystery Woman'. Interspersed with the articles were pieces cut out of *The Home*

Detective. They were scribbled over in some places and underlined in others. Nancy smiled to herself as she flipped through the pages. 'I know you and McKell were lovers,' she told Rebecca. 'I suspected it the first day you turned up out of the blue with your fancy clothes and your fancy airs! A postmistress indeed! McKell saying your name at the meeting only confirmed it. But what I didn't have was proof … until now!' She stopped at a page and pushed the scrapbook across the table towards where Rebecca was sitting. Rebecca looked down to see the article from *The Sydney Morning Herald*, the one with the picture of her and Ned leaving the Celebrity Club together. Rebecca was blonde in it and her face was hidden in the shadows.

'That's you!' Nancy said.

Rebecca kept her voice steady. 'That could be anybody.'

Nancy watched her keenly. Her eyes were bright and excited. 'Everyone has been speculating about the hair, the height and the figure,' she said. 'But Sherlock Holmes said, "To a great mind nothing is little." I've been saying that to myself about you over and over again. "Look for the little things. Look for the tiny clues." Then I found it.'

She opened her purse and took out a magnifying glass and held it over the image for Rebecca to see. 'There!' Nancy said, holding it over the hand Rebecca had linked around Ned's arm in the picture. 'The ring.'

Rebecca felt herself pale. She did see it. It was the white gold and onyx cocktail ring Ned had bought her at the auction, the one that Stefan had bid against him for.

Nancy straightened. 'I'm not going to stand by and let you destroy Doctor Litchfield. You will not be breaking his heart.'

Rebecca's muscles tensed. She drew up every ounce of courage she had in her to call Nancy's bluff. Nancy had never played bridge with the real Rebecca; she had only played it with the one who had deliberately *let* her win.

'He knows,' she said, flatly. 'I've already told him. He knows everything and he still wants to marry me.'

Nancy paused and frowned. Rebecca kept going. 'He hasn't told anybody because he wants to marry me more than anything. If you call the press it will be *you* who destroys his happiness.'

'What's going on?' a furtive voice called from the main area. It was Marge. 'I can hear you two arguing!'

Nancy gathered the scrapbook and narrowed her eyes at Rebecca. 'This isn't finished,' she said.

At that moment Johnny lumbered in the back door. His mouth dropped open when he saw Nancy standing in the sorting room. What he was thinking was written all over his face: 'What have I done now?'

Nancy looked from Rebecca to Johnny then stormed out. Rebecca rushed after her like a dog chasing an intruder out of its yard. She stopped when she saw Marge's distressed expression and deliberately relaxed her shoulders.

'Don't worry, Marge,' she said as Nancy slammed the post office door behind her. 'The shire secretary's wife and I just had some words. She keeps complaining about Johnny not whistling at every house. But I don't think it's necessary, do you? It's not as if everybody lives miles apart.'

Marge bit her lip as if she wanted to believe Rebecca but wasn't convinced. 'No, I suppose not,' she said, glancing over Rebecca's shoulder at Johnny.

'Good grief, Miss Wood,' said Johnny, approaching the counter. 'I didn't expect you to have to stand up for me. Mrs Pike's always got a bee in her bonnet about something.'

'That's right, Johnny,' said Rebecca, feigning calm although her heart was pounding in her chest. She rested her palms down on the counter. But when she glanced at her hands she saw how irrevocably she was doomed. On her left hand was the hideous engagement ring Timothy had proposed with and on the right was the white gold and onyx ring that had given her away.

★

After her encounter with Nancy it was impossible for Rebecca to carry on as normal. She was trembling so much that people would notice if she stayed at the post office. She needed peace and quiet to work out her next move. She feigned a migraine and asked Johnny to take charge of the post office for the rest of the afternoon. Back at her house she lay on her bed and stared at the ceiling. She really only had one choice now, and that was to tell Timothy the truth. She was certain he wouldn't want to marry her anymore, but he was an honourable man and might still wish to protect her. Perhaps he would be a buffer and stop Nancy alerting the press.

She sat up and swung her feet to the floor. The door to her wardrobe was open and she eyed a persimmon-coloured evening gown with a fitted bodice and a shoulder drape. She had bought it in Paris. She wondered why she had not tried harder to look like an ordinary postmistress, why she had not been able to let go of her delusions of grandeur? Stefan's words came back to her: *What if you were a great society hostess? What if the most brilliant artists, pioneers and statesmen of our time were guests at your dinner table? What if you travelled the world, read important books and filled your house with great works of art instead of children and toys? Would you still feel lonely then?*

'Yes,' Rebecca said quietly to herself. 'I would still feel lonely because I am a woman that men desire but don't love.'

★

Since Timothy had brought his mother home from hospital, Rebecca had been joining them every evening for dinner. But when she arrived at the house, Gillian was still napping upstairs and Timothy was alone.

'I have received the most puzzling message from Nancy Pike,' he told her. 'She dropped a note in the letterbox saying that she wants to see me this evening on an urgent personal matter. Do you have any idea what it is about?'

Rebecca had been determined to tell him the truth but now found herself unable to do so. Twinges of regret pained her. He was a good-looking man and so kind. There was a time when she had been hesitant about marrying him. Now the wedding was never going to happen. She was like a fly in a spider's web, trapped and helpless. Every part of her felt paralysed. All she could do was watch in horror now as Nancy waited to devour her.

She shook her head.

He smiled at her and nudged her with his arm. 'I have a feeling Mrs Pike wants a role in our wedding ceremony, that's what I think this is all about. She probably knows you aren't too keen on her, so she decided to try me. It's better that you come with me. We have to present a united front. We can't have her playing us off against each other now, can we?'

'No,' Rebecca replied, unable to look Timothy in the eye. She realised she might never have the courage – or the right – to do so again after Nancy revealed who she was.

Smiling, he put his arm out to link with hers. 'Come on then. Let's get this over with before dinner. Do you think we could offer her a role reading from the Bible to stop her interfering in anything else?'

On their way to Nancy's house, Timothy chattered about Iris Young's pregnancy, the new matron at Twin Falls Hospital and the vegetables he was going to cultivate that season, while Rebecca imagined the many different ways Nancy might reveal all to Timothy and the many ways he could react, none of them good. She disappeared somewhere inside herself, wondering what it might have been like to be a normal woman. Not a woman with a past, not a woman who had made terrible decisions, not a woman whose passions were about to destroy her. She didn't understand why she couldn't just stop and tell Timothy the truth right now, or why she was going with him to Nancy's house like a prisoner to the executioner. Did she hope that Nancy might see them together and change her mind?

Timothy knocked on the Pikes' front door but nobody answered. 'George and Earl are at a Boy Scouts camp,' he said, 'but the lady of the house should be home.' He hesitated and then knocked again. 'Mrs Pike?' he called. But there was still no answer.

Rebecca wondered if Nancy was already going house to house, telling everyone what she had discovered. Timothy walked around the rear of the house and she followed him. The glazed sliding door off the patio was partially open. Timothy opened it wider and peered inside.

'Mrs Pike!' he called again.

An icy sensation rippled over Rebecca's skin. It was something more than her dread of Nancy. 'Something's wrong,' she said.

Timothy turned to her and frowned. 'What makes you say that?'

Rebecca pushed past him and into the kitchen then towards to the sunroom where the card game had been played. She did not like creeping around someone else's home, but she desperately wanted to bring this thing with Nancy to a head. The house still reeked of Glamorene carpet cleaner and cigarettes but also something else that she couldn't identify. A blocked drain? A dead mouse? She pushed open the sunroom door and a shape on the floor caught her eye. In the fading daylight she thought she was looking at a pile of damask fabric, but then she saw a female foot with the toenails painted pink. She stepped towards it and realised the pile was Nancy, lying in the foetal position with her face turned towards the floor. Had she fallen?

Rebecca knelt beside her. The rug was damp on her knees. 'Nancy?'

She put her hand on Nancy's shoulder and recoiled when she found her flesh lifeless and cold. Then she saw the knife buried in her back, right up to the hilt. Rebecca reeled and stood up. Her hands were covered in blood. Then she realised the rug was soaked with it. Two large splotches stained her skirt at the knees. Her vision turned blurry.

'Help! Help!' she rasped breathlessly.

Timothy rushed into the room. He put his fingers to Nancy's throat but it was immediately clear there was no pulse. Rebecca leaned against a trophy cabinet, trembling with shock. Of all the ways that she had expected the evening to end, Nancy's death had not been one of them.

CHAPTER TWENTY-EIGHT

The morning light jabbed at Rebecca's eyes when she opened them. The room seemed to spin a few degrees. It was not her bedroom and yet the house seemed familiar, the cream walls and dark teak furniture. The bed cover was a muted shade of green. She squinted. Mrs Todd was sitting in an armchair by the window, knitting. She looked up when Rebecca stirred.

'Are you waking up, my dear?'

Mrs Todd went out the door and a few moments later Timothy appeared, holding a metal kidney dish. He took Rebecca's wrist in his warm fingers, feeling for her pulse. 'You're safe, Rebecca,' he told her. 'But you need more rest.'

He wiped something cold on her arm and then she felt the prick of a needle.

'She's had a terrible shock,' Mrs Todd said. 'Sleep is the best thing. Thank God you weren't both in the house while the killer was still there.'

'We can't be sure he wasn't …'

Rebecca's eyes closed and her limbs sank into the bed as if they were weighted down with lead. But her sleep was disturbed by terrifying images: Nancy's body lying on the floor, the blood-soaked rug. She recalled sitting in the parlour downstairs with a blanket over her shoulders but being unable to keep warm. The police sergeant had tried to ask her questions but her teeth were chattering and he couldn't make sense of her gibberish.

Sometime later she heard men's voices floating up from the floor below and caught snatches of conversations: 'detective', 'murder', 'maybe tomorrow'. Then Timothy's voice, 'Thank you. You have been most understanding.'

★

The sunset was sending rays of bright orange around the room when Rebecca's eyes opened widely this time. She blinked, and then pressed herself up into a sitting position. Her arms were wobbly and her skin felt clammy, as if she had a fever. The smell of tomatoes cooking wafted around the room. She pushed the covers off herself and saw that she was wearing only her slip. 'Mrs Todd?' she asked. But there was no answer. The room was empty. She sat up higher and ran her hand over her face. Then the events of the previous evening flashed before her again and she winced. She swung her feet out of the bed and tried to stand up.

'Rebecca. It's too soon for you to get out of bed.'

Timothy was standing in the doorway, a tray of soup and bread in his hands. She obeyed him and climbed back into the bed. He put the tray down on her lap and took the cover from the soup.

'You had better eat something,' he said.

Rebecca was conscious of him watching her as she tasted a spoonful of the rich soup. She didn't have an appetite but for some reason did not want to displease him by not accepting the food. When she finished the soup, he took the tray away from her and placed it on the table next to the bed.

'Is there something you need to tell me?' he asked. 'Was there some sort of trouble between you and Mrs Pike?'

She flinched at the sharpness of his voice. He had never used that tone with her before.

'No, I—'

He cut her off. 'Don't lie to me *anymore*, Rebecca. Please.'

There was a look of suspicion in his eyes that sent her floundering. She couldn't bring herself to speak.

'I've gone against God and my own moral code and lied for you, Rebecca. You owe me the truth.'

'You lied for me?'

He walked to the window and stared out at the garden. 'Can't you see the trouble you are in? Everyone knows that you and Mrs Pike weren't friends. Then Marge tells the detectives from Wollongong that she heard the two of you having an argument in the post office yesterday. Johnny, trying to be helpful no doubt, apparently told the police that you went home with a migraine.' He turned to her. 'Nobody can vouch for where you were for most of the afternoon. Nobody … except me.'

Rebecca couldn't feel her fingers and toes. She was turning numb, like someone slowly freezing to death.

'This morning the detectives were ready to arrest you. They said that they found evidence that Mrs Pike was blackmailing you – a scrapbook or something that linked you to Ned McKell.

As soon as they said that, I suddenly understood it all: your reticence to talk about your past, your reticence to talk about anything really. What could I do? Everything was pointing to you as a murderess. I gave you an alibi and then stalled the detectives by sedating you until we had a chance to speak.'

Rebecca had thought that the worst thing that could happen to her was to be torn to shreds in a press scandal over an affair. Now the fear gripping her told her that things could be much worse. She could be accused of murder, hanged for it even.

'I didn't kill her, Timothy,' she said, barely able to get her words out. 'Surely you can't believe that!'

Timothy stared at her, and then he pursed his lips. 'No, Rebecca, I don't believe you did. Otherwise I couldn't have lied for you. But you must tell me the truth now ... about everything.'

Rebecca's heart was racing so fast she could barely breathe.

'I was Ned McKell's mistress!' she blurted out. 'I am the mystery woman the press keeps talking about.'

There, it was out now. Her dirty little secret. She was a despicable woman for treating a fine person like Timothy so poorly. How could she even have considered marrying him when she had kept so much hidden from him?

Timothy sank into the chair next to her bed and pressed his face into his hands. 'Who are you, Rebecca?' He looked up at her, his mouth contorted with pain. 'Do you even love me? I was going to bring you into this house to live with my mother! And now I've lied to the police, to protect my future *wife*.'

The familiar bone-crushing fear of being rejected gripped Rebecca. She could see the esteem Timothy had once held her in vanish from his face, just as it had from her parents' faces the day Debbie died. Why had she not been honest with him sooner? He might not have liked her past, but he would have respected her more if she hadn't hidden it from him.

Rebecca dug her nails into her hands. 'What did you say to the police?'

'I told them that we were together at your house the whole afternoon … making love,' he said, looking away from her. 'It was the only thing I could think of quickly.'

'Timothy, I'm so sorry!' she cried. 'I never wanted to hurt you. I was so very afraid, and that's why I didn't tell you about my past.'

Timothy grimaced and shook his head. He walked to the door but when he reached it he turned back and looked at her, his expression cold. 'What will happen to Mum if I end up in prison as your accomplice? Just tell the police the same story I gave them. You're a seasoned liar, so it shouldn't be too difficult for you. I'm sure you will bear the humiliation with as much fortitude as I have had to. Then we'll leave it at that, shall we?'

He shut the door behind him.

Rebecca curled up her legs and pressed her chin to her knees. 'My God!' she said. 'What have I done?' But then an even more horrifying thought occurred to her. She hadn't killed Nancy. So who had – and why?

CHAPTER TWENTY-NINE

Iris Young peered into Rebecca's face before passing her the packet she had come to post. 'Should you be working today, Miss Wood? You look ill.'

Rebecca took the packet from her and placed it on the scales. Her mind was slow. If she'd had her choice, she wouldn't be at the post office. She'd have knocked herself out with Timothy's sedatives and spent the whole day in a coma, anything to stop the terror that was preventing her from thinking clearly. The police sergeant had telephoned to tell her that the two detectives from Wollongong would question her later in the morning. She had thought it best to try to act as normally as possible. 'It stops me thinking about what happened,' she told Iris. 'I'm better when I'm busy.'

Iris nodded. 'Yes, sometimes it is better to keep yourself occupied. It's such a terrible thing to have happened! Here in Shipwreck Bay!'

Rebecca could barely hear her through the blood pounding in her ears. She had spent the previous night being sick into a bucket. She wasn't sure if her queasiness had been the after-effect of the sedatives or a symptom of her stark fear. Timothy had given her an alibi, but what if the police hadn't believed it? And if they already knew that Nancy was threatening to expose her, then they would also know she was Ned McKell's mystery woman. Wouldn't that cast a doubt over anything she might say?

Iris left and Rebecca returned to her desk, her body stiff and leaden. She remembered the weeks leading up to the execution of Florence Dunne in Victoria the previous year. Whether a woman should hang for her crimes had been fiercely debated in parliament and discussed at every dinner party she'd attended. On one occasion the prime minister had asked his dinner guests if they thought Florence Dunne should be executed. 'It doesn't sit well with me to see a woman hang,' he said. 'Let her work for her crime, I say, and become a useful member of society. I believe she was exploited by the men who used her to lure victims.'

It was Rebecca who had spoken up in defence of the punishment. 'A person who has broken the law must be prepared to take the consequences,' she said. 'If she took part in a heinous crime, why is she less responsible than the men?'

A reporter who had been there to witness the execution had later described it in gruesome detail for Rebecca. 'Dunne fainted just before she was hung and had to be tied to a chair for the act. The choice of beige slacks was a bad one. She soiled herself, of course. There was no dignity about the thing at all.'

That last detail made Rebecca shudder. Nobody had been hanged in New South Wales since 1939, but if the public had been prepared to metaphorically lynch her over the affair with Ned, how much stronger would the outcry be against her for murder? She picked up her pen and notepad and tried to distract herself with correspondence, but her imagination conjured images of future dinner parties where guests were tut-tutting over the fate of Rebecca Wood. 'That sort of woman never comes to any good …'

★

The bell on the counter rang. The local police sergeant, Bill Hurley, was there with two men in suits. Bill had 'small town police sergeant' written all over him: beer belly, double-chin, puffy blue eyes. The two other men were sleeker, one in his early thirties, the other in his late forties. They both wore three-piece suits and their sharp-looking eyes scrutinised her from their freshly shaven faces.

'Miss Wood,' said Sergeant Hurley, his shoulders twitching nervously. 'This is Detective Blake and Detective Tarbell, from Wollongong. They want to ask you a few questions about how you and Doctor Litchfield discovered Mrs Pike's body.'

Detective Blake, the older of the two, pulled a pen and notepad from his breast pocket. 'Your full name, age and address, please, Miss Wood.'

He looked her in the eye and made her feel self-conscious. There was something lewd in the way he regarded her. Was it because he knew she had been Ned McKell's mistress or because her alibi was that she'd been sleeping with the town doctor?

After she had answered his questions, he asked her to explain how she had found Nancy. She was careful to relate the same story that Timothy had given in his statement, leaving out the indelicate detail of their lovemaking. 'My fiancé and I spent the afternoon together at my home and then we went to the Pikes' house to speak to Nancy before dinner.'

Sergeant Hurley stood at ease by the door but Detective Tarbell slowly paced the floor while Rebecca was talking. He glanced at the garden out the window, contemplated the portrait of the queen and studied the official noticeboard. He gave the appearance of not paying attention, but Rebecca could tell that he was listening to every word she said.

When she described the manner in which she'd found Nancy, Detective Blake flipped his notebook and revised something. Rebecca was conscious of a drop of perspiration running down her back.

'Doctor Litchfield went into the house with you but you were the first to come upon Mrs Pike's body, is that correct?' Detective Blake asked, finally.

Rebecca nodded. 'Yes, that's correct.'

Again Detective Blake went back over previous notes. He frowned, as if puzzling over some inconsistency. Her chest burned and she thought she was on the verge of being sick again, but she quelled her stomach by sheer force of will. She had to keep reminding herself that she hadn't actually killed Nancy.

Detective Blake looked up from his notes to Rebecca, and then back again. The floor felt as though it was vibrating underneath her feet, and she realised she was trembling. Then his eyes settled on her face once and for all.

'Can you tell me why you went to see Mrs Pike? What was the nature of your visit?'

Rebecca took a breath. 'We went there to speak to her about our wedding plans. We wanted to ask her to give a Bible reading in the church.'

Detective Blake wrote down her words but his expression gave nothing away. Then he abruptly closed his notebook and said, 'That's all we need.'

Rebecca paused, unsure if he'd meant that she had given him all the information he was after, or whether he now had all he needed to arrest her. She was relieved when he made ready to leave. He nodded to Detective Tarbell and Sergeant Hurley. It seemed the questioning was over and they were satisfied, but Rebecca couldn't leave it that. She had to know something of what they had suspected. 'Do you know who might have killed her?' she asked.

Detective Blake turned back to her.

'I live on my own,' she added, hastily. 'I'm afraid.'

Sergeant Hurley answered her question. 'There have been a number of burglaries along the coast,' he said. 'Mr Pike is confirming it for us, but it appears an item of his wife's jewellery is missing. If I were you, Miss Wood, I'd go stay with Mrs Campbell until we catch the culprit.'

Staying with Doris would be insupportable under the best of circumstances but she thanked Sergeant Hurley for his advice.

CHAPTER THIRTY

After she finished at the post office, Rebecca went to the beach. She sat on a rock and gazed out at the waves, trying to make sense of all that had happened. She would have to leave Shipwreck Bay now and start over again somewhere else. It was as if her affair with Ned had transformed her into a vagabond, destined to keep moving and never have anywhere to call home.

Her eyes followed the path of a seagull. She uttered a cry of surprise when she found Timothy standing behind her. He seemed out of place on the beach in his pressed trousers and shirt, his tie flapping in the breeze. His shoulders were slumped and his face was tired and sad. She loathed knowing she was the cause of his unhappiness.

'Hello, Timothy,' she said.

'Did the detectives speak to you?'

She nodded. 'I told them the same thing you did. They seemed to believe it.'

He didn't say anything, and glanced at the path as if he was thinking of leaving but remained on the spot.

'I'm going to apply for a transfer and make a fresh start,' she told him.

'You don't have to go, Rebecca. I won't tell anybody about your past.'

Her heart pinched at his kindness. 'I never meant to hurt you the way that I did. I hope you can believe that.'

He stepped closer to her. 'I assume you didn't, Rebecca. I don't have the impression that you are vindictive.'

'Don't be kind to me,' she said, looking away. 'I haven't been honest with you in other ways too. Stefan Otto and I were lovers, briefly. But that's over now.'

He sat down beside her. 'I know that,' he said. 'I'm not blind.'

She turned back to him, questioning him with her eyes.

Timothy picked up a stick and began drawing in the sand with it. 'I hoped you would eventually see Stefan Otto for the phoney that he is and choose me.' He stood up and flicked the stick out into the ocean. It bobbed on the waves for a few moments and spun, before it was washed away. 'I should have realised I'm not exciting enough for a woman like you,' he said, returning to his place on the rock. 'I'm just a country doctor, a rather sad and pathetic one who lives with his invalid mother.'

'That's not how I see you at all!' protested Rebecca. 'I think you are a very good man. *Too* good for me, if I'm honest.'

Timothy rubbed his finger over his eyebrow and frowned. 'Arabella's deceit nearly destroyed me. I can't stand lying, Rebecca. I simply cannot stand it!'

'I know,' said Rebecca, working the engagement ring off her finger. 'That's why I will go.'

Timothy's eyes rounded. 'Who says we can't still get married, if that's something you want too. I can provide a good life for you here in Shipwreck Bay.'

'Timothy, after all that I've done ...'

He took her hand and pushed the engagement ring back onto her finger. 'If a man truly loves a woman then he will forgive her,' he said. 'I know all about your past now, Rebecca.' His eyes looked over her face and he smiled. 'It doesn't matter to me who you used to be but who you will become.'

Rebecca felt panicked but elated at the same time. Isn't this what she had always wanted? To be loved and cherished? To be forgiven? 'I don't deserve you ...'

His features softened. Then he moved closer to her and brushed her cheek with the backs of his fingers. 'That's for me to decide. I think in time you will see how much you deserve me.'

'I look forward to that,' Rebecca replied, leaning against his shoulder and smiling.

CHAPTER THIRTY-ONE

Nancy's funeral was a showy affair. People flooded in for it from the surrounding countryside and as far as Sydney and Wollongong. The mourners filled the pews and the choir gallery and spilled out onto the church steps. The Country Women's Association committee formed a guard of honour and the flag outside the memorial hall was set at half-mast. Rebecca could barely bring herself to look at Nancy's casket, covered in white roses, when she and Timothy took their place in a pew. Doris was pumping out a hymn on the organ and Rebecca stared at her prayer book to shut out the memory of the night they had found Nancy's body.

She had attended funerals of people she hardly knew – public figures and socialites – but she had never been at a funeral for a woman who had hated her and intended to destroy her. Her nemesis was dead. She could no longer wreak havoc on her life. Timothy had told her that he had tactfully probed George to see if there was any evidence that could incriminate Rebecca, but it seemed there was none.

'The police must have taken the scrapbook,' he told her. 'It doesn't seem to be in George's possession.'

Indeed, Rebecca had heard nothing further from Detectives Blake and Tarbell. It seemed that any suspicion of her had amounted to nothing. They must have concluded that no one in the town had a motive and the murderer was probably long gone. They didn't seem to have any inclination to expose Rebecca as Ned McKell's former mistress either. For the past few days, Rebecca had expected to find the press on her doorstep at any moment. But nothing happened. She reached for Timothy's arm and squeezed it. For the first time since Nancy's death, she felt that she could breathe again.

★

After the burial the mourners met at the memorial hall for the wake. Rebecca stayed glued to Timothy's side, deliberately avoiding Nancy's clique, although Marge, Joy and Carmel kept glancing in her direction. How dare Marge have insinuated to the detectives that she might have killed Nancy! If Timothy hadn't lied for her, Rebecca could have been arrested and sent to prison – and worse!

But try as she might, Rebecca could not avoid Doris.

'Oh dear, oh dear,' said Doris, sidling up to Rebecca and blowing her nose loudly into her handkerchief. 'It's terrible, just terrible. A wonderful wife and mother cut down in the prime of her life. Our town will never be the same without Nancy.'

No, thought Rebecca, leaning backwards, trying to distance herself from Doris's phlegm. Thank God!

'I don't know who is going to organise things now,' continued Doris, patting at her red nose. 'We all looked up to Nancy, didn't we? She was one of a kind.'

'She certainly was,' agreed Rebecca.

'It will be hard for George and Earl,' said Timothy. 'I know they have appreciated all the women in the town who have been cooking and cleaning for them.'

'Oh, it's the least we can do,' said Doris, shaking her head. 'George wants to send Earl to Nancy's cousins in Bathurst for a while. He says the change of scenery will do the boy good.'

They all turned to Earl, who was standing near the food table and biting into a sponge cake, jam and cream oozing down his chin. Rebecca hadn't cared for Nancy and she didn't like George, but she did feel sorry for Earl. She hoped for his sake Nancy's cousins were nothing like his parents.

Bob Hill called Timothy over to join in a conversation that was taking place on the other side of the room. Rebecca would have liked to have gone with him but it was only men from the farms gathered together, so she had no choice other than to stay with Doris. Her landlady leaned towards her and said in a lowered voice, 'I believe it was that awful Stefan Otto who did it! Everybody knows he's never got over Nancy!'

Rebecca could feel her face flush. 'That was years ago,' she said. 'If Stefan Otto was so vengeful, why would he have waited until now?'

'Perhaps because of George's efforts regarding the factory ship. It stirred up memories of the first time George had got the better of him.'

Rebecca considered having someone arrested as a Nazi spy and sent to a camp a little bit more than just having 'got the better of him'. 'Then he would have killed George, not Nancy,' she replied, barely able to keep her irritation hidden. 'Besides that, Stefan Otto still can't walk normally after the skin grafts.' Out of the corner of her eye she spotted Mrs Turner, Johnny's mother. The woman wasn't much of a conversationalist but she'd bear anything to get away from Doris's smear campaign. She was about to make some excuse for why she needed to speak with her, when Doris grabbed her arm.

'It's the jewellery that gives him away, isn't it?'

Rebecca shrugged. 'The missing jewellery is probably what made the police believe it was a burglary gone wrong.'

Doris peered at Rebecca. 'It was her wedding ring that was taken. *Nothing else.* Nancy's pearls were still around her neck and her jewellery box wasn't touched. If it was a simple burglary, isn't that rather odd?'

Rebecca turned to the doorway and thought she was suffering a hallucination. Detectives Blake and Tarbell were standing there, looking directly at her. The hair rose on the back of her neck. Had they changed their mind about her innocence? They walked in her direction. The mourners noticed them and one by one turned quiet as the two men strode past Rebecca and Doris and towards George and Father Rob.

Detective Tarbell produced a pair of handcuffs. 'George Pike, you are under arrest for the murder of your wife, Nancy ...'

His words were drowned out by the collective gasp that rose from the mourners.

George clapped his hands over his face like a child trying

to hide. 'No!' he said. 'I did not kill my wife! You have made a mistake!'

Detective Tarbell grabbed George's hands and pried them away from his face. He pulled them behind his back to handcuff him.

'I didn't kill her!' George protested as the police led him out of the hall.

The mourners rushed out after the men. They blinked and gasped as the shire secretary, the most powerful man in Shipwreck Bay, was pushed into the back of the police car. George's face crumpled. He sobbed and shook his head when Detective Tarbell slammed the car door shut.

'Dad!' cried Earl, running towards the car and slapping his cake-smeared hands on the rear window. 'Dad!'

Frank gently pulled the boy away from the car and Elaine held him tight. 'Shh, shh,' she whispered, rubbing his shoulders, 'it will be all right.'

The mourners watched in disbelief as the police car took off and headed in the direction of the northern road.

'He couldn't have killed Nancy, could he?' Bob Hill asked.

The gathering exchanged glances but not one person had an answer to that question.

★

Rebecca and Timothy waited on the platform for the train from Sydney to arrive. When it came into the station, Johnny approached the guard's compartment to collect the mail but stopped short and gaped. Stepping out of the train in all her sartorial glory was Marion, accompanied by her poodle, Tipsy. The conductor placed the five suitcases she had brought with her on the platform. Marion was always one for having plenty of changes of outfits even when she was only staying for two days. Dressed in a Givenchy floral dress, she tilted her sunglasses and looked around the station. Despite the sea breeze, not a strand of her black hair moved out of place. She waved when she saw Rebecca and Timothy.

'Darlings!' she called out, sashaying towards them on her white pointed shoes. 'What a beautiful couple!'

Ernie burst out of his office, pushing a trolley. He loaded Marion's suitcases onto it without taking his eyes off her.

Marion kissed Rebecca then took Timothy's hands in her gloved ones.

'It's a pleasure to meet you, Miss Bedford,' Timothy told her, glancing at Tipsy who was sniffing his shoe. 'We've set up a room for you in my house where I hope you'll be comfortable.'

Marion's smile was like sunshine. 'Darling, I'll be comfortable wherever you put me. All that matters to me is that you will take good care of my friend Becky here.'

Rebecca liked seeing her friend with fresh eyes. Marion loved glamour. She sought the high life but she was never a snob. She was always so full of fun and adventure; it was true she probably would have been just as happy to have been given the spare bedroom in Rebecca's 'doll's house'. Friendship, clothes and fun were all that mattered to her.

When they arrived at Timothy's house, Marion admired every detail. 'Oh, charming! Charming! Charming!' she said, studying the floral paintings and running her hands over the seafoam-green furnishings. 'Green is such a soothing colour, isn't it?'

Rebecca caught Timothy's eye and he winked at her but a stiffness around his mouth made her wonder if he was not feeling as playful as his gesture seemed to imply. Was it possible he didn't like Marion but was trying not to show it? She very much wanted him to like her closest friend.

'I'm sure you two have a lot to talk about for the wedding tomorrow,' Timothy said, picking up his jacket and hat. 'And I had better see the last of my patients before Rebecca and I head off on our honeymoon.'

Timothy kissed Rebecca firmly on the lips and she put any doubts down to bridal nerves. Of course he would like Marion. Who couldn't like her?

Upstairs in the guest room, Marion whisked Rebecca's dress out of the largest suitcase she had brought. It was a fit-and-flare style with a puffy skirt and a bateau neckline. Rebecca fingered the delicate silk. 'It's perfect!' she said. 'I knew you'd pick just the right thing.'

Marion sat down at the dressing table and glanced around the room with a delighted expression on her face. 'Your fiancé looks so adoringly at you, Becky, I'm so happy for you. But why does he call you Rebecca and not Becky?'

Rebecca lay out the veil Marion had brought for her: waist-length lace attached to a crown of silk roses. She had purposely hidden her engagement ring as soon as Timothy had left the house. Marion wouldn't have said a bad word about it, but she didn't want her to think less of him because of its gaudiness. From the way she had designed the garden, Rebecca had perceived

Gillian as having had a keen sense of beauty. She found it hard to believe that her future mother-in-law could have ever worn the ghastly thing. 'I don't know,' she said. 'He is quite formal in many ways. Although he does call his mother Mum.'

'It goes with being a doctor, I suppose,' said Marion, calling Tipsy to her and playing with his ears. 'You know I had never heard of Shipwreck Bay until you mentioned it and then that terrible story of the man who murdered his wife.'

Rebecca sat on the edge of the bed. 'George and Nancy Pike were like the king and queen of this town and it has put such a dampener on everything. I suggested to Timothy that perhaps we should postpone our wedding, but he wouldn't hear of it. He thinks it's just the thing to lift everybody's spirits and that people will look up to us in place of the Pikes.'

'Doctors always tell you that life must go on, don't they?' said Marion. Then, thinking of something else, her eyes lit up. 'Anyway, I'm glad you didn't postpone it, otherwise I would have missed it. Guess where I'm off to next week? Egypt!'

'Egypt!'

'Yes,' said Marion, turning around to face the mirror and preening her already perfect hair. 'For five months! I'm travelling with the Nortons and a rather dashing retired naval officer by the name of Captain Campsie.' She clapped her hands together. 'Why don't you and Timothy come? You can make it your honeymoon!'

A sharp pain pricked Rebecca's heart. 'Unfortunately, that would be out of the question. It was hard enough to convince Timothy to take four days off to go to Penguin Bay. He has all his patients relying on him, and his mother of course.'

'Oh, that's right,' said Marion. 'She's an invalid, isn't she?

Well, never mind.' Then lowering her voice, she said, 'One day she'll kick the bucket and then the two of you will be as free as birds to go wherever you like.'

Rebecca smiled, but the truth had dawned on her a while ago. In marrying Timothy, the furthest she would get from Shipwreck Bay might be Sydney or Melbourne. Timothy had been quite adamant that since his war service he never wanted to leave Australia again. Rebecca saw she had no choice but to let the dream of being a world traveller fade; she had also been persuaded by Timothy to send all her fancy evening gowns and dresses to charity. 'You have got to let the past go,' he'd told her. 'You are not a glamour girl anymore; you are going to be a doctor's wife. Get a catalogue from Mark Foy's. Order yourself some smart things. Mum used to buy her clothes from there and always looked beautiful.' Rebecca acquiesced to his advice; after all, she had made the choice to change her life. But she did keep one of her former gowns tucked away in the back of her wardrobe, hidden under an organza cover. It was the emerald green dress she had worn to Nancy's bridge night. Her vixen's 'suit of armour'. Why she felt that she needed to keep it when she was marrying a respectable man and moving into a beautiful home, she had no idea. But no matter how much she tried to convince herself she was being irrational, she could not part with it.

There was a knock at the door and Shirley, the maid, appeared. She was a homely woman of sixty and she looked stunned when she saw Marion. Her eyes never left Marion while she spoke to Rebecca. 'Mrs Todd and I need to go and get things ready at the church for tomorrow. I was wondering if you could watch over Mrs Litchfield for a couple of hours?'

Marion stood before Rebecca could answer. 'Of course we can,' she said. Then smiling at Rebecca, she added with a wink, 'Come and introduce me to your soon-to-be *belle-mère*.'

★

Rebecca and Marion wheeled Gillian out to the garden and sat with her. Despite Gillian's lack of responses, Marion kept up a cheerful patter. 'Oh, the roses are marvellous, Mrs Litchfield! Such a pretty setting for the reception! Much better than the side room at the church!'

Gillian's eyes darted from Marion to Rebecca and back again. Rebecca could only imagine what she was thinking. Marion was striking and stylish and thoroughly modern. When she lit a cigarette, Rebecca was sure Gillian would be fuming. No doubt Gillian would tar Marion with the same brush with which she had tarred her.

'I have to telephone the post office,' Rebecca told Marion. 'I need to check how Johnny is managing while I'm not there.'

'They haven't found a replacement for you yet?'

Rebecca shook her head. 'No. It's difficult to entice people to such a remote town. I've agreed to work a couple of hours a day until they find someone.'

Johnny didn't answer when Rebecca telephoned. She assumed he was either out delivering mail or asleep in her chair with his cap covering his face. She sighed. She would have to let the post office go. She was proud of herself for having got it into good shape, but she would have a home to run now.

When she returned to Marion she was horrified to see that Gillian's arm was out of her sling and she was writing something on a notepad Marion was holding for her. Her hand was twisted, and clutching onto the pen seemed to be causing her pain, but she struggled to write with great determination.

'Oh, Marion!' said Rebecca, rushing to Gillian's side and putting her arm back in the sling. 'She's not supposed to have that arm out. She injures it.'

'Look at this!' Marion said, holding out the notepad. 'She's written the same thing over and over again. But I can't make out what it is.'

Rebecca took the notepad. It looked like a child had written on it or somebody using their non-dominant hand, but with all her experience at deciphering handwriting at the post office Rebecca immediately recognised the letters: *B-a-d*. Gillian had scrawled the word several times, obviously in some desperate effort to express her disapproval of Rebecca. She pursed her lips and gave the notepad back to Marion, then gestured for her to follow her inside.

'Gillian does not approve of me,' she whispered to Marion. 'That word is "bad" and she's written it multiple times, which was quite an effort for her. That shows you just how much she hates me.'

Marion rolled her eyes. 'Well, the idea that anyone could dislike you!' she said. Then, smiling again, she nudged Rebecca conspiratorially. 'Never mind though, darling. She can't talk. Half the women in the country would die for a mother-in-law like that!'

CHAPTER THIRTY-TWO

The morning of their wedding, Timothy went to his surgery to dress so as not to see Rebecca before the ceremony. While Rebecca sat at her dressing table, Marion, in a salmon silk dress trimmed with feathers, fixed her hair, strawberry blonde now that Rebecca had stopped dyeing it.

'You look good in white,' Marion told her. 'And I like the slight reddish tint in your hair.'

Rebecca chuckled at the memory of how her new hair colour had become the topic of discussion in the town for almost a week. The women were sure she was bleaching it to copy the movie star, Veronica Lake, while the men put it down to the lightening effects of the summer sun.

'Who could have imagined I'd end up a respectable doctor's wife?' she said. 'No more Christmases and holidays spent alone!' Her mind flashed briefly to Stefan and her heart ached, but she quelled the feeling before it grew. She hoped that she would get good at it with practice, not allowing herself to think of Stefan, like a weightlifter building muscle. 'My landlady was scandalised about my intention to wear white. She knows that

I was seeing Robert before he died in the war. I guess she's assumed that I'm not exactly inexperienced.'

Marion tittered and stood back to admire her. 'Never let anyone else tell you whether you are respectable or not, Becky. You decide that for yourself.'

The rumble of Frank and Elaine's truck pulling up in the driveway sent Rebecca to her feet. She looked out the window to see the vehicle parked in front of the fountain. Its cabin and bonnet were decorated with strings of paper flowers. Two velour armchairs had been secured to the tray. Elaine climbed out and waved to her. Rebecca drew her veil over her face. 'Come on, Marion,' she said. 'Our wedding car has arrived.'

*

The whole town had turned out for the wedding. Those who couldn't fit into the church waited on the footpath to watch Rebecca and Marion arrive. Frank lifted Marion and then Rebecca down from the truck and Elaine handed the bouquet Doris had made to Rebecca. 'You both look lovely,' she told her. 'You can't imagine how much this wedding has lifted everybody's mood.'

Rebecca and Marion took their places at the door and everyone in the church stood. Doris started up 'Pachelbel's Canon in D' on the organ. It was slightly out of tune but majestic nonetheless. Marion stepped down the aisle first, and Johnny applauded enthusiastically before his father clipped him over the head. People seemed unsure who to look at: the bride, beautiful on her wedding day, or the bridesmaid, who was as glamourous as Elizabeth Taylor. Rebecca almost lost her composure and laughed. Then she caught sight of Timothy standing at the altar; Carmel's husband, Pete, as his best man. Pete smiled broadly at her but Timothy's face was expressionless. She faltered. What had she been expecting? A man looking at her with a face flushed with pride? Or love? But Timothy had never really looked at her like that. How did he look at her? She tried to remember. Then she saw all the people that she detested in some way. The people who had stood by and watched Sanders Olsen nearly kill Stefan with a harpoon and then nearly kill him again when he set his house on fire. She couldn't bring herself to look at Marge. She was thankful that Timothy had not invited the Norwegians, but that was because they weren't really considered part of the town community and not because Sanders Olsen had killed his wife. Then there was Gillian sitting in her wheelchair next to the front pew, dressed in a garish shade of shamrock green and staring at her with wild eyes. She was struggling desperately with her bound arm and, as Rebecca passed her, managed to free it and grab onto Rebecca's veil, nearly tugging it off her head. The congregation gasped while Elaine raced to the rescue and gently pried Gillian's hand away, while Marion righted the veil. Rebecca was so humiliated that she would have run away then and there if Marion hadn't squeezed her arm and whispered, 'Chin up, darling. This is your day, not hers. Just look at that hideous green she is wearing. It's the colour of jealousy!' Rebecca calmed herself and, feigning a recovered dignity, stepped up next to Timothy. The man I am to marry, she thought, until death do us part.

★

At the reception in the garden, a lunch of coronation chicken, potato salad and herbed rice pilaf was served. There was no breeze blowing from the ocean to relieve the heat, but at least the air was untainted by the stink of boiling whale flesh. After the speeches were made, Rebecca and Timothy stood together and cut the white iced cake while Doris and Elaine distributed slices to the guests. 'I'll put the top section aside for the christening cake for your first baby,' Elaine told them with a wink.

They danced the bridal waltz before the other guests joined in with them. Then the gathering became a thrum of conversation. The children started a cricket match. Marion acted as the boxer for a rowdy game of two-up among the men.

'I'm not sure that's legal – or in good taste,' Rebecca said to Timothy, with a chuckle.

He took her arm. 'I guess we had better circulate. We are the star attraction today.'

They moved around the garden together, shaking hands and accepting congratulations and well wishes.

'How's the new grandchild?' Timothy asked one elderly farmer. 'Did you listen to the Willis and Anderson fight? Wasn't it a sizzler?'

'Will you be baking anything for the Twin Falls Fair, Mrs Litchfield?' the man's wife asked her.

Rebecca tried to think of a response but her mind went blank.

'There's so many things you can do with digestive biscuits these days,' the woman continued. 'I make mine with chopped nuts. My daughter uses marshmallow and chocolate.' She leaned in so close to her that Rebecca had a magnified view of the grey wiry hairs sprouting from the woman's chin. 'You can even add a little whisky.'

Another woman with drawn-on eyebrows and smudged eyeliner poked her in the hip with a bony finger. 'You'll be helping with the church flowers now, won't you?' she asked. 'I'll send you the roster next week.' Rebecca hated being poked as much as she hated whistling. She clenched her fists to stop herself screaming and smiled sweetly instead.

She thought of Marion's upcoming trip to Egypt and, for a stinging moment, missed Stefan. When Marion left, who would there be besides Timothy for her to talk to? Elaine was friendly enough, but her conversation was limited to babies and the bowling club. Then there was the insufferable Father Rob, the obsequious Mrs Turner and the bigoted and now very pregnant Iris Young. As for everyone else, she wouldn't trust them as far as she could throw them. Her gaze settled on Gillian, who had been placed in her wheelchair in the shade of a crepe myrtle tree. Tears were pouring from her eyes and Joy was holding her hand and dabbing at them with a handkerchief, trying to comfort her.

Oh, for God's sake, thought Rebecca. Why doesn't she just give up! We are married now and I've never been anything but kind and patient with her.

With a sinking feeling she slipped back to the bridal table and took a long sip from her champagne glass. Then her eyes settled on Marge. She finished the last of her champagne and put her glass down. She had a score to settle with Marge.

'It's really been a lovely wedding,' Marge told her, when Rebecca approached. 'It's wonderful to see a couple so in love.'

While Rebecca had seen Marge many times at the post office since Nancy's murder, the champagne had emboldened her and was making her light-headed. 'I want you to know that I don't hold it against you for implying to the police that I killed Nancy.'

Marge blinked at her. 'What on earth do you mean?'

'Oh, please don't let's start a quarrel on my wedding day,' Rebecca said. 'I know you told them that you had heard the two of us arguing in the post office.'

'I never told the police anything of the sort!'

Rebecca raised her eyebrow cynically but faltered when she realised Marge was genuinely dumbfounded.

'The only person I told about that argument was Doctor Litchfield, *your husband*,' Marge said, sticking out her chin. 'I went straight to the surgery after I left the post office and told him. I didn't hear everything the two of you said, but I did get the gist that Nancy was telling you that you shouldn't marry him and that you would break his heart.'

Despite the heat, Rebecca felt very cold all of a sudden.

'I told him because he was your fiancé,' Marge continued. 'I wanted to let him know that Nancy was trying to drive you away. I never spoke to the police. They never even questioned me.'

Rebecca couldn't breathe and couldn't think. She was sure Timothy had told her that Marge had spoken to the police. She frowned, struggling to recall his words. Isn't that what he had said? Or had she been so disorientated and confused that morning that she had misheard him? She glanced over her shoulder at Timothy and he smiled back at her and waved. She must have misheard him; Timothy was not a man to lie. Why would he lie about such a thing anyway? Rebecca ran her fingers down her throat. She must have misunderstood. But then another question prickled at her. On the day Nancy had been killed, for those hours that he was supposed to have been at her house making love to her, where had he actually been?

CHAPTER THIRTY-THREE

Rebecca viewed the breakfast table as if she was contemplating a piece of art: the sausages and scrambled eggs, cereal, strawberry jam and toast weren't merely items of food but elements of composition and colour. Everything looked just right on the milk glass and gold-rimmed plate set the town had given her and Timothy as a wedding gift. She had done it all on her own, including the centrepiece of miniature roses from the garden. Shirley was now only coming a few afternoons a week for cleaning duties and Rebecca had taken over all the meals. She was still shaky on roasts but all Doris's lessons in casseroles and chicken à la king were paying off.

Timothy sat opposite her, his face freshly shaven and his mind busy with *The Twin Falls Advocate* and an article about potential coal shortages. The days when newspapers and what they might contain had terrified Rebecca now seemed like a bad memory. She was Mrs Timothy Litchfield now, living respectably in a beautiful house by the ocean. She no longer feared waking up to find herself embroiled in a press scandal.

Timothy sensed Rebecca was watching him and glanced over the top of the newspaper. 'Do you have to go to the post office today?' he asked.

Rebecca poured a glass of orange juice and placed it before him. 'Johnny can't manage on his own. I'm sure it will only be for a little while longer'.'

Timothy put down the newspaper and cut up a sausage. 'Well, let's hope they find someone soon.' He glanced up at her and his eyes dropped to her waist. 'You know we have a project of our own.'

Rebecca pushed her scrambled eggs around her plate. He had not been coy about his desire to have a baby as quickly as possible. On their wedding night she had expected his lovemaking to be tender, given he had made no sexual advances towards her during their engagement, despite what he had told the police. But to her shock he was rough. He squeezed her so hard he left bruises, and the expression on his face had been angry not ardent. But afterwards, he returned to his normal, gentle self and she had lain awake, staring at the ceiling and wondering if perhaps she should be glad he was so eager to have children. For wasn't the creation of a new life the ultimate symbol of commitment?

'Besides that,' he said, folding the newspaper, 'I want you to take over looking after Mum.'

Rebecca fumbled with her serviette and dabbed at her mouth. It was the first time he had suggested it. 'But Mrs Todd is so good with her.'

She couldn't imagine anything worse than having sole responsibility for Gillian. It was bad enough having the woman eyeball her every time they sat down to dinner. Rebecca was getting used to it now, but at the first few meals the tension had given her indigestion.

'Mrs Todd will be retiring,' said Timothy, standing up and taking his jacket from the back of his chair. 'I would rather my wife have that duty than relegate it to a stranger. It makes us more like a family and sets a better example for the townspeople.'

He walked into the hallway to fetch his briefcase and hat. Rebecca followed him. She knew what caring for an invalid entailed, especially one that didn't like her, and she had envisioned a broader life for herself as a married woman. She hoped that she might head a charity to raise money for a hospital for Shipwreck Bay.

Timothy noticed Rebecca's discomfort when she handed him his hat. 'You needn't worry,' he told her. 'I'm only asking you to help with giving her meals and reading to her. I'll take over the other more difficult things. I am a doctor after all.'

'But you are so busy,' Rebecca said. 'It would be better for everyone if Mrs Todd stayed on at least until we find someone we are all comfortable with. What if your mother falls out of her chair and I'm here on my own?'

Timothy didn't seem to hear her. He was focused on straightening his cuffs. Then he looked up and kissed her on the forehead. 'I told you, there is no need to worry. I'll be back every day at lunchtime to help.'

'All right,' Rebecca agreed, reluctantly.

Timothy smiled at her and held her by the shoulders. 'There's a dance on at Twin Falls this Saturday. Why don't we go to that? You can get all dressed up and do your hair in that special way of yours. It's looking especially lovely now you are letting it return to its natural colour.'

Rebecca rubbed behind her ear. Timothy was very good at that. He was aware of her sensitivities, her likes and dislikes, and was always quick to reassure her when doubts assailed her.

'Thank you, I would like that.'

'Rebecca,' he said, brushing his hand down her cheek, 'I want you to be happy.'

'I am happy.'

He pushed a strand of hair away from her face. 'I want us to always be free to speak with each other. Never let there be lies between us.' He picked up his medical bag. 'I'll give you a call from the surgery.'

Rebecca twisted her wedding ring and followed him to his car. 'Timothy,' she said. 'There is something I have wanted to ask you … about Nancy's murder. You told me that Marge Mullens had informed the police that she had heard Nancy and me arguing at the post office. But she denies it. She claims she never said that to anyone else but you.'

He opened the car door and put his bag on the back seat, fiddling with it as if to make sure it was straight.

'Timothy? Did you hear what I asked?'

He closed the car door and glanced at her. 'No, sorry, I didn't. I was thinking about Mr Cooper. I'm worried he might have pneumoconiosis: the same thing that killed Corman Ryan. He's only young. He and his wife have three small children.'

Rebecca hesitated, not sure if she should persist with her own concern when Timothy had such a serious case on his mind. But she was his wife, she had to know. If there had been a misunderstanding, she wanted it cleared up.

'You told me the police said that Marge had told them that she'd overheard a fight between me and Nancy at the post office. Marge denies it. She said the only person she had told about the argument was you.'

Timothy stopped what he was doing and looked at her. 'Rebecca, I thought we had agreed to put all that unpleasantness behind us. I hate to remember it at all.'

'But Marge—'

'Marge is an old lady and a gossip!' he said, cutting her off. 'I lied for you, Rebecca. I'm a doctor, for God's sake! I have a position and a creed to uphold. I'm also your husband, for all that seems worth with your questioning of me.'

A deep sense of shame flooded over her. Of course she should believe him and not Marge. 'I'm sorry, I only wanted to—'

'I don't like to remember the whole thing,' he said, tugging open the driver's side door. 'We must go forward, Rebecca. We must forget that part of our lives. We have a whole future of our own to think about now.'

'I'm sorry,' she said.

Timothy became calm again. 'I know you are, Rebecca. You're overwrought. Try and relax now. Go and read to Mum. It will make you feel better.'

He kissed her again then got in the car, giving her a wave before he headed down the driveway. Rebecca turned back to the house. Something was wrong, very wrong, with her. How could she question Timothy like that? Perhaps Marge had been lying or Timothy was simply forgetful.

*

Rebecca was sitting in the parlour, reading *My Cousin Rachel* to Gillian, not daring to look up into her mother-in-law's disapproving face, when Shirley walked into the room carrying her bucket of cleaning polishes.

'Oh, sorry, I didn't see you,' she apologised, turning to leave. 'I'll do the other rooms first.'

Rebecca rose from her chair and followed the maid into the hall.

'Shirley,' she asked, trying to sound as casual as possible. 'The afternoon that Nancy Pike was killed, were you here?'

'Yes,' she said, taking out some glass wax and a cloth. She began rubbing the hall mirror.

'And my husband came home in the early afternoon to check on Gillian, as he always does?'

Shirley nodded and scrubbed at a smear. 'That's right. Doctor Litchfield does that every day without fail. Then he goes back to his surgery or out on house calls. He is such a dedicated man.'

Rebecca had to be careful not to open a can of worms by raising Shirley's suspicions. Why couldn't she bring herself to just ask Timothy directly herself, like a woman should be able to ask her husband? But if he had been in his surgery or out on house calls most of the afternoon, how could he have convinced the police that he had been with her at her house? That was the part of his story that was puzzling her.

Shirley picked up her duster and wiped down the mirror's ornate frame. 'Gives me nightmares to think while I was here cleaning, poor Mrs Pike was being murdered just a few houses away.'

Rebecca returned to the parlour and picked up her novel again. Timothy had come home and then left again. But where did he go? She looked up at Gillian, who was moving her mouth, trying to get some word out.

Rebecca's skin prickled. 'What is it, Gillian?' she whispered. 'What is the nasty thing you want to say about me? Vixen? Gold digger? Why can't you see how hard I'm trying to be a good wife to your son?'

The old woman drew up her chin. Her lips stretched with the effort to say the word. 'Odd,' she said. 'Oddie.'

Rebecca could decipher bad handwriting but not distorted sounds. What was Gillian trying to say? The name of a person? The name of a plant?

Something flashed in the old woman's eyes. For a brief second Rebecca felt she could see beyond Gillian's affliction. She was suddenly unsure that she was on the right track. 'Gillian, are you in some sort of pain?' she asked, moving closer to her but at a loss as to what she could do for her.

Shirley came into the room. 'It's all right, Mrs Litchfield. It's all right,' she said, putting an arm comfortingly on the old woman's back while patting her hand. 'Mrs Todd will come and visit you soon.' Then she looked at Rebecca, grimacing with embarrassment. 'Mrs Todd has looked after her ever since she had the stroke. You know how old people get, anything new takes a bit of getting used to.'

Rebecca sat back and folded her arms. So that's what Gillian had been trying to say. She wanted Mrs Todd back. Of course, anything would be better than her own daughter-in-law. She picked up *My Cousin Rachel* again, but this time she read it silently to herself.

★

The following Saturday night, Rebecca dressed in the new gown she had bought from Mark Foy's. It was an off-the-shoulder design with a fitted bodice and full skirt. The baby blue dress was pretty and well-cut, but Rebecca stared at herself in the mirror feeling strange. 'I should be happy,' she told herself.

It was hard to put her finger on exactly what was wrong, but it seemed that somehow, since the wedding, things had changed between her and Timothy.

The previous night she had taken particular care with the meal. With instruction from Doris, she had succeeded in making a crown roast with an apricot glaze. The browned sage and marjoram stuffing was something to be proud of: golden brown and crunchy on top with a soft, moist middle. She'd worn a fetching floral cocktail dress. The table was decorated with pink chrysanthemums from the garden and she'd opened a bottle of cabernet sauvignon. Timothy sat down at the table and made no comment. She watched him slice into the lamb and take a bite, frowning, before taking another. Why did Timothy keep scrunching up his nose like that? The meat was succulent and the gravy smooth. Even if he didn't like the food, surely he could at least recognise her effort?

She straightened her shoulders, trying to summon some of her former confidence. Cooking was new to her, but she'd once been viewed as an excellent conversationalist.

'So, how was your day?' she asked him.

'Not bad,' he said, stopping a moment to roll his tongue around his mouth as if trying to dislodge something from his teeth. 'And yours?'

'When a new postmaster is found they are going to have their work cut out for them. Telephone subscriptions, even in small towns like Shipwreck Bay, are going to double in the next couple of years. Someone will have to be hired to work the switchboard at night.'

Timothy didn't respond to Rebecca's statement. He pushed the food around on his plate as if he was reluctant to eat it.

'It might be good for you, of course,' she continued, feeling less and less certain of herself. 'You would be able to check on more patients by telephone instead of always having to call on them.'

She stopped. From the way he sat back and stared at his plate, it was clear he wasn't listening. Rebecca brushed the side of her neck with her fingers. What could she talk to him about if he wasn't interested in the post office? She didn't run in political circles anymore and was no longer privy to the secrets of the social set. She didn't even have time to read *The Twin Falls Advocate*. Every day she was at home with Gillian, except for those two hours at the post office.

And still Nancy's death lay between them. They hadn't talked it out enough, and every time Rebecca brought up the subject Timothy would shut it down. But she had to know, she couldn't keep wondering where he had been during those missing hours on the day of Nancy's death.

In the car on the way to Twin Falls, Timothy seemed to be in a good mood. He hummed the tune to *Green Eyes*, a rhumba, which was Rebecca's favourite dance style. Before they reached the town he patted her knee and smiled at her. 'You look lovely tonight,' he told her. 'That blue goes prettily with your eyes.'

Rebecca smiled, pleased. It was quite some time since he had looked into her eyes. 'Timothy, I know you don't like to talk about it, but I have to. I need to know one thing and then I promise I will never bring it up again.' She watched him for any change of mood or expression. But he seemed as he had been before, so she continued. 'I have to make sure because I feel uncertain about our alibi. I was home at the time Nancy was murdered. But where were you?'

'Not this again, Rebecca.'

'Please just answer this question. And then I'll never bring it up again.'

He flashed her a smile. 'Do you think I murdered her?'

'No!' said Rebecca, surprised that he was joking about such a serious matter. 'Of course I don't! But should George Pike be cleared of the crime the police might reopen the case. I have to know everything, Timothy. We have to protect each other.'

'Each other?' said Timothy, a crinkle of laugh lines forming around his eyes. 'I don't think I've ever been under any sort of suspicion.' He shifted gears to take a hill. 'But since you are so determined to be a detective, I'll tell you where I was. I went home to check on Mum as I always do in the afternoon, and then I went to Twin Falls Hospital to collect the latest X-rays for Mr Cooper. But halfway there I got a flat tyre, which turned out to be a bugger to change. By the time I finished, it was too late to go to Twin Falls, so I returned home. That's when I found the note from Nancy. Then you arrived and … well, you know how the rest of the evening went.'

Rebecca shivered as she saw herself, dreamlike, walking into Nancy's house in the dim light and finding her dead on the sunroom floor.

Timothy glanced at her. 'It was a close call for you, Rebecca. The police were on the verge of arresting you. If I hadn't stepped in and said we were together, you would be in jail instead of George Pike. They would have stopped investigating the case then and there.'

Feeling chastised, Rebecca turned to the sea. It was the same steel-blue colour as the darkening sky. It was impossible to tell where one ended and the other began.

★

The following Monday, the sky was grey and a strong wind was blowing in from the ocean. When Rebecca arrived at the post office, she found Johnny waiting for her. 'He's been charged with it, Mrs Litchfield!' He waved a copy of *The Twin Falls Advocate* at her. 'The shire secretary! Mr Pike!'

Timothy had left early in the morning to see some patients at Twin Falls Hospital and had taken the newspaper with him, so it was the first she'd heard of the news.

Johnny handed Rebecca the newspaper. On the front page was a photograph of George Pike being led to a paddy wagon and above it the headline 'Shire Secretary Charged With Murder of Wife'. Her eyes quickly scanned the article.

> *George Joseph Pike, 43, was charged today with having murdered his wife, Nancy, 32, of Shipwreck Bay. The Crown alleges that George Pike stabbed his wife in the back when she was alone in their home. The couple's son, Earl, was away at a scout camp at the time. Pike was supposed to be at the camp as well but apparently disappeared for several hours on the day of his wife's murder. Pike claims he was with 'some mates', but nobody has come forward to support his alibi. The Pike marriage had been troubled for some time and it is believed Mrs Pike refused to grant her husband a divorce for religious reasons …*

So George did do it, thought Rebecca, feeling an easing of tension in her body. It sounded like the Crown had a strong case against him. And after what Stefan had told her, she could believe he was entirely capable of it. She breathed a deep sigh. She didn't have to be so worried anymore. Of course, he hadn't been tried and convicted yet, but that would happen in due course.

By the time Rebecca had finished sorting the post office accounts and fixed Johnny's disorganised filing system, the sky was turning a strange charcoal colour. Thunder rumbled in the distance. On the way home the rain started to fall. She saw that Timothy's car was outside his surgery. He was back from Twin Falls. She wondered if he had read the news about George Pike. She ducked out of the rain and into his waiting room.

Timothy was talking to Nurse Gibbons. 'Iris Young is in the early stages of labour and is at her mother's place in town. She's always had difficulty birthing. It's going to be a long night.'

In minutes the rain turned from a patter to a thunderous deluge, the water cascaded over the gutters and flooded the footpaths and streets. Timothy turned to Rebecca, but she saw it wasn't the right time to bring up George Pike.

'You'd better go home, Rebecca,' he told her, 'and watch over Mum. Sit her near a window. She's always liked to watch storms coming in from the sea.'

Nurse Gibbons handed her a spare umbrella, although now the wind was picking up Rebecca couldn't see it being of much use. She was about to leave when there was a commotion of men's voices out on the street and suddenly three of the whalers burst in the door carrying something that at first sight was so bloodied and slick that Rebecca thought it was a slaughtered seal. Then she realised the creature had a human face, deathly pale, and that face was Sanders Olsen's. His eyes looked blank, like those of a fish that has been yanked out of the water, and his mouth was gaping open in an agonised cry but no sound was coming out.

'We tied a tourniquet,' one of the whalers told Timothy in broken English. 'But still he is bleeding.'

Timothy and Nurse Gibbons sprang into action, directing the men to carry Sanders into Timothy's office and lie him on the examination table. Rebecca hovered in the doorway, horrified at what she was seeing. The lower part of Sanders's leg seemed to be dangling, holding on to the rest of his body by nothing but a few tendons. Her stomach pitched at the sight of all the gore and blood. Timothy rolled up his sleeves. 'What happened?' he asked the whalers.

'He was hunting dolphins for crayfish bait,' said the whaler. 'But his leg got mangled in his winch.'

Timothy's teeth clenched when he looked more closely at the leg. He turned to Nurse Gibbons. 'We've got to amputate now,' he said. 'There is no time to get him to hospital.'

Nurse Gibbons took needles, bottles, forceps, scalpels and bandages out of the cabinet and placed them on a tray while Timothy scrubbed his hands and forearms in the sink. When Nurse Gibbons pulled out something that looked like the kind of saw Timothy might use to prune the citrus trees, Rebecca backed away and ran into the rain-lashed street.

The storm had intensified and the umbrella was as useless as a handkerchief against the tempest. The rain hit her face like needles as she ran down Mountain Road shielding her eyes rather than her head. The sea had turned black and on the horizon great streaks of lightning flashed across the sky. Once inside the house, she quickly pulled off her wet clothes in the kitchen and ran naked up the stairs to change into dry clothing. She caught a glimpse of herself in the dressing table mirror and started. The rain had been so fierce that it had washed away every trace of her make-up. There wasn't a smear of lipstick or mascara on her skin. She moved closer to the reflection and stared at herself as if she was staring at a stranger. She looked like a frightened young girl.

From somewhere nearby a crack came and she glanced out the window. One of the hoop pines had split in two. It must have been weakened by the dry spell. Then she remembered

Gillian and hurriedly dressed before rushing to her mother-in-law's room. The old woman was lying in her bed and trembling.

'Come on, let's get you up,' Rebecca said to her. 'Timothy said you like a good storm.'

Rebecca had taken to using Timothy's cheerful tone with Gillian, although it made little difference. The old woman was forever sending her expressions of annoyance. Rebecca managed to get Gillian into her chair and then wheeled it to the window so that she was facing the garden.

'Look at that,' said Rebecca. 'How high the waves are! No boats out there now, are there?'

Gillian looked from the window to Rebecca with wide eyes. Her hands were shaking. Rebecca assumed she was cold. She took a lap rug from the bed and placed it around Gillian's legs to keep her warm. The old woman began to whimper. Rebecca knelt down next to her. 'I know that you don't approve of me, Gillian, but please understand I'm doing my best. I don't have the most saintly of pasts, but I'm trying very hard to improve myself and be a better person. Timothy says we are a family now and that's what I would like us to be too. So please don't make things difficult for me.'

Gillian nodded her head towards her strapped arm but Rebecca shook her head. 'I can't let you hurt yourself.'

She sat with Gillian the rest of the afternoon, watching the ocean pitch and roll. Then voices from downstairs caught her attention. She went out on the landing and saw that Timothy and one of the whalers were carrying an unconscious Sanders Olsen into the house on a stretcher. Nurse Gibbons was following behind with a drip in one hand and Timothy's medical bag in the other.

'We'll put him in the downstairs guest room,' Timothy told them.

Rebecca was filled with a fury that matched the maelstrom outside. 'That man is not staying in this house!' she said, running down the stairs.

Timothy looked up at her. The whaler and Nurse Gibbons stood still. Then Timothy turned to them and urged the whaler and nurse to follow him into the guest room. Rebecca raced in after the three of them and saw they were moving Sanders onto the bed. She grimaced at the heavily bandaged stump of his leg. She grabbed Timothy's arm. He left the whaler and Nurse Gibbons securing Sanders to the bed with thick canvas straps, and nodded for Rebecca to come with him into the sitting room.

'May I remind you, Rebecca, that you are a doctor's wife!' he said under his breath. 'This is your duty to the town!'

'He can go to the hospital,' Rebecca said, her voice trembling. 'I will not have a murderer in our house!'

'*My* house, Rebecca,' Timothy replied. 'We can't get to Twin Falls now. There are landslides up and down the coast. We are cut off from Twin Falls and Wollongong. It might have been different if it wasn't for Stefan Otto stopping the factory ship, but as you might remember I still treated *him*!'

Rebecca flinched at the force of his anger. He took her by the arm and pushed her into the guest room. 'Iris Young has gone into labour,' he said, taking out syrettes of morphine from his bag and laying them on the bedside table. 'She and the child might die if Nurse Gibbons and I don't get to her.' He picked up one of the syrettes and took Sanders's arm and lifted the skin. 'You inject it here. It's not difficult. Every hour on the hour until I get back. He's unconscious now but when he comes to he'll go into shock on seeing that his leg is missing. Don't undo the straps. The last thing I need is for him to tear off the dressing. He could bleed to death. Dammit, Rebecca, have some decency. He might bleed to death anyway.'

After Timothy and Nurse Gibbons left to attend Iris Young, and the whaler returned to his home, Rebecca sat in the parlour shivering and crying. What was happening to her? What was she becoming? The town was cut off by flooding and landslides, but she was cut off in another way she couldn't explain. Gusts of wind howled around the house. She eyed the clock on the wall. 'Every hour on the hour,' Timothy had told her. Sanders was regaining consciousness. She could hear him moaning from the guest room.

She covered her ears with her hands. A gust of wind rattled and shook the windows then the lights flickered and went out. A twilight darkness fell over the house. She lit two gas lamps and took one to Gillian's room and placed it on the bedside table. The old woman was still looking out at the storm. Her eyes were wide and staring. 'Are you all right, Gillian?'

'My leg! My leg!' Sanders cried out from downstairs.

Rebecca had known enough veterans and former wartime nurses to have heard the stories of phantom limb pains. But it was not Sanders's physical or psychological needs she was thinking about when she walked into the guest room and looked at his fevered face. She placed the second lamp on the bedside table and eyed the syrettes on it. Sanders writhed on the bed under the straps, trying to reach the stump of his leg.

Another human being might have felt compassion or horror or fear. Rebecca felt nothing. A wide, black hole opened inside her. She sat down on the chair next to the bed and studied Sanders.

'Does it hurt?' she asked.

He gritted his teeth. His lips were dry and cracked.

'You must be thirsty,' she said.

His eyes followed hers to the water jug. Nurse Gibbons had left wads of gauze next to it. Perhaps a compassionate person would dampen the gauze and squeeze the water slowly into Sanders's parched mouth. She picked up one of the syrettes of morphine.

'Would you like something for the pain?' she asked.

He nodded, his eyes pleading with her.

Rebecca held up the syrette, looked at it for a moment and then put it down again. 'Did you kill Berit?'

Sanders's face froze.

'I know you did,' she said. 'I know she didn't hang herself. You strangled her, didn't you? Then you made it look like suicide. You hung her from the flensing deck winch. Such a horrific death for such a pretty girl. Why? That's what I want to know. Why?'

Sanders wriggled to free himself but it was futile. It reminded her of the way Gillian kept trying to free her strapped arm. But Gillian was a frail old woman. Here, tied to the bed, was a physically powerful man, a man who had made a living slaughtering the largest mammals on earth. Those great creatures had been at his mercy, but he'd had no mercy for them.

She played with the syrette in her fingers. 'Why?'

The sweat dripped down his face as he spoke. 'Because I am the man. My needs come first. Who was she to think she could do whatever she liked?'

'Berit was a person, Sanders,' Rebecca said, noticing the way his gaze was following the syrette. 'She didn't deserve to die. You could have let her go.'

Despite his agony, he laughed briefly then stared at her with a killer's coldness. 'I couldn't let her go any more than I could let a whale go. It's God's law. Man was made to dominate.'

Rebecca brought her face closer to his. 'Are you saying it's your God-given right to brutalise women? Is that what you are saying?'

Sanders didn't answer her. He was breathing heavily. She stood back and looked at the heavy straps that kept him secured to the bed. She took the cap off the syrette and Sanders watched her hopefully. Then she took the corner of the blanket and pushed the needle into it to release the morphine. The liquid dribbled to the floor. 'Go to hell, Sanders!' she said.

She left the room and shut the door behind her.

Sanders screamed but the thunder drowned him out. Rebecca walked out onto the veranda. The rain was coming in horizontally. The roof offered little protection against the onslaught, but she stood there watching the storm for what felt like an eternity until a seagull appeared from nowhere and nosedived into the garden. It floundered on the flooded lawn. The bird must have flown into something and become concussed. Rebecca saw it could not right itself. She took off her cardigan and ran out into the rain to scoop it up. She held it wrapped in the cardigan to her chest. For a moment she thought of Dunkel. Then she remembered the burning of Stefan's house. She looked up at her own house. *My* house, Timothy had corrected her. Then her eye travelled to the upper storey and she saw the light in Gillian's window. The old woman was staring at her, ghostly white with a halo pulsing around her head. Rebecca carried the bird into the house, which was now eerily quiet. She placed the gull in a box with a dry towel and left the box in the study so no one would disturb the bird until it recovered. She returned to the guest room and saw the dark puddle pooled on the floor. Sanders was staring at the ceiling, his eyes wide open and his mouth twisted into a frozen shout. She knew from the stillness of his features and the wax-like pallor of his skin that he was dead. Timothy had warned her that was a possibility despite all care. She picked up another syrette, took the top off and injected it into the air. Then she covered Sanders's face with a towel and left the room.

CHAPTER THIRTY-FOUR

A week after the storm, Rebecca was in the laundry ironing clothes when there was a knock at the door. She went to answer it and found Elaine on the doorstep holding a plate of digestive biscuits coated in pink royal icing and sprinkled with desiccated coconut.

'Hello,' Elaine said. 'I wanted to pop by and see how you are.'

Rebecca felt grateful to have company that wasn't Gillian or Shirley. 'Come in,' she said to Elaine, ushering her into the parlour. 'Let me put the kettle on. Gillian is having a nap upstairs.'

Rebecca carried the tea tray to the parlour and placed it on the coffee table in front of Elaine before taking a seat on the sofa next to her.

'The storm last week was horrible,' Elaine said. 'So many people have damage to their buildings and crops. Then of course the death of Sanders Olsen and Iris Young's baby dying three days after birth has just added to the distress everyone is feeling.'

Rebecca poured the tea. She didn't feel any responsibility for Sanders Olsen's death. She hadn't killed him. As far as she was concerned his demise was good riddance to bad rubbish. But the death of Iris Young's baby was another matter. When she had heard the news from Shirley, she'd wondered why Timothy hadn't rung and told her. When he came home that evening she'd expected that he would unburden himself to her, but he had simply washed up and sat down to dinner. Rebecca wondered if that was normal behaviour for a doctor. Patients must pass away on them as a matter of course, and perhaps they had to learn to deal with things philosophically and not bring their troubles home. Is that what Timothy had tried to do? To simply move on? But it didn't seem like the man she knew at all. Something had changed in him that she couldn't put her finger on.

'Anyway,' Elaine continued, 'some of the ladies and I were talking, and we thought it might be a good idea to throw a fundraising dance for the Flood Relief Fund. We wondered if you would like to be on the organising committee? All of us feel you would add a certain style to the event.'

Rebecca brightened immediately. 'I would love to …' Then, wondering if she should ask Timothy before agreeing, she added, 'If we could have the meetings for it here. I have to keep my eye on Gillian now Mrs Todd has retired.'

'Of course,' said Elaine, taking a nibble of a biscuit. 'It's really wonderful how Timothy and his mother reconciled.'

Rebecca started. 'Reconciled?' Had there been some sort of rift? Judging by Doris's comments at church the first time Rebecca had attended, Timothy and Gillian had the perfect devoted mother-and-son relationship.

'Yes,' said Elaine. 'I suppose he wouldn't want to tell you. They had an enormous falling out when Gillian went to Sydney to try and stop his marriage to his first wife.'

Rebecca sat back in her chair. That sounded like Gillian all over.

'They didn't speak for a few years,' Elaine continued, 'but then Timothy must have realised his mother had been right about his wife and then poor Gillian had that terrible stroke. He gave up his promising career in Sydney to come back here and care for her.' She looked around the room. 'He redecorated everything too. I noticed it when we came for the wedding reception. Very nice.' She took a sip of tea and then said, 'My mother used to bring me here to play with Timothy when I was a small child. I was six and he was eleven, so he was sort of an older brother for a while. On our way home my mother would joke with me: "Timothy's mother spoils him rotten. She never seems to be able to tell him no. He gets everything he wants. Don't expect that from me, young lady!"'

'Oh,' said Rebecca. 'I never imagined Timothy as a spoilt child.'

An odd sense of something shifting, something revealing itself, prickled her. She was learning so many things about the man she had married and was beginning to wonder if she really knew him at all.

'I think Gillian was making up for the lack of affection from his father. Old Doctor Litchfield was a very stern man. Everybody in Shipwreck Bay likes Timothy much better.'

'So you grew up together?' Rebecca asked, pouring Elaine another cup of tea.

'Not really,' Elaine answered, taking the refilled cup from Rebecca. 'My mother stopped bringing me when Timothy's baby brother was born.'

'Brother?'

Elaine glanced at Rebecca and lowered her voice. 'Yes, the poor child was sickly. He took all Gillian's attention and Timothy had to learn to entertain himself. I'm sure he didn't like that one bit. But then the poor little baby died. I don't think Gillian ever got over it. She became reclusive after that and even more so after her husband passed away. Up until her stroke, I only ever saw her at church.'

Elaine pulled out a notebook from her purse and began to tell Rebecca about her ideas for the fundraising dance. Rebecca nodded with a smile plastered on her face but didn't hear one word. Timothy had a deceased brother? He had given her the impression he was an only child. But hadn't she done that herself, with Debbie? Perhaps that was why he hadn't reacted the way she had expected when she had told him about her sister. It must have brought up terrible memories for him too.

When Elaine was ready to leave, Rebecca walked her to the door.

'The committee will be very excited to hear that Mrs Litchfield has agreed to join us,' Elaine said, beaming. 'Some of us have been a bit worried that Timothy was going to keep you all to himself. He's always been a bit possessive of people he loves.'

'Indeed,' said Rebecca, forcing a smile.

Elaine turned towards the path but a pressing question forced itself out of Rebecca's lips. 'What was Timothy's brother's name?' Then careful not to rouse too much suspicion she added, 'I would like to put some flowers on his grave.'

Elaine turned and nodded sympathetically. 'I'm sure Gillian would appreciate that. His name was Rodney.'

'Rodney.'

'That's right. That will be the name on the grave. But Gillian never called him that. She always called him ...'

Rebecca knew what Elaine was going to say before the words came out of her mouth. She recalled Gillian sitting in the parlour when she was reading *My Cousin Rachel* to her, the old woman's mouth twisting as she struggled to say the name.

'... Roddie.'

★

Rebecca sat at the dining table the following Saturday morning looking through her notes for the upcoming fundraiser. Timothy came down the stairs straightening his tie.

'I'll make your toast,' said Rebecca, putting down her notebook and standing up to go to the kitchen.

'How is all the planning coming along?' he asked, taking a seat at the table. 'Everything going all right?'

'I think the committee will be very pleased. Although it's short notice, I've booked a band from Wollongong and even managed to get some free advertising in *The Illawarra Mercury*.'

Rebecca went to the kitchen and sliced the bread. She turned on the toaster. Timothy hadn't asked her anything about the fundraiser dance since she'd told him Elaine had asked her to help organise it, and she was pleased he was taking an interest now. It took a certain amount of finesse to organise an event, and Rebecca was determined that any dance she was on the committee for would be an elegant and memorable affair.

The toast popped up and she cut it into quarters and inserted them into a toast rack. She carried it to the dining room and placed it before Timothy before taking her seat again. 'Do you think we might take your mother to the dance?' she asked him, unfolding her serviette on her lap. 'She might enjoy watching it.'

Timothy held out his cup for Rebecca to pour him some tea. 'That's out of the question, I'm afraid. The drive is too long and there are all the practical matters of being an invalid. We'll get Mrs Todd or Shirley to watch her that night.'

Since Elaine had told her about Roddie, Rebecca hadn't been able to get the poor infant out of her mind. Every time she looked at Timothy, and especially Gillian, she was overwhelmed by pity. It was devastating to lose a sibling, let alone a child. Even though Gillian continued to make faces at her, Rebecca wasn't as bothered by her behaviour as she had been before. In some ways she envied Timothy and his mother. There had been a rift in their relationship but they had managed to mend it. Rebecca and her mother had never done that. Her mother had gone to the grave estranged from Rebecca, even though her daughter had been her carer until her last breath.

Then, perhaps seeing Rebecca was crestfallen, Timothy added, 'But thank you for thinking of her, Rebecca. It touches me that the two women who mean the most to me in the world get along so well together.'

Getting on well together might be stretching it, Rebecca

thought. But whether it was the sympathy she felt for Gillian over the loss of her child or something else, she did have a sense that she and her mother-in-law had become inextricably linked in some mysterious way.

*

Rebecca felt a sense of triumph, standing in the doorway of the surf club auditorium and welcoming guests to the fundraiser dance. Every gasp of delight, every enchanted smile of surprise was a feather in her cap. The tables at the sides of the dance floor were covered in white cloths and decorated with candles and flowers instead of the usual garish balloons. Garlands of flowers and greenery hung from the walls, replacing the multi-coloured streamers some of the women on the committee had thought *de rigueur*. The effect was that of walking into a magical summer garden.

'Oh, it's so pretty and festive,' said Nurse Gibbons when she arrived with her husband. 'I've been hearing rumours that you did an extraordinary job.'

'The tickets were all sold out early,' Rebecca said, not afraid to blow her own trumpet. Why should she be? Thanks to her efforts not only would the dance be a success but donations had come pouring into the Flood Relief Fund from around the state. She'd developed her organisational flair and persuasive charm from all those years of promoting Ned's career. She may as well put them to good use. For Rebecca now had a plan: to run the biggest fundraiser the district had ever seen, to get Shipwreck Bay a hospital.

She saw Timothy speaking with Frank near the kitchen and squeezed her way around the dance floor to reach him, but Elaine intercepted her.

'Come and meet my mother and sister,' she said, taking Rebecca's arm. 'They have come from Penguin Bay for this.'

Elaine's sister could have been her twin with the same short bleached hair and olive skin. Their mother was finer boned with saggy cheeks, and lips that were naturally downturned at the corners so that even when she smiled she looked unhappy. 'This is Doctor Litchfield's wife,' Elaine said, leaning close to her mother and speaking directly into her ear. 'You remember Gillian Litchfield, don't you? From when you and Dad lived in Shipwreck Bay?'

Her mother stiffened, as if slightly offended her daughter should question her memory. 'Of course I remember Gillian! Always so beautifully turned out. Always so terribly particular. Her parties were such elegant affairs.'

Rebecca smiled. She liked hearing those things about her mother-in-law, although it saddened her too. If Gillian hadn't been crippled by a stroke, and such a damn snob, they might have been good friends. Rebecca may have even had a maternal connection she'd never experienced with her own mother.

Elaine's mother thought about something for a moment. 'I was very surprised when Elaine mentioned to me that Gillian was dressed in a green frock for your wedding,' she told Rebecca with a tone of rebuke in her voice.

But Rebecca hadn't chosen Gillian's dress that day. Timothy had. Rebecca took the empty seat next to Elaine's mother in order to hear her better above the music. 'Why is that?

Elaine's mother grimaced. 'Gillian always hated the colour green. She was adamant that it did nothing for a woman's complexion. She loved it in the garden, of course, but never on one's person and certainly not in the house.'

'Why not in the house?' Rebecca asked. She could understand certain colours not agreeing with someone's complexion, but furnishings were surely different. The colour of the interior of a home created an atmosphere and a backdrop. Her apartment in Potts Point had been decorated in silver and teal blue, while she favoured bright colours in her dress. If both the décor and her clothing had been in the same colour family, she would have blended in with the wallpaper.

Elaine's mother lifted her eyes to Rebecca's face. Her mouth shifted as if she needed to work herself up to what she was about to say. 'She believed it brought bad luck. I think she associated it with being ill … and with jealousy.'

'They do say "green with envy", don't they?' piped in Elaine. 'I wonder where that saying comes from.'

Their conversation was interrupted by the master of ceremonies calling for a Monte Carlo competition. Rebecca had been resistant to such a gauche game being played for the fundraiser, but it was a point on which she'd had to concede to stay in favour with the other women on the committee. Elaine waved Frank over. Frank nodded to Timothy and both men came to escort their wives onto the dance floor. While waiting for everyone to arrange themselves, Frank, who had been elected the new shire secretary of Shipwreck Bay now that George was in jail, leaned towards Rebecca and said, 'I've been telling your husband how everyone in the district has been singing your praises. First you get our post office in order and now you run a successful event that gets everybody's spirits up again. I told your husband he hit the jackpot when he married you!'

'Thank you,' Rebecca replied. A tingle ran through her veins. She was in her element again and she felt happier than she had in weeks.

The band started playing a slow rhumba and Rebecca looked into Timothy's face and smiled. But he did not look amused. 'Did you tell Elaine that you want to run a fundraiser for a hospital?' he asked.

Rebecca's muscles pinched. She was annoyed at Elaine for spilling the beans. She had wanted to surprise Timothy with that brilliant idea one morning over breakfast.

'Yes,' she told him. 'I think it's entirely possible. I don't have to limit events to only this district. I can use my contacts in Sydney. I would need you, of course, to come and speak about the importance of a hospital for the town.'

Timothy's face turned hard and dark. His displeasure took her by surprise. She felt suddenly unsure of herself. Hadn't he wanted a hospital for years?

'And what about a baby, Rebecca?' Timothy asked. 'And your responsibilities to my mother?'

Rebecca was lost for words. She had believed with all her heart that he would be thrilled with the idea of a hospital fundraiser. 'Well, of course I want a baby, but we have to let nature decide when,' she said. 'And I'll still take care of your mother.'

The music stopped and the couples moved to their assigned corners. Elaine and Frank's corner was eliminated, but Timothy and Rebecca were safe to dance another round. This time the dance was a foxtrot. They said nothing further to each other, but Timothy kept wiggling the hand Rebecca was clasping until she was forced to let go of it.

'What's the matter?' she asked him.

'You're gripping my hand too hard. You're crushing my fingers.'

'I'm sorry,' Rebecca apologised, feeling flustered. 'I didn't realise.'

'You always grip too hard. I've told you that before. I need my hands for surgery, you know.'

Rebecca's embarrassment turned to irritation. 'You've never told me that before,' she said. 'I don't grip your hand too hard.'

'You hold my hand like a man, Rebecca,' Timothy replied. 'If I want to dance with a man, I'll ask Frank.'

Rebecca stopped dancing. 'I've never been told by anyone before that I grip his hand too hard. No man has ever said that to me!'

Timothy's face turned ashen and his eyes blazed with anger. He stormed off and took a seat at one of the tables at the side. Feeling like a fool standing alone on the dance floor, Rebecca held her composure and sat beside him. She smiled away the concerned look Elaine sent her, as if she and Timothy were a pair of eighty-year-olds who were simply too tired to dance anymore. Rebecca fought back tears. How could he make a scene like that, especially tonight? After all her hard work for the fundraiser? She nodded and waved as a waltz was played and the other dancers whirled past her. The other couples looked so happy in each other's company. What was the problem with her and Timothy?

At the end of the night, when the kitchen was cleared and the floor swept clean, she said goodbye to Elaine and Frank and got into the car next to Timothy.

'What's wrong?' Rebecca asked him. 'What's wrong with you tonight?'

He turned the car ignition. 'I don't think I'm the person who has something wrong with them, Rebecca.'

His voice was cold. Rebecca's blood chilled at the sound of it. 'Are you so angry that I gripped your hand too tightly? I told you I was sorry. Or perhaps you'd rather that I didn't hold your hand at all. Is that it?'

Timothy sneered. 'I'm not the one who throws past lovers in your face.'

'What are you talking about?' Rebecca's mind felt like it was being tied in knots. She was totally bewildered.

'"I've never been told by anyone before that I grip his hand too hard. No man has ever said that to me!"' Timothy said in a whiny, high-pitched voice that was meant to imitate her but didn't match her tone at all. He turned to her briefly before looking back to the road, his shoulders hunched towards the wheel. 'Do you know how many lovers I've had, Rebecca? Just two. Both of them my wives. There were plenty of women in Greece who threw themselves at me and just as many who lusted after me when I was in Sydney. But I believe in the sanctity of marriage. That's why I never even made a move on you when we were engaged. I thought if I treated you like a lady you might become one!'

Rebecca's head was spinning. 'You knew about Ned McKell when you married me. Why are you so angry about it now?'

He'd also known about Stefan Otto, but to mention him would only be throwing fuel on the fire.

He didn't answer her and that long silence was worse than his rebukes. It made her feel like all the worst of her insecurities were coming to the fore, along with the painful memories of her parents' emotional abandonment of her.

'How have I not acted like a lady?' she asked.

Still he did not answer her.

'Timothy?'

They drove the rest of the way in silence. When they reached the house, Timothy pulled up in front of it and got out of the car without opening the door for Rebecca. She got out herself and followed him inside. Instead of having a cup of tea with her in the kitchen as he had done after the dance a few weeks earlier, Timothy went straight upstairs and slammed the bedroom door.

Rebecca stood in the entrance hall, shaking and disorientated. Then, exhausted, she turned on the lamp in the parlour and collapsed into an armchair. A button on a cushion behind her jabbed into her back. She pulled the cushion out and rested it on her lap. 'What's happening?' she asked herself. 'Why is he so angry at me?' She played with the fringe of the cushion then frowned. She looked around the room at the furniture. Her eyes drifted from the carpet to the curtains. She stood up, her heart beating furiously. She stormed into the dining room and stared at the tablecloth and the wallpaper. The door to the kitchen was open and she could see the counter tops and the refrigerator.

'Everything is green,' she said out loud. 'Every damn thing is green.'

★

My darling Becky,

*How I wish I could be there to comfort you. Marriage is not for
the faint-hearted, to be sure. That's why I've never attempted
it myself. How on earth can a woman be committed to a man
and at the same time be free to be utterly herself? You have an
adventurous spirit that you have had to tame. You have gone
from living in a whirlwind to living in a gentle breeze. That's
bound to cause all sorts of conflicts in your mind. Timothy
seemed completely devoted to his mother. I can't imagine that he
would deliberately have decorated the house in a way that would
distress her. What would be the purpose of that? Are you sure
you aren't overreacting? Men are clueless to female sensitivities,
even when we tell them a hundred times what we like and what
we don't. And as for the business about the hospital, no man
wants to be upstaged by his wife. Perhaps it is merely something
he wants to achieve by his own merit.*

*Unfortunately, men do seem to make less of an effort
after marriage, which leaves the wife responsible for making
the situation work. My solution to the fading of romance
and the beginning of familiarity has always been to move
onwards and upwards quickly before any sort of quarrelling
and bitterness can set in. But we want different things, my
sweetie. You desire the love of a lifetime with one man and
you want children, so in that regard I feel quite inadequate to
advise you. But from all the marriages I've witnessed, after
the honeymoon there does seem to be a rather turbulent period
of adjustment. You might just have to weather the storm and*

hope to find a deeper, happier and more comforting love on
the other side. I'll be back in Sydney at the end of winter and
if you come up to stay with me you might find a short break
away from everything will be good for the both of you.

As to contacting his former wife, I can't see anything
good coming of that. First wives are notoriously jealous and
I'm sure if you had any sort of dealings with her she would
inject your mind with poison with the deliberate intention
of killing any joy the two of you might share. But if you
really do believe that in some way it will reveal something
to reassure you, then I have enclosed the address of my good
friend Don Walsh. He is ex-ASIO and there is nobody that
Don can't find …

With all my love,
Marion

Rebecca sat at her desk in the post office and thought about what
Marion had written to her. She stared at the garden she and
Timothy had planted together. He had been so keen, so ardent
then, but the man she lived with now was very different. Colder
and more distant. Even Marion, so worldly, sophisticated and
experienced, had been at a loss to explain it. Was it really only
a normal adjustment to married life? Rebecca found that hard
to believe. This was something more than a storm that would
pass, giving way to calmer days. Rather, Rebecca sensed there
was something beneath the surface, something festering. Far
from being in a marriage going through a period of adjustment,
Rebecca felt like she was clinging to a raft that was being tossed
about in a violent sea. Six weeks had passed since the fundraiser

dance and Timothy had barely looked at her or spoken to her. It was putting her off balance and she had a growing sense that putting her off balance was exactly what he intended to do.

The stomach-churning smell from the whaling station permeated the air. The whalers had caught their first catch for the season. Rebecca's mind drifted to Stefan. How on earth can a woman be committed to a man and at the same time be free to be utterly herself? Perhaps Stefan had given her the answer and she had rejected it. But it was too late to think of that. She dug her fingernails into her palms so that the pain would stop her thinking about what might have been.

★

Marion's friend, Don Walsh, worked quickly. Within a fortnight he replied to her. Rebecca read his letter while Johnny was out on his morning delivery run. Timothy's first wife, Arabella, had remarried. Her last name was Cousins now and she had a young child. She lived in the country town of Tamworth in northern New South Wales, where she and her husband ran the general store. It seemed an unlikely place to have ended up for the sophisticated Arabella that Rebecca had conjured in her mind. But they had a telephone and she could make the call direct if she wanted. Did she want to? Could she stand it if her marriage failed? It would add to her list of fiascos: an unloved daughter, a rejected mistress, a divorced wife.

Rebecca stood up and went to the sorting room. She stared at the switchboard for a long minute before making up her mind. The new postmaster – a man with a wife and family –

was due to start at the end of the month. She may not have too many more chances.

She sat down at the switchboard and, with her hands trembling, connected the call.

There were crackles on the line. Then: 'Cousins' General Store,' a female voice answered. 'Mrs Cousins speaking.'

Rebecca's throat went dry. That soft, soft voice. It didn't belong to the Arabella she had imagined. It was not a siren's voice. It was not a sophisticate's tone.

'Hello?' Arabella asked. 'Who is calling?'

Rebecca tugged the plug out and disconnected the call, more from shock than anything else. It was as if a grave had opened up in front of her and that soft, whisper-like voice had arisen from the mouldy darkness. It was calling her to peer into the grave, to view what she sensed she would find there but was too afraid to confront. Something putrid and horrid. Something that she did not want to admit to herself.

CHAPTER THIRTY-FIVE

The church service on the Sunday after the trial of George Pike commenced was a sombre affair. The townspeople greeted each other but couldn't bring themselves to look into each other's eyes. Nobody mentioned the former shire secretary although several of them, including Doris and Elaine, had been subpoenaed as witnesses. The silence on the subject hung over everybody like a dark cloud. Father Rob did not preach on redemption or condemnation or forgiveness. His sermon that morning was on Genesis. 'Eve represents everything about a woman a man should guard himself against,' he said. 'A woman is by nature deceitful, seductive and untrustworthy.'

Rebecca found it ironic, seeing that George's victim had been female.

At morning tea, she ate a scone and watched Timothy play a game of tag with the children. He took one small boy and lifted him high in the air. The child gave a shrill cry of pleasure. The others soaked up his attention when he listened to their stories and he was a shining example of self-control when they argued or got too rowdy.

'Come on, fellows! Everybody share!'

He spent time talking to one of the farmers he'd treated that week, who had been kicked by a horse, and although the man had probably one of the greatest economy of words Rebecca had ever come across, Timothy managed to get him talking.

'Doctor Litchfield, I dinged myself up a little. Still I'd rather chew off my leg than get rid of that horse. His strength and pulling power make him worth his weight in gold.'

'Yes,' laughed Timothy, patting the farmer's shoulder. 'But don't let him get the better of you next time, Mr Austin!'

Before everyone headed home for Sunday lunch, Rebecca waited by the church gate while Timothy sidled up to Doris. 'I must say the flowers in the church today were spectacular, Mrs Campbell. You must tell me the secret to your magnificent rhododendrons.'

He is the same with everybody else, observed Rebecca. He has only changed in his behaviour towards me. Why? What have I done to deserve it? Have I disappointed him in some way?

The heat of the midday sun and her growing unease made her suddenly nauseous. She leaned against the gatepost and rubbed her head.

She heard Doris say to Timothy, 'Your wife is a bit peaky this morning. Is she unwell? Or are we going to hear the patter of little feet soon?'

Rebecca glowered. Could Doris have picked a more sensitive subject to bring up? Despite all Timothy's efforts, she had not fallen pregnant. She was beginning to worry that the abortion may have left her infertile. But how could she ever tell him about that?

★

After lunch, Timothy went out into the garden and Rebecca took some cold cuts to Gillian. Timothy did not take his mother to church anymore, claiming he was worried that with the cooler weather approaching she could catch a cold. Rebecca felt sorry for Gillian; that Sunday outing was probably all she had to look forward to each week.

Rebecca was surprised to find her mother-in-law still lying in bed; Timothy had not sat her up before they'd left for church. There was a stench in the room like rotting fish. Were they boiling a whale today? Sunday? She shut the window, but that only made the smell worse. She pursed her lips. Timothy mustn't have changed his mother's incontinence nappy. It wasn't easy for Rebecca to lift Gillian on her own. She deliberated whether to get Timothy from the garden, but could see from the window that he was absorbed with digging among the flowerbeds and she hoped the activity might improve his mood. Gillian emitted a whimper and Rebecca peered into her face. Tears were seeping from the corners of her eyes and when she touched Gillian's arm, her mother-in-law's skin felt clammy and feverish.

'Gillian? What's the matter? Are you too hot?'

Rebecca peeled back the new pink quilt she had bought from the Mark Foy's catalogue. Was it too thick for the weather? Gillian's nightdress was transparent with sweat and sticking to her skin. Rebecca would need to give her a sponge bath and change it. She lifted the hem of the nightdress so she could take off the soiled nappy and reeled back in horror. On the old woman's thigh was a crater-like sore, red at the edges and oozing with yellow pus.

'Gillian!'

She put the cover over her again and ran out into the garden. Timothy was bent over, pulling out weeds.

'Your mother!' she cried. 'Her leg … she has a terrible bedsore!'

Timothy stood up. He threw down his gardening gloves and walked towards the house. Rebecca was shocked by how calm he was. He saw grisly wounds as a matter of routine, but this was his mother. She followed him back into the house but could not bear to go into Gillian's room again. He came out a few minutes later and glared at her.

'How could you have let this happen? I trusted you with her.'

Rebecca wavered, unsure if she had heard him correctly. Was he trying to blame her for this?

'Go pack a bag for her!' he shouted, indicating a blue toiletry suitcase next to the dressing table in Gillian's room. 'She has to go to hospital, otherwise that sore will turn septic. I'll bring the car around the front.'

Rebecca was sure she was hurrying, but everything seemed to have turned to slow motion. The toiletry bag Timothy had indicated had a built-in cosmetic shelf and Rebecca couldn't fit Gillian's slippers into it. Did Gillian have an overnight bag somewhere? Rebecca peered into the wardrobe. On the top shelf she found a small blue suitcase that matched the toiletry bag and took it down. Her hands trembled as she packed underwear and nightclothes for Gillian. When Timothy returned, she passed the bag she had packed to him. 'Grab my jacket and hat, will you!' he said. 'Then help me get her to the car!'

After Timothy left for the hospital with his mother, Rebecca went to the kitchen. She paced from the refrigerator to the sink and back again like a mouse trapped in a maze. She tried to think, to reason out what had just happened but her thoughts wouldn't flow, they went round and round like leaves in a muddy whirlpool.

Four hours went by before Timothy returned. Rebecca jumped when she heard the car door slam. She could feel the fury emanating from him before he even appeared in the kitchen.

'How is your mother?' she asked. 'Will she be all right?'

Timothy looked at her from the corner of his eye, like a horse about to turn aggressive. His familiar voice did not match his altered behaviour. 'You know she needs to be moved every two to three hours!'

'You never told me that. You told me to read to her and feed her. I thought you were taking care of her other needs!'

No sooner had she spoken than she regretted it. Her challenge only made Timothy angrier. He moved towards her and she backed away from him. 'I thought you knew how to take care of invalids!' he said. 'Did you ever let *your* mother get into such an appalling state? You're irresponsible, Rebecca. I can't trust you with anything! Is that how you let Debbie drown?'

It was as if he had slapped her. Rebecca's cheeks stung with heat. 'You bastard!'

Timothy's eyes flashed. 'What did you call me? What did you call your husband? You foul-mouthed whore!'

Rebecca fled the kitchen and ran up the stairs. Timothy pursued her. 'I shouldn't have married you. I only married you because nobody else wanted you. I felt sorry for you, Rebecca. You were a ruined woman: a woman who had gone from man to man. I thought I'd give you a chance to make something of yourself. And this is how you repay me!'

Every word was like a bullet fired into her. Rebecca ran faster, but Timothy caught the edge of her skirt. She fell to her knees, tugged her skirt away and got up again. 'How dare you!' she spat. 'How dare you speak to me like that! I've done everything I can to make you happy.'

She ran into their bedroom and opened the wardrobe. Her suitcases were at the bottom of it; she pulled them out and tossed them on the bed. She swept items from her dressing table into one and piled some underwear into the other.

Timothy stood in the doorway, blocking it. 'What do you think you're doing?'

'I don't know why you're acting this way,' she said, folding a dress into the suitcase, 'but I'm going back to Sydney!'

Timothy slammed the door behind him. His face was livid. Rebecca's heart fell to her feet. He had never hit her but she was afraid he would now. She manoeuvred around the bed, away from him.

'Yes, that's what you do, Rebecca, isn't it? When you've made a mistake you can't face up to, you run away. That's how you ended up in Shipwreck Bay in the first place, remember. Running away from a scandal!'

Rebecca stared at him. The man before her had Timothy's eyes, Timothy's face and Timothy's stature but was not Timothy. Who was this? Rebecca had once read a science fiction story about aliens who created human clones, producing beings devoid of morality and emotion. It was as if Rebecca was looking at one of those abominations now. Her eyes darted around the room. How could she get away from him? If the window hadn't been so high, she would have jumped out of it.

'Where are you going to run to now, Rebecca? You're a murderess.'

Rebecca backed away as he stepped towards her. 'You know that's not true! You know I didn't kill Nancy!'

'How do I know that?' he retorted. 'The nurses at Twin Falls Hospital were horrified when they saw Mum's thigh. They couldn't believe her own daughter-in-law had neglected her like that! "She must have a mental incapacity!" the matron told me. "She should be put in an asylum!"'

'Is that a threat?' Rebecca asked him. 'Is that what you're saying you'll do to me?'

He laughed unpleasantly. 'It won't be so difficult to explain to the police that I lied about the alibi. They will understand that I was taken in by your Jezebel charms. Didn't Father Rob say a woman is by nature deceitful, seductive and untrustworthy? I will tell them you were Ned McKell's mistress; they will be interested in that. Where are you going to run away to then?'

Rebecca's mind was shattering to pieces like the Vallauris vase she had smashed in her kitchen on her first night in Shipwreck Bay. 'You told me the police already knew that. You told me they found evidence Nancy was blackmailing me.'

Timothy hesitated, turning something over in his mind. Then he shouted at her again: 'Put those suitcases away! You won't be going anywhere!' Then he left the room, slamming the door behind him.

Rebecca sank down on the bed, feeling as though she had survived a tornado.

CHAPTER THIRTY-SIX

The next day in the post office, Johnny had dozens of questions to ask Rebecca about forms and telegrams but she couldn't hear a thing he said. She felt panicked, anxious, like an animal in a trap.

After Johnny bundled himself out the door, Rebecca put another call through to Arabella Cousins.

This time a man's voice answered. 'Cousins' General Store. Tom Cousins here.'

'Hello,' Rebecca said. 'Shipwreck Bay Post Office on the line. Could I speak to Mrs Cousins, please?'

Rebecca was grateful he didn't ask her any questions. A moment later Arabella's voice came on the line. 'Hello? This is Arabella Cousins speaking.'

'Mrs Cousins, I am Rebecca Litchfield. I'm the wife of Doctor Timothy Litchfield. Your former husband.'

There was utter silence. Then Arabella spoke again. Her voice was no longer soft, but stiff and angry. 'What do you want? How did you get my number?'

'Please,' Rebecca said. 'There is something I need to ask you.'

Arabella lowered her voice. 'I've done everything to get away from him. I've not told a soul about what he did. Leave me alone!'

Her words were strong but there was a tremor in her voice. It was the voice of a terrified woman.

Rebecca sensed Arabella was about to hang up on her. Her own voice broke with panic. 'Is there something that I should know about my husband?' she pleaded.

There was a long pause. Rebecca wondered if Arabella had walked away from the telephone. Then her soft voice returned. 'Yes … your husband isn't who he pretends to be. He was dismissed from Sydney Hospital for inappropriate sexual conduct towards patients.'

Rebecca felt that the world was spinning out of control. Absolutely nothing was as it seemed. Everything was an illusion. Good people were bad, and bad people were good.

'You are in great danger, Mrs Litchfield. Very great danger,' Arabella whispered into the receiver. 'You need to leave now. Any way you can.'

Rebecca pressed the heel of her palm against her forehead. She knew this. *She knew this.* Why hadn't she acted sooner? Why had she continued to believe the farce that she had married a good man and that she was the problem in the marriage?

'And my mother-in-law … is she in danger too?'

'Gillian? His mother? He hates his mother. She knows what he is. She tried to warn me before I married him. But he convinced me that she was insane. She knew all about him and tried to tell me, but I laughed it off as bitter fancy.'

'She knew what exactly?'

But even before Arabella answered, Rebecca sensed what was coming. She couldn't breathe. Her face broke out into a sweat. Her hands were clammy. The world took on a dark shade as if something evil was looming over her.

'She knew that he killed his brother, Rodney. He smothered him with a pillow.'

CHAPTER THIRTY-SEVEN

Rebecca sat at her desk detached from the world around her. The reality she had lived in was coming apart and a new one forming. *Men are predators and we are the prey.* That is what Rebecca had said to Berit in their last conversation. She had thought she was the experienced, wiser woman when she had given that advice, but now she saw the horrible irony. Sanders Olsen had been a hunter with blood on his hands; he didn't disguise it. Ned was a selfish jerk who never pretended otherwise. But Timothy was something else – something malignant. From the moment he had laid eyes on her, he had identified her as potential prey. All those questions he had asked weren't out of friendly curiosity. There had been an ulterior motive. What had he gleaned? That she didn't have a family. That she was alone. She stared out at the garden. Even that had been a ploy, right there from the beginning. He'd fooled her and he'd fooled the whole of Shipwreck Bay. Getting her out in the garden with him was a way of scenting her, marking her out as his own. She was his possession and trophy.

She understood now why he had returned to Shipwreck Bay. It was not to care for his mother, but because it was the only place he could go where people wouldn't suspect his secret. How convenient for him for Gillian to have had a stroke. Why did fate so often favour evil? The whole time that Rebecca had thought that Gillian hated her, she had been trying to warn her.

Rebecca leaned back in her chair, the story Arabella had told her on the telephone rolling out in her head like a radio play.

I met Timothy when I was a nurse in Sydney. He was handsome and charming and set all the nurses' hearts aflutter when he made his rounds. It flattered me when he began to pay me particular attention. He took me dancing at the Trocadero and other nightspots that I would not have gone to on my own. I was an orphan who had grown up in a convent. I was swept off my feet by his sophisticated ways. When he asked me to marry him, I could not believe it. He was a 'catch', everyone said so.

At first, it was fun being married to Timothy and playing house with him in the apartment we rented in Paddington. But he began to change. He stopped taking me out. He accused me of embarrassing him with my lack of finesse. He became critical of everything I did from the way that I spoke to the way that I dressed. I kept trying to improve myself so that he would love me again like he'd done before. I was constantly trying to guess what made him angry, but it changed all the time. Sometimes if I didn't do something the way he wanted he would stop speaking to me for days at a time.

Then one evening he came home in a particularly nasty mood. Something about a change in the scheduling at the hospital had upset him. I listened and nodded as I went about making us dinner, trying not to inflame the situation. But I could feel his anger escalating. He was watching me, waiting for something. Then all of a sudden he grabbed me and threw me to the floor. His hands were around my throat and he squeezed hard. I struggled to get away from him, but his hands pressed more firmly.

I still have a ringing in my ears from the attack. Timothy told the hospital that I had tried to hang myself and he had saved me at the last minute. He had me committed to an asylum and managed to divorce me on the grounds that I was insane. I left Sydney as soon as I was released and moved to the country, terrified that he might find me. But he didn't even look for me. Whatever it was he had sought from me in marrying me, it was obvious I couldn't provide it, so he had discarded me as if I was a piece of rubbish. It was only by chance, from an old nursing colleague, that I learned the reason for his violent mood that day: he had been dismissed from his position at the hospital. It had been discovered he was interfering with female patients under anaesthesia. The hospital did it quietly to preserve its reputation, but those who worked closely with him knew. I have never revealed to anyone what he did to me. I've been too frightened. He is capable of anything to hide who he really is …

Rebecca stood up and stared out the window. She now understood why Timothy had not wanted her to fundraise for a hospital for Shipwreck Bay. He knew she was determined and capable enough to succeed. It would have exposed him to people in the medical profession who may have known about his past. He only pretended to campaign for a hospital when he was sure the town would never get one. Making the townspeople think he was a wonderful man allowed him to stalk women right under their noses.

Then something else dawned on her. What was it he had said about Anne Peberdy? That she was partially deaf and a loner, pretty but simple-minded. She went to the sorting room and threw open the cupboard where she had put the box of Mabel's personal items. It had never been collected. She pulled it out and took it back to her desk, cutting through the string with a pen knife. Her eyes moved over the contents as she took them out one by one: a comb, a Max Factor powder compact, two copies of *Good Housekeeping*, a scrapbook of recipes, a Butterick's pattern for a sun dress. Under a bolt of floral cotton she found a letter and she let out a breath when she saw the handwriting was Timothy's.

> *Dear Mrs Peberdy,*
>
> *I am deeply offended that you have questioned the amount of time Anne has been staying in my home for her course of treatment. As you know, for some weeks she has been unusually withdrawn but under my care she has been making progress. Or perhaps you would prefer for her to be put in a large public institution? A place where she would be in constant danger of violence? You do not have the means for a private asylum, and Anne displays the classic neuroses of a daughter deprived of a father at an early age. I had hoped that you might be more grateful to me ...*

Rebecca stopped reading and swallowed. Mabel had obviously become suspicious of Timothy's intentions towards Anne. But Timothy had masterfully turned it back on her.

> *There is a great deal of shame around your daughter's condition and I am trying to prevent the knowledge of it spreading far beyond our protective little community here in Shipwreck Bay …*

Anne had drowned herself, probably because Timothy had molested her. Mabel must have realised that she had been duped by Timothy and had then taken her own life. Timothy had tried to put the blame on Stefan for Anne's death. But when he'd said Stefan had 'seduced' women all the way from Wollongong to Penguin Bay, it had been a projection of his own predatory crimes. She glanced at the wedding ring on her finger and understood that he would kill her if she tried to leave. For it was obvious now that she was his greatest prize. Not a young, innocent girl but an experienced and desirable woman. He'd made her his wife, the ultimate male possession. But she had proved too much of a challenge, not as pliable and easily manipulated as he had hoped. He had tried to strangle Arabella prior to discarding her. What was he planning to do to her?

She sat back down in her chair. Her heart and her mind raced like galloping horses. There was no one in the town who she could talk to. Berit had found an ally in Rebecca, but Rebecca had no one in Shipwreck Bay. She rubbed her hand down the side of her neck. There was one small, slim hope. Provided he was still in Australia.

She went to the exchange and put through a call to the Menzies Hotel in Melbourne.

'Mr Otto is out for the day,' the receptionist told her. 'May I leave him a message?'

'Yes, tell him that Rebecca called and to meet her at sunset at the headland as soon as he can. Tell him to come quickly, by any means possible.'

★

Rebecca felt feverish when she sat down at the dinner table with Timothy that evening. Her skin was burning but her hands were ice-cold. She was conscious of him watching her. Beneath that handsome face, that English skin, lay a volcano: something volatile and dangerous. It could erupt at any time.

'You've undercooked the carrots,' he said, pushing his vegetables around his plate. 'You should try boiling them next time.'

Rebecca nodded placidly even though there was nothing wrong with the carrots. He was trying to provoke her. 'I'm sorry.'

He frowned and she was careful not to let her mask slip. She chewed a forkful of peas but struggled to swallow them. Her stomach was in knots. Don't let him see, she thought. Don't let him suspect I know his evil secrets. Opposite her was a man who had smothered his infant brother out of jealousy and had tried to strangle his first wife for who knew what reason.

'You were longer at the post office today,' he said, cutting into his steak. 'I was late back for Mrs McKenzie's appointment.'

'I'm sorry. I had some difficulty with the exchange. It won't happen again.'

She looked down at her food but she felt his gaze on her, travelling from her face to her hands. It took all her willpower to stop them trembling.

'Hmm,' he said, turning his attention back to his plate. 'It's not your fault, but it will be better when the new postmaster starts. Then you won't really need to go into town at all.'

I haven't produced a child for him, Rebecca thought. A child would have been the ultimate charade. It would have added to his parody of upright characters: the caring doctor, the devoted son, the adoring husband *and the loving father*. I haven't produced a child and that is why he is punishing me.

After dinner, Timothy went to read in the sitting room and Rebecca collected the dishes and took them to the kitchen. She stood at the sink and gripped the sides of the counter top, letting out a long, silent sigh. She hadn't realised until then that she had been holding her breath.

*

The next day at the post office Rebecca hoped there would be a call or some cryptic message from Stefan confirming that he would come. He was her only chance. She couldn't leave by train. Ernie would question her and, besides that, the station was visible to the whole town. Then she had the problem of Gillian. She had expected her mother-in-law would be kept at the hospital for at least a week, but now she had to make a plan for her too. Timothy had called Rebecca at the post office that morning to say that he would be picking Gillian up from Twin Falls Hospital in two days' time. Rebecca had been struck by how normal he had sounded on the telephone. It was as if his outburst over his mother's bedsore had never happened. But she knew now he wasn't normal. He was evil.

When Rebecca heard nothing from Stefan, she left another message for him.

'He didn't come back until very late and went straight to his room, but I will make sure he gets the message today,' said the receptionist.

Just in case, before going home, Rebecca went out to the headland. She could not bear to look at the ruins of Stefan's house. Instead she stood gazing out at the ocean. 'Please come, Stefan. I need your help.'

After two days more of waiting without any word from Stefan, Rebecca was sure that, for whatever reason, he wasn't coming.

*

That night, Rebecca lay next to Timothy, listening to his breathing. She squeezed her eyes shut to hold back the tears. All she'd ever wanted was to be safe. Now she was lying in bed with a man who was capable of killing his own brother. The knowledge that he might kill her too put her in such a state of fear that her teeth started chattering and she had to cover her mouth with her pillow so Timothy wouldn't hear. She clenched her fists and willed herself to think of a plan. If she could get Johnny's bicycle when he came back from the station, she could ride to Angelcliffe Station. Passengers were so rare there that it wasn't on any schedule, but all trains would stop if they were flagged down. Then she could take the train to Wollongong. It would be too risky to try to get all the way to Sydney in one trip, in case Timothy was alerted and followed the train in his car. But he wouldn't be expecting her to get off at Wollongong and therefore wouldn't go searching for her there. She would need all her strength for her escape, but she couldn't sleep. Images of Berit hanging from the winch on the flensing deck at the whaling station kept springing up in her mind. Berit had been so close to being free but somehow Sanders had caught her. Rebecca would have to be careful that the same thing didn't happen to her.

*

After Timothy left for the surgery the following morning, Rebecca stumbled around the house dizzy and off-balance, as if she was suffering vertigo. Her stomach lurched with every step she took. A strong wind was blowing in gusts, bending the treetops and making the walls creak. She put on a dark brown dress with deep pockets – the colour for camouflage and the deep pockets to hide the housekeeping money she'd taken. She checked herself in the mirror, careful that the pockets didn't bulge suspiciously or make jingling sounds when she moved.

When she fed Gillian she tried to behave normally, but the old woman could tell something was wrong. Her eyes followed Rebecca around the room.

'I'll send help for you, Gillian,' Rebecca promised her. 'As soon as I get away I'll make sure Mrs Todd knows the truth.' Then gently stroking Gillian's cheek, she added, 'I'm sorry I didn't understand what you were trying to tell me.'

She took Gillian's arm out of the sling and squeezed her hand. The old woman squeezed her hand back. Rebecca would probably never know how Gillian discovered that Timothy had smothered Rodney. When she looked into her mother-in-law's eyes she felt the burden she must have borne when she realised that one child had killed another, but to say anything to anyone would have been to lose them both. Poor Gillian. She must have hoped against hope that Timothy would grow up to be normal.

Rebecca opened Gillian's wardrobe and reached for the suitcase she'd used for her mother-in-law's visit to the hospital. She intended to pack the things that Gillian would need immediately, so that Mrs Todd could take her away as soon as possible. But the suitcase was caught on something. She tugged but couldn't free it. She moved the chair from next to Gillian's bed and climbed onto it. There was a small compartment at the back of the shelf and the luggage label was caught on its handle. Rebecca yanked the suitcase out and dropped it on the floor. Some instinct of curiosity made her return her attention to the compartment. Secret compartments at the backs of wardrobes had been popular during the war, but why would Gillian have one in hers? She opened the door and was surprised to find a document satchel inside it. Had Timothy hidden something there, not expecting Rebecca to be rummaging around in his mother's wardrobe? She reached both hands forward and pulled the satchel out. There was something heavy and flat inside it. She undid the buckle and opened the flap. Her breath caught in her throat when she saw what was inside. She took out the spiral-bound scrapbook Nancy had brought to the post office the day she had threatened to expose her. Rebecca flicked through it, her mind foggy and unclear. How had it come to be in Gillian's wardrobe? Then the fog cleared and she understood. Timothy had killed Nancy.

She leaned against the bedpost as the weight of the truth bore down on her. There had never been a note from Nancy. How could there have been? Nancy was dead by the time Timothy returned to check on his mother. Marge had told him about the argument and he had gone to see Nancy on his way home and she had revealed everything. Rebecca closed her eyes. But Timothy had already known about Ned McKell. He'd guessed already, hadn't he? *I believe something happened to you in Sydney, something that made you want to leave.* He couldn't bear to look like a fool instead of a saint in front of the townspeople. Then the deeper truth revealed itself to her. No, it had been something even more important than maintaining a front. The scandal was knowledge he was going to use to entrap Rebecca. As long as he held it over her, she wouldn't be able to leave him, no matter how hideous he revealed himself to be behind closed doors. He couldn't have Nancy spoil his plan, so he had killed her. Bile burned in Rebecca's throat. The police had not found this scrapbook because he had taken it. He had not been Rebecca's alibi. She doubted now they had ever suspected her. *She had been his!*

She was about to put the scrapbook back when something small fell out of it and tinkled when it hit the floor. Rebecca picked the object up. It was a gold and diamond wedding ring encrusted in a flaky brown substance. She recognised the bouquet design on it. It was Nancy's, and the brown substance was dried blood. She covered her mouth with the back of her hand, on the verge of being sick. Timothy had probably taken the ring to make the murder look like a bungled robbery, but a real burglar would have stolen more. Perhaps the missing wedding ring was one of the reasons the police had suspected George, apart from the fact that he and Nancy didn't get along and that he didn't have an alibi? Rebecca shook her head when she remembered Stefan telling her about George's shady dealings. He probably didn't have an alibi because he'd been meeting with his criminal connections when he should have been at the scout camp, and they were hardly going to expose themselves to save him. Taking the ring may have looked like the act of a vengeful husband. But why had Timothy kept it? The ring was incriminating evidence. Then it dawned on her. *It won't be so difficult to explain to the police that I lied about the alibi. They will understand that I was taken in by your Jezebel charms.* He'd warned her that if she tried to leave, he would pin the murder on her. What better way to confirm that than to plant some sort of 'souvenir' in Rebecca's possession?

Panic seized her but she stood frozen, aware she was losing precious time yet unable to move.

'*Go-e,*' Gillian urged, her eyes welling with desperation and … *sympathy.* '*Go-e!*'

Rebecca put the scrapbook and ring in the satchel and placed it back in the compartment. She couldn't risk what Timothy might do to Gillian if he discovered them missing. She packed the small suitcase and returned it to the top shelf. Then she kissed her mother-in-law on the cheek before heading for the door. She turned briefly and their eyes met. Who knew what the next few hours would bring? One of them – or both – could end up dead.

★

The last few minutes before midday were excruciating. Rebecca eyed the clock in the kitchen, her ears straining. The sound of Timothy's car in the driveway sent her scrambling to her feet. She picked up her purse and glanced around the house one last time. It was a beautiful house, it should have been a wonderful home. But she understood now that she would never see it again.

The motor on Timothy's car was still running. He hadn't got out of it. Then he tooted the horn. She opened the front door and looked out. He gestured to her to come to the car. The wind, which was blowing harder now, drowned out all sound. Her other senses had numbed too. Her vision had turned blurry and she swallowed to get rid of the sharp metallic taste in her mouth.

'I have to take some medicine to Mr Farrington,' Timothy said, leaning out of the window. 'I'll drop you off at the post office on the way. Mum will be all right for a few minutes.'

He sounded like a normal husband making a perfectly natural suggestion. For a fleeting moment Rebecca wondered if she had imagined the whole thing and maybe he hadn't done all those terrible things after all. Wouldn't it be easier then to not do this? But she knew the truth in her bones. Hadn't she witnessed his dark side herself? She climbed into the passenger seat and perched her purse on her lap, circling it with her arms to disguise its odd shape. She had been careful not to overpack it, but it was heavier than usual with her jewellery. She would need those items to sell to get herself started somewhere else. She had not taken the engagement ring Timothy had given her, but had hidden it behind a book in the library. She was certain Gillian had never owned such an ugly thing. It had probably belonged to one of his other victims and he got some perverse delight out of making her wear it. She turned and smiled at Timothy but couldn't bring her eyes to meet his.

'What's wrong?' he asked.

'Nothing's wrong.'

'You seem on edge about something.'

'Do I?'

He turned the engine off and scrutinised her. She thought of Berit again, and how one false move could be fatal. Then, by a tremendous exertion of will, she managed to compose herself.

'I suppose I am a little on edge about the new postmaster coming. I want everything to be running smoothly for when he arrives, but that trouble with the exchange the other day has me worried.'

Timothy restarted the engine. 'That's not your responsibility, Rebecca. You've got other things to think about now. Other responsibilities.'

'I know.'

'You've got to realise you're my wife now. That is the only duty you have.'

Timothy berating her had a strangely calming effect. Now she understood what he really was, his admonitions no longer hurt her. If anything they reassured her that he'd believed her explanation. When they arrived at the post office, Rebecca steeled herself before leaning towards Timothy to give him a peck on the cheek. The grocer and his wife waved to them, and Timothy got out to open the door for her, something he had ceased to do whenever they were alone.

'I'll see you at two o'clock,' she told him. But as she watched him drive away she muttered, 'I hope you rot in hell!'

There was no time to waste once she was inside her office. Rebecca wrote a letter to Marion explaining everything that she had found out about Timothy and a similar one to Mrs Todd to tell her why Gillian would need her help. She would post them both as soon as she got to Wollongong. She could not entrust either to Johnny. They could cost Gillian her life if he should give them to Timothy once Rebecca was reported missing.

Johnny was late back from the morning mail run. Rebecca bit her nails until they bled. Everything was tight now and she could not afford for one thing to go wrong, including missing the train at Angelcliffe.

'Sorry, I'm late,' said Johnny, wiping sweat from his forehead with the back of his hand as he hurried in the door. 'Mrs Davis wanted help hanging a painting. I can go out for the afternoon run straight away.'

'Not today,' Rebecca said. 'I need the bicycle for an errand. Could you watch over the post office until I get back?'

'Sure,' the boy replied, plonking himself down at the sorting table.

Rebecca eyed him for a moment. He did the most confounded things.

'Johnny, did you tell anyone that I went home with a migraine the afternoon Mrs Pike was murdered?'

He looked up at her and his goofy face turned serious. 'No,' he said. 'Only Doc Litchfield when he rang and asked where you were. You didn't fill out a leave form. I didn't want you to get in any sort of trouble with the Postmaster-General's Department. It was my fault that Mrs Pike got so angry at you that it gave you a headache.'

With an affection that surprised her, Rebecca smiled. Johnny was annoying and completely inefficient and yet he was a good soul. Good souls were rare in Shipwreck Bay.

'All the best, Johnny,' she said. 'You're a fine kid.'

He smiled shyly, bemused by her sudden warmth towards him but not suspicious. 'Take your time, Mrs Litchfield,' he said. 'If you're not back in an hour I'll take the afternoon post on foot.'

★

Rebecca's legs were trembling but she cruised casually through the town on the bicycle. It was important she didn't draw attention to herself. She waved to Gavin Young when he drove by her and stopped for a friendly word with Maeve Barney, who was tending the roses in her garden.

'It will be strange having a man as the postmaster,' the elderly lady told her. 'Still I suppose we'll manage.'

'I'm sure you will,' replied Rebecca, keeping the conversation short. 'He was a ship's captain, so I'm sure he will run things efficiently.'

She rode on and turned north on Ocean Road. She prayed that she would not meet anyone driving in or out of town. When she reached the top of the headland she was tempted to look back at Shipwreck Bay, but she willed herself to keep moving forward.

Once she was over the headland, she quickened her pace, cruising at breakneck speeds down the hills and pedalling up the inclines with all her strength. Her skin prickled, every nerve on high alert. If she hadn't had to wear a dress to make her escape, and had worn pedal pushers instead, her thighs might have been spared. But they were raw and burning. Her bra and girdle chafed her skin as if they were made of sandpaper instead of satin, but she had to push onwards. It was after two o'clock now and Timothy would be livid that she was late back from the post office. She wondered at what point he would start searching for her. Despite the ground she had covered, it wouldn't take him long to catch up in his car. She bit her lip, wondering if it would be wiser to steer off the road and use the bush track that ran alongside the rail line. But that would slow her down and she needed to get the train if she wanted to be in Wollongong by the evening. Spurred on by the fear that Timothy might catch her, she pushed harder, although her back was gripped by painful knots and her calves had turned numb. Then out of nowhere a car appeared on the road ahead. Rebecca veered off into the bushes before it passed. The blood drained from her face when she recognised the driver. Father Rob!

If he had seen her, Father Rob would be nosy enough to ask Timothy what his wife was doing so far out of town on a bicycle. There was no choice but to travel off the road now. The wind that had been blowing earlier had settled, but the bush track was littered with fallen branches. Rebecca had to stop several times to move larger ones out of the way. When the track veered away from the rail line and into a gulley, she was temporarily disorientated. Come on! she urged herself, although she was not confident that she was still travelling towards Angelcliffe. An unsettling feeling stirred in her stomach that she may in fact be looping back around to Shipwreck Bay.

When the little bushland station appeared up ahead of her, Rebecca cried out with relief. She glanced at her watch. The train for Wollongong was due in ten minutes. She propped the bicycle next to a eucalyptus tree. When she reached Wollongong she would send a note to Johnny, telling him where he could pick it up. If everything went to plan she would be safe. But if things didn't go to plan? She glanced nervously over her shoulder. She couldn't afford to think of that. It crossed her mind that perhaps she should hide in the bush until the train arrived, but that would be futile. Angelcliffe was a station in the middle of nowhere, so she would have to signal the train driver to stop. She was on edge until she heard the rumble of a heavy diesel engine. The train appeared through the trees and Rebecca waved it down. Only when she climbed into the first carriage did she even dare to breathe. She pressed her head against the cool glass of the window and tried to soothe herself. But she knew she would not be safe until she got to Wollongong. She would go straight to the police station and tell Detectives Tarbell and Blake what she had discovered. She didn't know how they would react when she told them about Timothy. There was a slim chance they might suspect her as an accomplice in Nancy's murder; after all, she had collaborated with Timothy's alibi. She'd have to take the chance that the evidence stacked up against Timothy, including his past history and his treatment of Arabella, would convince them. She no longer cared that she risked the press finding out that she had been Ned McKell's mistress. That problem seemed insignificant compared to the threat she now faced.

When the train passed the next station, Rebecca felt relieved. Then with the passing of each successive station she started to relax. She closed her eyes and felt the train's vibration. When she opened her eyes again she caught a glimpse of a tiny mining town through the trees. It wasn't a scheduled stop, so she was surprised when the train came to an abrupt halt at the station. She glanced around anxiously. The middle-aged man across the aisle grimaced and shrugged his shoulders. The other passengers, a group of old men in lawn-bowling uniforms, seemed as perplexed as she did. The conductor burst through the carriage.

'There's been a rock fall up ahead,' he told them. 'We have to wait here until it's cleared.'

'How long will that be?' Rebecca asked.

The conductor shrugged. 'Perhaps another half hour or so.'

Rebecca rubbed her hands down her skirt. In half an hour Timothy could be upon them in his car. She slipped her feet out of her shoes and cringed when she saw the raw blisters on them. Her bladder was full, causing a sharp twinge in her stomach. She couldn't use the toilet on the train while it was in the station. She gathered her purse and stepped out onto the platform. There was no stationmaster in attendance. He must have been supervising the workmen who, from the sound of voices and ringing shovels, were clearing rocks somewhere up ahead on the track. Passengers from the other carriages got off the train to stretch their legs too. Deciding that she would have enough time to relieve herself she walked to the ladies' room at the far end of the platform. Once inside the cubicle, she lifted her skirt and surveyed the damage to her thighs. Her skin had erupted into an angry red rash of oozing blisters where her girdle had rubbed. But she had nothing she could use to soothe it. At the basin, she slipped out of her shoes and placed each foot in turn in the bowl, letting the cool water give her some relief. The rumble of the train engine roaring to life startled her. She turned off the tap and slipped on her shoes. But when she grabbed the handle on the door, it wouldn't turn. She yanked it harder with no result. Her blood pumping in her ears, she shoved her shoulder against the door. Still it wouldn't budge.

'All aboard!' she heard the conductor call.

'I'm here!' she cried out, beating the door with both hands 'Wait!'

Then she heard the whistle and the rhythmic beat of the train shunting off. They couldn't have been in the station more than ten minutes! Why hadn't the other passengers told the conductor that she hadn't got back on the train? She flexed every muscle in her body and threw herself against the door. This time it gave way easily. But it was too late. She burst out onto the platform only to see the train moving out of the station.

'Stop!' she called, running after it.

But it gathered speed and continued on its way. Rebecca stood open-mouthed, watching it disappear into the distance. There would not be another train to Wollongong until later that evening.

'Rebecca.'

Her blood turned cold. She whispered a silent, feverish prayer that she had imagined the voice, but when she turned and saw Timothy standing behind her she knew everything was lost. For an eternity they stood staring at each other. His eyes had no soul behind them: they were like those of a statue. She realised then why the door hadn't opened: because he'd held it shut.

'I ...' she began but couldn't finish. There was no story she could make up for this. No excuse she could give. It was clear she had been running away, *from him*.

'All right,' he said, continuing to watch her with those empty eyes. 'Mum is on her own. We'd best get home then.'

He sounded calm but that chilled her more than ever. Her mind began working again. Without moving her head she tried to think where she could run. The station was too far from the town and she wouldn't be able to outrun him. She had to think of something else. Then she remembered what her father had told her once about stray dogs: *Don't run. If you run, you will set off their hunting instinct and they will see you as prey.*

The only choice she had was to cooperate with Timothy and look for another way to escape later.

★

Timothy had parked his car under a tree in the street that ran parallel to the station. He must have been following the train and seized the opportunity when it was delayed. Time and circumstance had been on his side. He opened the passenger door and she got in, then he went to the driver's side and started the engine. She winced at every headland they passed on their way back down the coast but kept her eyes ahead of her, doing all she could to avoid attracting his attention to her purse.

'Who have you been speaking to?' he asked. 'Who did you tell that you were leaving?'

He was assessing what other people knew. Rebecca hesitated, not sure how to best answer him. It would be safer if he thought at least someone else knew she was leaving and why, but it could also infuriate him that she had revealed his dirty, dark secrets. Unable to decide what to tell him, she made a last-ditch effort to appeal to his humanity. 'You were frightening me. I didn't feel safe with you anymore.'

'I had to come up with a story for Father Rob,' he said, ignoring her. 'He wanted to know if everything was all right. He saw you riding north on Ocean Road. I told him the most ridiculous story: that you were going to collect some waratah seeds for our garden.'

Rebecca nodded and nodded again. She was like one of Doris's nodding donkey ornaments. Keep your eyes ahead, she told herself, and he won't notice.

'What's in your purse?'

Rebecca tried to swallow but all the muscles in her throat constricted. 'My coin purse and some powder and lipstick.'

Timothy stopped the car. Keep breathing, Rebecca told herself, just keep breathing. She could sense his mind ticking over. At any moment he would figure it out.

'I have to go to the toilet again,' she said, opening the car door. 'I'll go behind a bush.'

She lurched out of the car, carrying her purse in front of her, her eyes darting from left to right. She could rip the letters to Marion and Mrs Todd into pieces and bury them.

'I'll only be a minute,' she called over her shoulder.

But she hadn't fooled him. He lurched up behind her and spun her to face him. 'What's in your purse?' he asked, trying to grab it from her. Rebecca tugged the purse away from him again. She didn't see his fist coming, it happened so fast. His knuckles struck her eye socket and knocked her off her feet. Her head hit the ground and everything went black. When she came to, Timothy was sitting on a log and the contents of her purse were scattered around him. He was holding the letter she had written to Marion, his eyes darting wildly over the words. Rebecca got up and tried to run but Timothy grabbed her around the neck in a stranglehold. She clawed frantically at his arms, trying to free herself.

'Where were you going?' he screamed in her ear. 'To the police?'

Rebecca's breathing was ragged and shallow. The sky was darkening and the trees were spinning. She was certain now of one thing only: Timothy was going to kill her.

CHAPTER THIRTY-NINE

It was stifling in the boot. Rebecca drifted in and out of consciousness. Her throat was parched, making it difficult to breathe. She squinted and touched the swelling around her eye. The throbbing pain in her head eclipsed the raw pain of her thighs. She couldn't tell where they were heading, but the car was moving fast. Then it came to a stop. Rebecca moaned and tried to lift her head. Timothy's shoes crunched on the gravel as he got out. A door creaked noisily nearby. Then the car rocked as he threw something heavy onto the back seat. The *ding* of metal striking metal made her heart beat even faster. What was it? A shovel? A spike? She hoped he would kill her quickly and not torture her.

The car started again and she sensed from the way the boot tilted that it was climbing uphill. Perhaps he was going to leave her in the car and push it off a cliff? Tears ran down her cheeks and dripped into her mouth. Either way she was going to die. She thought of Stefan. *You could go to university, Rebecca. You could study law and put that brain of yours to good use. Would you like that?* A wave of regret washed over her. Why had she not taken the risk and done more with her life? Now it was too late.

Timothy suddenly applied the brake. Rebecca was thrown against the front of the boot. She pressed her good eye to the sliver of a gap between the boot and the lid but couldn't see anything. A breeze was blowing outside and the car shuddered with its force. Timothy opened the boot. She blinked at the shock of daylight.

'Get out!' he said, grabbing her arm and yanking her to her knees.

Rebecca clambered out, unsteady on her legs. Timothy shoved her forward. His stale sweat was pungent. It was strange that she should notice it when her life was about to end, but it struck her as somehow important. Timothy had always smelt so clean, like Sunlight soap. Now he reeked like old cheese, as if his malevolence was seeping out of his pores.

'Do you recognise it?' he asked, grabbing her head so she was forced to look in front of her.

Rebecca lifted her eyes. Before her stood a single blackened wall surrounded by rubble. Weeds sprouted from gaps in the structure. Beyond it was an overgrown garden bordered by coastal scrub. A lonely grave stood surrounded by an iron fence. She knew where she was now. It was the ruins of Stefan's mansion.

'It's fitting that you should die here,' Timothy sneered. 'The whore in her place of defilement!'

He poked something sharp against her chin. Rebecca glimpsed the knife and her stomach plummeted. But she was not going to beg for her life. She would not give him that pleasure. One by one her senses sprang back to life. Her eyes smarted, her skin burned and her mouth tasted of acid.

'You're wrong,' she told him. 'We never made love here.'

Timothy's grip tightened then loosened again. He was distracted by something. Rebecca heard it too. The rumble of a car. 'Someone's coming,' she said. Timothy turned his head to listen. She took advantage of his distraction to slam her fist backwards into his crotch.

Timothy dropped to his knees. Rebecca raced towards the road. If she could reach it in time she might be able to flag down the car's driver. She was almost at the gate, but Timothy had recovered and caught her. He threw her on the ground and dragged her backwards by the collar of her dress. Her arms and legs flailed in the dirt but she managed to twist herself onto her stomach then onto her knees and Timothy lost his grip. She fled again, this time in the direction of the scrub. Branches whipped her face as she threw herself into the trees and dropped down behind a large boulder. Her legs were a mess of scrapes and cuts and her head was spinning. She leaned against the boulder for support, terrified she would pass out.

A twig snapped. Timothy was somewhere nearby. She could hear his agitated breathing. 'You won't get away,' he said. 'There is nowhere to go.'

A shrill noise pierced the air. Rebecca started. It was the whaling station alarm. The chaser boat must be on its way to pursue a kill just outside the bay. She willed the whale to sense the danger and move on. It at least had the open ocean. She was certainly about to die, but she clung to every last second of her life.

'They won't get out fast enough to harpoon it. It's already moved on.'

Rebecca squinted and cocked her head. A man's voice, but not Timothy's. It was low and gruff. Had she imagined it? She strained to hear it again.

Then another voice carried on the breeze, this time very familiar. 'I give them no more than ten years before governments around the world see that killing whales doesn't make sense when there are other products available. It's all the whales that will die before they come to their senses that I worry about.'

Stefan! Rebecca's skin tingled with electricity.

He had brought someone with him, and both men were only a few yards away but hidden from her view by the trees. If she called out to them her voice might be lost in the wind, or they wouldn't be able to tell quickly enough where it was coming from. The danger of alerting Timothy to her hiding place was too great. If she stayed hidden, she might still have a chance. The sun was beginning to set and if she could hold out, keep playing cat and mouse with him, she might be able to last until nightfall.

'Whose car is that?' asked Stefan's companion.

Rebecca's breath caught in her throat. Timothy had left the boot open. Would the men sense that something was wrong?

'It's Litchfield's! Rebecca must be nearby,' Stefan said.

Her heart skipped with hope. She raised her head above the boulder and filled her lungs with air.

'Stefan!' she called out.

Her voice died in the wind. Nobody answered her. But Timothy had heard her. Leaves rustled as he stalked towards her in the underbrush. Then in a flash he was upon her, his eyes bloodshot. She scrambled up and ran for her life.

'Stefan! Stefan!' she screamed, hurtling herself forward. She was running out of track. The coastal bush cleared and she was on a bare rock now with the sheer drop to the ocean in front of her. The sun was sinking in the sky, shooting out rays of violet and blue.

'Rebecca?'

'Stefan! Stefan! I'm here!' she cried. But when she turned it was Timothy standing behind her.

'Who are you calling to? There is no one here but us.'

Rebecca's heart sank as the world around her turned shades of gold. Of course it was sheer folly. Stefan couldn't be here, at this precise moment. In her desperation she had imagined it. Miracles did not happen, not for her. She glanced at the rocks below then back to Timothy, understanding that she had a choice now. Mabel and Anne had made that choice, and she could too. She stepped back towards the edge of the cliff. She would not give him the pleasure of killing her. Then a maniacal glint came to his eyes and a nasty smirk to his face and she realised that either way he would win.

'Rebecca!'

From the corner of her eye she saw movement. Two men were pushing through the trees. Stefan was hobbling along with a walking stick and Rebecca realised he must have needed the other man to drive him here. His companion was elderly, with a grey moustache and a homburg hat perched on his head. He wasn't going to reach her any faster than Stefan. Timothy saw them too. His lips curled into a snarl. Then he was upon her, jabbing at her with the knife. She drew her arm up to protect herself and fell backwards, closer to the edge. He lunged at her and she kicked as hard as she could to keep him at a distance. He was bigger than her – and stronger. It shouldn't have been a fair fight, but somehow she managed to knock the knife out of his hand. It landed next to her hip.

'Rebecca!' Stefan screamed.

Timothy's hands were around her neck now. She thrashed her arms and legs to try to get him off.

'We'll *both* die,' he said, his face in hers. Then he pressed himself against her and kissed her hard on the mouth. She knew he now meant to kill her and then himself.

Her arm was pinned under her body. She struggled to wiggle it out. Her vision blurred and she felt like her head might explode. She thought of Debbie, the water filling her lungs, and saw herself as if in a dream, sinking below the surface of the waves.

'Rebecca!' Stefan called.

She burst to the surface. Somehow she managed to free her arm from under her. She grabbed the knife and with every bit of strength she had left she jabbed it into Timothy's back. She felt it slice into his flesh and stick there. His eyes opened wide and he jumped to his feet. Reaching for the knife, he lost his footing and fell backwards, rolling closer to the sheer drop. When he realised where he was his fingers dug into the sandstone, but he couldn't get a grip. He stared at Rebecca in horror. Then his lips formed into a curse that he had no chance to utter before he went plunging over the side. His arms made clockwise movements until he hit the rock platform below with a loud, sickening thud. Rebecca recoiled. Timothy's lifeless body lay face up, staring at her from a pool of blood.

She felt two strong arms pull her backwards. Stefan had her in his grasp.

The elderly man peered over the cliff and screwed up his face. 'Good God!' Then he looked at Rebecca. 'Who was that man? Why was he trying to kill you?'

'My husband,' she said, her voice raspy and breathless. She turned to Stefan, who looked at her questioningly. She had no explanation for him. All she could think was that she should have been dead and yet somehow she was alive. She turned her face towards the horizon. The sun was a red globe sinking into the ocean. It set the sea on fire. Then its last rays shot out into the dusky sky and it vanished. Somewhere on the other side of the world it would rise again and a new day would begin.

CHAPTER FORTY

The Daily Telegraph
The Courts Today
Inquest into Doctor's Death

After the evidence of several witnesses, including the deceased's widow, had been heard in the Coroner's Court today, the Coroner, Mr J. Ward, closed the inquest into the death of Doctor Timothy Robert Litchfield who fell to his death from the headland at Shipwreck Bay on 26 March. Giving evidence, Mrs Rebecca Carol Litchfield, who is blonde and attractive, said that her husband had threatened her shortly before his death. According to Mrs Litchfield, her husband had been showing increasingly perverse behaviour towards her since their marriage. On finding jewellery in his possession that belonged to Mrs Nancy Pike, who was murdered in Shipwreck Bay last November, Mrs Litchfield tried to flee from her husband but was pursued and caught by him.

Detective-Sergeant McCarthy examined the witnesses, who included Mr Stefan Otto and Mr Bill McLaren, an insurance agent, who had driven Mr Otto to Shipwreck Bay after Mr

Otto received a message asking for help from Mrs Litchfield. Mr McLaren was of the opinion that when the two men arrived at the headland Doctor Litchfield was attempting to kill his wife with a knife. He testified that the doctor had lost his grip of the weapon and Mrs Litchfield had then stabbed him in self-defence. The shock of the injury then caused him to lose his footing and he plummeted to his death, a distance of some 100 feet.

When interviewed by police in regard to Mrs Pike's murder, Mrs Litchfield had supported her husband's statement that he had spent the afternoon of 12 November with her; however, the coroner concluded that Doctor Litchfield would still have had time to murder Mrs Pike before visiting his then fiancée to create a convenient alibi. Further evidence presented by Doctor Litchfield's former wife, Mrs Arabella Cousins, led the Coroner to conclude that Doctor Litchfield was a covertly violent man who preyed on women. He had, in fact, been dismissed from Sydney Hospital in 1948 after several allegations of misconduct towards female patients. Mr Ward conceded all evidence pointed to Doctor Litchfield as responsible for the death of Mrs Pike, and that her husband, George Pike, who is currently on trial for her murder should be immediately acquitted …

The Twin Falls Advocate
Scenes at the Court
A Great Crowd

Upon her exit from the court yesterday morning, Mrs Litchfield was quickly whisked away in a motor car from the back entrance *by her lawyer. A battery of photographers finding that they were defeated by the speedy escape, positioned themselves on lorries and other vehicles and took pictures of the crowd of people outside the courthouse. Before long, heated arguments broke out between the onlookers. Residents of the town of Shipwreck Bay claimed that the finding of Mrs Litchfield as innocent of all wrongdoing was a travesty of justice. Nurse Gibbons who worked for Doctor Litchfield's father for over 20 years described his son as 'a gentleman through and through'. She reported that in the days before his death Doctor Litchfield had been distressed to discover his wife had been neglecting his invalid mother after he had entrusted her with her care. 'The poor bedridden lady had a bedsore the size of a moon crater,' the nurse said. Mr Ernie Mullens, the long-serving stationmaster of Shipwreck Bay, claimed that Mrs Litchfield had a wandering eye and had approached him on several occasions with inappropriate suggestions. 'Doctor Litchfield was a much-loved and respected member of our town,' wept Mrs Doris Campbell. 'I knew that woman was trouble the moment I laid eyes on her. When a good man is driven to insanity, there is only one question we can all ask ourselves: what did his wife do to provoke him?' ...*

*

'Are you ready?' Stefan asked Rebecca. He was sitting next to her in the back of the taxi as it pulled up at the passenger terminal. The massive white ocean liner that would take them to England was in port. The dock was bustling with cranes and forklift trucks loading cargo. The great funnel was blowing steam in preparation for the journey. But Rebecca wasn't looking at the ship. Her eyes settled on the pressmen gathered like vultures outside the passenger terminal.

'Did you hear me, Rebecca?' Stefan repeated, gently. 'Are you ready?'

Even now it stunned Rebecca that it was her marriage to a country doctor that had led to her name being splashed across the front page of every newspaper and not her relationship with Ned McKell, as she had once feared. For the past few weeks she had been living in a goldfish bowl as columnists, radio announcers and even fashion reporters speculated on the many different versions of what had happened. Was Rebecca Litchfield a helpless victim or a femme fatale? Her life had made the perfect story: an opportunity for the self-righteous to preach and for the masses to satisfy their insatiable appetite for scandal. She thought she would go mad, hiding away yet again from public view and waiting for even more catastrophes to be unleashed. But so distracted were the reporters by the fact that she had stabbed a man to defend herself, they didn't bother to check too deeply into her past. Despite their clamour and their prying, not one of them picked her to be Ned McKell's 'mystery woman'. As for the scrapbook of articles Nancy had collected to incriminate her, that was lying on the bottom of the ocean and disintegrating. She and Stefan had taken it to the same spot where Rebecca had set Dunkel free. *Didn't Stefan once say that we would all return to the sea one day?*

A slow, cat-like grin settled on her face. 'I'm ready,' she said.

Flashbulbs popped like gun shots when Stefan opened the door and helped her out of the taxi. The pressmen crowded around them, lunging at her with their microphones. They made her ears ring with their barrage of questions.

'What are your plans now, Mrs Litchfield?'

'How long do you intend to stay in Europe?'

'Will you be returning to Australia?'

The more the reporters harassed her, the less she heard them. Their voices faded and she was filled with a strange sense of calm, as if she were standing in the eye of a storm as it whirled around her. *This* is what she had most feared? *This* had been the reason she had fled to Shipwreck Bay? In the light of all that had happened since then, it did not seem so bad.

Once inside the terminal, the press were kept back behind a barricade. She squeezed Stefan's arm. He looked at her and smiled.

'Think of the future,' he said, taking out their passports and handing them to the customs officer. 'You'll put this behind you, Rebecca. This will all be forgotten and in a few months you won't even have to carry that monster's name.'

She wasn't sure that nearly being murdered by your husband was something you could put behind you, but she would try. More terrible than the prying of the press had been the letters of sympathy she had received each day:

You have such a sweet, sad smile, I don't understand how any man could ill-use you.

We all learn our lessons, dear. You will know what to look out for next time.

She did not want to be *that* woman, the kind that people felt sorry for and wanted to protect. She did not want to be a victim.

She thought of Gillian, now safe in a comfortable old people's home in the leafy Sydney suburb of Roseville. The Litchfield estate had been transferred to Rebecca by default on Timothy's death and she had made sure that Gillian was well provided for. She had taken care to select a place with a beautiful garden.

She and Stefan moved towards the gangway and her eyes travelled over the grand ship. A moment of hesitancy struck her. She glanced at Stefan leaning on his walking stick. He had been her rock the past few weeks: keeping her hidden away in his Melbourne hotel suite, holding her hand when she nearly broke down the night before the inquest, supporting her throughout the ordeal. He had promised her a new life in Europe, one where she could be utterly and truly herself. But what if in the end he turned out to be another Ned? Someone who promised her the world but eventually tired of her as he was tempted by other conquests?

She straightened her shoulders. So what if he did? She had survived far worse and if necessary she would get herself through new misfortunes again. Her eyes drifted past the ship to the wide ocean beyond it. Ahead lay a world of possibilities and she would seize every one of them. She had once tried to protect herself, to keep safe, by grasping at a tenuous security. She saw the error in that now. Sometimes the safest thing you could do was to take a risk.

AUTHOR'S NOTE

Those readers who are familiar with my historical works of fiction may wonder if Shipwreck Bay is based on the NSW South Coast town of Eden, because of its past association with the whaling industry, and whether characters like Ned McKell and Stefan Otto are modelled on real people.

I confirm that they are not. *The Mystery Woman* is a complete work of fiction and Shipwreck Bay and its characters did not appear from anywhere other than my imagination.

It was my aim to focus on the Gothic and thriller aspects of the novel, rather than to bring history to life. I placed the story in the setting and time period I did because they were perfect for the themes of the contradictory ways in which women are viewed, hypocritical morality, and the ever-present fear of societal rejection.

However, while the story is a work of fiction, I undertook much research in order to give an authentic feel to the setting. Given that Australia is a country famous for its whale watching and its strong stance on protection of all species, many Australians are shocked to learn that whale oil exports used to be one of the country's most important primary industries and only came to an end in the late 1970s after whales were hunted to near-extinction. At that time, many Australians also began to oppose the industry on the grounds of its appalling cruelty.

Stefan Otto represents a 'lone voice in the wilderness', one of those individuals who speaks up against an injustice long before it reaches a groundswell and becomes a movement. We've seen these courageous and unconventional people in all of humanity's major steps forward, in the campaigns for women's liberation, equality and peace, and against slavery, and we are seeing it coming to fruition now in the growing movement for animal rights. A genius, and far ahead of his time, Leonardo da Vinci was speaking up for the humane treatment of animals back in the Renaissance period.

So if you are one of those lone voices in the wilderness now, standing up for an injustice that nobody else seems to care about and being ridiculed for it, I not only applaud you but encourage you. Your road may feel like a lonely one, but future generations will thank you!

ACKNOWLEDGEMENTS

Writing *The Mystery Woman* has been an exciting journey. I would like to thank everyone who helped bring the book to fruition.

I'm grateful to my clever agent, Catherine Drayton, for encouraging me to try a new direction in my writing, and to my enthusiastic publisher, Anna Valdinger, and savvy senior editor, Scott Forbes, and the rest of the talented team at HarperCollins Publishers Australia for working closely with me to achieve it.

I'd also like to thank the wonderful people who shared their firsthand knowledge of small country towns and their post offices to lend authentic detail to the story: Harry Nowak, who was once the delivery boy and later the postmaster for Stratford, in Victoria, and his wife, Joy; Ron Martin, who was a volunteer with the Rural Fire Service; and Judy Mactier, who gave me some delightful detail regarding the telephone service in the 1950s and also inspired the idea for the 'Tree of Knowledge'.

Thank you also to my perceptive editor, Alex Craig, for her help regarding plotting and structure and also to the astute Maddy James for her proofread. The sagacious Roslyn McGechan, my first reader, was extremely generous with her time and provided insightful feedback on historical detail and language. Thank you also to versatile Lily Testa for her help with nautical and mechanical questions.

I feel deep appreciation for my precious friends and family and all the support they always give me (and also for my gorgeous companion animals for their peaceful presence during the long, solitary hours required to produce a novel). Life would be a dull affair without them all!

With thanks and love,
Belinda Alexandra

READING GROUP QUESTIONS

1. What do you think of the relationships between the female characters in the novel? Are they all antagonistic or are some of them supportive?

2. How do you think Rebecca sees herself in relation to men? To what extent do you think society has shaped this view and to what extent do you think it stems from her own personality? Do you think Rebecca would see herself differently if she had been born after the 1970s?

3. Do you think Rebecca changes over the course of the novel? In what ways?

4. Timothy is a master of the technique of psychological abuse known as 'gaslighting' (manipulating someone's perception of reality in a way that causes them to doubt themselves). What particular instances of him doing this in the book stand out for you? How do you think he manages to fool someone as worldly-wise as Rebecca?

5. 'One in four women will experience domestic abuse in her lifetime.' This is a frightening statistic. Do you think

society has come a long way in its understanding of the dynamics of domestic abuse – or do we still stereotype and blame the victims?*

6. Do you think what Rebecca did to Sanders Olsen was justified? What would you have done in her place?

7. The author describes the book as a 'Modern Australian Gothic Romance'. Traditionally, Gothic novels have the following elements: an atmospheric setting; a damsel in distress; mystery and suspense; a ghost/monster or a beast within; a burdened male protagonist; horror and death. How does *The Mystery Woman* fulfil these characteristics and in what ways does it deviate from them?

8. Do you think Rebecca's relationship with Stefan is a classic romance? Do you see them living 'happily ever after' – or not? Why?

9. What do you think about the double standards with which both the press and public view Rebecca's affair with Ned – for example the idea that he's been led astray but she's a homewrecker? Do you think these double standards still prevail today?

---

* For readers interested in gaining a better understanding of the often covert nature of domestic violence and the methods of psychological control that abusers frequently employ, the following are recommended reading:

Lundy Bancroft, *Why Does He Do That?: Inside the Minds of Angry and Controlling Men*, Penguin Putnam, New York, 2002.

Don Hennessy, *How He Gets Into Her Head: The Mind of the Male Intimate Abuser*, Cork University Press, Cork, 2012.

Carol A. Lambert, *Women with Controlling Partners: Taking Back Your Life from a Manipulative or Abusive Partner*, New Harbinger, Oakland, 2016.

10. The cruelty of whaling isn't even a consideration for the citizens of Shipwreck Bay. The town's economic prosperity is the first priority. Can you think of specific examples today where economics overrides animal welfare? Do you think this imbalance will change in the future as people become more concerned with animal welfare issues?

11. What surprised you most in the story?

12. What scene did you most enjoy and why?

13. If you were to choose a soundtrack for the novel, what would it be?

Discover the world of Belinda Alexandra ...

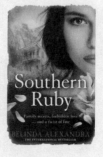